Our Story began in...

The Kind of a Girl...

as Lorraine Innis, a man in disguise trying to avenge the death of his girlfriend, accidentally foiled the assassination attempt on Russian president Kropotkin.

It continued in...

The Girl in the Diamond Studded Heels...

as Lorraine, now famous, became an international symbol of peace!

Then came...

The Girl in the Aubergine Sandals...

and we met Lorraine's Aunt Elinor and started to learn about the tragic flaws in Lorraine's past.

Now get ready to meet...

The Girl in the Lime Green Wellies!

ALSO BY G.C. Allen

The Kind of a Girl

The Girl in the Diamond Studded Heels

The Girl in the Aubergine Sandals

Coming Soon...

The Girl in the Saffron Espadrilles

The Girl in the Blood Red Stilettos

The Girl in the Sky Blue Plimsolls

Visit www.iLorraine.com

The Girl in the Lime Green Wellies

G.C. Allen

The Fourth Book in the
Lorraine Innis Series

Daley•into•Print LLC
Mundus Est Vestra Locusta

"A minist'ring angel shall my sister be."

- William Shakespeare

For Bambi Sue,
Ministering Angel, Sister, and Friend

Hope deferred makes the heart sick...

- Proverbs 13:12

The Girl
in the
Lime Green
Wellies

Clodagh Clott couldn't recall ever being in Delaware. Well, not on purpose, at least.

It was such a small state, she thought as she drove her Toyota Camry down Interstate 95. It was possible she may have stepped in it by accident. She thought of her childhood when she would walk along a crack in the sidewalk and pretend she was on a tightrope above a circus ring. She recalled walking heel-to-toe along a line, only to lose her balance and fall off the imaginary rope. If she had been to Delaware before, she concluded, it must be something like that: focused on another goal, another destination, and then there you find yourself... in Delaware.

Now, however, she was going there on purpose.

As she crossed the Pennsylvania state line, Clodagh recalled the mysterious call that had summoned her to Wilmington with the promise of a lucrative assignment. As a self-employed motivational consultant, she couldn't afford to pass up any leads, especially not with a bank. Big companies often looked for unique motivational strategies. Her sister, Denise, called her business a "racket," but then Denise was a lawyer: very analytical; very skeptical. Denise thought you just had to point people at a job, tell them how to do it, and then leave them to do it. Denise thought that way because that's what Denise would do. She didn't understand the need to motivate people.

Clodagh admitted some motivational experts were scam artists, but then such an inexact science naturally attracted its share of snake oil salesmen. The CEOs and company presidents she met were all self-motivated men and women. They hadn't needed anyone to light a fire under them to succeed. Often they were easy prey to someone coming along with a slick package, catchy jargon, and "proven" methods guaranteed to make employees perform. Clodagh didn't us those tactics. More than once, she had turned business away because she had been expected to change people's personalities magically; to impart a work ethic and an innate drive. It couldn't be done, she told more than one disappointed CEO. Her competitors might promise something they knew could never be delivered, but Clodagh wouldn't.

It might be interesting to work for a bank, she thought as she took the off-ramp onto Delaware Avenue. She wondered what sort of motivation a banker would require. Don't embezzle? Make more money? Cheat widows and orphans while looking benevolent? She could only wonder. There it was: Fourth Fiduciary Trust. Clodagh pulled her car into the garage beneath the building and parked. Then she double-checked her instructions. The administrative assistant, a woman named Patricia Einfalt, hadn't said whom she would be meeting with, only the place and the time. Oh, yes, and, she was warned that her meeting would be strictly confidential.

Clutching her handbag and her leather folio, Clodagh entered the elevator. Once inside, she checked her appearance in the mirrored doors. It was her best suit, but whenever she wore it around corporate types, she felt inadequate. It was powder blue, and all the executives she met wore dark blues and grays. She had to remind herself that wasn't her style, but that didn't help her feelings of inadequacy.

Fourth Fiduciary Trust: where had she heard that name before? It wasn't a bank near where she lived, but there was something familiar about it. The door opened on the executive floor, and she stepped out. In the first twenty yards, she counted at least three gray suits, two in navy blue, and two in black. Clodagh sighed. Her anxiety was relieved when she entered the executive suite. There, behind the first desk, was a woman who looked like she had a home-perm and was wearing a dress that looked like it came from a mid-range department store. Maybe Clodagh's suit would be okay. What made her even more at ease was that the name on the desk, P. Einfalt, was her contact.

Even before she spoke, Clodagh was welcomed by a cheery smile that seemed more appropriate in a neighbor's kitchen than in an executive suite.

"May I help you?" The woman's tone was sincere as if she really wanted to be of assistance. Most executive assistants Clodagh encountered made that phrase sound more like: "Can't you see I'm very important? What do you want?"

"I'm Clodagh Clott. I was contacted about some consulting work."

The cheery expression grew even more genuine if that were possible. "Oh, yes, I called you. I'm Patsy... that is, Patricia Einfalt, oh, never mind, you can call me Patsy. I called on behalf of... oops, never mind who."

"Oh," said Clodagh. "Will I be meeting with you, then?"

"Me? Oh, no," she giggled as if the suggestion were ridiculous.

"Your boss then?"

For the first time, Patsy's smile darkened as if a tender nerve had been touched. "My boss is… well, no, the man I used to work for…" she stopped and reached for a tissue from the box on her desk. She gently daubed her eyes and then aggressively blew her nose.

"Excuse me," she said, regaining her composure. "I took off all last week, but I guess I'm still very upset when I think about poor Mr. Liverot."

"Mr…"

"Liverot," said Patsy Einfalt. "He died suddenly a few weeks ago. Poor Mr. Liverot." She blew her nose again, though not as vociferously this time.

Clodagh recalled the name. Liverot; he was the banker who died along with President Merton in that attack at the White House. They were killed by the deranged old lady.

"If this isn't a good time," said Clodagh, "I can come back."

Patsy Einfalt stood up and returned the smile to her face in a series of short spasms that reminded Clodagh of a light bulb flickering on. Once it had returned, her smile shone as brightly as a floodlight.

"Oh, no, that's okay, thank you," said Patsy, "thank you for being so sensitive. You're not meeting with me, you're meeting with… oops; I almost said it again. Never mind. Please, follow me."

Patsy Einfalt led her into a side office.

"Please," she said indicating a table with two wing chairs on either side of it, "have a seat, she, that is the person you're meeting with will be with you in a few minutes. Would you like coffee, tea, water…"

"Tea, please," said Clodagh sitting down.

Patsy Einfalt nodded and began to leave when she stopped herself and scurried back into the room.

"Oh, I almost forgot," she picked up a file folder from the desk and handed it to Clodagh. "If you would, please read this, and if it's okay, that is, if you agree, please sign the letter inside." She said this in an official-sounding tone. Then her sunny side returned as she exited with a promise to hurry back with the tea.

Clodagh stared at the closed door for several seconds and then looked down at the file folder. Inside was what seemed at first like a routine confidentiality agreement. She had seen those before: promising not to share any company secrets or procedures with competitors or the general public. There was a lot of legal phrasing, though none she couldn't decipher. She shook her head at the document. Its stilted language reminded her of a normal conversation with her sister, Denise. It wasn't until she studied it more closely, however, that Clodagh noticed the difference in this agreement. It wasn't about the company. It was about the individual with whom she was to meet. Though that person wasn't named, the document made it clear that until she signed the agreement, she wouldn't meet this mystery figure. And if she did sign it, and did meet the person, she was not to divulge the identity of said person, or more importantly, anything shared by the same.

She was still studying the piece of paper when Patsy Einfalt returned with a tray with the tea set and a plate of cookies.

"Is everything clear?" asked Patsy.

Clodagh looked up into the secretary's guileless face. She wondered if her genial manner was some sort of con. Had she walked into something shady? What nefarious secrets were hiding beneath that simple grin and spiral curls?

"Uh, yes, it's clear," said Clodagh. "It's just that this is a rather unusual agreement."

"Oh? Is it?"

"Yes, I've never seen anything quite like it."

Patsy shrugged.

"Well," Patsy concluded, "I don't know about that, but if you don't sign it, you can't meet with Mrs. Innis."

"Mrs. Innis?" Clodagh's eyes widened. Of course, Peter Liverot, Fourth Fiduciary Trust, they were all connected to....

"Patsy!" A voice scolded from behind.

Clodagh turned. There in the doorway stood the most famous woman in the world: Lorraine Innis.

- 2 -
A Mystery, Wrapped in an Enigma, Wrapped in a Tyrian Purple Suit

Patsy," chided Lorraine Innis, "the purpose of having a person sign a confidentiality agreement is to keep what you divulge to them a secret after they sign it. If you let them know the secret before they sign it becomes rather pointless."

Patsy Einfalt lowered her head.

"But it's okay," said Lorraine embracing her. "There's no harm done."

"There isn't?" said Patsy.

Lorraine shook her head. "No, I think we can trust Clodagh, that is Ms. Clott." She looked directly at Clodagh, and her face seemed to brighten, making Clodagh feel like a long lost friend.

"Now," she continued, "please leave us alone for a bit. I have a lot to discuss with Ms. Clott."

Patsy began to leave and then stopped.

"Oh, what about the..." she nodded towards the unsigned document.

"I'll take care of it," said Lorraine. "Oh, and we don't want to be disturbed by anyone."

"Not even Valerie, that is, Ms. Fierro?"

"I thought she was still on leave," said Lorraine.

"Oh, right," said Patsy.

"But not even her," said Lorraine. "I don't want anyone else to know with whom I'm meeting." The stern tone returned to her voice, and Patsy's face grew serious, and she nodded. Before the door closed, Lorraine Innis was careful to add a warm "thank you" that reinstated Patsy's smile.

Lorraine Innis stared at the door for several moments after it clicked shut. Clodagh observed her in profile. She looked just like she did on television, standing there in an impeccably tailored suit of Tyrian purple. Tyrian purple, thought Clodagh, looking down at her own powder blue outfit. Why hadn't she thought of purple? It was business-like and feminine without seeming frivolous. Her face, viewed from the side seemed vaguely familiar, but, then she'd seen that face countless times since the previous October... just never in person.

Lorraine turned to her and again smiled so genuinely that it was almost artificial. Clodagh reminded herself that she had never met this woman before. If it were insincere, the smile would rank right up there with politicians and used car salesmen.

"It's a pleasure to see you... to meet you, Ms. Clott," she said. "May I call you Clodagh?"

"Um, uh, sure, yes, I guess so." Being tongue-tied on top of wearing the wrong color suit made her feel even more inept.

"Thank you, Clodagh," said Lorraine, sitting beside her. "And, please, call me: Lorraine."

Clodagh just nodded.

"Shall I play mother?" asked Lorraine as she arranged the teacups and began to pour.

"Mother?"

"Yes, sorry," said Lorraine concentrating on the tea, "that's a British phrase. I've spent some time in England. I... I almost married a British... person."

"Martin?" asked Clodagh and then grimaced. She shouldn't mention Lorraine's bigamist husband who had been the subject of a worldwide search the previous autumn. "Oh, I'm sorry."

"No, not Martin," she said. "Someone else entirely." She paused with a distant look in her eyes before recovering her composure. "Milk?"

"Just sugar, two, please," said Clodagh, "I don't like milk in tea...sorry."

"Don't apologize," said Lorraine spooning the sugar into Clodagh's cup and handing it to her. She then poured milk in her own tea. "Another British affectation," she said, nodding towards the milk pitcher. "I've come to prefer it, but in a way, it's almost in honor of... someone."

Lorraine Innis seemed on the verge of being upset. She shook her head as if she were dispelling a bothersome fly, and continued. She swirled her spoon through her tea, then lifted the cup to her lips and took a sip. By the time she lowered the cup, she was back in control

"Excuse me," said Lorraine, "I drifted into an area that I didn't intend to go, at least not yet. Cookie?"

"Thank you," said Clodagh, taking a cookie without taking her eyes off Lorraine's. "Not yet?"

"Excuse me?"

"You said: 'not yet,'" said Clodagh. "You said you drifted into an area you didn't intend, at least not yet."

Lorraine took another sip of tea, eyeing Clodagh over the rim of the china cup.

"Clodagh," said Lorraine, lowering the cup, "have you wondered what you're doing here?"

Clodagh fidgeted in her seat for a moment, but then wondered why she should be nervous. She was being honest. It was these people, that goofy secretary and Lorraine Innis that were making it a big mystery. She felt indignation rising in her. "Yes! Yes, I am!"

"Good."

"I mean, I know you're a famous person, but this whole thing of asking me to come here under a shroud of secrecy, then this... this agreement." she picked up the piece of paper and then let it flutter back to the table. "It's all pretty strange, and forgive me if I feel that I'm being kept in the dark and that you're not being very forthright with me."

Lorraine smiled. "Same old Clodagh."

"What do you mean? 'Same old Clodagh?' That's another thing: you keep looking at me like you know me. I've never met you before in my life. You may be an important person, and I'm just an insignificant consultant. But still, I thought from all I've ever read about you that you were nicer than to toy with a person."

"I need your help, Clodagh," said Lorraine ignoring her tirade. "And you're the only person who can help me."

"How do you even know me, Mrs. Innis?"

"That's a fair question. And please, forgive me for being so mysterious, but you'll understand once I explain."

"After I sign your confidentiality agreement?" said Clodagh.

Lorraine pushed the document aside.

"I trust you," she said. "That was only a formality. I know you're the same person you've always been. You haven't changed, though I have."

Clodagh tilted her head to the side. "I know you?"

Lorraine nodded. "And I know you. And I know I can trust you. I have something very important to do, and only you can help me."

Clodagh studied her eyes. Lorraine Innis was the head of a global charity, she had inspired an international peace plan, she was the most influential woman in the world... and she needed Clodagh Clott?

"Do you need your employees motivated?" asked Clodagh.

"No, it's nothing like that." Lorraine put down her teacup and rose to the window. "No, I know you do that sort of thing. I saw you being interviewed on television. You were on one of those cable shows talking about your business, and then you mentioned your other interests, and I remembered it all. And I knew that I needed to talk to you. You followed in your father's footsteps, but of course, in your own unique way, didn't you?"

"You know my father?"

"And your mother, and your sisters. I saw Denise last year."

"Denise? She didn't mention meeting you."

"Legal ethics," said Lorraine. "Attorney-client privilege..."

"Yes, that's Denise," agreed Clodagh. "And she introduced you to the rest of the family at the same time?"

"I already knew them," said Lorraine. "How is your father? Does he still practice psychology now that he's retired from the Air Force?"

"No, he and my mother moved to Arizona..."

"But you got your degree in psychology, among other studies."

"Yes, but..."

"And your other sisters, Rhoda and Caprice? I understand Caprice is still an excellent golfer."

"She is but," Clodagh stopped herself, and stood up. "Look, Mrs. Innis, I don't know how you know all this and how I fit into your little scheme..."

"Please, don't call it a scheme."

"Call it whatever you want, but stop toying with me."

"I want you to help me, Clodagh."

"Help you? To do what?"

"Do you remember Chesney Potts, I mean, Chesney Potoski?"

Clodagh's racing thoughts came to a dead stop. "Chesney? Of course, I remember him. I grew up with him."

Lorraine Innis turned to her. "Yes, well, I want you to help me kill Chesney Potoski."

Clodagh staggered backward into her chair. Her mouth fell open.

"Kill Chesney?"

An enigmatic grin played around the corners of Lorraine Innis' mouth. "Yes, well, just for a little while."

- 3 -
A Smart Slap
for a Stupid Boy

Lorraine Innis sat down next to Clodagh and reached for her hand. Clodagh recoiled from her touch.

"No," said Lorraine, "I'm not a murderer, and I don't want you to be one either. Clodagh... Clo..." Lorraine leaned forward and whispered in a deeper voice: "Clo, it's me. It's Chesney."

Clodagh leaned further away.

"Really," said Lorraine in her normal voice, "it's true."

Clodagh eyes darted around the features of Lorraine's face. It was almost as if she were in shock.

"Oh, I was afraid of this," said Lorraine.

She had tried to ease into the revelation. The moment she saw Clodagh after all these years, Lorraine wanted to hug her but hadn't. She fought the urge to blurt out: "it's me, your best friend from Earswick, New York." She thought it would be a shock, but now realized it would be jarring no matter how she broached the subject.

"Clo, Clo," she continued, again trying to speak in a more masculine register. "I can't do the voice, my old voice, too well. I'm out of practice. Not that you really ever knew my adult voice, still, it's me: Chesney. I lived down the street from you. We had the tree fort. We read books there. We went to school together until you had to move. You were my best friend. You always told me to stand up for myself. You helped me..." She almost brought up the revenge against Stosh but stopped short. Then she remembered a more intimate fact: "You gave me my first kiss!"

Clodagh made direct eye contact with Lorraine. With that encouragement, Lorraine continued.

"It was the day of the golf tournament. We called it the 'Stupid Golf Tournament,' remember?" Lorraine said, taking her hand. "You were sitting on your bike, and you leaned over, and you kissed me on the lips."

Clodagh's brow furrowed, and she nodded. Lorraine smiled and nodded in return. Then Clodagh removed Lorraine's hand from hers, reared back, and delivered a hard slap across Lorraine's cheek.

"Stupid boy!" said Clodagh.

"Oww!"

Clodagh recoiled as a stunned look spread over her face.

"I'm sorry," she said. "I'm really, really sorry, Mrs. Innis. It was just a knee-jerk reaction. I thought about Chesney, and when I kissed him. He was the first boy I ever kissed, but he didn't kiss me back, and it upset me. I'm so sorry. I don't know what came over me. If it's any consolation, you're the first stranger I ever hit."

"That's okay, I suppose," said Lorraine rubbing her cheek. "It must be a bit of a shock, but there was no other way to break it to you."

Clodagh scowled. "Still, you're supposed to be a very nice lady," she said. "You shouldn't go around broadcasting intimate details from a person's past, especially not ones that are, well…"

"Embarrassing?"

"I was going to say: 'private.'"

"I didn't broadcast them," said Lorraine, "I hardly whispered them."

"But still, you know. I don't know why he told you."

Lorraine shook her head. "He didn't tell me."

"Then how else would you know?"

Lorraine reached out and took Clodagh by both hands, not only to convey her friendship but to prevent another assault. "Clodagh…Clo," she said. "You're not hearing what I'm saying. I tell you I am Chesney."

A flurry of expressions swept across her face as she tried to process the information. In a matter of seconds, she seemed to deny, believe, speculate, trust, and ignore the evidence before her. Finally, a healthy skepticism won out.

"If you're Chesney…"

"Shh, not so loud," cautioned Lorraine.

"If you're," she said more quietly, "…who you say you are, prove it."

"How? I already told you about the kiss."

"Well, Chesney could have told you about that. Tell me something else."

"You have three sisters…"

"That's public knowledge…"

"Okay, well," said Lorraine, "the anagram of your name is 'Gold Cloth Cat.'"

"Anyone who does anagrams could figure that out."

Lorraine wracked her brain. It was getting harder all the time to prove who she used to be.

"I know…you once got back at your sister Rhoda by sabotaging her bra straps."

Clodagh's eyes shot up. "Yes, that's pretty good," she admitted. She tilted her head and studied Lorraine's eyes for several seconds.

"Oh, and your parents almost named you something else."

Clodagh blushed.

"Don't say it," she warned, and then, after a moment's thought, "okay, go ahead. What did my parents almost name me?"

"Myfanwy."

Clodagh, almost Myfanwy, winced.

"Sorry," said Lorraine.

"Okay," she concluded, "for the moment, let's say you are Chesney Potoski who has now become Lorraine Innis."

"Yes..."

Clodagh's mouth twitched as if she were weighing a puzzle in her mind. "...so, you're the most famous woman in the world."

"Okay..."

"Okay, so what do you need me for?"

Lorraine sighed. Her shoulders slumped. "I was trying to bring this person to justice, and it was the only way I could figure out how to do it."

"By becoming world-famous?"

"No, I didn't want to be famous at all," said Lorraine. "I figured I would take care of this villain and then disappear, that is, Lorraine would disappear, and I'd go back to being Chesney. But things happened, things I didn't figure on, and now this..." Lorraine gestured towards her own body. "...now I'm famous, and I'm stuck, and I don't know what to do, and I need your help. I really, really need your help, Clo. I really screwed up..."

Clodagh's mouth dropped open. "It is you!"

"Yes!"

Clodagh's free right arm cocked back as if to deliver another assault to Lorraine. Lorraine flinched and braced for the blow, only to have Clodagh stop, stare for a moment and break into a fit of giggles.

Lorraine relaxed. After sixty seconds of snickers, Clodagh daubed her eyes. Then after several deep breaths, her gaze turned critical once again.

"Yes, Ches," she nodded before Lorraine raised a finger to her own lips. "Oops, sorry," Clodagh whispered, "sorry, Mrs. Innis..."

"Lorraine..."

"Sure, whatever, Lorraine...well, *Lorraine*," she said Lorraine with added emphasis, as if she were sharing an inside joke, "you finally took my advice, *Lorraine*."

"Your advice?"

"Don't you remember? When we both were banned from the Earswick Public Library by Mr...oh, what was his name?"

"Mr. Repaupo... the Penguin!"

"Yes, that was it! Anyway, you had to get that book, and I told you to disguise yourself as Margaret Legotti?"

Lorraine felt her face redden. "Oh, yes. Actually, it wasn't that incident that gave me the idea."

"Still," she said, "you turned out pretty good."

"Pretty well," corrected Lorraine.

Clodagh sighed. "Yes, there's no doubt it's you in there. Still correcting everyone's grammar, I see. Good or well, you make a fine woman. You fooled me."

"I did?" asked Lorraine, though it was apparent she had.

"I've got several Lorraine Innis dresses at home, and…" she reached for her handbag and fished out a lipstick and powder compact. "…Lorraine Innis cosmetics. Yes, I wanted to be just like you, too. And to think, that I, along with half the women in the world, want to be just like a chubby little boy from Earswick."

"That was never my intention," said Lorraine.

Clodagh pulled out another lipstick. "I bought a Valerie Fierro lipstick, too… but I don't wear it."

"Why not?"

Clodagh grimaced. "I don't know; it's a little too…"

"…bold? Assertive?"

"Tarty," concluded Clodagh.

Lorraine grimaced.

"Oh, sorry," said Clodagh, "she's your cousin. I'm sorry."

"She's not really my cousin," said Lorraine, "but she is a close friend."

"Sorry."

"I know Valerie can seem very sexy to those who don't know her, but she's actually a very caring, understanding, compassionate person."

Clodagh nodded. "I'm sure she is, sorry. I'm sure I'll get to see that side of her when I get to know her."

Lorraine shook her head. "Oh, no, you'll never meet Valerie; not if I can help it. I need you for something completely secret." She retrieved the confidentiality agreement from the table. "Before I go on, maybe you'd better sign this after all.

– 4 –
Love and a Cast of One

A t that moment, the very caring, understanding, compassionate Valerie Fierro was exercising all those emotions on herself. "Ow," she cried, "that hurts."

"Sorry."

"I've got my arm in a cast here, you know!" snapped Valerie.

"I'm trying to avoid it, but if you want to know the truth…"

He paused for a moment. Valerie didn't answer. She didn't care about the truth at the moment but knew he was going to continue anyway.

"…to be perfectly honest… dear… you hit me with your cast. I didn't hit your cast." He paused before adding. "If you want to know the truth."

"I'm sorry," though she wasn't. She was irritated.

"Maybe it's just too difficult," he said, trying to lie beside her and not to disturb her arm. "Maybe we just wait a little longer to fool around… that is until your arm is out of the cast."

"Maybe," she muttered.

Mike Valvano leaned on his right arm and looked at her. Valerie's brow furrowed.

"You keep sitting there like that, and I won't be able to wait," she purred, "not even if I were in a body cast."

His boyish smile made her want him that much more.

"Cut it out," said Valerie, "or I'll grab you right there. I'll grab you by that gorgeous curly hair of yours, I'll jump on top of you, and I'll bang your brains out right now."

"You'd bang my brains out with that ten pounds of plaster," he said, pointing at the cast.

Valerie smiled back and felt very catlike. "It would be the most satisfying death a man ever had."

She arched her back and thrust her breasts towards him, but this lithe hallmark of her sexual repertoire just wasn't the same with a broken arm. She let her buttocks drop back to the mattress with a less than alluring "flump."

He tried to hide a frown.

"It's not my fault," she said.

"I didn't say it was," he said. He sounded sincere, but, she reminded herself, he had been a priest. Sincerity was standard-issue along with the backward collar.

"Stupid Lorraine," she muttered, though loud enough to be heard – as she intended.

"Oh, you shouldn't blame your cousin," he said. "You were driving when you had the accident, not her."

"Yes, but I wouldn't have been there if it wasn't for her."

"Maybe so, but you can't blame her. If you want to blame anyone, blame the one who designed it all."

"The guy who designed the bus that hit me, or the guy who designed my Lexus?"

He smiled indulgently and pointed skyward.

She rolled her eyes. That's what she got for bedding an ex-priest. He was always bringing his former boss around when she least suspected it.

"Let's leave him out of this," she said. "I'd rather blame Lorraine."

"God made Lorraine," said Mike.

Valerie laughed out loud. God made Lorraine? That was a good one. She made Lorraine Innis. Lorraine Innis, created by Valerie Fierro, based on a stupid idea by Chesney Potts.

"Besides, your cousin seems like a very nice woman," continued Mike, "even if she doesn't like me all that much."

"Well, that's reason enough," said Valerie, reaching out to stroke his arm. "If she doesn't like you then…"

"She was just being protective of you," he said, "There I was, by your bedside in the hospital; you, in a coma; me, captivated by your beauty. She was doing what any woman would do for her cousin."

Valerie smirked. Stupid Lorraine. What any woman would do? She's not a woman, and she's not even my cousin. Valerie had wanted to tell him all about Lorraine, but couldn't. She had too much responsibility for it all. Mike might think she was twisted or kinky or something. Well, she told herself, she was sort of kinky. She adored sex when he was wearing his clerical collar. That was fun. Not as much fun as when he wore it and had still been a priest, but she could pretend. That was playful, she reasoned, not kinky, and even if it was somewhat perverse, it was clean perverse.

Mike Valvano was still talking, and, she noticed, he was now half-dressed.

"Are you going?"

"Got to, Babe," he said, glancing at his watch as he strapped it to his wrist. "I told you I only had a little time. I've got to meet a man."

"Stupid cast," pouted Valerie, lifting her arm and then letting it drop.

He leaned over and kissed her.

"It won't be on much longer," he consoled her.

She stroked his face as he stood up, almost scratching his cheek with her nails. "You could..."

He cut her short as he pulled on his silk sports coat.

"...not today, Babe, I've got to make a living now. Not as much time for afternoon fun. I'm working for myself now."

Valerie grimaced. Some of his allure had faded. Oh, Michael was as sexy as ever, in some ways even more now that he was pulling in good money. But there was a degree of excitement that was missing, the sense that they were being naughty. It was that wonderful, clean perversity...

With his back towards her, in the darkened room, his gray jacket looked almost black, like a priest's. If she squinted the illusion was even more believable. If it weren't for this damned cast, she would have lunged at him, flying naked through the air, landing atop him and having him undressed by the time they hit the floor. She knew she could do it. She had done it before. Damned cast.

"What time will you pick me up," she asked him.

"For what?" he asked his back still to her.

"Dinner," she said, suppressing her annoyance at having to reply to the obvious.

"Dinner tomorrow?"

"Dinner tonight! I eat dinner every day, you know."

"Sorry, *Cara Mia*," he said, turning around. "I've got meetings this evening..."

"Michael."

"I told you, didn't I?"

She thought for a moment. He had told her. She almost accused him of not loving her but was already bored with using that tactic.

"We'll go out tomorrow," he promised.

"Michael?"

"Yes, *Bella Cara Mia?*"

"Do you love me?"

He tilted his head to the side and smiled. It was such a devoted look, such an understanding look, so full of love she almost forgave him for leaving.

"Michael?"

"Yes, love?"

"Do you still have your collar...your priest collar?"

"I've probably got one around. Why?"

She writhed seductively and batted her lashes at him. "I might need a visit from *Father* Valvano."

He wagged his finger at her. "That might be arranged. I'll pass that message along to Father Valvano…"

"Tell him," she cooed, "tell him I'm so lonely here, all alone…"

He was already out the bedroom door.

"Why don't you call your cousin?" He called over his shoulder. "I'm sure Lorraine will come over to keep you company."

Valerie seethed to a full boil by the time she heard the front door shut. Call Lorraine?

"Why would I talk to that stupid bitch?" muttered Valerie. "She wouldn't even talk to me all the way back from Washington."

Valerie punched the pillow with her good arm and then punched her head into the indentation and lay back down. She let out a deep sigh and settled into a calm that lasted all of thirty seconds. Then she sat up again.

"Stupid, stupid bitch!"

She looked around for something to hit. But the only thing that would give her real satisfaction to wallop was miles away.

"Probably still hasn't said a f**kin' word, f**kin' stupid bitch!"

Valerie rose and pulled on her silk dressing gown.

Michael would have to remind her of Lorraine and everything that had happened. Why couldn't he just have wild, satisfying sex and keep his mouth shut about Lorraine? Now the thoughts that she had been pushing from her mind came rushing back. The broken arm was bad enough. The accident that had totaled her new car wasn't much fun either. The other major event of the day, Peter Liverot being blown to bits on the White House lawn, could work to her advantage. What really annoyed her now, however, was that Liverot had said something to Lorraine on his deathbed. Valerie was having her arm set in another part of the hospital. Whatever Liverot said had plunged Lorraine into total silence ever since.

Valerie began pacing her bedroom. Had Liverot told on her? Had he revealed to Lorraine that Valerie was working against her wishes; that she had agreed to keep Lorraine under control in return for lucrative financial considerations? Had Lorraine let Liverot know that she wasn't really Lorraine Innis but a former employee of his by the name of Chesney Potts?

"Who cares what she said to him," she said aloud. "He's dead now, so who cares what she said?"

What Lorraine said to Liverot didn't bother Valerie. It was what Lorraine didn't say to her for over three hours. It was like taking a road trip with a brunette Harpo Marx; not a single sound apart from the occasional tooting of a horn.

"Stupid bit…"

Valerie stopped in mid-rant and smirked. She's even got me doing it, she thought. She was the only person in the world who knew that Lorraine Innis, the beloved idol of womanhood, the worldwide icon of the best of feminine attributes, the role model for a generation of empowered girls was really a man. Valerie had been there from the beginning, and while the whole idiotic scheme wasn't hers, she as much as anyone had helped make a doughy little loser into a universally admired figure. She stopped in front of the dresser mirror and looked at her own reflection. Figure! Her figure was better than Lorraine's. Hers was real; no padding. She could do a *Playboy* photoshoot. Lorraine couldn't do that. Lorraine wouldn't do that. No, Lorraine Innis was too pure for that! Lorraine didn't know how to capitalize on a tenth of what had been thrown her way.

"Stupid…"

She caught herself again. She had a hard time not thinking of Lorraine as a woman. The longer the whole charade went on, the more Chesney Potts faded away. That's why Lorraine wanted to retire. She wanted to disappear before he did.

"Who cares?" she muttered aloud to herself. Who cares if Chesney Potts disappears? No one except Chesney Potts and he's half-way gone. After all, no one missed him. All the people who'd ever cared about fat, dumpy Chesney were dead. What did Lorraine care if she had to go on being Lorraine? Hell, thought Valerie, if she had the world handed to her on a silver platter she'd agree to spend the rest of her life as a longshoreman, or a wildebeest, or one of the seven dwarves.

"Stupid… person!"

That didn't feel right.

"Stupid, stupid, bitch! BITCH! BITCH! BITCH!"

Yes, that was satisfying. It was right. "He's Lorraine now, and he's going to stay Lorraine," Valerie growled, "at least until I get everything that's coming to me." She punctuated "me" with a swift jerking of her arm towards her chest. Unfortunately, she was so engrossed in her tirade that she did so with her plastered arm. She fell back on the bed with a moan, cradling her right breast.

"I'll get you for that one, too, Lorraine!" she vowed.

She would get everything that was owed her: all the fame, all the adulation, all the money… especially the money. Lorraine will just have to like it, Valerie would see to that.

Valerie's determination faded as she realized that she couldn't even get Lorraine to open her mouth on the way back from Washington. How then, Valerie wondered, could she make Lorraine do what she wanted her to do?

She thought for a moment then a deliciously devious smile spread across her lips.

Maybe she couldn't get Lorraine to do what she wanted, but she could always manipulate Chesney, or at least that little bit of Chesney that was still there under all that Lorraine. She could twist him around her little pinkie. She had mastered handling men from a very early age.

Valerie reached down and fingered the small gold pendant around her neck. Most people just thought it was an abstract design. Only she knew what it really was.

"*Prima I dente, poi I parenti...*" she whispered. Her eyes moistened. "*Prima I dente, poi I parenti,*" she repeated. "I haven't forgotten, Daddy."

Valerie closed her eyes and could almost see him again. So strong, so loving; stern outwardly, but inwardly tender, especially to her, his *Piccola Principessa* – his little princess.

She rubbed the gold charm between her fingers, and she was there again.

◆

It was her thirteenth birthday. Her father pulled her aside, in private and gave it to her. Though she had never had any grown-up jewelry before, Valerie instinctively knew it was real gold, and that excited her very much...in spite of the odd shape. Her expression must have betrayed her puzzlement, for her father took her chin in his rough hand and stroked her cheek with his thumb.

"Happy birthday, *Principessa,*" he said. His English always sounded a little stilted, but his Italian sounded like a beautiful melody.

"Thank you..."

"Already you are growing up, this is why I give you this," said Giorgio Fierro. "Wear it always. Always to remember, and never forget, will you do that?"

"I will, Daddy," she said. "I'll always remember you, and never forget you gave me this... this... gold thing."

He smiled and wiggled her chin in his hand. "No, Valerie. I know you'll always remember me. I want you to remember the tooth."

"The tooth?" She looked down at the gold charm. It did sort of look like a tooth.

"I didn't want it to look too much like a tooth. What would my *Principessa* look like with an ugly old tooth around her neck?" He lifted the delicate chain and placed it around her neck. After fumbling with the tiny clasp, he secured it and let it drop. The charm fell just between the cleft of her developing breasts. "I know it's a tooth, and you know it's a tooth, and that's enough so you can always remember."

"Remember what, Papa?"

"*Prima I dente, poi I parenti,*" Giorgio Fierro said, almost as if it were part of some sacred incantation.

Despite having spent thirteen years with a native-born Italian, and having a mother who was second-generation Italian, Valerie was not fluent in the language. Her older sister Rose was much better at it, but Valerie struggled to pick out the words that sounded familiar.

"First... something," she began. His face contorted as he rooted her on. "Then, something, something... parents?"

He reached out and hugged her in his powerful arms. Then pushed her back to arm's length, smiled, and said: "No!"

"No, *Piccola Principessa. Prima I dente, poi I parenti.* 'First,' you got that right. '*Parenti*,' that means relatives. *Prima I dente, poi I parenti.* It means first your teeth, then your relatives. I want you to always remember that. Will you do that, Valerie?"

She nodded. "I promise," she said. "I'll take good care of my teeth."

He gave her another smile, followed by a shake of his head. "That's a saying, a, uh, a *proverbio*, a proverb. It means: look out for yourself first. After that, you can worry about your family. But you've got to take care of you first."

Valerie smiled. She liked that advice. After all, who better to look out for you but yourself? Then a thought darkened her mind.

"What about you, Papa?" she asked. "Does that mean you won't look out for me first?"

He hugged her.

"*Mio Piccola Principessa,* you are more precious to me than my teeth. In your Papa's case the saying is: *Prima Principessa, poi I dente, poi I parenti!* And it will always be that way."

He repeated the phrase several times more, and she echoed it until she had committed it to memory.

◆

Valerie Fierro opened her eyes, pressed the gold tooth to her bosom, and renewed her vow.

"Lookin' out for number one..." she said and rolled over for a nap.

- 5 -
Giorgio vs. the Swazzy-Stickers

Giorgio Fierro's earliest memories in his native Sicily were of teeth. His mother was always mentioning teeth to his father. He often wondered why. His father wasn't a dentist. His father ran the family's small café until he was conscripted into the army. By the time Giorgio figured it out it didn't matter. By then he was an orphan in another country.

His father was a big strong man, but then most men look big and strong when you're two-years-old. By the time Giorgio turned three his father was gone, like most of the other local men.

Giorgio remembered asking his mother why his father and all the other men, all except the old ones, had to go away.

His mother would just say: "*Il Duce.*" Then she would look at the picture of the bald man with the big jaw hanging in the café. If no one were around, she would spit on the floor. The spitting stunned Giorgio because his mother scrubbed the floor every day.

His father going away was fixed in Giorgio's memory. There was a lot of hugging, and there were tears in his father's eyes. He had hugged Giorgio before, but never with tears. Not soon after he went away he came back, but now he was in a tan uniform, as were the other men who went away but never came back. After that, Giorgio never saw his father again.

Ironically, while most of the village men went away in uniforms, other men, not from the village, took their place. The uniforms of these men were gray. Many of them had yellow hair, pale skin, and they spoke a different language.

His mother told him they were *Tedeschi* – Germans. The Tedeschi were nice to Giorgio. They would come into the café, rub his head, and make remarks in their strange language, smile, and laugh. They would often make other comments to each other that Giorgio sensed were about his mother. These also were accompanied by smiles and laughs, but they were different kinds of smiles and a type of laughter that Giorgio did not understand.

He could tell that his mother did not think these remarks were nearly as amusing as the Tedeschi thought they were. She didn't laugh, at least not in the kitchen. Still, out in the café, she smiled a pretend smile. Giorgio had a harder time pretending to be pleasant, but it didn't seem to bother these soldiers. They didn't care what a little boy thought of them, except for one. One Tedeschi seemed nicer than all the others. He didn't joke the same way. He didn't even rub Giorgio's head, but instead patted him on the shoulder as if he really liked Giorgio. He spoke to Giorgio's mother in Italian, or at least he tried, and even when his vocabulary fell short, there was always a sincere *grazie* on the end of every sentence.

One day the nice Tedeschi brought Giorgio a toy plane. It was made of wood, and the Tedeschi had made it himself. At first, Giorgio thought he was just showing it to him. After admiring it, Giorgio started to hand it back only to be encouraged to keep it.

"Tell *Capitano* Zimmer 'thank you,'" said Uncle Roberto, who was very old. He must have been the oldest person in the world, Giorgio thought, because he was always telling other people what to do.

Giorgio took a step back.

"Would you like to give the nice plane back to the Capitano?" asked Uncle Roberto.

Giorgio clutched the hand-carved toy to his chest and shook his head.

"Then thank the good Capitano," said Roberto.

"Grazie," said Giorgio shyly.

Capitano Zimmer nodded and said, "*prego*," but with that odd Tedeschi accent. Then he reached out his gray sleeve and patted Giorgio. It was a friendly pat, and Giorgio relaxed. He looked at the toy and smiled, but wished he had something to offer in return. He had an idea.

"I... I can do a tumble," he said. His father had taught him some tumbles. Giorgio had performed his little tricks before, but only for his aunts and uncles, never for one of the soldiers. It was the only thing he had to offer in return for the toy airplane.

Captaino Zimmer gave Giorgio and then Uncle Roberto a puzzled look. Perhaps, Giorgio thought, they didn't have tumbling where he came from. Uncle Roberto nodded at Giorgio and said: "Giorgio, go ahead, do your tumble."

Giorgio placed the airplane on the table, gave himself plenty of room and then did a forward summersault. When he came up from the flip, Giorgio saw a fresh smile, a smile of understanding and of pleasure on the Capitano's face. He started to applaud.

"Wait, wait," said Giorgio, setting his feet just the right distance apart just as his father had taught him. He looked behind to make sure the area was clear, and then, with all the concentration he could muster, executed a rather awkward backward summersault. Giorgio had so much momentum that he fell down at the end of it.

"Bravo, bravo," said Capitano Zimmer. "That is very good. Where I come from we have acrobats, in my wife's family, they are almost as good as you!"

Giorgio was so encouraged by the Capitano's response that he wracked his brain for an encore. Knowing only two tumbling tricks and having exhausted those, Giorgio settled on the only other talent he could think of.

"I can sing a song," he said to the Capitano, who unsure of the translation looked to Uncle Roberto for an interpretation.

"*Was? Uh, che cosa?*" asked Zimmer.

"*Cantare...*" Uncle Roberto, knowing very little German, scratched his gray head for a moment then put his right hand to his chest, stuck his left index finger in the air, and mimed an aria.

"*Ach! Ein Leid!*" Capitano Zimmer smiled and nodded.

"Go ahead, Giorgio," said Roberto while lifting his skinny body atop a nearby table.

Giorgio looked around. He had never been allowed to stand on a table before. From his vantage point, he could see all over the café. The soldiers all looked up at him.

Giorgio froze with all those faces staring up at him. It was the first time in his life he could recall people looking up at him. He glanced down at Uncle Roberto, who nodded for him to continue.

"Tell them," said Roberto, "tell them what you are going to sing."

"*Una canzone... Come sentito alla radio da* Mr. Hugh Goode..." said Giorgio.

Most of the Germans looked to Zimmer, who attempted to translate.

"*Ein Lied... als im Radio gehört.*"

A song, as heard on the radio. The other Germans put down their glasses and stuck their cigarettes into their mouths to free their hands for applause. Giorgio bowed, cleared his throat, and sang loud and clear the song he had heard many times on the radio.

Who's that man with the funny little mustache,
Spouting all his bile?
The one that all the jackboots follow,
While they shout Sieg Heil?
It isn't Charlie Chaplin, he isn't clever, not half,
And though he talks old cobblers, He never gets a laugh

Adolph Hitler, with your silly swazzy-stickers,
Adolph Hitler, all your girls have Nazi-knickers...

By the time Giorgio reached the chorus the novelty of a little Italian boy singing atop a table had worn off and the English lyrics, albeit sung with a heavy Italian accent, were deciphered by many of the Germans. There were some snorts of derision made through an alcoholic fog, but the majority of soldiers present weren't drunk enough to excuse the matter. These exchanged confused looks and the question *"Englisch?"* was heard on more than one pair of lips.

Unaware that he was mocking the leader of an ally, Giorgio continued, his singing, in fact, grew louder. Uncle Roberto, even worse in English than in German, was unaware of the content of the song until he heard the name of Adolph Hitler voiced in the language of the enemy. He tried to hush the boy, but it was too late. Giorgio's mother emerged from the kitchen. Her eyes grew large at the scene which she had overheard and was now seeing. As she entered from the kitchen, a large imposing officer was filling the cafe's main entrance with his military decorations, and substantial girth. His heavy scowl attested to his ability to understand English, even when filtered through the mouth of a three-and-a-half-year-old Italian.

"Halt! Arrestare!" demanded the officer.

Giorgio's mother clapped her palm over his mouth in mid-verse. Giorgio stood there, atop the table, with his mother and Uncle Roberto shielding him from the irate officer who seemed intent on scolding all the other soldiers present. All of them, even the ones who had seemed relaxed by the wine, suddenly looked very sober. Stony expressions now graced every face; except that is for Capitano Zimmer's. Capitano Zimmer seemed to be trying to explain, or apologize, or do something that Giorgio couldn't understand. Occasionally, Zimmer would turn to try and translate the fat officer's tirade, but always in softer, understanding tones. This concession only brought a fresh wave of yelling from the fat man.

Finally, the fat officer barked some commands to the soldiers who dashed from the cafe, all of course, except Capitano Zimmer. It seemed that Zimmer was left behind to translate.

"Seniora," Zimmer began, "the boy, he should not sing that song..."

At this point, the fat man interrupted and barked some orders at Zimmer. Zimmer turned. With his back to the fat one, he rolled his eyes as if to apologize in advance for what he was being compelled to do.

"This café is off-limits to all personnel of the Third Reich!" he said sternly and then turned to the fat man who nodded his approval of the change in tone. Zimmer turned and made another grimace to personally disavow the message.

"This boy has shown great disrespect to our beloved Fuhrer, and to all the German people!"

The fat officer prodded him to continue. It was evident that he comprehended Zimmer's softened tone much more than the broken Italian he was speaking.

"The Fuhrer and the German people are the friends and protectors of the Italian people..." he paused here to glance back at his superior, who prompted him with more words.

"...We are protecting your island from the English and the Americans... and, and you throw this back in our faces by listening to illicit radio songs designed to insult our Fuhrer, and to sow discord between the German and Italian people..."

Giorgio's mother and Uncle Roberto made many apologies, though Giorgio couldn't understand why. He thought his singing was quite good; nearly as good as his tumbling had been, so he just stood there atop the table scratching his head until the fat man seemed satisfied, barked something at them in his strange tongue, wagged his pudgy finger, and then turned on his heel and marched out of the café. Capitano Zimmer remained behind for at least a moment.

"I'm sorry, sorry for..." he said, then rolled his eyes in the direction of the door and ran out after the fat man.

After he had left, Giorgio's mother stood there with her face frozen in a very heroic expression. But after a motor started up and drove away, she slumped into a chair put her face in her hands and began to cry. Uncle Roberto sat beside her, shaking his head.

Giorgio felt responsible for what had happened, but still didn't fully understand. He bent down over his mother and patted her head.

"I will sing better, Mama," he said. "Don't cry. I will practice, and next time I will sing much better for the Tedeschi."

Instead of comforting her, Giorgio's assurance made her cry harder.

"Don't worry," said Uncle Roberto, but he appeared worried enough for all of them. Giorgio wasn't sure who wasn't supposed to worry, it was all so confusing. Things didn't get any clearer when Roberto called out for Rosa, his daughter, and his mother's cousin bustled into the room from the kitchen.

Giorgio liked Rosa. She was a bouncy lady, and not just because she was shaped like a rubber ball. She was almost always cheery, and would always share her candy with Giorgio and even give him the biggest piece. Rosa was often in the kitchen, concocting a massive pot of red sauce. Despite her size, which was exaggerated due to her lack of height, Giorgio never actually saw Rosa eat, not the way most people ate, at least, not sitting down with a knife and a fork. Instead, she seemed to sample things continually.

"*Io sono solo un piccolo assaggio,*" was her favorite phrase. "I'll just have a little taste..." More than once, Giorgio would hear an adult remarking: "here comes piccolo assaggio," and there was Cousin Rosa.

Roberto asked Rosa to take Giorgio into the kitchen and then muttered something under his breath. Rosa's face appeared serious for a moment, then she looked up at Giorgio and suddenly seemed to brighten even more than usual.

"Come, come here, with Rosa," she said, though the command was unnecessary since she carried him away in her arms. Once in the kitchen, she sat him on the counter and returned to one of her large kettles of sauce. She sampled a bit from the tip of a wooden spoon, nodded her approval, and then ladled some onto a dish. Then she tore the end off of a crusty loaf of bread and handed them both to Giorgio.

"Here, eat, Giorgio," she said before asking: "Are you hungry?"

Giorgio waved his head as he had seen her do and replied: "I'll have a little taste."

Rosa seemed oblivious to this appropriation of her personal phrase and returned to her pot. Giorgio dipped the corner of the bread in the thick sauce, started to bring it to his mouth, and then stopped.

"Rosa," he said.

"What?" she said, not looking up from the pot.

"The Tedeschi..."

"What about them?"

"Why don't they like my singing?"

"What do you mean?"

Giorgio related as best he could what had just happened. After listening to the disjointed account, Rosa put her arm around Giorgio.

"This is a big world," she said. "It goes past this little village. You know that, don't you?"

He nodded his head. "Yes, there's Trapani." That was the big town where he had gone once with his parents.

"Yes, well," she said, "it's even bigger than Trapani."

Giorgio was amazed.

"It's a very, very big world," said Rosa, "and it's much, much bigger than Trapani, or Rilievo. There are bigger parts of Sicily and even bigger parts of Italy, and even that isn't the end of it. There are other countries bigger than Italy, and then there are countries over the seas bigger still."

Giorgio was astonished. Where, he wondered, would it all end?

"And, you," Rosa pinched the end of his nose, "you, my dear Giorgio, are a very little boy in a very little village. Do you understand?"

Giorgio thought for a moment and then nodded his head.

"All except..."

"All except what?"

"Why the Tedeschi don't like my singing?"

Rosa grimaced and thought for a moment.

"I don't think it's your singing. You are a very nice singer. It's just like I said, you are a little boy in a little village, and you are not the center of a very big world. You are the center of your Mama and Papa's world, and you're a very precious part of my world and your Uncle Roberto's world, but as precious as that is, it's not a very big world to anyone outside of it."

"Not the Tedeschi?"

"Especially not the Tedeschi," said Rosa with a scowl. "The Tedeschi and all the soldiers and airmen you see are very busy. They are much too busy to worry about little boys singing. So even though you might think they don't like your singing, you shouldn't worry about it."

"No?"

"No," said Rosa. "Remember, *Prima I dente, poi I parenti.*"

"That's Papa," said Giorgio brightly, "Dente! That's what Mama calls him."

"Dante," laughed Rosa hugging him. "Dante, that's your Papa's name. He's not a tooth!"

Giorgio felt his own teeth and felt a great relief for this explanation.

"The soldiers do not worry about you," said Rosa.

"Capitano Zimmer is very nice," said Giorgio.

"Yes, I'm sure he is," said Rosa, before adding, "for one of *them.*"

"He asked me to sing, he likes my tumbling."

"Yes, yes, I'm sure he does, but even this Capitano Zimmer, he has bigger problems to worry about. I'm sure he's very nice and likes you and your tricks all very much. But he looks out for him, and you look out for..."

"Teeth..."

"No, what I meant..."

"Papa, Dante..."

"No, no, Giorgio, listen, when I say first your teeth, then your relatives, I don't mean your teeth..."

"Papa's teeth?"

"No, no..."

"Your teeth?"

"No, it's a saying. It's just a way to say you look out for you. Those soldiers don't care about you, they care about themselves, they look out for themselves, and then maybe after that, they think about their family."

"Their mamas and papas?"

"Yes, or their wives or children, do you understand what I'm trying to tell you?"

"I, uh..."

"Don't think the big world revolves around little Giorgio, and don't worry that someone doesn't like your singing or your tumbling or whatever it is you do. *Prima I dente, poi I parenti.*"

"*Prima I dente, poi I parenti,*" Giorgio repeated it slowly as he pondered the words, and then a second time to help make it stick in his head.

"Good!" said Rosa.

"And I only worry about what I do good," said Giorgio and don't worry about what anyone thinks."

"Right," said Rosa as she stirred the sauce.

"And you, too."

"Me, too? What?"

"Don't you worry about what you do. Who cares what anyone else thinks?"

"What?"

"Like your sauce..."

Rosa turned and rolled her eyes at him. "I make the best sauce!"

"In all the village?"

"In all the world!" said Rosa, as she began to stir the pot. "Sometimes you learn too much, too quickly, too well."

– 6 –
A Grammatical Matter
of Life and Death

It was like a festival, only there weren't any flags, or processions, or special food. Everyone was excited, shouting, and running. Giorgio Fierro was sitting on the steps outside the café when it began. An old man leaned out of his window and yelled: "*Invasione, INVASIONE!*"

People repeated the word, often while they ran about. It was almost like the way everyone shouted "Merry Christmas," or "Happy New Year," only they didn't run around when they did that. Nor did they ask questions when someone said: "Merry Christmas."

Everyone seemed to have a different question.

"Where? When? Who was it? Which way are they going? Where did you hear it? On the radio? Whose radio?"

This last question was often whispered. Not many of the people listened to the radio. Aside from the café, there were only five sets in the town, and only three of those worked.

After watching the commotion for several minutes and realizing there wouldn't be a parade or any treats handed out, Giorgio went inside the café. It was empty. Certainly, it was devoid of Tedeschi. A few times after the fat Tedeschi had made such a fuss over Giorgio's singing he thought Capitano Zimmer had come to visit, but this was always after Giorgio had gone to bed. Giorgio thought he heard the Capitano's voice, but he had never seen him. He could hear him across the hall in his mother's room. Giorgio stole from his small bed and crept across the hall. He could hear whispers inside, but the door was locked. When he rattled knob, it grew very quiet on the other side until Giorgio's mother called out. Her voice sounded odd; like she was out of breath. She told him to go back to bed. Giorgio told his mother the door was locked. She told him she would fix it in the morning. Then he heard a giggle; like it came from a man. So

Giorgio went back to bed, wondering how his mother learned to giggle like a man.

The mornings after he thought he heard the night visitor, there would always be hard-to-find canned meat for breakfast.

Other things had changed too. His mother had grown fatter, just around her middle. Giorgio marveled at this since their already meager diet was even more so of late. But still, his mother grew. Other women, the older women shook their heads and whispered. Giorgio heard his mother explain to the other women that Papa had come back for a very short visit. When Giorgio interrupted, tugging on her skirt and asking why he hadn't seen Papa, his mother's face turned the color of Rosa's sauce. Then she would explain that he had been asleep.

The women had exchanged smirks, nods, and disapproving looks, but Giorgio wasn't concerned about that. What he didn't understand is why his father hadn't woken him up.

That was months ago now, and Papa hadn't come back for any more visits.

Now Giorgio looked around the empty café. He heard a racket in the kitchen and ran to see what it was. Giorgio saw his mother wrapping plates in old newspaper and then packing them into barrels.

"Mama," said Giorgio rushing to her side, "today is an invasion."

"Yes, Giorgio," said his mother somewhat out of breath. She seemed to be more and more out of breath as she grew fatter and fatter.

"Can I go?"

"Go? Go where?" she asked.

"...to see the invasion."

"No!" she snapped. "Don't worry, the invasion will come here. You won't have to go see it. It will be here soon enough."

"Are you going to see it?"

"What? No, Giorgio, why would you ask such a thing?"

Giorgio pointed to the crates and the dishes. "I thought maybe you were taking the plates to have a picnic at the invasion...and you weren't going to take me."

Her cross expression melted into a smile. She crouched down as far down as her belly would allow and hugged him.

"Are you worried that I would ever leave you, my little monkey?"

Giorgio nodded. "I don't want to miss it."

"Miss what?"

"The invasion."

His mother sighed and shook her head. "You don't understand. The invasion is a lot of soldiers coming."

"Even more soldiers? Are they more Tedeschi?"

"No. No, they are not, they are *Americani* and *Inglese*."

Giorgio thought about the toy plane that Capitano Zimmer had given him. "Will they bring airplanes, too?"

"Yes, and soldiers, and tanks."

Tanks! Giorgio didn't have a tank. He would like a tank very much. "Will they get here soon?"

"Soon enough," she said and resumed wrapping the dishes. "That's why we must wrap up what we can and store it down in the basement so that it doesn't get broken. Do you understand?"

Giorgio nodded. Perhaps Americani and Inglese were clumsy and broke plates. He knew very little about the Americani, so he hoped the Inglese would come, too. He knew Inglese songs, especially the ones that Hugh Goode sang on the radio.

"Will he come, too?" said Giorgio completing his thought aloud.

"Will who come?"

"Mr. Hugh Goode? I know his songs. Will he come, too?"

"Don't ask so many silly questions," said his mother.

Giorgio turned away, uncertain if it was a silly question because it would happen or because it wouldn't happen. Another question sprang into his head, and before he could decide whether it was silly or not, it gushed from his lips.

"How many days until my birthday?"

"What? Oh, today is..." she glanced up at the calendar on the wall, "... today is the 10th. It's still two more weeks until then."

"How many days is that?"

"Fourteen," she said without looking up.

Giorgio nodded to himself and then looked at his fingers. He only had ten of those. He looked down at his bare feet. There were another ten of those, but he wasn't exactly sure how many more he would need to make the fourteen. He hoped the Inglese would come before his birthday and that Mr. Hugh Goode would bring him a tank.

The ensuing days dragged on in the hot July sun as the world baked into an impenetrable crust. Each day the adults were even more anxious than the day before about invasions and approaching soldiers. This Giorgio found puzzling since they already had soldiers. Why should more soldiers be an occasion for news? A fellow's fourth birthday, now that was something exciting. More strange men in uniforms? Not so much.

The day before his birthday, he woke with a palpable excitement in the air. People were leaving town, and there seemed to be a considerable amount of activity coming and going from the nearby airfield. Before he could even go downstairs for breakfast, his mother came to his room.

"Giorgio," she said urgently, "we're going to the basement."

"Is there a party in the basement?"

"Party?" she asked, looking out the window. "There's no party. It's the Americani."

Giorgio was surprised. They'd had spiders, and once even a snake in the basement, but never Americani.

"Can I talk to them? Can I tumble for them? Do they like Inglese songs?"

"I don't know, you can ask them when they get here, but until then we have to stay in the basement. It's safer."

Giorgio shrugged and followed his mother down the stairs, though she was now so fat it was a slow process.

They were halfway through the cafe when his mother lurched forward and let out a sharp cry and sat down. She was clutching her belly and panting. Tiny beads of sweat popped out all around her face.

"You'll be cooler in the basement," he said, not sure of what else to say.

His mother started to rise and then plopped down again. Her eyes looked towards the ceiling, and all Giorgio could see were their whites. Giorgio's right foot stood on his left foot to keep himself from running away. He often did this when he was afraid.

"Mama?" he said after a moment in which the only sound was her deep panting. "I'll help you... down... stairs?"

Her answer was long in coming and followed a deep swallow.

"No Giorgio," she said, trying to smile. "No, my... my time has come."

Giorgio wasn't sure what time this was since he didn't know how to tell time.

She reached out and grasped his hand.

"Giorgio," she said, now she was speaking in shallow but determined gasps, "my boy... you must go get..."

She paused.

"Go, and see if Rosa is around, and tell her to come quickly..."

"Rosa," Giorgio repeated. "Is she going to cook?"

His mother shook her head, her long dark hair now matted with sweat.

"No, no," she smiled, though with great effort, "no... tell Rosa: 'Mama's time has come.' Now say that back to me."

"Tell Rosa: Mama's time has come."

"That's good, very good..."

He smiled at her, she smiled back, and then as he remained frozen to his spot, she winced in pain and barked: "GO!"

Giorgio stood still for a second, and then like a tightly coiled spring bolted out the door and into the street. The village was in a state of pandemonium. Several of the neighbors he passed shouted to him, but Giorgio paid no attention. He ran as fast as he could, repeating his message lest he forget a word of it. He reached the street where Rosa lived with Uncle Roberto, darted up their lane, and up the handful of stone steps to the door. It was ajar, and so he dashed inside. There Rosa, not surprisingly, was holding a stockpot. What was surprising was that the pot was empty. She stared at Giorgio, startled by his abrupt entrance. He stared back, equally amazed by the sight of Rosa holding a pot devoid of food.

"Giorgio," she began, "what are you..."

Giorgio gulped a deep breath and blurted out his urgent message. "Tellrosamamastimehascome..."

She shook her head "I can't understand you. Slow down, Giorgio," she said, "what is it?"

Giorgio started pulling on her plump hand, repeating the command several times as he did so. Finally, either through repetition or the fact that Giorgio's was winding down, Rosa's face lit up.

"Her time! Your Mama's time has come!"

Giorgio gulped another slab of the sultry air, nodded and slumped into a nearby chair. Instead of running out the door, Rosa began gathering a collection of towels and things from the cupboard. Before he knew it, she had packed her supplies in a basket and was out the door. He sat in silence for a moment before she rushed back in.

"Giorgio," she said and repeated his name a few times. "Come with me, no, wait here, no, you can come, no, you'd better not, oh, I don't know what to... no, you'd better wait, here..."

Giorgio interrupted with a suggestion. "Uncle Roberto..."

Rosa stopped and nodded. "Yes, Uncle Roberto will be back soon... I hope. Wait for him and tell him I am helping your Mama. *Mio Dio!* What a day for all this to happen. What a time for your Mama to have her time!"

"Yes," agreed Giorgio, "my birthday is tomorrow!"

Rosa shook her head. "And you may have to share it. You wait here, do you hear me?"

"Can I watch the parade?"

"Parade?"

"The Invasion," said Giorgio, "the Americani." He was still not sure what an invasion entailed, but he was reasonably certain there would be a parade, perhaps in honor of his fourth birthday.

"No, no," said Rosa. A worried look clouded her face. "Don't watch the parade, stay inside, don't go near any soldiers. Stay here!"

Giorgio nodded. "What if I have to go?"

"Go? Go where?"

"Go!" He made a gesture with one hand towards his groin, and with the other pointed in the direction of the outhouse.

Rosa rolled her eyes and sighed. "Okay, you stay inside. Don't go out, but if you have to go out, stay away from anyone, especially any soldiers."

"Tedeschi, too?"

"All soldiers," she said, "if you have to go, go, and hurry back here and wait for either me or Uncle Roberto."

"If I see any soldiers..."

"If you see any soldiers... well... play dead."

"Dead?"

"Yes, lie down. Don't look at them. Pretend you're dead and they'll leave you alone. Now, if you have to go outside, what are you?"

"I'm Giorgio!"

"No, you're dead," she said.

They rehearsed this scenario several times until Rosa was confident it had taken hold. Then she gave Giorgio a kiss on the forehead followed by a slap on the backside, and a warning to remember, before rushing out the door.

Giorgio sat very, very quietly for a long time before deciding he must go to the outhouse. It must have been nearly two minutes. Then, moving as if he had a very full bladder to convince himself, he walked outside to the outhouse. Once inside, he stood almost another two minutes to coax out a trickle to justify the trip. He was leaving the outhouse when he heard a roar of a motor coming up the main street of the village. Momentarily forgetting his coaching from Rosa, he ran up the side street to see if the parade had begun. It wasn't a parade, but it was a gray motorcycle with a sidecar. On the side of it was painted a black cross.

Not an Americani, thought Giorgio disappointedly, just a Tedeschi. Then Giorgio recognized the man in the sidecar. It was Capitano Zimmer. He started to wave, but then he remembered Rosa's instructions and dropped to the pavement.

The motorcycle roared up to him and came to a stop. He opened his eyes to see Capitano Zimmer jump out and rush to his side.

"Are you okay?" he said in his broken Italian.

"Yes," said Giorgio opening his eyes.

"I was at your house, at the cafe," said Zimmer fumbling for the words, "but it was closed up. Where is your mother?"

"Her time has come," said Giorgio, then thinking Rosa was part of the equation, he added, "and Rosa, too."

Zimmer seemed visibly shaken by this information. The man on the motorcycle said something in the Tedeschi language indicating he was in a hurry. Zimmer said something back to him and then turned to Giorgio.

"So," said Zimmer in his halting Italian, "*sei morto?*"

Giorgio's face lit up. Capitano Zimmer appreciated another of his performances. "*Si, si! Sono morto!*"

Capitano Zimmer lowered his head and seemed upset by it all. Had he had a better grasp of Italian grammar, he would not have done what he did next. For while he meant to say: "*sono morti* – they're dead," he actually said "*sei morto* – you're dead." This, coupled with Giorgio's agreement to the statement, and the apparent rush he was in, resulted in Capitano Zimmer scooping up Giorgio, jumping back into the sidecar with him, and speeding off through the town.

Before Giorgio knew what was happening next, he was on an airplane flying over the water. He began to understand what an invasion truly entailed.

- 7 -
She Could Never Be Me
While I Was Around

Lorraine Innis stared at the document.

"You saw me sign it," said Clodagh.

"Sorry," said Lorraine, smiling faintly, "I'm not questioning your word, or that you'd keep what I'm going to share a secret. You'd do that even without this paper. I was just thinking of people, things, and what's about to happen…"

"Well, I'm glad one of us knows what's happening," said Clodagh. "As much as I like to catch up with old friends, even in new forms, I still don't understand what you want."

Lorraine walked to the window and looked out over the Wilmington skyline. She could see the twin spans of the Delaware Memorial Bridge leading into New Jersey where so much of her history lay. In the same direction, thousands of miles beyond the sea… she sighed.

"I'm not very good at all this," Lorraine started with her back to Clodagh. "I've made a terrible mess of things, as usual."

"Not very good? You're the most famous woman in the world. You save world leaders, inspire peace plans …"

"Okay, okay," said Lorraine, "let me put it another way. Chesney Potts…"

"Potts?"

"I mean Chesney Potoski, I, that is he changed his name… that's another long story. Anyway, whether he's a Potts or a Potoski, Chesney isn't very good at this. Lorraine Innis was really behind all those other things."

"But there's only one person," said Clodagh.

"Chesney gets it all wrong. He, that is I, always have. It was Lorraine who did all those things. And she did them correctly. Most of it happened when she didn't know there was a Chesney."

"But how could you not know who you really are?"

44

Lorraine shook her head. "It wasn't easy. I had assumed the guise of Lorraine Innis, and then I was traumatized into forgetting who I really was. So, when I was doing all those heroic things and making all those wise decisions, I only thought I was Lorraine."

Lorraine paused. After thirty seconds of silence, she turned around.

"Go ahead," said Clodagh.

"You understand?"

"Sure. I've studied the mind enough to know that just about anything is possible, especially under severe shock or stress."

Lorraine nodded. "Well, at least I don't have to convince you of that. It's when I know I'm playing Lorraine, like an actor's role that I get in the way, that is, Chesney gets in the way. Do you see what I mean?"

"I believe so. You've come to the conclusion that Lorraine Innis is a better woman than Chesney Potoski can pretend to be."

Lorraine slumped down in the chair, her legs splayed in a very unfeminine manner, and she sighed. "That's about the size of it. Lorraine is not only a better woman, but she's also a better person. She doesn't mess things up the way he does." She looked down at her stance. "See? After being Lorraine 24 hours a day, seven days a week for nearly a year, I still slip, especially if I'm around someone who reminds me of my other self. And it's not just the sitting, standing, walking, talking parts, I rarely mess those up. The worst is the thinking. When I think like Lorraine, I'm flawless. I'm smart, I'm kind, I'm compassionate…"

"And why do you think that is?"

"Because Lorraine Innis was designed to be that way. She's the person I'd create if I could build an adult from scratch. She doesn't have all of the fears, the self-doubts, the hurts, the baggage that we all pick up in our journey through this crazy world."

"And that's why everyone loves you," she said. "Because you're the person we'd all like to be, the person we'd all like to know."

Lorraine Innis sat up and pounded her fists on her knees. "But can't you see? That's the problem. I can't be her and him at the same time. At times, when I'm talking about both of them, I don't feel as if I'm either. That's why I need your help. I saw you on television. You were talking about the many techniques you used as a management consultant."

Clodagh smiled. "Oh? Which one was it that you needed? My Visualizing the Rungs on the Ladder of Success, or my 37 Tough Love Habits of a Compassionate Manager?"

Lorraine waved her hands. "No, no, I don't need any of that silly stuff…"

Clodagh grimaced. "I see what you mean about your being too Chesney at times."

"It was when they were mentioning your other qualifications; specifically your license as a hypnotherapist. I want you to help me get rid of Chesney."

Clodagh recoiled. "You want me to use hypnosis to eradicate Chesney?"

"No, it's not like that…well, yes, it sort of is like that, but…"

"But nothing," said Clodagh. "It's called hypnotherapy for a reason. Half of that word is 'therapy.' I take it very seriously. It's not some stage trick where someone winds up clucking like a chicken. I learned those skills to help people."

"Then help me," implored Lorraine. "I know your hypnotherapy isn't a gimmick. That's why I called for you because you're serious and sincere. Clodagh…" Lorraine took a deep breath and consciously tried to lower her voice to its more masculine timbre. "Clodagh, I'm a screw-up. Sometimes I feel that I've never gotten anything right. I'm always doing things from the best intentions and completely messing them up. You remember how I ruined that whole golf tournament plan; how I wound up putting my mother and brother in the hospital, how my mother lost the…"

Lorraine felt a lump in her throat and sought to hide it behind a short cough. Then she took a sip of tea and continued.

"Since then I've lost nearly every person I cared about, and while it wasn't my fault, not directly at least, still, there was nothing I could do to stop it either. And when I tried to do something, again for the noblest of reasons, I always messed it up and made things worse."

Lorraine bowed her head and started to weep. In a moment she felt Clodagh's hand atop her own.

"You're too hard on yourself," said Clodagh. "You're the kindest boy I ever met."

"Maybe, but I'm also the most ineffective person you ever met."

"You're right. You're so screwed up," Clodagh teased before adopting a more clinical tone. "Okay, so, what do you hope to achieve through these sessions?"

"Sessions?"

"You didn't think I was going to wave a pocket watch in front of your eyes, say a few magic words, and turn you into a full-time international heroine, did you?"

"I suppose not," said Lorraine. "I guess I hadn't thought about it that deeply."

"Same old Ches," said, shaking her head. "Looking at the big picture, missing the details; eyes on the mountains in the distance and falling into the first pothole in front of you. Well, don't worry. We'll straighten you out; as much as possible. But you didn't answer the question. Sit down, relax, take a deep breath." Lorraine did as Clodagh requested. "Okay, now, Mrs. Innis, before we start, I'd like to know what your goals are. Visualize… imagine you're Lorraine Innis and only Lorraine. You're a confident, warm, caring person. You're admired by millions. The world is yours. There is no Chesney. It's just you. What would you do?"

Lorraine took a deep breath. "I suppose I would find out who really was responsible for Martina's death. Yes, that's what I would do. I'm sure I could sort it all out."

"And who is Martina?"

Lorraine opened her eyes. "Oh, Martina Fergus, she was my, that is Chesney's fiancée."

Clodagh mulled over that admission. "Martina Fergus, so she was the blueprint for Martin Innis?"

"Well, sort of, I suppose," said Lorraine. "I needed an imaginary husband. It was easier to keep it straight if the names were similar. I was either Martin or... never mind."

"But," interjected Clodagh, "there is no Chesney in this new reality you want to create, is there?"

"No, but..."

"Then why would you, Lorraine, worry about something in Chesney's world?"

Lorraine grimaced. "That's very logical."

"So, you don't really want to eradicate Chesney, do you?"

"No, I not completely," said Lorraine. "No, I don't want to get rid of Chesney. Actually, someday I want to get rid of Lorraine and go back to being him all the time. But right now, I want Lorraine to operate as his agent. When I was Lorraine and didn't know who Chesney was, I somehow did what was right for him without even trying or thinking about it."

"And you think that if Lorraine were fully in charge, she would make everything turn out right?"

"I've never known her to fail," said Lorraine. "I don't want to erase Chesney completely, I want to temporarily forget about him. I can't be two people at once and do either of them justice. So, right now for all the challenges that are facing me, I'd much rather have Lorraine around. Do you think you can do that?"

Clodagh stared at Lorraine for a minute. Finally, she leaned back and nodded her head.

"I can send Chesney on the 'vacation' you're looking for, but that doesn't mean I will. This isn't a game. There are possible repercussions when you start moving the furniture around in a person's head. I don't want to wipe out something you might need."

"You make me sound like a computer hard drive," said Lorraine.

"Not a bad analogy," she agreed. "I don't want to mess up your operating system. Some parts that you think are exclusively Lorraine may be connected to Chesney."

"So you can help me, but you won't."

"I didn't say that, either," said Clodagh. "But this request is coming from Chesney. You remember; the guy who screws everything up."

"Don't split your infinitives...sorry."

"The guy," repeated Clodagh, "who screws up everything. I know you think you've thought it out…"

"I have," insisted Lorraine.

"And you thought out the golf tournament, but didn't figure I'd get a flat on my bicycle and that vicious dog would get loose. If, and I emphasize if, if we go ahead and temporarily make you a full-time Lorraine, it will be after I examine you and see what needs to be done. Then, after some intensive therapy sessions, if I determine we can do it and do it without any harm to you, we'll try it."

– 8 –
Invitation to the Trance

A re you sure we can't do this in the office?" asked Clodagh that evening, as they entered Lorraine's townhouse.

"Not if you're going to do hours of therapy on me," said Lorraine. "I can't be sure who would walk in on us. At least here you won't be disturbed while you do... whatever it is you're going to do."

Clodagh looked at the living room. "Very comfy, tasteful, feminine without being too girly."

"Yes, well," said Lorraine hanging up their coats, "that was the idea once I, she, had to get a permanent residence. I want to reinforce Lorraine as best I can while I have to be her, without going over the top. Well, where do you want to do this?"

Clodagh pointed at the sofa.

"And I can sit there," she said, sitting in an adjacent armchair. "Do you want to change?"

"Into whom?" asked Lorraine. "Whom do you want me as to do this? Do you want Lorraine Innis? I don't think I could be all Chesney at this point."

"Why don't you just get as comfortable as you usually would for an evening at home. Okay?"

Lorraine agreed and excused herself. A few minutes later, she came back downstairs wearing a blue lounging outfit. "Is this okay?"

"Yes, very comfy."

"Only it's the most neutral thing I've got now," said Lorraine sitting on the edge of the sofa. "I'm fairly straight now, too."

"Straight?"

Lorraine held her arms out to the side and indicated her body. "Straight up and down." She pulled out the front of her top. "No curves, no padding."

"No make-up either," noted Clodagh.

"So, you can Chesney now?"

Clodagh scrutinized her. "No, not really, at best, you're sort of in-between."

Lorraine sat on the sofa. "Well, that's what we're here to work on, getting me out of the middle and putting Lorraine in control, for now."

"I'm not sure that's what will happen. I want to find out some things first. I need to know why you've done all this to yourself, what you were trying to accomplish, and why you think you need to erase yourself from the picture temporarily. So why don't you just lie down, make yourself comfortable, and we'll begin."

Lorraine laid on the sofa and adjusted the pillow beneath her head. Once she had gotten settled, Clodagh placed a blanket over her.

"Just to keep you warm," Clodagh explained.

Lorraine nodded, closed her eyes, took in a deep breath, and slowly exhaled. Then she waited. After several seconds of silence, she opened her eyes and craned her neck sideways to see Clodagh, just looking at her.

"Well? Aren't you going to get going," said Lorraine, "you know, put me under?"

"Close your eyes. Alright. Relax. Now, the last I knew of you was when we moved from Earswick."

"And so did we," said Lorraine, "about two years after you did."

"Ah, I didn't know that."

"You didn't ask," said Lorraine. In her relaxed state, her voice took on a somewhat dreamy quality.

"And where did you move to?"

"Colts Neck, New Jersey. My father's company moved to New Jersey."

"So you went to high school in New Jersey?"

"Yes."

"Anything remarkable happen in high school?"

"No, not even in college. I mean, I did what I was supposed to do. I got good grades. My parents were happy, or at least they were satisfied."

"Were you happy?"

"I wasn't even satisfied," said Lorraine. "We might as well have stayed on Long Island. I was still a little fat kid. I got along with everyone for the most part, but..."

"But what?"

Lorraine shrugged her shoulders which now felt heavy. "I was the same person. I had the same eclectic tastes in music, books, and hobbies. When everyone else was listening to rock music, and learning to play the electric guitar, I was listening to old stuff that my Aunt sent me and playing the ukulele."

"Not exactly with the times, were you?"

"The last time I was with the times was when I was four years old. Since then, I've felt as if I've been going backward while the world was going forward."

"You always were good in history. And did your unusual tastes cause you any trouble in high school or in college?"

"I was teased, but there was never any real malice behind it."

"I always admired you for that," said Clodagh. "It's very easy to go along with the tide. You swam against it. You were a rugged individualist."

"More like a flabby individualist. I was elected that in high school and college."

"Flabby individualist?"

"Class Individualist."

"That's a great distinction."

"Not when I overheard a classmate asking another kid what the category was, and he was told: 'just vote for the weirdest person you can think of.' Then I won in a landslide."

"Still, at least you weren't a sheep," said Clodagh. "Not many people have the courage to stand out from the crowd in high school or college."

"I was just being me."

"And that's even rarer, but let's go on," said Clodagh.

Lorraine wasn't sure if she imagined it, but Clodagh Clott seemed to be speaking more softly, and almost sounded as if she were moving away.

"Go on?"

"Yes," said Clodagh, "what is your most distinct memory from that time?"

Lorraine kept her eyes closed. She felt her eyelids flutter rapidly while also feeling quite heavy.

"That," said Lorraine, "that would be the day I graduated college, it was the last day we were all together…"

"Good," said Clodagh, "then let's go there…"

"Alright," said Lorraine as she felt herself go.

- 9 -
Celebration with a
Banjulele Solo

It was as picture-perfect a day as could occur in New Jersey. The sky was a blue so deep that it almost hurt to look at it, with only innocent fleecy clouds to contrast with the azure background.

Chesney Potoski sat in his graduation robe on the college lawn listening to the inspiring words of the guest speaker, a woman of whom he had never heard. The program identified her as an award-winning contributor to the local newspaper.

He agreed with the message even if it was a bit vague. He recalled his high school graduation four years earlier. It was pretty much the same. He thought of the high school graduation gift he had received from his parents: a stereo turntable. He took it to college and played it proudly until a music major with perfect pitch heard it.

"Is that your stereo?" asked Colin, the music major from across the hall.

"Yes, it is," said Chesney.

"Well, it's too fast."

"Huh?"

"*Ticket to Ride*," said Colin. "It should be A Major."

"A major what?"

"Not a major what, the key of A Major, that's the key the song is in. Your turntable is too fast. It's playing it in B Flat."

"How do you know?" asked Chesney.

Colin rolled his eyes as if it were evident to anyone with at least one ear. He exited, taking care to shut the door on Chesney and his offensive music machine.

Now four years later, Chesney saw Colin sitting with the music majors, his long brown hair sticking out from beneath his black mortarboard. The month before Colin held his senior recital, playing a composition of his own. Chesney attended, and though he couldn't tell what key Colin's opus was in, he knew the effort was more abrasive to his ears than the Beatles played on a poorly calibrated turntable.

"Will the communications school stand up..."

The Dean's command, along with a sharp poke in the ribs from the graduate to his left, jarred Chesney out of his reminiscence. He stood with the other 137 communications majors, and then immediately sat down again: a graduate. After all the other schools had stood up and sat, they were dismissed, unleashed into the waiting world.

"That was pretty cheap, Sphincter Face... not reading out everybody's name."

This observation came from behind him and was punctuated with a whack to the back of his head. It was five minutes after the recessional and Chesney was standing beneath a magnolia tree amidst the milling graduates and well-wishers trying to find his own parents in the crowd. Unfortunately, his brother found him first.

"Oh, Stosh, uh...thanks for coming, I guess."

"Yeah, well, you came to my graduation," said Stosh, who had mellowed in the past ten years. He still stood a good head taller than his younger brother and was still thin and wiry, though the first outcropping of a beer-induced paunch sat above his belt buckle.

"Yes," agreed Chesney. "and they read every name."

"We earned it."

"Over 2,000 graduates..."

"That's because I went to a real University, not some half-assed little state college."

"What a hot day," said Chesney recalling the day five years earlier.

"It didn't bother me," grinned Stosh. "I was naked under my gown, and so was the chick next to me..."

Chesney pulled out the front of his graduation gown beneath which he sported a full suit and tie. He shook his head.

"When's the baby due?" Stosh asked poking Chesney's protruding belly.

"Cut it out..."

"You look like a knocked-up nun in that get-up." Stosh's observation was vocal enough to cause several people in the vicinity, including a cute girl, to turn around. "Sister Mary Bun Up the Chute, eh?"

"Knock it off..." said Chesney under his breath.

"What'll Mother Superior do with her fallen angel..."

Chesney saw his parents approaching.

"Little Sister Immaculate Constipation!" continued Stosh.

"At least," Chesney whispered, "at least, my bags are full of nuts..."

"Why you, little..." Stosh drew back his fist.

The scheduled knuckle sandwich was preempted as Mrs. Potoski threw her arms around Chesney.

"Oh, my baby!" She cried. "My baby's graduated from college!"

Chesney could feel his face redden as he looked in the direction of the girl, hoping she hadn't heard. She had. Being referred to as a baby was even worse than being likened to a pregnant nun. He looked over at his father, who was standing silently. At that moment Chesney wished all his relatives were like his father, or that he had come from a long line of mutes.

For the next minute, Mrs. Potoski engaged in the type of overt doting that should be confined to children under the age of two. While she was doing this, Stosh stood behind her, making mocking faces at Chesney. His father was oblivious to it all as he admired the new greenhouse that the college erected next to the quadrangle.

"What are your plans now… Chesney?" his father asked as they strolled to the family car. Chesney noticed his father still paused uncomfortably before saying his name.

"Yes, dear," added Mrs. Potoski, "what will you do, work for a newspaper?"

"He could get his old paper route back," said Stosh, "but the twelve-year-old girl up the street who has it now has a better arm."

"I don't have to work for a paper," explained Chesney. "I'm qualified for any job that entails writing."

"Oh, you could work at Stosh's company," exclaimed Mrs. Potoski. "They put out a catalog. You could write that. Wouldn't that be nice? Both my boys working together?"

"NO!" Instant replay would have been necessary to ascertain who had reacted first and more vociferously to her suggestion: Chesney or Stosh.

"Why not?" said Mrs. Potoski.

Both brothers fumbled for reasons before Mr. Potoski interrupted.

"Prudence, let Chesney make his own way in the world," said Mr. Potoski, "it'll make a man of him."

Chesney sighed. What, at the age of twenty-two, did his father think he was: a homunculus?

"I never helped my sister get a job," continued Mr. Potoski.

"Your sister lives in England," noted Mrs. Potoski, "besides which she doesn't even care about glass or windows."

"She'd miss them if she didn't have them," he noted.

"Oh, that reminds me," said Mrs. Potoski as they reached the car, "we have some gifts for you."

She nodded to her husband, and he unlocked the trunk. Inside were several gift wrapped packages. Mrs. Potoski pointed to a rectangular one.

"Open that first," she said, "that's from your father and me."

"Here?" asked Chesney looking around the parking lot. He had assumed they were going to take him out to dinner, or at least have a cake at home. After four hard years of study, he had never envisioned his graduation celebration taking place at the rear end of a Dodge Reliant.

His mother looked at her watch.

"We've got plenty of time," said Mr. Potoski in a low voice, "the dinner doesn't begin until seven."

"Dinner?" asked Chesney.

"Yes, they're having a function at the golf club," she said.

"Oh," said Chesney.

"Go ahead," encouraged his mother, indicating the package.

Half-heartedly he tore away the paper.

"A typewriter…"

"It's electric," said his father.

Chesney nodded and smiled, hoping the smile was broad enough to hide his disappointment. Some of his classmates had already invested in those new word processors.

"Thank you," he said, "I'm sure I'll get a lot of use out of it."

"This one's from me," said Stosh handing him a square package. "Congratulations, Cheese Nit."

Chesney unwrapped it to reveal four cut-glass tumblers.

"Oh, how lovely," said his mother, "you'll need some nice glasses when you get your own apartment one of these days."

"Yes, thank you," said Chesney hesitantly. He glanced at his father, who was viewing the gift with the same skepticism as Chesney. They were probably dribble-glasses. Not surprisingly, Stosh worked for the North Jersey Novelty Company: "Purveyors to the Jape." Chesney returned the box to the trunk of the car lest they explode or provide some other "rib-tickling" surprise.

One last box remained.

"That's from your Aunt," said his father, nodding to the final and largest package. It was wrapped in heavy brown paper, tied up with binding twine. Chesney removed the parcel slowly from the trunk of the car and ran his hand over the top. The upper corner was liberally plastered with several rows of British stamps, bearing the profile of the Queen.

"Well, aren't you going to open it?" asked his mother, who was habitually curious about unopened gifts.

"Yes, of course," said Chesney, still staring at the package. He was enjoying the moment of anticipation, which, given his Aunt's track record with delightful surprises, was considerable.

"She didn't give me anything when I graduated," Stosh could be heard muttering.

"Yes, she did," said Mrs. Potoski, "she sent you that pen and pencil set."

"Big deal," said Stosh, "I could buy a lead pencil and a Bic at the drug store for a quarter."

Chesney ignored his family's remarks as he luxuriated in the moment. He untied the knots on the string, enough to loosen it from the package, and then slid it off. Then he methodically undid the taped edges of the brown paper.

"It's a box," said his mother, though given the rectangular shape of the original parcel one could expect nothing less under the wrapping.

"Open it, already," snapped Stosh.

Chesney lifted the lid of the box to reveal another case inside. This one was oddly shaped like a scalene triangle but with curved edges on its longest side.

"Oh, wow, if it's what I think..." Chesney caught himself. He didn't want to appear more impressed by Aunt Elinor's gift than the one his parents had given him.

"What is it?" said his mother.

Without replying, Chesney lifted the case from its bedding of excelsior packing. Then he undid the latches of the case.

"That must be at least forty years old," noted his father.

"Couldn't afford something new," snorted Stosh.

Beneath the lid there it was: what Chesney had hoped for.

"It's a banjo," said his mother, "a little banjo."

"It's a banjulele," whispered Chesney.

"What?"

"A ukulele."

"I thought you already had a ukulele," she said.

"I do," said Chesney. Aunt Elinor had sent him his first ukulele when he was still in high school.

"But this is a ukulele with a resonator," he said, picking it up carefully. "And..." he fingered the metal plate screwed into the headstock, "...it's a Hugh Goode."

"I thought you said it was a banjulele," said Mrs. Potoski.

"It's a Hugh Goode model, the type he used to play in his films."

"More musical diarrhea," muttered Stosh.

"Stosh," said Mr. Potoski in the cautionary tone that had become automatic after two decades of practice.

"It's bad enough that she sends him those records without turning him into the evil spawn of that cornball."

Chesney ignored the comments, preferring instead to soak in the magnificence of the instrument, its worn vellum head, the shine of its steel rim, the imitation ivory tuning pegs, the patina of the wooden back. Aunt Elinor had wisely loosened the strings before packing it to avoid straining the neck. Turning it over, he saw a note attached in his Aunt's handwriting. He faced his family so they wouldn't be able to read over his shoulder.

"My dearest Chesney," it began. *"I've been saving this for a few years for an extra special occasion, as I suspected it was something you would appreciate. There are only a few events more momentous than graduating from college (take it from a silly person who didn't). Enjoy the uke, and think of me from time to time when you're strumming away. Hope to see you soon,*

Love,
Your Aunt Elinor"

Chesney stared at the note for a full minute until his father's voice broke the spell.

"Well, congratulations again," he said, "hate to run, but we've got dinner at the club."

"Are you coming right back home?" asked Mrs. Potoski as she hugged him, "or are you going to celebrate with your friends?"

Chesney smiled, hoping his eyes didn't betray any sadness. "I, uh, I guess I'll be home later tonight, or tomorrow. I'm almost done packing."

"Are you going to a party?" she asked.

Chesney shrugged. He thought he would have been celebrating with his family, but apparently, they had other plans. His few friends had made other arrangements.

"Or are you going out with Joanne?"

"We're not seeing each other anymore, Mom," said Chesney.

"Since when?"

"Since last semester," said Chesney recalling the girl whom he'd dated for nearly two years. "Remember?"

"Oh, yes, that's right," said Mrs. Potoski with a smile that drooped into a frown of condolence. "I remember now. That's too, bad, she was very nice."

"Yes, she was."

"I always thought you two would get married."

Chesney shrugged.

"Come on, Pru," interrupted Mr. Potoski, "we've got to get going. Chesney will be fine. I'm sure he's got something lined up."

"Probably a party with Mary Palm and her five daughters," snickered Stosh just out of earshot of his parents.

Mr. Potoski went to close the trunk with Chesney's gifts inside of it.

"Wait," said Chesney, and he retrieved the banjulele. "I think I'll take this with me."

"What do you want to lug that around for?" asked Stosh. "I can take it back home for you." He smiled, sincerely. Stosh doing anything sincerely was a warning that he was plotting something harmful.

Chesney looked down at Aunt Elinor's gift in his arms and then back up at the malicious glint in his brother's eyes. It was reminiscent of how he had looked at Chesney's leather-bound copy of *Great Expectations* years earlier; the one he glued together. He clutched the instrument to his chest.

"No, I'll keep it," he said, before adding in a very low voice: "And if you touch even one string of this…" he glanced down at his brother's crotch, "I swear I'll have the other one."

– 10 –
A Quinquennial Review
Doesn't Happen Every Day

Years passed.
Chesney fidgeted in his seat while the human resources director of Marlton Press studied a file. The nameplate on the desk read: Dennis Ullmer. The anagram was obvious, Chesney thought: "Sullen Remind."

Ullmer hummed monotonously as he read Chesney's file, almost like a machine.

Chesney looked around the office decorated with framed book covers. Next, Chesney examined himself. He pulled at his blue JC Penney sports coat then tugged at his necktie draped over his belly. He would have to try and slim down. Perhaps that was what Mr. Ullmer wanted to talk to him about. The HR director was always trying out improvement schemes on employees. Ullmer saw himself as some sort of social engineer; building a better human race, to create a more efficient, more dependable, more robotic workforce. He recalled an incident last December at the Ullmer's Christmas open house. It was an uncomfortable social occasion made more so when Ullmer's scarecrow of a wife got tipsy on mulled wine and launched into a rambling discourse on George Bernard Shaw, Heinrich Himmler, and the virtues of eugenics. Ullmer looked embarrassed, but his reaction indicated he didn't disagree with his wife's rant.

Maybe he had eaten too much at the party, thought Chesney. Maybe he was to be the guinea pig for some employee weight reduction initiative, and if that failed, maybe he would be liquidated. Chesney pulled at his snug waistband. He would like to be thin, but not through the re-education efforts of Dennis and Imogene Ullmer.

Finally, the personnel manager closed the manila folder and looked up.

"You've been with us five years now," said Ullmer with the same condescending tone he used for everyone aside from Ms. Marlton.

"Four and three-quarters," said Chesney.

"What?"

"I've been here four and three-quarters years, Dennis, I mean, Mr. Ullmer."

Company policy dictated that everyone was supposed to call everyone else by their first names. Ullmer had instituted the procedure, but like most of his rules, he excluded himself.

Ullmer reopened the file and quickly closed it again, then cast a suspicious eye towards Chesney. He forced a smile on his face.

"Sorry," he said, though his tone was far from penitent. "We're a bit early. I blame my own efficiency. You're due for your five-year annual review..."

"Quinquennial," interrupted Chesney.

"What?"

"You can't have a five-year annual review since an annual review occurs once a year. You could conduct a fifth annual review, but technically it should be termed the quinquennial review, that is, the fifth anniversary, or something that's done every year and is now in its fifth year..."

Chesney stopped. Ullmer eyed him contemptuously.

"Sorry, Den... Mr. Ullmer."

"Yes, well," said Ullmer straining to un-squint his right eye. "Then, for the sake of accuracy, let me say welcome to your quick-quen-quin..."

"Quinquennial..."

"Yes! Yes! That!" snapped Ullmer. "This is that review..."

"Albeit a few months early," noted Chesney under his breath.

"You damned editors," muttered Ullmer grabbing papers as if they were the necks of employees. "You're all so damned persnickety and accurate. I wish we could put out books without you. For that matter, I wish we could do it without the authors, as well. This whole place would run much more smoothly..."

"Excuse me, Mr. Ullmer, Sir..."

"What?!"

"Excuse me, I don't want to be overly pedantic..."

"And I don't want to be five-foot, nine, but that's exactly what I am!"

"...but, I'm not an editor, I'm an assistant editor..."

Ullmer leaned forward and grinned malevolently. It was as if he was holding Chesney fate in his hands.

"Yes, well, you *used* to be an assistant editor," said Ullmer.

Chesney grimaced and nodded his head. He wasn't being called in for his review, after all. This was his exit interview, and that could take place on nearly any day. Of course, he thought, he couldn't be fired on a weekend, as Marlton Press was closed Saturday and Sunday, but as this was a Thursday, he could be fired today. He started to rise.

"Where are you going?" said Ullmer.

"I don't work here any longer," said Chesney.

"Sit down," said Ullmer. "I love it when you anal-retentive little fact-checkers, you grubby little grammarians, get it wrong."

"Excuse me?"

"When I said you're an editor, it's because you're an editor."

"Sir?"

"This is your review, your..."

"Quinquennial..."

"Your fifth-anniversary review. Potoski, you're being promoted. Ms. Marlton had recommended, and me, in my benevolence..."

"*I, in my benevolence...*" whispered Chesney.

"...have decided to promote you to a full editor."

Chesney sat silently until he realized that Ullmer was awaiting a reaction. "Thank you," he finally croaked.

"You're welcome," sneered Ullmer.

They sat facing each other for several painful seconds. Chesney wasn't sure what he was supposed to do next. Normally, his "thank you" would be the end of it, but from the look on his face, Chesney felt Ullmer was waiting for him to kiss his ring or sign away his soul.

"Well?" Ullmer finally said. "Don't you have any questions?"

"Should I?"

Ullmer rolled his eyes. "Editors! Not an original thought in your heads! You only know how to correct somebody else's punctuation. Can't even ask a simple question about your own future, can you?"

Chesney thought for a moment. "I've never been promoted before. What I am supposed to ask?"

Ullmer sighed as if he were dealing with yet another infant in his nursery of slow-witted children. "You're supposed to ask: how much more money do I get; do I get more vacation; do I get profit-sharing; can I increase my contributions to the 401K; do I get my own parking space; do I get an office with a window; and a dozen other things!"

The questions were rattled off so quickly all Chesney could manage was a sheepish grin and add: "Do I?"

The grin slipped off Ulmer's face like snow off a tin roof. "You get some more money..."

He shoved a piece of paper at Chesney, who said "Oh!" in anticipation of the increase, and then "oh," again when he saw its disappointing size.

"And the other questions," said Chesney after he had digested his new salary and found he was still hungry. "Do I get more of, you know, offices, and vacation, and those other things you said?"

"No," said Ullmer. "You don't."

Still, Chesney told himself, he was an editor. He must have been doing a good job to be promoted. Ullmer was smiling again, though now it was the sort of polite smile he wore when he kicked someone out of his office.

So, Chesney started to leave. He was halfway to the door when finally a question came to mind.

"Oh, Mr. Ullmer," he said, "I thought of another question."

"What?"

Chesney fumbled with his necktie. "As an editor, do I have a say in the books I edit? I know that editors are mainly supposed to edit other people's work, but I have a project..."

"A project..."

"Yes, you see, I'd like to edit a book on windows...for my father."

"Your father has written a book on windows?"

"No," said Chesney, "that's not it. He's not a writer. He's a fenestrator, that is, he designs windows; they're his whole life, just about. I just thought perhaps, if it was okay with Ms. Marlton, that I could write a book about windows...for my father."

"And put his name on it?"

"No, I'd write it so he could read it. It would be like a tribute to him."

"You want to write a book about your father's windows?"

"No, not a tribute to what he does, but a tribute to him for what he likes. Do you understand?"

"No," said Ullmer.

"Well, what about your father?"

"What about him?"

"Well," said Chesney, who by now wished he hadn't broached the subject. "I mean, what did he do for a living?"

"He was in personnel," said Ullmer. "They didn't call it human resources back then, they called it 'personnel.' All the same, he was in the same line of work as me."

"You're in the same line of work as he," corrected Chesney.

"That's what I said."

"No, you said your father was in the same line of work as you, indicating that you were in the field before he was. Sorry."

"Yes, well," seethed Ullmer, "we were both in the field of personnel."

"And that's my point."

"What is your point, Potoski, what?!"

"Your tribute to your father was following in his footstep," said Chesney, "but I can't do that. I suppose I could, but I'm not very good at designing windows, or engineering, or anything like that. My mother was going to be an English teacher, and so..."

"And so what?"

"I guess that's why I have a facility with words. So, I'd like to write a book about windows to honor my father."

"I thought you said you wanted to edit a book about windows."

Chesney grinned. "First I'd have to write it."

"Well, you go ahead," said Ullmer, who by now had his head down and was waving Chesney out of his office.

"Thank you, thank you very much."

"But do it on your own time," added Ullmer. "Write your book on windows, write your life story, write your grocery list, write whatever you damn-well please. Just write it on your own time. And when it's done, you can submit it just like any other author. And if it's any good, and Ms. Marlton thinks she can sell more than three copies off the dollar table to frustrated fumigators…"

"Fenestrators," mouthed Chesney.

"…then we'll publish it. But until then you're an editor, and while I hate to admit it, you're the pickiest, most particular, and finicky one I've ever seen, which means you'll probably be running the whole editorial department before too long…"

"Thank you, Sir, for your vote of confid…"

"It's not a compliment! Get out of here before I lose my professional demeanor!"

Out in the hallway, Chesney looked again at the letter announcing his promotion, along with the increase in salary. He had moved out of his parent's house in Colt's Neck the year before to a small apartment. A large raise would have made it possible to move to a bigger apartment, or perhaps even a small house. The increase he received wouldn't even allow him a better car. Still, the extra money was nice. He could save it. There wasn't much else he could do with it. Maybe, he'd finally have enough to visit Aunt Elinor in London. They hadn't seen each other in more than ten years. They wrote to each other about a reunion, but there were always circumstances that prevented it. Yes, that extra money would go toward visiting Aunt El. There wasn't much else on which to spend it. His social life didn't put much of a strain on his finances. In fact, Chesney hadn't any social life to put the least bit of exertion on anything. He hadn't had a date in several months and only one steady girlfriend since graduating from college. Chesney paused for a moment and thought of her. She had been nice, so nice that he had thought of asking her to marry him. Before he had the chance to do so, she married a young undertaker who was adept at embalming. No, he concluded, it didn't matter how much his raise was. He didn't really have anything on which to spend it.

Still, it was good to be an editor. He returned to his desk and avoided mentioning his promotion to the assistant editors and proofreaders around him. They might resent his new position, and he didn't want to be resented.

Chesney was editing a travel book when the phone rang.

"There you are, Kid," said the voice on the other end. It took Chesney a few seconds to recognize the voice.

"Stosh?" said Chesney. He was surprised, not just by the fact that this was the first time his brother had ever called him at work, but that Stosh hadn't used some crude nickname.

"Yeah, where have you been?"

"I was down talking to human resources," said Chesney. He paused, expecting Stosh to ask if Chesney was there applying for a promotion to the human race.

"Yeah, well, Kid," said Stosh, ignoring the opening for an insult, "how are you doing?"

"Uh," Chesney didn't know what to say. His brother had never asked him how he was before without an insult. The last time Stosh had called Chesney anything it had been "Scrotum Head" and that had been in church on Christmas Day. By comparison, "Kid" was a verbal hug. "I guess I'm okay."

"Good. Holding up okay?"

"Uh, yeah."

"Good, good, that's good, Kid," said Stosh. "Look, can you do me a favor."

"A favor?" Chesney nodded to himself. The reason for this kinder Stosh was coming into view.

"Yeah, Kid, can you go to the airport?"

"Airport?"

"Yeah, Kennedy," said Stosh, "only I got to go to Newark at the same time to meet Mom," said Stosh. "You sure you're okay?"

"I guess..." said Chesney his confusion growing. His mother was with his father on a business trip, but there weren't due back for several days. Why would his mother be coming back early? "Kennedy Airport? Whom am I picking up?"

"Dad's sister."

Chesney felt his pulse quicken. "Aunt Elinor?"

"Of course, Aunt Elinor, she's the only sister he had," said Stosh. "You sure you're okay?"

"I'm fine," said Chesney. This was good news. Funny how he had just decided to go see her and here she was coming for a visit! He'd be happy to pick her up at the airport, he could... Suddenly, his mind jumped back to what Stosh said. "Wait, the only sister he *had*?"

"Right," said Stosh.

"What do you mean, 'had?'"

There were several seconds of silence on the other end of the line.

"Oh, shit," Stosh finally said, "didn't anybody call you?"

"Call? When?"

Another several seconds of silence followed as Chesney felt the anxiety building inside him.

"Sorry, Kid," said Stosh, "Dad's snuffed it."

"Snuff..."

"He's dead."

– 11 –
The Princess and the Oft-Told Tale

"Daddy, Dadddyyyy!"

Giorgio Fierro opened his eyes as his daughter, Valerie, clambered on his lap.

"Oh, yes, *Principessa*," he mumbled as he stroked her dark brown hair.

"Daddy, why are you falling asleep already? It's not bedtime, yet."

He smiled, nodded, and half-closed his eyes.

"Daddy!"

"Daddy's very tired, Principessa." He considered educating Valerie on the demands of working a double shift in construction, and the economic realities of providing for a wife and two daughters, but condensed that into: "Daddy worked very hard today."

He was starting to drift off again, the taste of his wife's lasagna lingered on his palate coaxing him towards an after-dinner nap. This luxury was again interrupted by a stab to his groin as Valerie shifted on his lap and kneed him in the crotch.

"Oh, yes, Valerie," he said, "what is it?"

"Daddy..."

"Principessa?"

"Daddy, tell me a story."

"What kind of story?"

"Tell me how you met Mommy and fell in love...pleeeeease!"

"Oh, not again, *Piccola Principessa*. You've heard it so many times..."

"It's my favorite story, Daddy, my absolute best favorite. Please!"

This last request was spoken as a command.

"Eight-years-old and already a woman," he sighed.

"Now, go slow, Daddy," said Valerie, nestling into her father's lap. "Don't leave anything out because it's such a nice story."

"Story," repeated Giorgio as he collected the fragments of the tale from the corners of his sleepy mind. "Yes, alright, I met your mother…"

"No, Daddy, you used to start it: 'many years before you were born.' Do it like that. That's the way you always do it."

He nodded. "Yes, fine: it was many years before you were born. I had just come to this country…"

"Valerie!" A stern voice made Giorgio jump in his recliner.

"Mommy, Daddy's just about to tell me…"

"And you are supposed to be helping your sister dry the dishes, not bothering your father."

"But.."

"Go! Go help your sister Rose."

Valerie climbed off her father's lap and disappeared into the kitchen. As she did so, Connie Fierro, Giorgio's wife, came into view holding a dishcloth. He smiled in a mute apology for indulging his youngest child.

"Honestly, Giorgio," she said, "she's just using you."

"For a chair?" After twenty-years Giorgio's accent had lessened, but English was his third language, and he still took some idioms literally.

"She doesn't want to hear that silly old story again," said his wife. "She's only trying to get out of doing the dishes."

He smiled contritely. He knew his wife was right, but he could never deny his Piccola Principessa. Connie never understood why, and Giorgio was never going to tell her. Connie was a good woman, second-generation Italian, a good wife, a good mother, she still had her looks and her figure, but that didn't entitle her to know every thought in his mind.

"You work hard enough," said Connie, "without constantly spoiling her."

"Yes, Connie, I was only…"

"Daddy," Valerie reappeared around the corner, "don't tell any more of the story until I come back…"

"I won't…"

"OUT YOU!" Her mother delivered a sharp swat to Valerie's behind with her dishtowel. "Go dry the dishes!"

With that, they both left Giorgio in his recliner with his thoughts.

How had he met his wife? It was, by her own admission, his daughter's favorite story. Story. That was an accurate description of the version he shared with Valerie. It was largely made up, but the truth wasn't something you told to a child, especially not to your daughter. For that matter, he never even told Connie the whole story. She knew her part in it, of course, but her part didn't even embrace the half of it. She came in at the end, after Beryl. And she didn't know Beryl, nor would she ever, and that was fine with Giorgio. No reason to bring up the past now. Giorgio Fierro never was the type to talk much, but you couldn't really blame him.

◆

"I'm in love with Beryl," he said. "I'm going to marry her."

A stunned look crossed his friend's face, which dissolved into a wide grin before finally breaking out into an uproarious laugh. This was followed by several slaps on Giorgio's back.

"You dog! You are full of surprises, you are! I don't believe it!"

"I mean it, Lenz, I'm going to marry her."

"I don't doubt you, old fellow," said Lenz, "I didn't mean that. I just meant that it's astounding news...good news, but astounding."

"Oh," said Giorgio.

"You always did take things too literally," said Lenz, with a laugh. "I still remember how you used to stare up at the ceiling every time Herr Purzelbaum would tell us" '*Es ist noch kein Meister vom Himmel gefallen.*'

Giorgio shook his head. "I didn't know much German at the time, did I? Besides, it's a silly saying, isn't it? 'No master has yet fallen from heaven.'"

Lenz repeated the phrase, imitating their old taskmaster. Giorgio would have laughed if it hadn't been so chillingly accurate.

"Yes, well," said Giorgio, "I still don't understand it, literal or not."

"Practice makes perfect, that's all it means. Practice makes perfect, my dear Giorgio. And though Purzelbaum was a fat old goat, he was right about that, eh? I still recall when first I laid eyes on that grubby little war orphan."

"Wait a minute. You were a grubby little war orphan, too."

Lenz smiled at him in that way that indicated he was always two steps ahead of Giorgio. Still, Lenz's confidence wasn't malicious. He was like a brother to Giorgio.

"Ah, yes, I was a grubby little war orphan," confessed Lenz, "but you were grubbier, smaller, and not at all initiated into the new life in which fate had thrust you. And while fate might have been unkind to you: so young and defenseless in the middle of a war, with your parents snatched away from you at so tender a point in your life..."

"It was my birthday," said Giorgio.

"And while fate took away your parents with one hand, with the other hand she gave you a brother who has worked hard to be a mother, father, grandfather, uncle, and whatever relatives you may have lost... namely: me."

"And *Capitano* Zimmer," added Giorgio, removing his cap.

"Ah, yes, the good *Kapitan* Zimmer," said Lenz, who placed his hand over his heart.

"He was the one who fell from heaven," said Giorgio, "and then he was taken up there again."

"Shot down by the U.S. Army Air Corps," said Lenz. "Just as well..."

"Lenz!"

Lenz shrugged. "No disrespect, but he couldn't know what his in-laws were really like. After all, with his big heart, he rescues orphaned children around Europe only to bring them back to..." He rolled his eyes, jerked his thumb in the direction of Germany, and made a sour face.

Giorgio didn't argue the point. He never won an argument with his friend, and besides that, Lenz was right. Capitano Zimmer had already rescued four children, all boys, all war orphans from 1940 to 1943. His missions of mercy came to a dead halt when he was shot down on one of his regular missions for the Luftwaffe.

Recalling the day that he was scooped up by Capitano Zimmer, driven to the nearby airbase, and spirited out of Sicily, always made him feel as if he were four-years-old again. The memory of his family brought tears to his eyes, though he tried to hide them now in front of his friend. His excitement over his first ride in an airplane was tempered when Zimmer gave him a waxy candy bar in the back of a transport plane and then told him that he was taking him to a new home now that all his family was dead. Dead? At first, Giorgio sat in stunned silence and then tried to bargain with the kindly Capitano, only to be told that it was no use, that they were gone. But, Zimmer informed Giorgio that he was taking him to a place where he would be cared for. That since he no longer had a family of his own, Giorgio could be in his family, or more accurately, his wife's family.

"You see, Giorgio," Zimmer explained in his broken Italian, "I lost my mother and father, too, when I was not much older than you are now. We orphans will stick together, you'll see. It will be all right."

With that, he gave Giorgio a blanket and then gave money to the man on the transport plane, who accepted the bribe as he had other times. Exhausted from the events of the day, Giorgio fell asleep, only waking after they had landed and he was being carried to a truck. Soldiers were shouting things to one another in German. It was much colder, colder than it had ever been at home, but then the foothills of the Alps were bound to be colder than sunny Sicily.

Garmisch-Partenkirchen, the name sounded so odd to his Sicilian ears. He would spend the next years of his life there, on a farm just outside the town. Until he was eighteen, he would be there with Zimmer's in-laws, the Purzelbaums. At first, the farm seemed all that Zimmer had promised. There was peace and quiet and safety, especially for being deep within the Third Reich at a time when the war had turned against it. A farm afforded more food than the rest of the population had. There was little evidence that there was even a war going on, aside from the occasional sight of a military airplane. No bombs ever fell on the Purzelbaum's farm, and even when Nazi Germany collapsed, the area around Garmisch-Partenkirchen remained in Axis hands. It wasn't until May 1945 that Giorgio had his first glimpse of one of the American soldiers that he'd been waiting almost two years to see.

While the larger conflict had left the farm untouched, Giorgio still found himself in the middle of a war. Upon arriving at the farm, Giorgio learned that Frau Zimmer and her parents were not nearly as benevolent as the Capitano. They were always barking out orders.

The other four boys, all of whom were bigger than Giorgio, responded as if there were a penalty for disobedience. Giorgio just stood there. He knew he was supposed to do something, but because he knew no German, he had no idea what that was. Frau Purzelbaum, a broad, hearty woman with a bust like a Panzer tank, called the burst of activity to a halt, and then posed a question to them all. After a moment's hesitation, one of the boys, a dark-haired fellow just a little bigger than Giorgio, nodded and raised his hand.

He said something in German to the woman, and then turned to Giorgio and said in very good, if a bit too refined, Italian: "They want to know if I speak Italian," he said.

"Yes, Italian!" said Giorgio, happy to hear his native tongue in this strange land.

The boy said something to Frau Purzelbaum and then turned to Giorgio to explain that he spoke a more classic, Northern Italian, while Giorgio spoke a Southern, peasant dialect. Still, he assured them he could translate. After getting a series of detailed instructions from Frau Purzelbaum, the boy grabbed Giorgio's hand, and with a brief "*andiamo*," led him outside.

– 12 –
You Could Be Handy Lighting a Fuse

My name is Lauritz," the boy explained as they stood in the crisp alpine air, "but they call me 'Lenz.'"

"Lenz?" The name sounded strange to Giorgio, as did most of the names he had encountered in the last few days.

"What's your name?"

"Giorgio."

"No, your last name? Your family name?"

Giorgio confessed he didn't know. Lenz rolled his eyes.

"Come on," he said, leading him to a barn built into the side of a hill. "It doesn't matter, anyway. They'll call you what they want to call you. Just as well you don't have a last name. They'd only ruin it."

"Is this where the cows sleep?" asked Giorgio, pointing to a herd on a nearby hillside.

"This is where we all sleep," said Lenz.

"What? Everyone?" Giorgio pointed back to the neat, white stucco house. "Doesn't anyone sleep in the house?"

"*They* sleep in the house," said Lenz. His tone conveyed that "they" were the three adults. "The rest of us sleep in the barn."

"With the cows?" Giorgio was excited, as any four-year-old who wasn't familiar with cows might have been.

"Don't be a little *Einfalt*," said Lenz teaching Giorgio his first practical German word. They passed the milking stalls and continued to a rickety ladder that led to the loft. There Lenz showed Giorgio a row of beds. Actually, they looked more like nests surrounded as they were by straw. He pointed to the second to last one.

"That's mine," he said in a territorial tone, before waving to the end. "You can have that, and that's your nail."

He pointed to a nail upon which hung a leather harness.

"What do I do with the nail?"

"Hang your clothes on it, don't be an Einfalt."

Giorgio looked down. The only clothes he had were there on his back. He almost pointed this out, but he didn't want to be an Einfalt.

Despite this earnest desire not to be an Einfalt, the word was soon drummed into his head. Frau Zimmer and her parents, the Purzelbaums hurled it at him so often he was afraid it would become his name. The only advantage to becoming Giorgio Einfalt was that it would have given him a score of relatives since that was the epithet attached to just about everyone and everything in whom the Purzlebaums found disfavor – which included just about everyone, even each other.

He hadn't been on the farm for more than an hour before Giorgio realized he was there to work. This wasn't a harsh slap of reality. He had helped in the café back home from the time he could walk. What did take some getting used to, however, was the type of work and the people for whom he worked. He was accustomed to the atmosphere of a cozy little restaurant where the customers were guests, and they were there for a convivial meal or drink. On the farm the work was much harder. The clients and bosses were more demanding, and conviviality never entered into the equation. Also, the clients and the bosses were practically the same. Giorgio spent most of his time trying to please both the cows and the Purzelbaums, with very little discernible difference between them. Both groups took his efforts for granted and often repaid him crudely. Never was he offered a kind word. After a while, he'd sooner expect one from a cow than from a Purzelbaum. More often than not his efforts were rewarded with a kick (from either cow or a Frau) or a pile of effluence (physical from the cows, verbal from the humans). The only consolation was that he was kept so busy that Giorgio had little time to reflect on his lot. It was only in his small cot in the loft at night that he would think about home, his mother's gentle caresses and then break down and cry.

"Shut up," Lenz would whisper in the dark, whenever Giorgio's sobbing became too loud, "don't let anyone think you're a baby. Be a man! Like me!"

Though he was barely one year older than him, Lenz did indeed represent masculine maturity to Giorgio. The only other male role models were the other three boys, all of whom were older, bigger, and unable to speak any Italian, and of course Herr Purzelbaum. Herr Purzelbaum with his straining belly, his heavy handlebar mustache, and his puffy head didn't appear to be something any human being would emulate. That left Lenz, who became Giorgio's guide through the strange world in which he had landed.

The farm wasn't all work, Giorgio discovered. There was also work. Not the same type of work. After the day's farm work was done, Herr Purzelbaum would put the boys through training for their secondary occupation.

It seemed that Purzelbaum was not the family's actual name, but was their professional appellation. Their uncorrupted name was "Pfirsichbaum" which literally means "peach tree," but given the fact that theirs was a dairy farm and peaches didn't grow locally, Herr Purzelbaum changed it. Purzelbaum meant "tumble" or "somersault." Though he had a fine dairy herd, Purzelbaum's first love, was acrobatics. Though it was hard to believe, Herr Purzelbaum was hiding a trim, limber acrobat beneath his layers of fat. In fact, his aerial accomplishments were what first won the heart of his future wife, the only daughter of Bavarian dairy farmers. Though injury cut short his professional career, Gustav Purzelbaum never lost his love for a well-executed triple backflip or his appreciation for a snug-fitting pair of tights.

Purzelbaum's dream of a turnverein or acrobatic club lay dormant. The only possible recruits for his circus were his wife, his daughter, and the cows. Given that his wife and his daughter were even more bovine than the cows, he would have had greater success teaching his herd to do triple pikes. This changed in 1938 when young Kurt Zimmer, a local boy, was showing a romantic interest in Louisa Purzelbaum. Kurt's frequent visits to the farm started Purzelbaum thinking about reviving his act, though Gustav knew that one athletic boy does not a turnverein make. Still, the Purzelbaums consented when he asked for their daughter's hand in early 1939. If nothing else, Gustav told himself, he could use the farmhand immediately, even if the rest of the acrobatic corps never materialized.

Soon after the wedding, the Second World War began, and Kurt was elevated from the Hitler Youth to the Luftwaffe. Within a year he earned his pilot's wings. Although a good enough pilot, Kurt Zimmer was soft-hearted earning him the nickname of *Miezekatze*, or Pussycat. Despite having no reluctance at shooting down an enemy plane, Pussycat Zimmer was forever adopting small animals, the more helpless they were, the more irresistible to his tender heart. War being what it is, especially the type of Blitzkrieg practiced by the Third Reich, Kurt Zimmer was rarely without some object of pity to look after. It wasn't long before Kurt found his first war orphan, a young Dutch boy whom he befriended in the spring of 1940. The two grew closer, and just before Kurt's unit was about to move, the young flier got the bright idea that he and Louisa could adopt the boy as they could have no children of their own. Initially, his wife was cool to the suggestion until her father talked her into the idea. The boy, an eight-year-old named Jon, soon arrived on the farm and proved to be a willing worker and an excellent physical specimen for Herr Purzelbaum's dreams of acrobatic glory.

While his wife seemed ambivalent to Kurt's humanitarian efforts, his father-in-law praised them and encouraged more of it...especially with boys of a certain height and build. A year later, during the invasion of the Soviet Union, Kurt was able to fulfill Gustav's request with not one, but two boys - nine-year-old Ukrainian twins. In 1942, Kurt Zimmer found

Lenz in the Balkans and sent him back home to what he thought was a growing family. His visits on leave were short enough to keep Kurt in the dark to the fact that he was building less of a family and more of a slave labor circus. He watched with blind innocence the various tumbling routines Herr Purzelbaum had taught the boys. Kurt thought it was all just good clean recreation and not a blossoming act. He was also pleased that his mother-in-law had sewn up special costumes for the boys in which to execute their little tricks.

Kurt Zimmer failed to notice the critical edge to Herr Purzelbaum's voice when he brought Giorgio home.

"Another one, too young, and even scrawnier than the last one," Gustav muttered, as he nodded in the direction of Lenz. "Still, we'll make do."

He did make do, and it wasn't long before Giorgio was being put through the paces, helping with farm work and acrobatic exercises. Though a bright boy, Giorgio still needed Lenz to translate Purzelbaum's commands. Giorgio, when he realized that they were being trained to do tricks, displayed his crude somersault that had always been well-received back at the café. Instead of applause, Purzelbaum rolled his eyes, slapped his fat palms against his even fatter forehead, and muttered: "Einfalt!"

Giorgio was just too small to do the same tricks as the larger boys. Soon he was put to work running in and out with props, holding up hoops, and being tossed through the air by the other boys. Being a dead weight didn't offer much of a future, but Giorgio's life was forever changed the day Purzelbaum added a human cannonball routine to the act. Lenz was chosen to fly out of the cannon and land atop a pyramid formed by the other three boys. Giorgio's part was to light the fuse. It wasn't a real charge. The cannon itself was a prop that contained a spring-loaded platform. The exaggerated-sized fuse and small bit of powder at the end of it were merely for theatrical effect.

Giorgio's duty was simple, though the timing was critical. The three boys couldn't maintain their human pyramid for more than sixty seconds. When Purzelbaum started his drumroll, Lenz was to stride to the cannon and be helped inside by the two Ukrainians. Then, after Lenz disappeared down the barrel, the boys rushed to a spot ten yards away and formed their pyramid by hoisting Jon on their shoulders. This was the cue for Giorgio to march to the rear of the cannon take out an oversized match, strike it and light the fuse. It was simplicity itself, but Giorgio being only four-and-a-half had a hard time remembering all the steps. He always remembered the solemn stride, and nearly always to light the match, but this is where he grew confused.

"Giorgio, *Feuer! Feuer!*" Herr Purzelbaum would urge under his breath as if they were in front of a real audience. But Giorgio's only reaction was a confused look, while the match burned down towards his fingers.

"*Feuer*, Giorgio, *Feuer!*" He would repeat, joined in the chorus by his wife and his daughter.

Finally, he would shout: "Lenz!"

Lenz, inside the cannon, knowing he was being called on to translate, would holler: "*Fierro!* Giorgio, *Fierro!*"

"*Ja*, Giorgio, *Fierro!*" Purzelbaum shouted.

In this way, Herr Purzelbaum learned his first and only words of Italian: Fierro. It was always spoken as a command and always coupled with Giorgio's first name. Soon "Giorgio" and "Fierro" became inseparable, and ultimately Fierro became the last name of the orphan from Sicily. It was as good as any other; better than a German one. At least he could understand it, he reasoned. A name was a name. It was just another fact of life that was forced upon him, like the death of his family, being an orphan, and the daily shoveling of manure.

– 13 –
The Fixed Tombola
and the Broken Heart

Those days are long past, now, eh? Eh, my friend? My brother?"
Lenz squeezed Giorgio's shoulder as they walked through the
funfair.

"Yes, long past," said Giorgio glancing over his shoulder as if the past
were sneaking up to take him back to Germany.

"You never did master old Purzelbaum's triple flip, did you? Ha, always
a half-twist short. How he yelled at you! *'Einfalt! Einfalt!'* Remember?"

Giorgio grunted.

"Oh, but that was so long ago," said Lenz. "But how red in the face he
would get with you every time you failed! Ha! 'Einfalt! Einfalt!' Eh?"

"I had forgotten," muttered Giorgio, though he never had.

"But now, my little brother, the little orphan is going to marry. Eh, old
fellow? You will be an orphan no more. Now you will have a family, one
you build yourself."

Lenz tousled Giorgio's hair as he often did. Giorgio had almost grown
to like it after all these years.

"So, do you have plans? Are you going to take your new bride to
America with us? You and I, building houses, while at home your little...
uh, what was her name again?"

"Beryl..."

"Yes, thank you, old fellow, Beryl... Beryl keeping your house while
we build houses for others. Eh?"

Giorgio nodded. That had been the plan. After the war, they had
stayed with the Purzelbaums because they had nowhere else to go. The
Americans who occupied Bavaria weren't terribly concerned with the case
of a handful of foreign orphans. For more than ten years Giorgio and the
other boys were led around Bavaria performing their act. In time Giorgio

grew stronger and was a full member of Purzelbaum's troupe despite never mastering the triple flip.

Purzelbaum's turnverein came to a sudden end when Giorgio was seventeen. It was then that the two Ukrainians abandoned the group on tour. They disappeared near the Czechoslovakian border. Lenz guessed that they preferred Soviet rule to that of Purzelbaum. For several performances, they tried to continue with a reduced line-up, but it soon became evident that this wouldn't work.

"Do not worry, my boys," Purzelbaum assured his remaining three performers, "we'll go back home, and my Louisa will help us find some new recruits to the act. Don't worry."

None of the boys were worried about the end of the act. If anything they feared that Frau Zimmer would find a few poor stooges to replace the ones that had flown the coop. When they returned to the farm, however, they learned that Louisa rather than restocking her father's supply of acrobats was about to take flight herself. An American stationed at a nearby base proposed marriage to the German widow, and she accepted.

With the turnverein at an end, the three remaining boys were an afterthought. After being told that they were nearly family and being worked like poor relations, Giorgio, Lenz, and Jon were on their own. Jon, being twenty merely shrugged and walked away, presumably back to the Netherlands. Giorgio couldn't walk back to Sicily, even if he knew from where on that island he had come. Besides, at the age of seventeen, Giorgio spoke Italian like a four-year-old. He spoke some German and a smattering of English but was dependent on the more linguistically fluent Lenz. Instead, he used his large hands, and his strong muscles and his brawny back to speak fluent manual laborer. With the skills they had learned on the farm, the pair set off with some money and tools borrowed from the Purzelbaums without their knowledge.

As the leader of their two-man crew, Lenz decided their best chance for a prosperous future lay with the Americans. The Americans seemed to have the most money of any nationality around. Lenz surmised that if they had so much cash in Germany, they must have even more back home in the States. With this goal in mind, Lenz and Giorgio set off towards America, working odd jobs to support themselves. In a year they had made it to Great Britain.

It was in England, just south of London, in Croydon, that the pair found work in a brickyard. England, having been bombed severely during the war, was in great need for rebuilding, and so the duo found steady work. It was there that Giorgio met Beryl. He soon fell in love with her, and she agreed to marry him.

"I'm not so sure about this," said Giorgio looking over his shoulder. He felt as if he were being shadowed by fate in some form or another. "Something will go wrong."

"Nothing will go wrong, old fellow! Eh?"

Apparently, Giorgio's expression betrayed a lack of confidence in Lenz's assertions.

"Look, look," said Lenz, rubbing Giorgio's neck as they walked through the fairgrounds, "you and the girl, what's her name?"

"Beryl," said Giorgio.

Lenz slapped his forehead. "Yes, I cannot remember that name. I don't know why not, old fellow. It is an ordinary name, but I'm sure she is a nice girl..."

Giorgio pulled away. "She's beautiful, she's like a goddess..."

"No offense, no offense, old fellow, none at all," said Lenz pulling him into a warm embrace. "She is beautiful... to you. She is a goddess... to you. And that is how it should be. You have only eyes for her, this..."

"...Beryl."

"Yes, yes, I know, eh. This Beryl is yours, and you are hers, and that is how it should always be. To me, she is like any other girl, like any other one in a crowd of thousands... just a girl. But to you, the sun rises with her and sets the same with her. She is your light, your love, and I, as your brother, I rejoice. Even though I am losing my brother, I rejoice that you have found your one true love."

Giorgio smiled, nodded, and repeated that last phrase. "One true love. I love her so. She is my life, my angel, my *Principessa*..." He thought a moment, and his anxiety returned. "But..."

"Nothing, nothing!" Lenz reiterated his assurances with a backhanded slap to Giorgio's chest. "Nothing will go wrong, my old fellow. And do you know why? Because nothing can go wrong, that is why." He looked Giorgio in the eye. "This is my gift to you. We've been through too much, too many nights in that loft, too many flips, too many falls, too much muck, and manure. Do you think I could let you down after all that?" He stared intently into Giorgio's eyes, the utmost seriousness furrowing his brow.

Giorgio studied his brother's expression for a moment, then smiled, and shrugged.

"No, no, of course not," he said, "it's not you, I just worry..."

Lenz broke into a beaming smile and pulled Giorgio to him and kissed his neck. "My brother, my old fellow, you always worry. Too much you worry. This is easier than a single somersault. I know a chap. It's all set. You need a little honeymoon trip. You have no money. I have no money. I know a fellow. He's running the tombola, the raffle, at this fair. The top prize is a trip for two to a beautiful seaside resort..."

"*Si*, Bognor," interrupted Giorgio. "I've never been, is it beautiful?"

"Bognor? It's not just Bognor... they call it Bognor Regis, that means the King went there. If it's good for the King, it must be good for my brother and his princess. But does it matter? When you're in love, the whole world is Bognor. As I was explaining, you've got the winning ticket in this raffle, this tombola..."

"But it hasn't been drawn yet."

Lenz jerked his head from side to side in a playful, mocking way. "No, it's not been drawn, but it's been won... by you." He pushed an envelope into Giorgio's hand. "Here's the winning ticket... no, don't open it, yet. Not here, not now!" He forced the envelope into Giorgio's jacket pocket. "Don't be so obvious, eh? Not so conspicuous!" He pulled Giorgio closer and stood by his side. "See over there," Lenz nodded towards the stage of the fair. Giorgio started to raise his hand to point but was slapped down. "Shh, come on, blend in. Be blasé like me. See the stage? Good. That's where they will draw the winning ticket, your winning ticket. But you won't be there."

"No?"

Lenz shook his head. "It's too obvious. You must not be too eager. If you're standing next to the stage waiting for your prize, it makes it look fishy, like it's all been set up."

"But you said it has been set up."

"Of course, but it mustn't look like it has been set up. You bought this ticket for a lark."

Giorgio started to reach into his trousers for his wallet. "That reminds me, I didn't buy the ticket..."

"Shh, it's my gift, remember? Even the price of the ticket is my wedding present to you and, uh..."

"...Beryl."

"Yes, that's her. I'm not talking about what you actually did. This is not a time for the pure truth, old fellow. This is your story, the make-believe. This is what has to look like what happened unless you want your oldest and best friend, your brother to land in the police station, as the English say 'in the nick.' Is that what you want?"

"Oh, no..."

"Good," said Lenz, "we're in agreement on that much, eh? Now, you bought this ticket, pretend, eh? You bought this ticket for fun. You didn't think you'd win. You never even thought of Bognor. You and your girl came to the fair for a day out, a lark. You bought the ticket. You stick it in your pocket, and you go see the fair. You eat, you listen to the music, you ride the rides. You forget all about it. You take your girl on the rides, up on the romantic wheel, maybe you kiss her, maybe you kiss her again..." Lenz nodded across the fair at the Ferris wheel. "Eh? You ride, you kiss, very nice, very romantic, you and your girl. You forget all about the tombola, and then they pull your ticket. You're not even there when they do it..."

"Will I still get it?"

"You already got it," said Lenz. "It's like they say 'in the bag,' eh? You're up on the wheel, you see your best friend... that's me... he's by the stage, he's excited, he meets you at the wheel, he brings you and your Beryl... see I'm learning...he brings you and your Beryl the good news... you're going to Bognor! Perfect, eh?"

Giorgio nodded and smiled uneasily.

"What?" said Lenz. "You're still nervous?"

"It's just complicated."

"Complicated? It's the simplest thing in the world. They pull a ticket, you win. What's so hard about that?"

Giorgio shook his head. "It's so much to remember. It's not like work."

"It's easier than work. I've done all the work for you..."

"Work is easy," said Giorgio, "I go to work, I lay bricks, I eat lunch, I lay more bricks, I go home..."

"It's even easier than that," assured Lenz, "even easier than eating lunch. Look, you have the ticket in your pocket... no, don't touch it, leave it there. You have the ticket. You get on the big wheel. You ride the wheel. You get off. You win!" He glanced at his watch. "But if you keep worrying then you really will have something to worry about. They're going to start the tombola any minute. Come on..."

Lenz hustled his brother to the Ferris wheel, pausing only long enough to purchase a ticket for the ride and shove it into Giorgio's hand. "Another gift from me..."

"Wait, I can't go, where's Beryl?"

"Who? Oh, yes, where did you see her last?"

"About fifteen minutes ago, she was going to, you know..."

"I told her to meet you here, don't worry..."

"But I can't kiss on the ride by myself..."

Lenz looked at his watch again, straightened his tie, looked nervously around the immediate vicinity, and made one of those snap decisions which Giorgio had come to rely upon.

"Okay, look, don't worry. I'll worry," said Lenz. "The main thing is to get on the wheel. I'll tell the operator..."

"Who?"

"Him," Lenz pointed at a man standing beside a large lever, "the guy running the wheel. I'll tell him you're expecting your girl, and when she comes, he will let her on. I'll take care of it, but you've got to be up there when they pull your name, or it will land us all in the stew, old fellow, okay?"

Without waiting for a reply, Lenz ushered Giorgio on to the seat of the Ferris wheel, closed the bar, and nodded to the operator who threw the lever setting the ride in motion. As he retreated backward, Giorgio could see Lenz take out some cash and explain the situation to the man running the ride. From Lenz's gestures, Giorgio could tell he was giving the operator complete instructions. He breathed a sigh of relief. Lenz was taking care of everything.

After a few minutes, the wheel had completed its loading revolutions, and the ride started in earnest. As he rode, Giorgio could catch snippets of what was happening around the bustling fairground. Each time he rose toward the top Giorgio would scan in the distance, trying to find Lenz near the main stage. As he descended, his focus would switch to the base of the ride, hoping to see Beryl. It was on one of his ascents that Giorgio finally caught sight of Lenz near the stage. From the sound of the tinny loudspeaker system, the drawing was already underway, and several of the tombola prizes had been awarded. On the next go-round, he was just able to make out the words "Bognor" and "Grand Prize." Where was Beryl, he wondered. She was missing it all.

As the wheel spun, and Giorgio was once more on the upswing he heard the announcement for the grand prize: the trip to Bognor. Then he heard the resulting commotion, but as he reached the height where he could see the stage, he saw a stranger jumping up on to the stage. He was a bald little man. He was waving a raffle ticket. The master of ceremonies was shaking his hand. The man was waving to a fat woman in the crowd, presumably his wife. He was motioning for her to accompany him on the stage. She wore a loud, flowered dress and a hat too small for her head. It took two men to help her on to the stage, and when she joined her husband, he almost disappeared in her embrace. As he took in this scene, Giorgio realized the wheel had come to a stop with him at the very top. Other patrons were starting to shout, but the operator was ignoring them.

Giorgio stared down for a moment, not comprehending why the man had stopped the ride. Then he looked back towards the stage. There must be a mistake. The bald man with the fat wife wasn't going to Bognor. He was going to Bognor, with Beryl, his goddess, his Principessa. Lenz had it all worked out. There must be a mistake. He had the winning ticket. The ticket! Giorgio began to reach into his coat pocket when something caught his eye in the distance, beyond the booths, beyond the food tents, beyond the stage. He saw Lenz. He saw Beryl. They were getting into a car. Neither of them had a car. And they barely knew each other. Maybe there was something wrong. Maybe Beryl was sick. Maybe…

Giorgio joined the chorus of shouts for the operator to get the ride moving. He had to get off. Still, the operator was deliberately ignoring them. Giorgio looked down in his hand. There was the envelope. He tore it open, expecting to find a ticket. Instead, he found the note. He read it several times before all the words sunk in. He wasn't going to Bognor. Beryl wasn't going to Bognor. She wasn't going to marry Giorgio. She and Lenz were going to America. They were going to get married. There were several phrases expressing warmth and fondness, several "old fellows" and "brothers" thrown in as well, though these, it was now obvious, came cheap. They had always come cheap.

He wasn't sure when the wheel finally started again. Giorgio didn't notice. Nor did he notice that it had begun to rain. It must have been raining hard for his clothes were soaked through. He wasn't sure, as he staggered off the Ferris wheel who had betrayed him first, or if it had been a joint betrayal. A flurry of thoughts and emotions in several different languages flooded his mind as he pushed through the crowd of fairgoers running for cover in the cold Kentish rain. Finally, one voice pushed through the rest, clearly and distinctly...

It was Rosa, from back in Sicily: *Poi I dente, poi I parenti!* – First your teeth, then your relatives.

He had no relatives. He had thought he had a brother, and he thought he was about to have a wife. But now all he had were his teeth. He nodded to himself in the downpour. He finally understood.

◆

"The dishes are all dry, Daddy."

"Hmmm, oh, yes, good thank you Principessa," Giorgio sat up in his recliner.

"So now you can tell me."

"Tell you what, my little love? Oh, yes, the story..."

Valerie clambered onto her father's lap. "Okay, Daddy..."

Giorgio looked onto her large brown eyes, and for a moment, he was a little boy again, back in the café, and they were his mother's eyes. He smiled.

"Daddy!"

Her insistent plea brought him back to Delaware and middle age.

"Oh, yes, Principessa, well, as you know, I was not born in America. I came here as a young man..."

"...and you got off the boat in Philadelphia."

"Yes, I got off the boat..."

"And you saw Mommy..."

"Yes," he nodded, "I saw your mother, and right then I said: 'That's the girl for me.'"

Valerie pressed her cheek against her father's rough, weathered face.

"That's a lovely story, Daddy."

"Yes, Principessa, a lovely story," he agreed, "yes. It is."

– 14 –
The Flat Rate Funeral

Kennedy Airport had changed since he was twelve-years-old. Chesney sat in the same spot where he'd broken down in tears after running away from home. The molded plastic seats which had seemed so futuristic at the time had been replaced by ones made of metal and fabric. They were more comfortable if less "space age."

He looked across the concourse. The restaurant where Aunt Elinor had consoled him was now a private lounge. Good thing he wasn't a kid running away from home now. In the current layout, he might never have run into Aunt Elinor. He was glad to have gotten there before progress had.

"Chesney?"

He stood up and turned. There was Aunt Elinor standing in a black dress, her arms stretched out to meet him. They hugged each other tightly before she pushed him back to arm's length. Her eyes were still vivid with their multi-colored irises.

"My you've grown," she said beaming at him. He self-consciously pulled at this shirt.

"Yes, I need to lose some weight," he said, looking down.

"No," she said, "you've gotten taller. We see eye-to-eye now."

They were the same height, and while she was average for a woman, he was shorter than the average man.

"Stosh is over six-foot-tall," he sighed, "well over it."

"That's nice," she said in an airy way that indicated that she couldn't care less if Stosh were a pigmy or the center for the Boston Celtics. "But look at you!"

She smiled at him, and he felt the warmth of her unconditional love wash away his anxieties. Aunt Elinor looked much the same as she had all those years ago. Her hair was a little grayer, and perhaps she a few wrinkles, but these were outshone by her radiant smile.

"So," he said awkwardly, "am I still your favorite relative?"

Her smile broadened. "Of course, you are," she said. "Am I still your favorite Aunt?"

It was a silly question. He had no other aunts. Favorite aunt? Try favorite person in the whole world. Instead, Chesney just nodded and hugged her again.

"I didn't find out until yesterday," said Chesney as he changed lanes to escape the exhaust of a tractor-trailer.

"Couldn't they find you?" asked Aunt El.

"I suppose they could have," said Chesney with a shrug. "But I guess they forgot. It happens, I mean with Dad passing away so far from home. Mom naturally called Stosh first. Then there was so much to arrange. They had to call you; what with you being in England, and his sister."

"But you're his son."

Chesney shrugged again. "But he has… he had two sons. He only had one sister. Besides, I didn't have to travel very far. I was already close to home. They didn't need me."

"I need you," said Elinor touching his shoulder.

"And I'm here," said Chesney, "picking you up from the airport."

"I won't listen to you tearing yourself down. I need you. I never did have any children. You're the closest thing I have to that. Everyone likes to feel a bit of immortality, you know. Most people do that through their children. You're my bridge to the future, Chesney. You're the only person in my family who seems not only to understand me but acts like they're enriched by the experience."

Chesney pretended to concentrate on the traffic on the Belt Parkway while thinking about what she had said.

"Ironic," he finally said after several miles had passed, "that Dad would be killed by a window he designed."

"He was always so dedicated to whatever he was doing," she agreed. "Even as a child, if he were working on some little project, he would drop everything until he got it just the way he wanted. What kind of window was it?"

"It was a special glass. Dad was worried about earthquakes and high rises, and the glass shattering and then falling from skyscrapers onto pedestrians. Apparently, this design would help the glass and frame stay in place under the strain."

"He must have been very proud of it."

Chesney nodded in agreement. If the window had been in a building, it might have stayed in place forever. But while they were setting up the prototype for the press conference, a cable snapped, and the huge frame came crashing down on Rodney Potoski. Had his design been less perfect, it might have given way on impact. As it was, both the glass and frame held, flattening its designer like a bug on a windshield. The only consolation was that his mother hadn't witnessed the accident. According to eyewitnesses, he didn't even see it coming. He died at the apex of his career: a happy man.

After a few more miles of silent reflection, Chesney spoke up.

"I was going to write a book."

"A book?" said Elinor. "That's very exciting, Chesney. What type of book?"

"For Dad."

Elinor remained silent, allowing him to bare his inner thoughts at his own pace. Nearly a mile went by before he filled in the space. "It was going to be about windows. I'm not exactly sure what about windows, a history, or maybe some famous window pioneer, I was trying to get my employer to publish it. They told me to write it first. On my own time," he said. A few more exits went by. "I suppose it was a dumb idea."

"Yes," said Elinor, "I suppose you're right."

He stole a quick look over at her, surprised at her response. He said very little for the rest of the ride, not really knowing what else to say.

Due to a traffic jam on the Jersey Turnpike, they went directly to the funeral home, arriving just minutes before the start of the viewing. Stosh was there, tall, and proud in his dark suit; looking like a man any corpse would be proud to call his son. His mother was in black with a lace veil framing her face. She greeted Aunt Elinor with a hug that seemed warmer because of the circumstances.

"Closed casket?" Chesney whispered to his brother.

Stosh rolled his eyes as if it were obvious. "We're lucky they could fit the old man in that one."

Chesney wanted to punch Stosh for referring to him as "the old man." It was one of his favorite expressions for their father, and while he never thought about it before, now it bothered him. Rodney Potoski had only been in his mid-fifties. Still, given Stosh's usual tact, it was fortunate he wasn't calling him "the dead man."

"I saw him," said Stosh muttering in muted tones out of the corner of his mouth. "I had to identify the body. You know, so Mom wouldn't have to."

"Surely they had to know who he was," said Chesney.

"Don't be a dope all your life," said Stosh. "It's a legal thing. You should have seen him. Did you ever see a guy flattened under a wall of two-and-a-half-inch thick, unbreakable glass?"

Chesney stood there with his mouth open for a moment until he realized it was a rhetorical question.

"Well," continued Stosh, "it ain't a pretty sight. It was like frog guts mashed between two slides in biology class. They could have sent him home in an oversized manila envelope." Stosh looked down at his shorter, rounder brother. "It would have even thinned you out,

Porky... granted you would have wound up about fifty feet tall." Stosh snorted but possessed enough decorum not to emit a full belly laugh.

Chesney sighed and moved away, as Stosh began greeting the mourners, some of whom had driven from the old neighborhood in Earswick; others were more recent friends from Colts Neck. Aside from the almost obligatory crudities murmured in Chesney's ear, Stosh was the picture of dignity. He looked the role of a good son, standing there, accepting the condolences of the mourners. He stood tall and strongly supported their mother, who after hugging Chesney, and consoling him briefly, took up her widowing responsibilities next to Stosh. For his part, Chesney tried interacting and exchanging appropriate words with familiar faces from his childhood, but somehow he still felt like a fat little kid around these adults. They all looked up to Stosh and treated him like an equal, if not a superior since he represented vital youth. Chesney felt patronized, and almost imagined several of them starting to pat him on the head. Chesney wanted to shout and proclaim that Rodney Potoski was his father, too, and that he tried to be a good son, and that good children aren't measured just by their height and how they looked in a dark suit. When some old neighbors asked the obligatory question on what he was doing now, Chesney mentioned his job at Marlton Press and his promotion to editor. But after a few times, Chesney felt this was being poured into disinterested ears, and he merely said he was "still working." He wanted to stand on a chair and announce he had wanted to write a book for his father. The fact that he hadn't made it all seem hollow, even to himself. If he couldn't impress even his own imagination, why should he burden these people there to pay their respects? Chesney felt a poor legacy to the man who had loved his career and had given his all to it.

He looked to the other end of the room where his Aunt was speaking to guests, none of whom she knew. Occasionally he caught her looking at him with a thoughtful look, but one that was oddly vague. Perhaps she thought he had let his father down as well. It was much easier, he told himself, for him to keep up a long-distance relationship. Even Aunt Elinor couldn't help but be disappointed in the sort of ineffectual adult he'd become.

"I wish I could trade places with you, Dad," he whispered while standing alone by the casket, "it would be a relief for everyone."

– 15 –
Liar, Liar,
Leg's on Fire!

The funeral the next day was more of the same: dignified, plenty of neighbors and business associates of Rodney Potoski paying their respects. Stosh performed as if his father's stately mantle had wafted down on a breeze, coming to rest on his shoulders. He acted like the patriarch now. Stosh only stepped off his new pedestal briefly, and then only to Chesney, confirming the transformation was just on the surface.

"Got a peek at the will," he muttered to Chesney as they stood by the doors of the sanctuary before the service.

"What?" Chesney was stunned that he'd thought of an inheritance, while their father wasn't yet in the ground.

"Mom showed it to me."

"Mom? Why?"

"I'm the executor of the will," said Stosh.

"Oh," said Chesney, "yes, well, that makes sense if you're executor."

Stosh paused to greet a mourner. After the man had passed, Stosh rubbed his hands together.

"The old man was pretty shrewd."

"Pretty shrewd?"

Stosh tapped the side of his nose. "Smart investments."

Chesney struggled to keep his composure. "Yes, I... I would think that's all for Mom, to take care of her..."

"Sure, sure," said Stosh.

Chesney breathed a sigh of relief. Even Stosh couldn't be so mercenary at such a time as this. They stood in dignified silence as the last guests filed into the sanctuary.

"Mom's well taken care of," said Stosh. "The old man saw to that..."

"Old man!" thought Chesney.

"But there's the trust fund," said Stosh. "Nice tidy amount…"

"I don't believe it," said Chesney raising his voice loud enough to make the last row turn around. He lowered it again. "I don't believe you!"

"Don't get your little soldier in a knot," said Stosh with a wink. "You got one, too… nearly as big as mine. Of course, I had a five-year head start, but still, you'll be taken care of in a few years."

"I don't care," said Chesney. "And I hardly think …"

"Can't touch it until you're thirty, Jock Wipe," said Stosh, "course, I passed that, so I get mine right away. I'm going into business for myself; been wanting to do that for a while, but didn't have the mazumas."

"Mazumas?"

"I'll make the old man proud," said Stosh, starting up the aisle to join his mother. "Chip off the old block, eh?"

Chesney stood there for a moment, almost wishing he could run out and find another giant dog to bite off his brother's remaining testicle. He wondered if his father's flattened condition precluded him turning over in his grave.

The funeral service began. Mrs. Potoski sat between her two sons, wiping away an occasional tear and nodding at the words of comfort. Stosh sat bolt upright with a proud look on his face as if he had received his birthright. Chesney almost expected him to appropriate one of the altar candlesticks as his scepter and proclaim himself "King of the Potoskis."

Aunt Elinor arrived late and slipped in the back, saying nothing to him. Chesney wondered if she were angry with him, though she didn't seem so. If anything, she wore a pensive look on her face. Perhaps, he told himself, this was her way of dealing with grief. He hoped he hadn't done anything to upset her.

Chesney was lost in thought as they stood for a hymn. Suddenly, the singing had stopped, and Stosh was tugging on the back of his coat, pulling him back into his seat. When he looked up, Chesney was stunned to see Aunt Elinor standing in the pulpit. He glanced down at the program. She was not part of it.

"For those of you who don't know me," she began in a soft but clear voice, "I'm Roddy's sister. I asked Prudence if I could share a few brief comments on my brother, and she graciously agreed."

Chesney hadn't noticed it before, but years of living in England had given her the trace of an odd accent, or at least a blending of her native speech patterns with some British pronunciations.

"I just wanted to share a memory I had of my brother. Odd, but I haven't thought about it for years. It occurred when we were children. Roddy was probably ten-years-old, and that made me almost nine. I suppose the tragic circumstances of Roddy's untimely passing brought it back to my mind as if it had happened yesterday.

"My brother was a passionate person, as I'm sure many of you will attest. I don't mean that he was emotional or sentimental, far from it. Still, he loved his family very much, even if that affection was rarely expressed in the usual outward manifestations of love."

Chesney caught his aunt's eye. She quickly looked away.

"He was passionate about his work, for his work seemed to define him. I believe this is called 'tunnel vision' and is often couched in negative, obsessive terms by the psychologists that always seem to be finding fresh reasons why we're all a bit balmy. In Roddy's case, however, I prefer to recall him with more favorable adjectives: steadfast, resolute, and determined. True, he was obsessive, but his compunction was directed towards a greater good. You didn't have to be in his presence for more than a few minutes to learn that he was absolutely potty about windows. This wasn't some strange attachment, but rather he understood that simple invention in a more profound way than most of us, and he saw that they were his means to make the world a little better place than he had found it. That realization is a wonderful gift. If we take nothing else from Rodney's life, it is the lesson that each of us can do no better than to find his or her gift and use it to the betterment of the world around us.

"But I'm wandering. I promised you a reminiscence of Roddy. As I said, we were children. Our father was a veteran of the First World War, and as a result of that conflict, he had lost a leg. Father only celebrated one holiday: Veteran's Day, or as they used to call it back then, Armistice Day, the day that commemorated the end of the Great War. Christmas, Thanksgiving, birthdays, none of them really mattered to our father; it was first and foremost Veteran's Day. He worked as a night watchman, as that was one of the few jobs a man with a wooden leg was afforded back then, and he was grateful to have it. In those days a watchman didn't have days off or holidays. There were only two watchmen, and they each worked twelve-hour shifts. If one wanted a day off, the other would have to work a double shift. Consequently, they each only took one day off a year. Our father's counterpart chose Christmas. Father always took off Veteran's Day.

"Roddy was probably about the age of ten when he realized the distinct difference in our father from those of the other kids. He somehow understood how important that one day of the year was to our father. Roddy realized how much father had sacrificed for his country and how much he continued to give in the same spirit every day for his family. That was the first time I saw that spark of purpose ignite in my brother. Roddy got the idea to honor Father on his most special day: on Veteran's Day.

"Perhaps it wasn't a practical idea or even a very good idea, but it was a notion that came from his heart, and that made it a great idea. Roddy took it upon himself to fix up a special wooden leg for our Father just to wear on Veteran's Day. Dad had two wooden legs. One for every day, and the other, an older one, that he kept in case anything happened to his good one. Every year he'd get a new one from the government, and then he would take the old one and throw it out, and rotate them like that. About mid-October that year, just after Dad had gotten his new leg, Roddy took the old, old leg from the trash, and he sneaked it out into the back of the garage. There he set about refinishing it and decorating it, especially for Veteran's Day. He worked like mad on that piece of wood, for three weeks, polishing, staining, and who knows what else. It was really something, at least by the standards of a ten-year-old boy. Then the day before Veteran's Day, Roddy was all done, and he decided to inscribe it. He borrowed a friend's wood-burning stylus. That was a sort of a cross between a pen and an electric iron. You could use it for burning designs in wood. Well, Roddy decided to add some words of tribute to the leg, but he hadn't realized that the varnish he'd used was flammable. When he applied the heat, the leg caught fire. He just managed to put it out before burning down the garage, but the leg was ruined. Roddy was crushed. He worked so hard on it, and he never got a chance to give it to Father. Our father hadn't even known about it, and he never found out.

"I somehow was reminded of that day, and how hard Rodney had worked on it when I heard about how he left us a few days ago. Again there was a project he put himself into for the benefit of others, another accident, this one even more tragic, and once more he never got to see how much others appreciated all his efforts."

Now Elinor's eyes were fixed on Chesney.

"There's a story in the Old Testament. Where King David wanted very much to build the temple, but was not allowed to. His son, Solomon ultimately built it."

Elinor reached down, slipped on a pair of reading glasses, and read: "And in 2nd Chronicles 6:8 Solomon says: 'But the Lord said to David my father, Forasmuch as it was in thine heart to build a house for my name, thou didst well in that it was in thine heart.'"

Elinor put down her glasses and looked into the first row.

"There are no regrets," she said, "when you're heart is in the right place."

Then she looked around, and as if she suddenly realized that she was once again speaking to a large group, smiled bashfully.

"And that's all I wanted to say."

Elinor returned to her pew, amidst the nodding of heads, the wiping of eyes, and a smattering of noses blown.

◆

"That was beautiful, Aunt El. How did you know?"

"How did I know what, Chesney, dear?"

Chesney stood once more in the international terminal of Kennedy airport, saying goodbye to his aunt.

"That story about, Dad, and the wooden leg, and doing well in the heart, and all that," he said. "It was perfect."

"Thank you."

"You never told me about that before. Dad never told me that."

"Well," said Aunt Elinor, "he wouldn't, would he?"

"No, I suppose he wouldn't. Dad wasn't one to display his emotions like that."

She nodded. "Not only wouldn't he, he couldn't."

"Excuse me?"

"He couldn't have told that story," she explained. "I only just made it up last night."

"You..."

"Yes, well," said Elinor, "I know it's not very honest telling a lie to cover up another lie."

"Another lie?"

"Yes, when I agreed with you that your idea for a book about windows was a dumb idea. Actually, that was only a half-truth, though normally I don't approve of such distinctions. I mean, a lie is a lie. But I was just agreeing with you."

"But why did you agree with me that it was a dumb idea? I don't understand."

She smiled again. "Apparently you thought it was a dumb idea, and I've learned not to argue with someone when they're putting themselves down. If they really believe it, it won't do any good, and if they're just wallowing in self-pity the more you try to pull them out the more they'll use you to pull themselves in deeper. Do you understand?"

"I think so," said Chesney.

"I had to show you," she continued, "but I didn't know quite how at the moment."

"Is that why you didn't talk much at the wake and the funeral?"

"That and I didn't really know anyone. I was thinking, and then I remembered that verse."

"But why the whole story about the leg?"

She shook her head. "If I just came up to you and chucked a verse at you, it wouldn't stick. You'd just think I was a nice old lady spouting some platitude..."

"You're not old..."

"A middle-aged woman, then," she said. "Either way, if you wrap something in a story first and then stick on the commercial it works better; makes it more memorable, if you know what I mean."

Chesney agreed and accompanied his aunt through the terminal, stopping on the way to purchase a few magazines and a paperback book for her flight. At the newsstand, she picked up a book of word puzzles and held it out for him.

"Am I still 'Nature's Lion?'" she asked with a tiny grin.

For a moment, he was at a loss for words, forgetting the anagram of her name he had devised in his youth.

"No,'" he said.

"No?"

"You're now 'A tardy menu,'" he let her ponder the letters for a moment before providing the solution: "My dear Aunt."

With that, he leaned forward and kissed her on the cheek. Then he paid for her selections and guided her to her gate.

"You know," she said in a slightly scolding tone, "you really do need to come and visit me in London. I've only been waiting since you were twelve."

Chesney was about to apologize when he recalled his promotion and raise. "I'm an editor, now," he said almost as much to himself as to her.

"Really? That's wonderful, dear! You didn't mention it in your last letter."

"It only just happened."

"I always knew you'd get on well," she said. "Does this mean you'll be able to come and visit?"

"Well," Chesney looked down at his shoes. That had been his first thought. Still, that would be better as a surprise. He tried to adopt a disappointed expression. "I really don't know. I mean, as an editor I'll have a lot more work and responsibilities."

"Oh, I see…"

Perhaps he had overplayed it, Chesney thought. He tried to soften his remarks. "Still, I mean, you never can tell what will happen, can you?"

"No," said Elinor smiling, "no, you never can tell."

– 16 –
Digging a Rut
Two Minutes at a Time

Although he was being coy with Aunt Elinor, Chesney was correct. He couldn't tell if he could afford a trip to England. He couldn't tell much about anything. Oh, he could spot a dangling participle, a split infinitive, or an abused gerund, but away from manuscripts, he was as clueless as ever. Very few people noticed it, especially at work. To them he was the quiet, conscientious editor, reading behind a pile of work with his ever-present Coca-Cola at his side. He rarely strayed from his spot from eight in the morning until four in the afternoon. Like some musty Dickensian clerk plodding away atop a tall stool, or a Roman galley slave pulling on an oar hour after hour, Chesney Potoski flipped page after page, correcting an endless march of words he had not written.

One day he saw an assistant editor looking at him from over the cubicle wall. In her hand was a stopwatch. He put down his pencil and asked if he could help her.

"Did you know," she said, "you edit at the rate of one page every minute and forty-five seconds?"

"Pardon?"

She pushed down on the plunger on the watch and held it out to him.

"A minute and forty-five seconds," she said.

"Is that fast?"

The girl shrugged her shoulders. "Speed doesn't enter into it. It's not the speed, but the consistency. And I'm not timing everyone."

Chesney fidgeted in his chair, reached for his Coca-Cola.

"Don't get all defensive," she said.

Chesney looked at her. Suddenly he felt old and foolish though they were around the same age.

"You're just so consistent," she continued. "You show up at the same time, you arrange your desk the same way, get your first soda from the cafeteria, and then you start editing. And you turn a page every minute and forty-five seconds, give or take a second or two, but never more than a second or two."

"So?"

"So nothing," she said.

He would have been angry, but there wasn't a hint of mockery or condescension in her voice. It was almost as if she were an anthropologist studying an aborigine in the Outback.

"It's just interesting," she continued. "Whether you've got a lot of corrections to make on a page, or if the page is flawless, you spend one minute and forty-five seconds on it. Then you reach up, put a dab of Tacky Finger on your index finger, turn the page, wipe your finger, reach up, take a sip of soda, and then start on the next page. With the turning and the sipping, it comes out to exactly two minutes."

"Some people," he said, "don't have enough to do..."

"And then every tenth minute, you don't sip the soda."

"I don't?"

"No, you do this." She jerked her head to the left, then to the right, and then rolled her shoulders.

He stared at her for at least as much time as it would have taken to edit half a page. When it was clear she had nothing more to add to her detailed study of the habits of the New Jersey book editor, he spoke.

"Well, glad I could be of such interest to you."

"Oh, it's not just me."

"What?"

"No, we all noticed it."

"All of you?"

"I don't mean everyone, like the whole building, or the whole floor..."

"Well, that's a relief," he said, trying to temper his sarcasm.

"Just the fiction readers and editors," she added with a nod over the cubicle wall. Chesney stood halfway out of his chair and observed the half-a-dozen girls who suddenly put their heads down and pretended to be working.

"I see," he said, sitting back down. He felt silly.

"I...I didn't mean to upset you."

"Upset? I'm not upset," said Chesney though his voice wavered.

"Good," she said. "We just noticed, that's all."

"That I'm a qualified timepiece if the clocks should ever malfunction."

"No, it's nothing like that," she said. "It's just that you're reliable."

"...reliable..."

"And steady. You're consistent and predictable. And those are all good things, you know."

Chesney stared at the girl for a minute. He didn't even know her name, but she was attractive, especially for the fiction department. Most of the women in the section were bookish even for employees at a publishing house. They wore bulky sweaters over shapeless figures, and thick reading glasses with over-sized frames and half of them had their hair pulled back, making them look like little bookworms. Still, he imagined underneath their bulky wrappers, with their hair unfurled and their glasses off they were probably very alluring. He had seen one take off her glasses once and found her watery myopic eyes captivating. And now he was actually having a conversation with one of them, and the most attractive one of the bunch. He wondered if he should ask her out. Abruptly asking out a strange girl was not predictable. Asking her out would be daring, impulsive, and terrifying.

He looked away for a moment, then, thinking of nothing else to say, said it: "My name is Chesney Potoski."

"Yes, I know," she said. She didn't offer her own name in reply. She just pointed to the edge of his cubicle. "It's on your nameplate."

He nodded. He could learn her name, but to do so, he would have had to venture into their department uninvited, a liberty which his shyness would not permit.

She looked at him for a moment. He wondered if she were waiting for him to say something else, but before he could decide, she spoke again.

"Well, hope I didn't upset you," she said as she turned to go.

"No, not..."

"Good, okay," she said, and then she was gone.

He stared at the wall of his cubical for the amount of time it would have taken for him to edit five-and-a-half pages of text, including the intervals to moisten his finger and sip his Coca-Cola. In that time, Chesney wrestled with what had just transpired. He spent the first page-and-a-half worth of time wallowing in self-pity over the realization that women were watching him for their amusement. After this, he wondered if perhaps there was a possibility, small though it may be that the girl was actually trying to meet him. She could have easily studied his habits from a distance, couldn't she? After all, anthropologists rarely chatted with their subjects. Maybe, he thought, just maybe she was using this as a way to start up a conversation, to draw him out so that he might ask her out. Maybe that was all nonsense about so many seconds per page, the Tacky Finger, and the sip of soda. Perhaps she made it up. How would he know? Now that he was aware of the hypothesis, he couldn't study himself. Still, whether the girl had been studying his habits or whether she had just made it all up, one thing was clear: she was watching him. Was she watching him because she was interested in him?

He sat for several moments nodding, relishing the idea that a somewhat attractive female would also find him somewhat attractive. Yes, that was a possibility, but he really didn't know what to do about it if it were true.

He tugged on the worn cardigan that he always wore at his desk. It was dark and oversized. He used it as much to mask his weight, as to shield himself from the overzealous air conditioning. Why did he have to be overweight? That was a stupid question. He had long concluded that he overate to compensate for his lack of confidence. This, of course, resulted in him feeling even less confident, which made him eat even more.

No, Chesney thought, the pendulum of his mind swinging back to its starting point, this girl wouldn't be interested in him. She had come over to amuse herself his expense. Chesney sighed. Nothing was likely to change. He would go on being a fat little guy who was very fussy about words, who wrote long letters to his maiden aunt, played the ukulele in private, and went without a meaningful love in his life.

He would have been content if not for that last item. He started to reach for his Coca-Cola and then froze with the cup halfway to his lips. He stared at it for a moment and then put it down. He looked down at the manuscript and the blue pencil resting across the page. He glanced at the clock and watched the second hand rhythmically jerk along. These had been the constants of his existence, and they would serve as such for the rest of his life...unless.

Constant and predictable, that's what she said. Or you could call it plodding along in a rut. Rut? No, he thought, it was more like falling into a deep hole and waiting until someone filled it in. He stood, and for one moment, considered throwing his soda against the wall, tearing the manuscript to shreds, and walking out of the building forever. But, he reasoned, Coca-Cola splattered against the wall would only make a mess for the janitorial staff. The manuscript he was editing was quite interesting, and he couldn't destroy someone else's hard work. Lastly, he needed a job, and he had just recently been promoted. It would be very ungrateful to repay them with a tantrum.

He sat down again. Absent-mindedly he began reaching for his Coke but stopped himself. No, Chesney thought. He would break out of his rut, not through some ill-conceived impulse, but with a steady, determined effort to... to... not do the same thing.

– 17 –
The Perfect Dress and
the Reason for Leashes

Valerie Fierro turned the page, and her life changed forever.

Though at sixteen she had long given up on fairy tales, Valerie couldn't help but recall their magic as she flipped the page of *Cosmopolitan* and saw it: The Dress. It was daring, it was sophisticated, it was sexy, it was... her. In that dress, Valerie would no longer be just her father's little princess. In that dress, she would be the most beautiful girl at the prom.

"Oh, Reggie, Reggie," cooed Valerie to her companion on the bed beside her, "isn't it just perfect? Look at this dress! Did you ever see anything so passionate in all your life?"

Reggie looked soulfully into Valerie's eyes but uttered not a word.

It was all working according to plan, she thought as she mentally checked off the items on her agenda for the prom. Although she was just a junior, she had it all figured out. She would maneuver a dating relationship with a senior, and not just a senior, but a suitable type, either an athlete, or someone with money, or both. He would have a cute face, and a great body, nice hair, and his coloring would complement hers. Not too dark, not too blonde, sort of light brown that would contrast nicely with her dark brunette hair. He would be tall, that was important, she noted as she looked at the dress in the magazine again.

"Three, maybe four-inch heels," she said, chewing on the corner of her bottom lip. "So he'll have to be tall, don't you think so, Reggie?"

Reggie glanced at Valerie but offered no opinion on the matter.

"Yes, tall." Valerie sprung off the bed and stood on her toes. She kept one eye on the mirror, while with the other she looked at the photograph of the dress. "This would be three-inch heels." She held the pose for a moment. "And this would be four." She lifted herself another inch. Then she raised her hand level with the top of her head and then raised it another three inches. "There, that's about how tall he has to be."

Reggie yawned and looked away.

"You've got to think of these things, Reggie," she scolded. "You've got to think of the pictures. The boy should come up to here. Now, if I'm five-five, and have four-inch heels, just likes these ones in the picture…if I'm wearing these shoes he… wait, he'll be wearing shoes, of course, probably with a one-inch heel…that will be perfect! My eyes will come right about to the bottom of his nose. You've got to think of these things. This is going to be the most important night of my life, and I don't want to be looking up at his neck, or worse, be towering over him. Six foot to six two is perfect for this. Plus it will have to be someone going to a good college. Don't ask me which one, just as long as it's a good one. That means college dances and frat parties. But that's next year."

Valerie jumped back on the bed. Reggie rolled over and looked at her. She smiled at him and winked.

"And this dress, well, it's just perfect. Look how it's cut." Valerie reached down and cradled her well-developed breasts into her hands and pushed them up, approximating the lift of the dress' tight bodice. "Irresistible," she concluded, "totally! That's how I'll be." She winked at Reggie. "And, I'll let you in on a secret. This dress, on my body, well, I won't be a little princess any more after that night if you know what I mean. Don't you dare tell anyone, will you?"

Valerie nudged him with her toes. Reggie stirred and sprang on top of her.

"No, no, Reggie!" She tried to cover herself with the comforter, but it was too late, no matter how she protested Reggie was inflamed with a desire that mere words wouldn't quench.

"Reggie!" Valerie screamed at the annoying pitch that only a teenaged girl can achieve. Footsteps were heard up trodding up the stairs, followed by the door bursting open.

"What's going on in here, why are you… SCOREGGIA!"

Reggie ignored Connie Fierro, even though she used his full name, indicating he was in big trouble.

"SCOREGGIA!"

"Reggie! No, mother! Don't hurt him!"

Valerie's plea was in response to her mother raising the back of her hand to the excited collie attempting to impregnate the left leg of a family member. Connie Fierro smacked the dog's rear end, knocking him from the bed. Unlike a cat which lands on its feet, Reggie the Collie landed on his pointy snout. Despite belonging to such a majestic-looking breed, the Collie rolled clumsily on his side. Then, encouraged by a kick up the rear from Connie's size-nine flat, Reggie hurried out the door.

Valerie sat there, staring at the doorway. She didn't want to look at her mother. Her mother never took her side. She would blame Valerie instead of Reggie. And she had also just kicked the poor dog. Valerie sat there, unsure where to look, or whom to be angry at, or whom to accuse. Before she could reach any conclusion, her mother pounced.

"Valerie! What were you doing?"

Valerie looked up. Her mother was standing in her favorite blame Valerie pose: one hand on her hip, the other elbow drawn in tightly to her side, allowing her to swing her arm like a construction derrick.

"ME?!" Valerie feigned shock.

Her mother looked around the room. "Do you see anyone else here?" Connie Fierro lifted up the corner of the bedspread. "I don't see anyone else." Her daughter fidgeted. "Well?"

"Well, what?" said Valerie modulating between defiance and innocence, hoping one of them would work.

"What were you doing?"

"Me?" she said as if she had been an inert object since the beginning of time. "Me? I was just reading a magazine." She tried to hide the cover, but her mother snatched the magazine from Valerie's hand.

"No!"

"What?"

"No!"

"You said you wanted me to read more," protested Valerie.

"Yes, books. Things that will improve your mind, not trash like *Cosmopolitan*." Her mother flipped through the magazine and stopped at a photograph of one model. "Look at this one! What do you call that?"

Valerie studied the woman in the picture for a moment. Her first instinct was to call the woman, the dress, the pose, all of it: "hot." However, she knew that would not help her win this debate. Instead, she tilted her head to one side, as if she were pondering a philosophical subject. She nodded. "Yes, I might call that ...provocative...maybe...just a little bit."

Connie Fierro stared at her daughter and then nodded. "Provocative?"

Valerie relaxed a little. She liked the word "provocative." It was much more mature than "sexy." In her estimation, it was a champagne word, while those other descriptions were beery. She wanted a life with champagne words, champagne moments, and champagne relationships.

"Yes, mother," agreed Valerie, feeling quite mature. "Definitely provocative."

"Provocative," Connie repeated, this time with a much more pejorative intonation, "provocative? You're almost right. You call her provocative? I'd call that girl a *puttana!*"

Valerie's mouth dropped open. A whore? A whore? In *Cosmo?*

"Valerie, look at this girl..." Connie continued.

Girl? That wasn't a girl, she thought, the person in that photo was definitely a woman. She wasn't just a model, she was a role model.

"…you can see all the way up her thigh, her boobs are nearly hanging out, she obviously isn't wearing a bra. Look at all that make-up! It only says one thing: how much does she charge? *Puttana!*"

Valerie repressed the urge to roll her eyes. It would only prolong the lecture. Her mother just didn't understand style.

Connie Fierro was now flipping through the magazine, stopping to point out every little flaw she imagined. She was almost to the page that featured the dress… The Dress… Valerie's perfect dress for the prom. Valerie held her breath, it would be fatal if her mother saw the perfect dress in the middle of her other petty complaints with the content of *Cosmo*. If she saw that dress, now, in that magazine Valerie's life would be over. Valerie opted for a tactical retreat while her mother was still unaware of her larger prom campaign.

"…You're right, Mom…mmy." She played the little girl card. She had given up "Mommy" years ago, though she reserved the title for appropriate moments. It always had an emotional effect on Connie Fierro, especially when Valerie remembered to raise her voice half an octave. The key was not to overuse it. Her father, on the other hand, was still and would always be "Daddy." With Giorgio, it would never lose its potency. Fortunately, it worked now. Her mother closed the magazine and tucked it under her arm, but the lecture wasn't over.

"I know that this must seem all grown-up to you, Valerie," her mother continued. Valerie looked innocent while waiting for her to get to the end of her rant against stylish women.

"…this isn't real life, Valerie. You wouldn't see me or your sister dressing like this…"

Valerie bit her lip. Her mother or Rose in one of those dresses? Neither of them had the body for those dresses. She loved them both, of course, but her mother was skinny, almost bony. She hadn't enough curves to hold up a chic strapless number, while Rose was way too round. In a strapless dress, she'd look like the butcher's wife rolled up in a sausage casing. Yes, Valerie concluded, that was why her mother and her sister didn't appreciate real style because neither of them could pull it off. If you can't join them, tear them down. It was sad. Valerie would need to be more understanding… after the prom. While she ruminated on this theme, her mother had moved on to a fresh subject.

"…and I've told you before you shouldn't let that dog on your bed…"

"Reggie?" How could she blame that poor collie? It wasn't his fault. He was just a dog. Being at the lower end of the family pecking order, Valerie understood too well how these things worked. The innocents always were blamed. Poor Reggie, even his name, short for *"Scoreggia,"* the Italian word for "fart," was unfair. After all, it wasn't the dog's fault that he was flatulent. She'd never met a dog, or a man for that matter, who wasn't.

"…Reggie is too easily excited…" said Connie.

"…but I barely brushed against him with my foot, it was an accident…"

"...that wouldn't have happened if the dog hadn't been on the bed..."

"...he gets...excited."

"That's why you don't let him on the bed, Valerie," said Connie, "and you shouldn't dress like that either."

Valerie looked down at herself.

"What's wrong with this?" Her mother had seen the shorts and top she was wearing before.

"There's nothing wrong around the house or in your bedroom..."

Valerie looked around as if to indicate that's where she was.

"You know what I mean, young lady," was her mother's quick retort. Valerie said nothing. "It's not appropriate to wear... not when..." Valerie kept quiet, sensing her mother's reasoning was falling apart. "...not on the bed....with..." She paused to regroup mentally. "You wouldn't wear those short shorts and that short top on the bed with a boy."

"So?" asked Valerie.

"So...Reggie's a boy," her mother concluded.

"Reggie's a dog."

"A boy dog," Connie sat down on the edge of the bed, and gently pushed a lock of hair from her daughter's cheek. "Valerie, Reggie is a dog, of course, but he's also a boy. And trust me, you'll soon learn that there's not a great deal of difference between dogs and boys. I know you think they're all cute..."

"Not all of them," interrupted Valerie, "not all dogs, certainly not all boys!"

"Some of them," conceded Connie Fierro, "can be very cute, and you look into their big eyes, and they just seem so happy and innocent, and lovable. But just like Reggie, it doesn't take much to turn them from cute puppies to wild animals. When they cross that line, you'll find that you can't control them. That's why you need to be more careful. You're not a little girl anymore."

Valerie nodded. Inwardly, however, she had reached a different conclusion. She wasn't a little girl, she thought. She was a damned sight more than just a little girl. And as for controlling dogs and men, well, she reasoned, she was ready for either of them. That's what leashes were for.

"Well, I'm glad you understand," said Connie. She started to return the *Cosmopolitan* to her daughter. Then she looked at Valerie and then at the magazine, and then back at Valerie before tucking the issue under her arm. "I think I'll hold on to this for now," she said. To Valerie "for now" usually meant "forever," or at least until Valerie was an old lady and everything in that issue would be out of style.

Connie Fierro turned to leave, taking with her the dress that would change Valerie's life. Valerie tried not to show her disappointment or her desperation, but somehow, in that cruel sixth sense that mothers seem to have, her mother stopped, turned, and delivered a devastating parting shot.

"Oh, that reminds me, sweetheart," she said, sounding like she cared about her daughter's life, "the prom is coming up, isn't it?"

"Yes, the senior prom."

"Do you think you'll be asked?"

Valerie shrugged her shoulders while thinking: "I'd better damn well be asked."

"Well," continued her mother, "if you do get asked, I've got some catalogs downstairs," she continued. "We'll have to go through them. Sears and Penney's have cute dresses for the prom."

Then with the grace of a Gestapo agent, her mother turned and goose-stepped from the room. Valerie sat on the bed, staring at the space where her mother had been. Her jaw felt like it must be dislocated. Sears or Penney's? Valerie just learned in school about how cruel and unusual punishment was forbidden. Apparently, the Founding Fathers hadn't been specific enough. Obviously, none of their mothers had ever even suggested that someone should have to go to the prom on the most important night of their life wearing a dress from the J.C. Penney or... Ick! The Sears catalogs!

Valerie refocused her thoughts before she retched. She buried her face in her pillow and tried to think pleasant thoughts. But no matter how she tried, big pink Sears dresses with ugly rows of lace and puffy sleeves kept banging down the doors of her mind and forcing themselves upon her imagination. Ewww! It was bad enough to think of those horrid creations, but soon, despite her best efforts, she saw herself wearing them. They clung to her body like some sort of repulsive alien in a horror movie affixing itself to its victim and sucking the life out of her until she became a tacky zombie. She imagined herself in the middle of the dance floor with all the cute girls laughing at her, all the good-looking boys running away, and a row of pimply, myopic dorks in ill-fitting, powder-blue tuxedos lining up to dance with her.

Valerie screamed into her pillow, but then heard a sound that broke the catalog dress spell. It was a car door slamming. Valerie sat up. Her eyes narrowed into determined slits. She had lost the first battle, but she would win this war.

– 18 –
Albrecht and the
Icky Store

Her initial impulse was to run to her father, smother him with affection, and then ask for the dress. Her mother would launch a counterattack, followed by tears from Valerie, and then days of pouting. The end result would be Valerie's life ending as she was forced to attend the most important event of her life wearing some dorky dress from the Sears catalog.

A direct assault would doom her to slumping off to the prom looking like a cute little girl and dragging herself home again no more a woman than when she had left. She would have to approach this problem as a sophisticated woman. This event was too crucial for childish tactics. This was not a game. This was a fight for the rest of her life.

Suppressing the urge to grab for her dress of destiny, Valerie went downstairs as if she desired nothing more than the company of her family and her mother's baked ziti.

The next day, after school, Valerie was at the local pharmacy. In addition to prescriptions and the usual stuff, they sold magazines. Towards the back of the rack, behind the copies of *Ladies Home Journal*, *Family Circle*, and *McCall's*, sat the more sophisticated periodicals. Those other magazines had mundane articles on cleaning, sewing, and vapid suggestions for new twists on old chicken recipes. The other magazines, those towards the back, had practical topics like makeup, fashion, and most importantly of all: sex. No wonder her mother was prejudiced against magazines like *Cosmo*. Connie Fierro had no use for their wise counsel. She didn't need to know about fashion, and Valerie doubted whether even a top cosmetologist could elevate her mother beyond looking like a middle-aged housewife. As for her mother and sex – Valerie banished the consideration of two such contradictory ideas from her mind. Ewww!

Valerie felt a pang of sympathy for her mother. At the advanced age of forty-one, Connie wouldn't be anything more than a suburban housewife in the jerkwater of Delaware. Valerie decided she would be nicer to her aged mother, especially after she'd become a successful executive married to a tall, handsome man in a custom-tailored Brooks Brothers suit.

Valerie returned to the matter at hand. How could she convince her parents to spring for her *Cosmo* dress for the upcoming prom? She couldn't march into the house with this replacement copy of *Cosmopolitan* plop it down on the dining room table and make a straight sales pitch. Her mother was already prejudiced against anything sophisticated. How could she put this one over?

Valerie's eyes wandered to the more juvenile publications like *16* and *Tiger Beat*. Years ago, she had once been an avid reader of those magazines. She noticed the headline on the cover of *Tiger Beat*: "The Hottest Styles for This Year's Prom," and shook her head. She remembered sharing their idea of "hot"... when she was about nine-years-old! Nobody she knew would think much of those dresses...

Valerie's eyes narrowed. No one would think much of those dresses except maybe her mother. She plucked the issue of *Tiger Beat* from the shelf and flipped open to the dresses. If only the dress of destiny, her *Cosmo* dress, were among those in *Tiger Beat*, then her mother wouldn't object to it. Valerie held up the two magazines. They were the same size. She could easily paste the one page into the other, and then show it to her parents.

Congratulating herself on her sophisticated wiles, Valerie started for the cash register, and then realized she'd need some glue. She quickly took a jar of paste from a nearby shelf and examined the label.

"...ideal for paper..." she read aloud to herself.

"You don't want that," said a voice from behind. Valerie jumped. The voice was sort of deep, but with still a juvenile quality to it. She slowly turned; hoping to see a member of the football team, not first-string, she knew all of their voices by heart, but some athlete nonetheless. She looked up, expecting someone tall and good looking, but then lowered her gaze to someone her own eye level.

"Oh," she said, trying to hide her disappointment. Valerie tried to appear genial, even to nonentities. And Albrecht Eckner was as "non" a nonentity that she could think of while still knowing his name. "Hello, Albrecht."

"Hello, Valerie."

Albrecht spoke so smoothly. His voice sounded like maple syrup being poured over a swatch of velvet. At least that's the image that came to her mind. Valerie had never actually poured a viscous liquid over any fabric.

They stood facing each other for a moment. Valerie made only cursory eye contact, much as she had seen royal people do in movies when they were forced to look at commoners. When she did steal a glance at Albrecht, she couldn't help noticing that he was looking at her very closely indeed.

It was an admiring look, yet not one that conceded that he was out of her league… which he obviously was! However, it was a disconcerting look. It was the stare of someone looking at something they knew they couldn't afford but were confident they would somehow obtain.

They stood there for several uncomfortable moments as he gazed upon her, and she avoided looking at him. She did make passing glances at him as she scanned the store, paying him no more mind than that bottle of Calamine lotion over there, or that box of tampons on the shelf. Looking at him indirectly, Valerie had to concede that Albrecht Eckner wasn't completely repulsive; after all, she did know his name. She wouldn't socialize with him, of course. He had nice dark brown hair and a reasonably good body. She did detect a slight paunch over the top of his belt, but then he wasn't an athlete. Valerie could well imagine that little roll developing into a full-size belly when he was older. Still, she thought that was no concern of hers. His face was interesting, Valerie concluded, though not quite attractive. He had good bone structure, which was more important in a girl than a boy, but still, her years of studying beauty had taught her to appreciate good bone structure when she saw it. His eyes, on the other hand, were narrow, almost like a lizard, or someone who had forgotten their sunglasses for a day at the beach. Good nose, she thought and had to concede it was more attractive than her nose, which was one more reason not to hang around with him; as if she needed one. It was his mouth, though that was most bothersome. It was surly, with a slight curl to the corner, even when it was in neutral. Yes, it was surly, no doubt, but Valerie couldn't decide if it were surly in an attractive way, like Elvis Presley in the old movies, just before Ann Margaret would kiss him; or if it was surly in a cruel way that would grow, with his potbelly, into an ugly sneer by middle age… at about thirty.

"Well…Albrecht, it was nice seeing…" Valerie began, attempting to break away from him. She had tolerated him in her presence long enough.

"You don't want that," said Albrecht. His voice carried such a degree of authority that she stopped turning away even though she wanted desperately to do so.

Valerie looked down at the items in her hands and then back up at him. A smug smile spread across her lips, and she tilted her head to one side.

"I think I know what I want," she said, trying not to sound overtly snotty, but meaning to convey that sense just the same. "Besides, what do you know about women's magazines?"

Without flinching, he returned the look and the tone with the same degree of snot and perhaps even more cattiness.

"I wasn't talking about the magazines." He then dropped the edge from his voice. "I was talking about the paste."

"Paste?"

"You don't want the paste," he said.

"I don't?" She said, feeling her confidence slipping away. "Why not?"

He shrugged. "Nobody wants paste, unless you're a pre-schooler with an unhealthy appetite or if you're making paper chains. You're not doing anything like that, are you?"

She shook her head.

"Then you want rubber cement," he said.

"I do?"

"Most likely," he said authoritatively. He nodded towards the paste. "What were you going to use that for?"

Valerie wanted to say: "None of your business, you horrid amphibian," but somehow his tone carried such certainty she found herself explaining despite herself.

"I was going to...cut some pictures out of this magazine, and...paste them into this one."

His narrow eyes closed even further, and a smile spread over his closed mouth, though the sneer remained in the corner. Albrecht Eckner nodded as if he knew Valerie was up to something sneaky and he heartily approved.

"Then," he said, "you definitely want rubber cement. I use it all the time on the yearbook."

"Oh," she said, "are you on the yearbook?"

"I'm the photo editor," he said as if it were common knowledge.

Valerie nodded. "Oh, right, I've seen you at games, and plays, and things... with your camera."

He smiled as if he were patronizing a slow child. Valerie felt her cheeks glow red. How dare this little dweeb, with his dorky camera, make her feel this way? He might go around taking pictures, but she and her friends were in those pictures. How dare he try to make her feel like she was, well, like she was him?! Still, when it came to gluing photos, he was a pro, and she was a novice. After all, she reminded herself, this wasn't about popularity and cliques, not at the moment. This was about the perfect dress for the prom. She could suffer the insufferable Albrecht Eckner for a moment if it helped her plan succeed. Later she could crush him like the bug that he was.

"Oh," she forced a smile, "so I don't want paste. I want rubber cement."

"That's right," he said. "Paste would be lumpy. You want to use rubber cement if you want your efforts to be clean and... undetectable."

Valerie smiled and nodded in agreement, but then came up short. She looked Albrecht in his beady eyes. He knew something. Why else would he add the word "undetectable?"

She pushed the paranoia from her mind. She reminded herself that she would be the most sophisticated girl at the prom. And standing before her was a... peasant, yes, that was it. In the high school hierarchy, she was royalty, and he was a peasant.

"I've got some."

"I'm sorry?"

"I said I've got some rubber cement. I can let you have it," said Albrecht.

"Oh, no, that's alright," said Valerie, putting the jar of paste back on the shelf, "I'll just get some here. I don't want to put you to any trouble." She also wanted to get away from him. She had already afforded him more time than manners dictated she squander on him.

"They don't sell it here, and it won't be any trouble," said Albrecht. He sounded sincere.

"Okay," she said, forcing a smile, "I guess you can bring it to school tomorrow."

"You can have it right now."

She looked him up and down. Surely he didn't have a jar of rubber cement on him.

"I just live a few doors down," he said. Without actually touching her, Albrecht steered her to the counter where she paid for the two magazines. In another minute, she was walking out the door with Albrecht Eckner. Valerie looked up and down the street. They were in the middle of the town's small shopping district. There were no houses for blocks.

"You live..."

"Just over the family store," he said. He nudged her elbow, and she found herself, against her better judgment, walking down a public street with Albrecht Eckner.

Live above a store? Eww, that was a bit grotesque, wasn't it? She tried to recall the stores on the block, but couldn't bring any to mind. It was like taking a test in school. The harder you tried to remember something, the more you couldn't think of anything beyond the fact that you were trying to remember something. She'd been down this street since she was a little girl, but couldn't recall a single shop. Her mind tried to plug in generic shops. A bakery? No, that was the other way. A dress shop? No, most of those were at the mall. She glanced at Albrecht, and he returned the glance. His eyes exuded an eerie confidence as if he were in on some scheme with her. That was ridiculous, she thought. All he knew was that she needed to glue paper together and needed to do a neat job. She was letting her imagination run away with her.

"Here we are," said Albrecht.

"Where?" Valerie looked up at the glass doors with two large display windows on either side. "EWWW!" She tried to stifle her reaction, but it had already escaped. How could it not? The window had gilt letters painted on it proclaiming "A-1 Home Medical Supplies." It wasn't the writing on the window that was repulsive, but the display behind them. There, as if they were actually proud of them was the ickiest collection of things Valerie had ever seen. There were crutches and braces and wheelchairs and walkers and rubbery complicated-looking corsets and yucky tubular contraptions that looked like they would fit over toilets. Ewww, EWWW, thought Valerie as she tried to look away but for some reason couldn't. This was all old-people and sick-people stuff. EWWW! In that corner of her mind that she tried to reserve for compassion, Valerie reminded herself that some people might need these things. Still, the rest of her brain interjected, that was no reason to fill a store with them. EWWWW!

If Albrecht had taken any notice of Valerie's reaction, it didn't register on his face. If anything, he seemed to have a tiny smile tucked just beneath the curl of his lip.

"Won't you come in?" he asked, holding the door for her. She could have sworn she had heard the same intonation used by some hunchbacked butler towards the pretty heroine in some creepy horror movie. She always thought the girls in those movies were so stupid when they accepted such invitations, but like those girls Valerie found herself giving in without a word of protest.

Unlike those cobweb-filled castles, Valerie found the inside of the Eckner's store very bright and airy. The walls were a cheery yellow. There was a high-ceiling with florescent lights, modern glass counters and cases, and soft music playing. It would have been a very nice store, she thought, if it wasn't filled with all those horrible, icky, old, sick people implements.

"Come on in," said Albrecht, who seemed to brighten inside the store, or maybe it was just that he seemed more normal against such a creepy backdrop.

A couple approached from the back of the room, whom Albrecht introduced as his parents. They were older than Valerie's parents. Mr. Eckner was tall, taller than his son. His mother was short, plump, and though she looked older than her husband, showed signs of once being quite pretty. The couple treated Valerie as if she were somehow attached to their son; like she was his girlfriend. As if the contents of their store weren't enough, that misconception was enough to mortify Valerie. She tried to smile politely, though she heard very little of what they said. She was too busy wracking her brain for an escape route. Finally, she recalled how she had been lured in there in the first place.

"Uh, Albrecht," she said through clenched teeth, "I really have to go home; the rubber cement?"

"Oh, yes," he said, turning to his parents. "I'm helping Val out with a little project."

Val? Valerie loathed the diminutive of her name, but just took a deep breath and closed her eyes. When she opened them again, Albrecht was retreating up a side staircase. After he had gone, Albrecht's parents stared at her for several uncomfortable moments before Mrs. Eckner spoke up.

"So! You like our Albrecht!" She spoke with some sort of faint accent. Valerie, having an immigrant father herself, didn't mind the accent. It was what she was saying with that accent that bothered her. Mrs. Eckner wasn't asking if Valerie liked Albrecht, rather she seemed to be telling her that she did.

Valerie smiled weakly. She would have liked to say that she thought their son a loathsome, spotty, little gecko, but didn't think this was quite the time or place.

"Someday," interjected Mr. Eckner, who had no accent whatsoever, "all this will be Albrecht's." Mr. Eckner, by outward appearances, was normal, except for the fact he thought his son inheriting a collection of crutches and surgical corsets was something to brag about. He looked around his store admiring all he surveyed, and then filled with genuine pride in his accomplishments, looked at Valerie and asked: "Do you like home medical supplies?"

Valerie contemplated screaming at the top of her lungs at this latest question. She would have, but her impulse was interrupted by a clattering and banging from the staircase. She looked over, expecting to see Albrecht and a jar of rubber cement. Instead, Valerie was shocked to see one of the oldest, fattest men that had ever existed bumping and shuffling his way down the stairs, puffing and swearing (or at least that's what it sounded like) as he came. With each step, he lurched to one side, until some inner pendulum caused him to sway the other way. In this manner, he made his way down the stairs. At first, Valerie thought he had done this with his eyes closed, but as he neared the bottom steps, she realized that his eyes weren't closed. Rather, his cheeks were so fat that they forced his eyes into a perpetual squint. His cheeks would have no doubt allowed his eyelids to relax, had they not in turn been pushed upwards by his jowls, which were kept in position by his enormous neck. It was at his neck that her observations came to an end since the rest of his fat was covered by his clothes. Still, Valerie imagined that his entire mass was a series of adipose layers supporting the tier above it.

As if the physical appearance of this old man weren't remarkable by itself, he embellished his visual impression with a series of grunts, rants, and bellows in some strange language. At first, Valerie guessed he was some client, some lunatic old person in need of just about every geriatric appliance the store sold. He was obviously senile, she thought, given the incomprehensible gibberish coming from somewhere under his bushy mustache. She would have continued in this belief had not Mrs. Eckner started speaking back to him in the same weird tongue, though in much softer and refined tones. It was then, Valerie came to the conclusion they were speaking Transylvanian.

"That's Opa," explained Mr. Eckner, "my father-in-law, Albrecht's grandfather."

Valerie could merely nod with her mouth agape at the sight of such a repulsive being lurching about in the middle of a store filled with such revolting wares.

"He lives with us," said Albrecht's father, as Opa and his daughter conducted a lively discussion between themselves. "He's from the Old Country."

Valerie nodded again. She wondered which old country Mr. Eckner meant, but judging from Opa's appearance, it must be the oldest country on Earth. Valerie watched in astonishment as the old man continued to bicker with his daughter. Finally, after repeated efforts to interrupt him, Mrs. Eckner pointed out that they had a visitor. Opa forced his eyes open wide and ogled in Valerie's direction. Apparently, the old fart was nearsighted for he wobbled nearer for a better look. Valerie stood stone silent, hearing that such a tactic was effective with menacing bears.

Not having a bear's keen sense of smell, Opa refrained from sniffing Valerie, though his head did scan her from the top of her head to approximately halfway down her torso. Valerie looked sideways towards Mr. Eckner, expecting some sort of advice, but receiving none. Albrecht's father simply returned her look, in mute approval of her strategy to stand still and stay quiet.

Finally, the old man stood back, looked at his daughter, nodded, and said: "*Schön Möpse!*"

Valerie had no idea what that meant, but he was smiling, which was always a good sign. His daughter, however, apparently disagreed with whatever he had said, because she scolded him in his native tongue, starting a new argument. Not wanting to be in the middle of a family squabble, and in fact not wanting to be there at all, Valerie wondered if anyone would notice if she made a break for the door.

Carefully pointing her left foot towards the door, Valerie steeled herself for the dash, when Albrecht returned clutching a brown glass bottle. Albrecht forced his way between his mother and his grandfather, asking something in their common tongue. Valerie never knew he could speak another language, but then, she conceded, it didn't matter since she had never even wanted to talk to him in English. Valerie surmised that Albrecht was trying to learn what the argument was about. Opa muttered something, punctuating it with a shrug. Mrs. Eckner resumed scolding him, and apparently gave her version of what had happened. The worst part came when all three turned and looked at Valerie.

"What?" said Valerie. "What are they saying about me?"

Albrecht smiled and then tried to wipe the smile off his face. "Nothing. It's just that, Opa, my grandfather, thinks you're my girlfriend."

"Girlfriend!"

Albrecht said something to his grandfather.

"I told him," confirmed Albrecht, "that you're not my girlfriend."

Opa looked at his grandson, and then at Valerie, and then back at his grandson.

"*Nicht deine Freundin?*" said Opa.

"*Nicht meine Freundin,*" said Albrecht.

The old man again looked at him, then at Valerie, and then back at Albrecht. A sneer similar to the one he had passed down to his grandson curled upon his lips.

"*Einfalt!*" The old man turned and shuffled away.

Albrecht's face turned red, and his mother followed her father, nitpicking at him as he went. Mr. Eckner pretended to rearrange a display of trusses.

"Here's your rubber cement," muttered Albrecht handing her the bottle.

"Thanks," said Valerie, "I'll, I'll bring it back… at school."

"Keep it," he said.

"What did he call you, your grandfather?"

"Nothing…"

"He said, 'Einfalt.' What's that mean?"

He looked away, and for the first time since she had known him, Valerie felt sorry for Albrecht, but only a little bit. She had to remind herself he had brought her to this disgusting place. Still, he seemed terribly deflated.

"It's just an old German word," said Albrecht. "He uses it on everyone."

"Oh," she said, then, without knowing why exactly, she repeated it several times. "Einfalt…Einfalt…"

"I think you'd better go," said Albrecht. "You have to work on that project of yours."

Valerie looked down at the bag in her hand.

"Oh, right, yes, I do have to go," she said. "Well, thanks."

He nodded, and she felt a fresh wave of compassion for Albrecht. Fortunately, it evaporated as soon she turned, and all the icky, yucky, old, sick stuff assaulted her senses.

She rushed towards the door without looking back, and promising she would never, ever enter that place again… ever!

– 19 –
Every Parent's Sincere Desire
for Better Emollients for Their Children

W hat are you doing?"

Valerie Fierro jumped, almost spilling the rubber cement all over the copy of *Tiger Beat*. Fortunately, Valerie caught the applicator brush in her hand before it dribbled on the page. She hunched over the desk to conceal her work.

Big Old Rose with her Big Old Nose! A long-forgotten taunt for her older sister came to mind.

"What are you hiding?"

Now Valerie felt Rose's hand on her back.

"What?!" snapped Valerie. She craned her neck around, still keeping her project from the prying eyes of her sister.

"What are you up to?" asked Rose, ignoring Valerie's attempts at privacy. "What have you got there?"

It was too late. Rose was nearly on top of her. She was taller than Valerie and outweighed her. Rose had all the leverage or the fulcrum or some physics thing that her science teacher was always talking about. Reluctantly, Valerie showed her the magazine.

"*Tiger Beat?*" said Rose, removing the magazine from Valerie's grasp. "I haven't seen this in years. I didn't think you still liked *Tiger Beat*. How cute!" Rose wasn't being sarcastic, which made her even more annoying.

"Yeah, it's real cute," said Valerie. "It's adorable, now give me my magazine, and leave me alone."

Rose ignored her and thumbed through the pages of the periodical. "Joey Travolta in Love – TRUE!" Rose read the headline and then laughed. It wasn't a teasing laugh, but more a nostalgic laugh. "The names are different, but the headlines haven't changed." Rose tucked the magazine under her arms as she looked toward the ceiling. "Remember when I was in love with Wayne?"

"Wayne? Who's Wayne?" said Valerie. "And don't wrinkle the pages. I'm not done with...done reading it yet."

"Wayne Osmond," said Rose with a wistful look in her eyes.

"Donny Osmond's brother?"

"Donny's his brother," said Rose. "Wayne's older. Remember Wayne Osmond?"

"Yeah, okay." Valerie didn't remember, and she didn't care. Rose was ancient. Even though she was only four years older than Valerie, it might as well have been a hundred years. Their tastes never were in-sync. That never bothered Valerie until Rose said she thought Valerie's appreciation of the movie *Grease* was "jejune." Valerie had to look that one up, but even before she had found it in the dictionary, she knew she wasn't going to like it. Big Old Rose with the Big Old Nose! Still, she didn't want her plan uncovered, even if she'd have to get smacked with another "jejune."

"Okay, okay," said Valerie, returning the brush to the bottle of rubber cement and reaching for the issue of *Tiger Beat*. "Let me have my magazine. Why don't you go write a letter to Wayne, and give him my love while you're at it!"

Rose rolled her eyes in that superior, older-sister way that always made Valerie seethe.

"Here," she said, handing the magazine to Valerie. "I don't want your magazine." She began to turn and then stopped. "What's with the rubber cement?"

"What rubber cement?"

"The rubber cement in your hand."

Valerie looked down and feigned surprise as if the bottle just mysterious materialized.

"Oh, relax, will you," said Rose as she turned. "Who cares if you're keeping a scrapbook of your teen idols..."

"Scrapbook?"

"I don't care," said Rose, turning. She was at the door. "If you want to follow puerile pursuits, it's no skin off my nose."

"You could stand a couple of inches off of your nose," muttered Valerie as she crossed to the door and closed it. Valerie looked at her own nose in the mirror. She flashed a practice smile, quickly followed by her sultry look (the one with her eyes half closed), and then reached up to touch her proboscis. It was Italian, she concluded and conceded that it was larger than some girls' noses. But it wasn't unattractive, even if it did have a slight kink in it. At least it was pointy. Not bulbous like Rose's. It was cute and pointy...like Reggie's snout. Yes, of the entire family her nose was most like the dog's, and she liked it that way.

"Puerile pursuits!" said Valerie, repeating her sister's parting shot. She didn't know what puerile was, and she didn't care. Valerie wouldn't waste her time looking it up. Why should she? She knew it wasn't nice. She returned to her desk and glanced back at the closed door. Why couldn't Rose be nice... like she was?

Valerie listened for a moment to verify that no other interlopers were loping around in the hallway, and then, satisfied the coast was clear, returned to her work. She opened the issue of *Tiger Beat* to an article entitled: "Gnarly Fashions for the Perfect Prom!" The dresses weren't too bad, some of them were almost acceptable. There wasn't anything too Sears Roebucky or J.C. Pennyish. Valerie recalled the previous evening when she had been forced to sit down with her mother and look at those two catalogs. She rolled her eyes and mimed sticking her fingers down her throat. They were all perfect... perfectly gross!

She flipped the page of the article, revealing what was supposedly the highlight of the spread: a peach colored-dress with layers of ruffles in the skirt. It looked like it had escaped from Cyndi Lauper's Goodwill bag, but still, that wasn't entirely bad. Anyway, this would be the last time that dress would see the light of day in this particular magazine. Glancing over her shoulder to make sure there was no one coming, Valerie slid open the drawer and drew out the latest issue of *Cosmo*.

With what she imagined to be surgical precision, Valerie cut the page of her dream dress from *Cosmopolitan*. She was careful not to wrinkle or fold the photograph, lest she be out another $1.95. Then, with the page removed, she sized it up against the page of *Tiger Beat* into which she would insert it. The *Cosmo* page was slightly larger, which meant she could, with careful trimming, glue it directly over the page in the teen magazine. After trimming it down, however, she placed it over the other page only to realize that the color scheme of the page clashed with the layout of the page facing it.

Valerie studied the two pages. She looked at it beneath the harsh illumination of her desk lamp, and then in ambient light. She scrutinized it from various angles. She tried to imagine how her mother might see it when it was casually handed to her. She squinted at the two pages and then glowered at them with eyes nearly bulging from her head. Finally, she came to the conclusion that no one, not even her mother, would be fooled. She was almost ready to give up when she noticed that the woman in the sophisticated *Cosmo* dress had the same stance as the fresh-faced little teen queen in the *Tiger Beat* spread. The *Cosmo* picture was slightly larger, large enough to cover the other girl.

Stashing the fragments of her plot in the drawer, Valerie rushed to her parent's bathroom and opened the medicine cabinet. As a child, she often recalled sitting on the hamper and watching her father shave using an old-fashioned razor, the kind with the removable double-edged razor blade. There had been something so romantic about watching her father shave. He would lather up his face from the can of Foamy shaving cream. "Rich in emollients," promised the writing on the can.

She remembered asking her father what exactly "emollients" were, but he didn't know.

"They must be pretty good, *Piccola Principessa*," he concluded. "Rich people use them."

Valerie nodded in agreement. "When I grow up," she proclaimed, "I'm going to marry a man with lots of emollients!"

"Just as it should be for a *Principessa!*"

He would then continue to lather up while humming some tune. Towards the end, he would mutter something that sounded like "swazzy stickers." Then, the best part would come when he twisted the bottom of the handle of his razor, and the top would open like the jaws of some tiny mechanical monster. Giorgio Fierro would carefully slide a double-edged blade from the container and drop it into the middle of the jaws, closing it again with a few twists of the handle. Then came the climax, as her father dragged the sharp blade across his face. It was such a marvelous scraping noise. The only other sound like it was when her father would shovel ice from their driveway. The scraping was interrupted on average three times a shave as her father nicked himself. This was accompanied by a short oath, either in German or Italian. Then he would reach behind him. This was the cue for Valerie to tear off a little bit of toilet paper, and place it on the tip of his calloused outstretched finger.

"*Grazie,*" he would say without looking.

"*Prego,*" she would reply, happy that she was an integral part of the process even if her father had to draw blood for it.

By the time he was finished Giorgio Fierro would have jagged dots of toilet paper all about his face that would remain there for at least a half an hour until his wife reminded him of them as he was walking out the door.

Every few days, corresponding with an increased number of cuts to his face, Giorgio would decide his current blade was all used up. Then he would open up the tiny jaws, remove the blade, and stick it in a little slot in the back of the medicine cabinet.

"Where do they go?" she recalled asking her father the first time she saw him dispose of an old blade.

"They disappear…it's magic!"

Valerie loved that answer. It was right out of a fairytale, and of course, in all of her father's fairytales, she was the princess. She eventually realized that the used razor blades just fell down into the space behind the wall. Still, she never told her father she knew, nor did she ever correct him when he dropped a razor blade down the slot and said, with a twinkle in his eyes: "*Presto, Principessa!*"

Valerie jarred herself from her reverie and retrieved a razor blade, taking care not to cut herself. She rushed back to her room with the blade carefully concealed in her palm. After a painstaking operation, she had surgically extricated the model from *Cosmo*. She then unscrewed the cap from the jar of rubber cement releasing its built-in brush along with its mind-altering fumes.

"At least Albrecht Eckner is good for something," she muttered as she brushed a thin layer of the cement over the model in *Tiger Beat*, before making another application to the backside of the *Cosmo* picture. Albrecht was right; rubber cement was the adhesive of choice. Unlike white glue or paste, it dried flat and didn't stain. The excess, after it had dried, was easily rubbed away.

Holding out the open magazine at arm's length, she had to admire her handiwork. Now, no less an authority as *Tiger Beat* had endorsed the most fabulous, perfect, sophisticated dress ever designed for the form of a woman; a woman like her.

She could hardly wait to show it to her mother.

– 20 –
A Ticket to Write
(But Only Half-Fare)

"Would you like another drink?"

As with most questions Chesney Potoski fielded in the past month, he pondered his response. It was all part of his decision not to be predictable. It was started by that girl at work, the one who intimated he was in a rut. Since that day, Chesney resolved not to be predictable, even when it ran contrary to his deepest felt wants: like right now. He really wanted a soda. The long flight was playing havoc with his sinuses, his mouth was dry, and his throat was crying out for the bubbly carbon-filled delight of a Coca-Cola.

But that was just how the world would expect him to react in such a situation. He looked over his shoulder even though he was sitting in the last row of the airplane. He felt as if that girl from work was watching him. Someone, somewhere, was certain he would ask for a Coke.

Chesney swallowed hard, and looked up at the flight attendant, who was waiting, unaware of the great struggle going on before her eyes.

"Sir?"

"Uh, thank you," said Chesney with a faint smile. "Do you think I could have a cup of water?"

A few minutes later, his thirst slaked but not really satisfied, Chesney congratulated himself on yet another small victory, albeit over no one but himself. Still, he conceded, those are often the most difficult battles. He shifted in the uncomfortable airline seat. He had never been on an international flight before. Still, it would have been even more uncomfortable a month earlier. One of the unintended consequences of breaking out of his usual routines was that he had lost nearly fifteen pounds. He could still stand to lose at least twenty, or thirty more, but he was making progress. And, if he hadn't shaken up his habits, he wouldn't have been on the plane at all. He probably would have been sitting in his cubicle, plodding along at his editing at his pace of one page every two minutes. He looked out at the approaching sunrise and then glanced at his wristwatch. He had already switched his watch to London time. If he were in New Jersey, he would have been asleep. He would have gone home at five-thirty, fixed dinner, eaten, watched television alone until ten, brushed his teeth, read in bed until ten-thirty, turned out the light, and gone to sleep. That is what he would have been doing if he hadn't purposely altered his habits.

It hadn't been easy; he had nearly given up numerous times. Why change, he had asked himself, why disrupt comfortable, time-proven routines? Then he realized that would be admitting to the girl at work, and the whole world that Chesney Potoski was safe and subdued in his cage. That notion didn't bother him too much, except when he realized he was trapped in a prison of his own design. No one had gotten the better of him; no one had bested him; no one but himself. It was that realization that gave him the strength to break out of the shackles he had forged.

At first, no one had noticed his private war. They didn't see him wake up fifteen minutes earlier; go to bed at odd times; walk where he would have driven; or turn down his favorite foods. And he hadn't missed any of those routines. They weren't necessary, just comfortable. Those habits had been a substitute for thinking. Chesney found his thought processes invigorated by using parts of his mind that he hadn't flexed for years.

The first time that anyone else noticed the new Chesney was at the monthly editorial meeting. As the newest editor on the staff, Chesney would hide in the most unobtrusive seat. It was from there, as invisible as he could be, Chesney would wait for assignments to be tossed his way. This meant that he wound up with the tasks none of the other editors wanted. He didn't particularly like the jobs he got this way but didn't want the others to think he was pushy. Now, he couldn't worry about that. He had to push if he was to break out of the predictability prison.

More than a few eyebrows were raised at that meeting when Chesney charged into the conference room and commandeered the seat across from the boss, Beverly Marlton. And instead of slumping inconspicuously in his chair, he sat up straight and leaned forward. He even wore a bow tie for a bit of fashion rebellion. Before going into the meeting, Chesney resolved that he would demand the very first assignment offered.

It was more of a meat market than a meeting. Ms. Marlton came with a full menu of projects, like so many succulent chops and tantalizing cuts, to throw to her editors. Like a kennel of dogs, they would jump at the offerings. The bigger dogs, the more experienced editors, would snatch the choicest bits first. Now, he would spring first, and grab the prime cuts if for no other reason than it was contrary to his usual way of doing things.

"First up this month," began Ms. Marlton, looking over the pile of assignments over the half-rims of her designer glasses, "I've got a project here that…"

"I'LL TAKE IT!"

The room, which had already been absent of noise grew even quieter.

Chesney felt his cheeks glow red. He was looking across the table at Ms. Marlton, but he could feel all eyes in the room riveted upon him. He almost looked around, as if he too was looking for the source of the impetuous eruption. Instead, he reminded himself that his strategy had been to be unpredictable, and he had just succeeded beyond his most optimistic expectation.

After five seconds, the silence was broken by the sound of the air conditioning coming on. Five seconds later, human speech returned to the room courtesy of Beverly Marlton.

"Chesney?" she began.

"Y-yes," he said, haltingly at first, but regaining his newly-forged initiative. "Yes, Ms. Marlton, I'll take it."

"What?"

"That first assignment," he said. "It is an editorial assignment, isn't it?"

"Why, yes, it is," she said, pushing her glasses atop her red hair. She looked him square in the eye, almost as if she were scanning for some evidence of latent lunacy that human resources had failed to detect in him.

"Then I'll have it," he said, "that is, it's mine." Chesney paused a moment, still feeling the stares focused on him throughout the room. "If it's okay... that is, if no one else wants it." Inwardly he kicked himself for turning deferential at the end.

Ms. Marlton looked at him, unblinkingly for a moment. "No, it's fine," she said, "it's just that, well, you usually just... well, you usually just wait. If no one else objects, you can have this one, Chesney."

One of the more senior editors interrupted.

"Excuse me, Bev," she said, taking a familiarity that Chesney wouldn't dare to employ, not even now, "before we surrender to the impetuosity of youth, just what is the book?"

Beverly Marlton lowered her glasses. "It's a biography..." she began. Immediately others around the conference table began to clear their throats, and jostle in their chairs presumably to object. "More specifically, a ghostwriting assignment."

A collective sigh of relief went through the room, along with several chortles, a few snorts, and grunts, and more than a few editors nodded knowingly.

"So," concluded Ms. Marlton, "no one objects to Chesney having this one."

The silence was palpable. It was not an envious assignment.

"Yes, well," said Ms. Marlton, "it's a little out of your field, Chesney, but I think you're certainly up to the challenge."

"Thank you," said Chesney, as he accepted the file folder across the table, "thank you for your confidence in me... I think."

And that was how Chesney Potoski found himself crossing the Atlantic in the last row of coach on a budget airline.

Chesney took a sip from his morally superior cup of water and sighed. Ghostwriting was rarely interesting, at least at Marlton Press. Oh, it might be fascinating at some of the big New York publishing houses. There, the rich, famous and heroic are given seven-figure advances to "write" their autobiography only to have the real work done by an editor. Those life stories allowed one to mingle with big-name politicians and legendary film stars. A ghostwriter at those levels could even make a name for himself. He could wind up with an "as told to" credit.

That wasn't how ghostwriting worked at Marlton Press, however. There, editors had to milk pedestrian life stories from equally pedestrian lives. Co-stars of old television shows, and second-rate politicians, those were the types who trickled down to Marlton Press after being rejected by the more prestigious publishers. Occasionally, Beverly Marlton accepted fees from the subject of an autobiography. She didn't like to do so since that put the company into the realm of a "vanity publisher," a printing press for hire.

Chesney opened the folder again. "Lord Bagnall of Staffordshire," it said. Lord Bagnall: that certainly sounded impressive, as did Staffordshire. According to the proposal, Lord Bagnall of Staffordshire wanted his story saved for all posterity. It was a remarkable story, according to no less an authority on the subject than Lord Bagnall of Staffordshire. It was a story of remarkable success, though not necessarily exciting success. Lord Bagnall was an industrial success, as his own proposal attested. And while he wasn't exactly a rags-to-riches story, his success was entirely his own... at least in his field. In fact, there were so many qualifiers and what felt like unfinished sentences in Lord Bagnall's proposal that Chesney wondered what was left unspoken. Perhaps, he thought, His Lordship was hiding something. Maybe that's why a peer of the realm was coming to a small American publisher instead of one in his own country. Chesney would have thought that British publishers would have been familiar with his story. Maybe, thought Chesney, that was the reason that Bagnall had come all the way to Marlton Press... he was too well-known in the UK. Perhaps he had paid Beverly Marlton to get his version of his story in print. Whatever the reason, Chesney concluded this would be his challenge as a writer. He had to make the mysterious Lord Bagnall the hero of his own autobiography. If Bagnall was dull, it was Chesney's job to make him interesting. If he were an unsympathetic figure, he would have to make him more likable. After all, Lord Bagnall was the client, in one way or another, either in cash or in prospective sales, he was paying for the services of Marlton Press... even if it was only just enough for a seat in the last row of a cut-rate airline.

– 21 –
The Erratic Shopkeeper and the Stunningly Average Girl in the Lime Green Wellies

L ondon was just as Chesney always imagined it would be: damp, drizzly, and a little melancholy. And he loved it. The train trip from Heathrow Airport to Paddington Station traversed rows of brick houses interspersed with factories that had seen better days and warehouses that if they weren't yet abandoned seemed to be patiently waiting for that prospect. But there was something about it all that called to his soul. Perhaps it was his preference for that climate. Or maybe it was his admiration for the island that fought alone against Hitler when the rest of the world was either defeated or sitting on the sidelines. It could have been the bits of British culture sent to him by Aunt Elinor via books and records. Probably, he concluded as he walked through the bustling concourse of the station, it was all of those things, the affinity for all his heroes who had walked these same streets: Charles Dickens, Winston Churchill, and Hugh Goode.

He stopped outside Paddington Station trying not to look like some lost tourist. Although he had plotted the route to Aunt Elinor's flat numerous times, including twice on the airplane, Chesney still dug into his pocket for a small London atlas. He glanced around to orient himself before confidently starting down the street. It took him half-a-block to realize he was going the wrong way and turn around. Chesney tried to walk briskly like the natives seemed to be doing, and not be too in awe of the sights, though a few glances confirmed there was not all that much to look at in this neighborhood. He passed more than one tube station, which made him think that perhaps he should have taken the Underground, especially as his suitcase was growing heavy. As Lord Bagnall hadn't provided any stipend for the Tube, he decided to walk. He also didn't want his first impressions of London to be subterranean.

He turned onto Marylebone Road. To celebrate this milestone, the sky, which had been gray and misty, welcomed him to the borough by gushing forth with a heavy shower. Despite his raincoat, Chesney soon felt the lack of an umbrella. As luck would have it, he passed a small shop which sold umbrellas and ducked inside.

"Hello, umbrella?" said Chesney, to the shopkeeper.

"No, Witherby," said a middle-aged man with a graying brown hair.

"Witherby?" That must be a local term, Chesney thought. "Well, I'd like to buy a Witherby."

"That's entirely out of the question. The Witherbys are not for sale!"

Cheney picked up an umbrella. "Is this a Witherby?"

"No, that's an umbrella."

"Well, then what's a Witherby?"

"I'm am a Witherby." he pointed towards the door. There, in gilt letters on the glass was painted: "S'YBREHTIW." Chesney had done enough anagrams in his life to recognize that this was "WITHERBY'S" backward.

"Sorry," said Chesney, though he wasn't exactly sure why he was apologizing, "I'm new here."

"And old somewhere else, no doubt," said Mr. Witherby.

At least if he were teasing him, Chesney thought, he was genial about it.

"Now, sir," Witherby said, "you need something for the weather."

"I want to buy an umbrella."

"I see." The man nodded.

As Chesney neared the counter, the man recoiled.

"I didn't mean to startle you," said Chesney, though he wasn't exactly sure that he had.

The man scrutinized him carefully, almost squinting at him, until he finally relaxed into an amiable smile.

"Startle me? Me, sir? No, sir, not at all, not one whit. It's just, well, we don't get many of your kind in here, no offense... by your kind, I mean young men all the way from the Antipodes."

"The Antipodes?" said Chesney. "But I'm not from Australia."

The man winked as if he were in on a subtle joke. "Yes, but that can also refer to your home... New Zealand!"

"But, I'm not from there either. I've just flown in from..."

"Don't tell me, Canada! The Northern Lights, oh absolutely..."

"America, the United States," said Chesney. "New Jersey."

The man gently flicked at the right side of his jaw with his index finger, as if he were giving a flea a backrub. "Well, that's a new one on me," he said. "New Jersey?"

"Yes."

The man flicked at his jawline another moment before slapping his hand flat upon the countertop and then pointing at Chesney with his free hand.

"But you have spent considerable time in Australia."

"No, this is my first time out of the United States…"

"That you know of…"

Chesney pondered the possibility of having wandered out of the States without being aware of it. So as not to prolong the debate, he nodded. "Yes, I suppose…"

"Ah!" The man thrust his pointing finger up into the air. "I knew it." He then rubbed his hands together, as if some great matter had been settled, and normal business could resume. "Now, what can I do for my honored visitor?"

"An umbrella?"

"Ah, yes, we have several umbrellas as you can see from our mellifluous stock."

Chesney looked around the small shop. There was a wide selection of umbrellas, but something else caught his eye.

"What about those…" said Chesney pointing to a rack filled with flat caps. Mr. Witherby sidled up to the rack and scrutinized it.

"No, no," said Witherby, "these aren't umbrellas, these are caps."

"I meant, what about a cap?"

"Yes, these would fall into that category of accouterment, broadly speaking. Yes, these are caps, given a liberal application of that term: 'cap.'"

"I meant, what about a cap for me?"

"For you?" Mr. Witherby looked judiciously at the caps and then studied Chesney's head. "Well, they go on your head," said Witherby.

"It would save me carrying around an umbrella," said Chesney picking a gray tweed model off the rack.

"And unless you're adept at balancing an umbrella on your head it would be much more fashionable. And you could wear it even when it isn't raining."

"Yes," said Chesney putting the cap on his head, then turning to the shopkeeper. "How's that?"

"It's not for me to pass judgment on such matters, sir. Fortunately, we have a device that takes the question away from the objective observer and places it upon your own head, much as the cap is now. I call it our 'Decisionator.'"

"Decisionator?"

Mr. Witherby reached under the counter and placed a free-standing mirror on the counter. He beamed as if this was the latest technology and he was the first in all London to possess it.

"The Decisionator?" Chesney smiled.

"Yes, sir," he replied, caressing the brass frame.

"Thank you," said Chesney, glancing once more at Witherby, looking for the slightest sign that it was all a joke. Finding none, Chesney returned his attention to his cap. He tried it at several angles on his head and turned his head various ways to see different views. He looked back at the shopkeeper, who was silent as if he were respecting a private moment between prospective buyer and potential cap.

Chesney looked back at the mirror. There, something suddenly caught his attention; in fact, it not only caught him, but it grabbed him and refused to let go.

There, in the mirror, over his shoulder, through the display of items in the window, he saw a pretty girl. No, that was incorrect. She was beautiful, simply beautiful.

Chesney looked up at the shopkeeper who stared back at him. His impish expression was now replaced by one of concern.

"Are you okay, lad?" Witherby asked.

Chesney realized his mouth was agape. He closed it and then attempted to open it again in the formation of an explanation, but the words would not come. He looked back in the mirror, over his shoulder through the window... but... she was gone.

A wave of panic raced through his mind, though he didn't fully understand why. So what, he reasoned. You saw a girl; a pretty girl; a beautiful girl. There are dozen of them walking around; you're in a vast metropolitan area, a world capital; there must be millions of...

Though it only took him a second to wrestle with these thoughts, the delay was too long. Throwing logic aside, his heart took charge. He spun around, rushed to the window, and leaned over the half-wall that housed the store's display. There she was, across the street; she had moved across the street. Now he had a full view of her from head to toe. He could drink in her entire form. She was beautiful. If he had been marooned on a desert island for decades, cut off from all human influence, and then asked to describe his ideal of feminine grace, he would have come up with the precise description of the girl now standing on the opposite side of the street.

Thinking this moment would never end, that he would never leave this shop and that she would stand forever on the sidewalk, Chesney studied her as if he had all eternity to do so. She was... well... average: average height, average weight. Her nose was average: neither too large nor too small. Her chin seemed average. Her mouth also appeared to be average. Her hair, now, her hair was long, well, perhaps it was longish. He didn't know the average length for a young woman's hair, but maybe that was average, too, hanging straight just past her shoulder. The color was a stunningly average brown, not as dark as perhaps coffee or chestnut brown, but darker than an ash brown; it was more a brown brown. In the front it was arranged in bangs across her forehead, nearly coming to the tops of her glasses. Her glasses, yes, Chesney noticed she wore glasses. The frames weren't heavy, or light either, they were average. But still, there was something very extraordinary about her glasses, at least to him. They made her eyes, her face, indeed her whole being attractive to him. He couldn't really see her eyes behind her glasses, not at that distance, but he had to guess they were probably brown, or blue, or hazel, or some variation on a color that millions of other people shared. She wore an ordinary beige raincoat with ordinarily beautiful legs sticking out from underneath. She wore short rain boots of bright green, and carried a green umbrella. Topping it all off was a cute beret that matched the boots. The ensemble was neither trendy nor traditional but seemed perfect for the person wearing it.

Chesney felt his face redden. He didn't even know her, not the least bit about her, but he found that she stirred desires within him that he'd never experienced before. Not just carnal urges, but feelings that went deeper than that; soul-calling-to-soul feelings; desires that projected beyond the moment and into eternity. He wracked his mind. He searched his memory for a similar feeling in his past but could find none. With no other response forthcoming, his body bypassed his mind and took matters into hand, and in a most extraordinary way. His knees buckled.

"Steady on, lad," said the shopkeeper grabbing Chesney's elbow.

Chesney looked up at him. He had been taller than Witherby when he'd entered the shop, hadn't he? It was all quite disorienting.

"You'll do yourself a mischief, sir," the man was pulling him up to his full height.

"My knees..." he finally managed to say.

"Your knees, sir?" The shopkeeper's genially flippant manner was replaced by concern.

"Yes, they buckled," said Chesney looking down at his knees as if they were foreign to him.

"Extraordinary, sir," said Mr. Witherby. "Is this a regular occurrence?"

"No, it's never happened to me before."

"Perhaps it's the air travel," suggested the shopkeeper. "Not that I travel much by airplane. I don't like to travel more than any journey beyond three hours in duration. Coming all the way from New Jersey, and in one of those pressurized sausage casings, well, I'm no aeronautical engineer, but I imagine such an experience is libel to be fraught with all manner of residual effects."

Chesney shook his head.

"Plane? No, no, it couldn't have been the plane, it was the girl."

"Girl, sir?" Witherby looked around the shop.

"No, the girl out there. There across the street..."

He pointed out the window, but instead of the fascinatingly average young lady, he found his index finger indicating an old man carrying a plastic Sainsbury's bag.

Witherby looked at the old man across the street, and then back at Chesney. "Airplanes, it's the pressure, the pressure..." he tapped his own head but was clearly doubting a full accounting of Chesney's marbles.

Panic swept through Chesney. He darted sideways in short spurts, much like a dog that needs to go outside. She was gone. The girl was gone. The girl whom he saw wrapped in the mantles of forever had used her two average feet in the lime green boots and legged it out of his life.

"She's gone!"

"Well, thank heaven for that, sir," said Witherby. "I was afraid you were going a bit funny up in the bonce, sir."

"Bonce?"

"Your head, sir…"

"Don't…" he was about to instruct to the shopkeeper not to worry about bonces, or heads, or whatever, but he hadn't time now for that. He had to act, didn't he? Wait, he asked himself, what would the old Chesney have done in this circumstance? He paused for half-a-second and then answered himself aloud.

"I wouldn't have done anything…"

"Sir?"

"…because I wouldn't have even been here. I'd have been sitting in my cubicle…" Chesney paused to glance at his watch to confirm the time back in New Jersey. "…or almost, I'd be getting ready to go to work…"

"Sir, perhaps you'd like to have a sit-down…"

"…but I wouldn't have been here. So, who cares what…"

He wasted no more time debating possible courses of action or inaction. No matter which version of Chesney Potoski was reacting at the moment, the best course of action was action itself. He turned and grabbed Witherby by the shoulder.

"Where does this road go?"

"Everywhere, eventually, until you get to the sea," spluttered the shopkeeper, "but if you take it to the airport, it can go practically anywhere on the Earth…"

"Right," concluded Chesney as if that narrowed his choices. He would go to the ends of the Earth if need be to track down the ordinary girl with the extraordinary power over his knees.

Chesney rushed to the door and dashed out into the street. In his haste, he barely noticed Mr. Witherby calling after him.

"Wait! Stop… Chesney!"

– 22 –
P.C. Rundleson Knows He's Got a Balmy One

The policeman brought him back, his right hand clutching the collar of Chesney's raincoat, the tweed cap in his left hand. He only got across the street, only far enough to look round one corner. The girl wasn't up that street. By now she could be anywhere, down another street, up in a building, on a bus, down the Tube… anywhere. He felt miserable.

"I can explain, officer," said Chesney as he was marched back to Witherby's.

"Yes, sir," muttered the policeman.

"I saw this girl…"

"Someone you know, then?"

"Uh, no," said Chesney, "not exactly. Do you believe in love at first sight, officer?"

The policeman stopped in the middle of the street.

"Love at first sight, sir?"

Chesney noticed a ring on the officer's left hand, the one holding the cap. His name badge read: "Rundleson."

"Yes, you seem to be a married man, Officer Rundleson…"

"P.C. Rundleson."

"P.C.?"

"Police Constable."

"Yes, well," said Chesney, "P.C. Rundleson, you seem to be a married man…"

"Oh, yes?" said P.C. Rundleson. He said it in the same skeptical way that Chesney's father had used the phrase.

"Yes, well, if you're married, and there is a Mrs. P.C. Rundleson," Chesney swallowed hard, "d-didn't you fall in love with her, maybe at first sight? I mean, maybe the first time that you saw her, and you thought: there's a girl I could love. There's a girl who encompasses my whole future. There's the girl I've always been waiting for but had given up all hope to ever find. Maybe?"

P.C. Rundleson's stoic expression eased, and his grip on Chesney relaxed slightly. Chesney detected a wistful glint in the corner of the eye of P.C. Rundleson.

"The wife, I am referring of course to Mrs. Rundleson, the wife and I," began the P.C., "we dated for almost three years."

"Oh, yes?"

"Then I got her in the club, so we got married."

"The club?"

"Up the spout, bun in the oven!" Any hint of sentiment evaporated from the P.C.'s voice.

"Oh, pregnant," said Chesney, getting it on the third euphemism.

"Not to put too fine a point on it, lad, Yes! Now, come along..."

P.C. Rundleson escorted Chesney back to Witherby's shop.

"Now, sir," said Rundleson in his most authoritative voice, "is this the man?"

"No, it isn't!" said Chesney.

"I wasn't talking to you, sir," said Rundleson to Chesney.

"But this isn't Mr. Witherby," said Chesney pointing at the man behind the counter. "Mr. Witherby has brown hair, and he's shorter than me. And he has a funny manner."

"Funny?"

"Well, facetious, but not in an abrasive way," said Chesney. "It's almost genial; in fact, it was quite genial, and not at all insulting, it was almost as if he were performing a one-man show for a one-man audience."

"I am Mr. Witherby," said the man behind the counter.

"No, you're not," said Chesney, before turning to P.C. Rundleson, "no, he's not. He's too fat, well, I mean, Mr. Witherby's not as fat as this gentleman, and he doesn't have a mustache, and his hair wasn't slicked back like his..."

The man produced identification and handed it to P.C. Rundleson who read: "Jonas Witherby."

"And you," continued Rundleson to the authenticated Witherby, "saw this man running out of your shop with this merchandise, vis, one tweed cap?"

"No, I didn't," said Witherby.

"But you put out the hue and cry that you were being robbed..."

"No, I didn't."

"I ran out of the shop," offered Chesney, "to follow that girl, the one I was telling you about. That's when Mr. Witherby, the real one, called after me to tell me to stop. I was running across the street. In my excitement to catch up with that girl, I forgot that I had on the hat. The first I thought of it was when he yelled after me, he said 'wait, stop Ches...'"

Chesney stopped.

"Go on," encouraged P.C. Rundleson.

"He said 'Chesney.'"

"And?"

"Chesney's my name."

"And what's so unusual about that, then?"

Chesney paused and looked around the shop. "I never told him my name."

P.C. Rundleson rolled his eyes. "Let me repeat the facts so far as I've been able to ascertain them. You ran out of this shop to chase a girl you didn't know but had fallen in love with, and you were told to stop by a man who calls you by your name which he doesn't know, and this man has the same name as this gentleman, the proprietor of this shop, but it isn't him. Is that correct, sir?"

Chesney nodded. "Yes, that's about it."

"And at the nub of it all," said P.C. Rundleson with a triumphant air, "the crux of the entire affair is that you were fleeing from this shop, wearing a cap which you had not paid for."

"For which I had not paid," said Chesney.

"What?"

"A cap for which I had not paid…"

"That's what I said," said Rundleson.

"No, you said: 'a cap which you had not paid for,'" corrected Chesney. "You ended your sentence in a preposition."

"So?"

"It's not done," said Chesney, "especially not here, in the cradle of the English language."

"He's right, you know," agreed the other Witherby. "You shouldn't end a sentence in a preposition."

"Look, the both of you, but mostly you," Rundleson pointed at Chesney. "I am a member of the Metropolitan Police, not the grammar police, my propositions, or prepositions are not the question here. What is the question is that you, clever Yank, ran from this shop with this cap on your head, a cap for which you had not paid… for!" Chesney guessed he added that last "for" just to assert his authority to do so. "Now, isn't that right?"

Chesney, while correct in the rules of language, realized he was equally in the wrong by the rules of law. He nodded in agreement to the charge.

"Right, then," said P.C. Rundleson, "or is that a preposition?"

"No, sir," said Chesney softly, "it's an adverb."

"Good, well, then, you and I are going down to the station, if you don't mind…"

"Wait a minute, Constable, I don't think that will be necessary."

Chesney turned and to see his Aunt Elinor standing in the doorway.

"Aunt El…" he cried.

"Ms. Potoski," said the shopkeeper.

"You all know each other," asked Rundleson.

In a brief flurry of admissions, Aunt Elinor confessed she knew both Chesney and the shopkeeper, the shopkeeper admitted he knew Aunt El, but not Chesney, and Chesney that he only knew his aunt. None of which seemed to placate the constable.

"Jonas," said Aunt Elinor, ignoring the cop, "what's going on here? Why are you having my nephew nicked?"

"This young man," said Rundleson waving the cap, "stole this piece of headgear: one cap."

"Ridiculous," said Elinor, not bothering to even look at Rundleson. "Chesney, you didn't steal that cap, did you?"

"No, I was running after this girl," he said, "I just forgot I'd been trying on the cap..."

"There, you see," said Aunt Elinor, before doing a double-take. "What? Chasing a girl in the street?"

"Do you believe in love at first sight, Aunt El?"

She smiled. "Of course I do." Then she turned to P.C. Rundleson. "There it is. A simple mistake... is that the cap?" Aunt Elinor plucked it from the constable's hands. She examined it, shook her head, and handed it to Mr. Witherby. "Here's your cap, Jonas."

"It's not so simple, ma'am," said Rundleson.

"It's not as difficult as you'd like to make it either," she said, looking at the floor in front of the counter. "Chesney, is that your suitcase."

"Yes, Aunt El."

"The fact that he left without his suitcase," she concluded, "confirms that this was not a case of premeditated daylight robbery. Even if he hadn't come back, which I'm sure he would have, what he left behind far exceeds the value of that... thing. It's not a crime, other than a crime of judgment. Really, Chesney, chasing after girls in the street and in that cap!"

"She was beautiful, Aunt El," said Chesney wistfully, "her soul was calling out to mine..."

"A piece of advice," she began. "When you're listening for souls calling out to your own, don't do it while wearing caps that don't belong to you. Is that clear?"

Chesney agreed.

"And," she continued, "I'm sure my friend, Mr. Witherby, here, wouldn't want to prosecute my favorite relative, would you Mr. Witherby, especially when there are extenuating circumstances..."

At this last remark, Aunt Elinor rolled her head in one direction while making her eyes dart in the other in some sort of signal to the shopkeeper. Mr. Witherby seemed mystified before her meaning dawned on him. He then looked over his shoulder towards the back of the shop and then back at Elinor and nodded.

"He's been up to it again, hasn't he?" said Mr. Witherby.

Aunt El pursed her lips and nodded. "Apparently so."

Mr. Witherby smiled at P.C. Rundleson, and tentatively patted him on the arm, as one would a big dog that was hoped to be friendly.

"Well, Constable," said Witherby, "I guess that settles that, eh?"

Rundleson cocked a skeptical eye at Witherby and then another at Aunt Elinor. "Yes, sir," he said slowly. "I'm not exactly sure what this…and that all was." He made a series of tics and grimaces that approximated those that Elinor and Witherby had exchanged. "But…" the P.C. looked around for some way of reasserting his authority. He took the cap from Aunt Elinor, "…but, I'm sure that this young gentleman will be purchasing this cap, won't you, sir?"

Chesney looked at the cap and nodded, convinced of P.C. Rundleson's authority to make him do so.

"I'll be glad to buy it," said Chesney. He took out his wallet, but only had American money. He looked at Aunt Elinor, who sighed and pulled a twenty pound note from her purse. He thanked her and handed it to Mr. Witherby, who rang up the purchase, and then gave Chesney the change. He started to hand it back to his Aunt, who waved it away. Finally, to complete the transaction, Mr. Witherby cut the tag from the back of the cap and handed it to Chesney, who put it on his head and turned to P.C. Rundleson.

"That about wraps that up," said Rundleson giving one last cautionary look to all involved, but especially to Chesney before starting from the shop. In the doorway, the constable turned. "And don't go chasing English girls around the streets like some balmy cowboy. This is not the Wild West!"

Chesney assured him he wouldn't while restraining Aunt Elinor.

"Cowboy," said Aunt El once the cop was out of earshot. "How dare he compare my nephew to some Wild West hooligan! This is why you shouldn't leave your shop, Jonas."

"I have to go to the bank some time," he explained.

"I'll go for you," she said, "or I'll come and watch your shop. This wouldn't have happened if you'd been here. Wait until I give Postie a piece of my mind."

"Postlewaite doesn't mean it," said Witherby. "You know how he is."

"Postlewaite," interrupted Chesney, "was that the first man? That's Mr. Postlewaite, your friend, Aunt El?"

Aunt Elinor rolled her eyes. "Yes, that's Postlewaite," she said, trying not to smile. "Silly Postie! He almost got you arrested. If I hadn't come by… imagine that benign fool! It's not unusual for him to impersonate Witherby or anyone else to strangers, but now he's inciting them to run after women in the streets!"

"Oh, he didn't do that," said Chesney. "That was my idea."

She gave Chesney a censorious glance and then turned to Mr. Witherby. "Well, we've taken too much of Mr. Witherby's time, Chesney… oh, yes, by the way, you've not been properly introduced." Aunt Elinor completed these formalities and then herded her nephew out of the shop. Chesney picked up his suitcase and put on his new cap, which elicited another pursed expression from his aunt.

"It's stopped raining," said Chesney, looking upward as they exited the shop.

"Never mind the rain," said Aunt Elinor. "I want to understand why you're running after women on the streets."

"It's where she was," said Chesney. "You could hardly expect me to chase after someone where they're not. Besides, it's not practical to chase someone around a shop is it?"

"I suppose not. You're not some cardboard lover in a French farce. At least you're still pedantic, that's a consolation…"

"What do you mean, Aunt El?"

"It's a good sign that you're not completely around the twist."

Chesney put down his suitcase and gently steered his Aunt's bottom atop it. Once she was seated, he recounted the experience that had struck him like a thunderbolt.

"You should understand," he said after he had described the girl in every inch of her ordinary details.

"Me? Why should I understand? I've never chased anyone in public."

"You told me you understood, you said you had fallen in love at first sight."

She smiled. "Yes, I remember falling in love the first time I saw you, you chubby little boy – although you're not so chubby anymore. Probably all this running after unsuspecting women!"

He sighed. "I'm afraid she is completely unsuspecting. She doesn't know I'm alive."

"Then she doesn't know what she's missing, the silly girl!"

Chesney sat beside her on the suitcase. There, on the sidewalk, he explained the life adjustments that had brought him to London.

"You almost got married once, didn't you, Aunt El?" he asked, returning to the topic of love.

"I didn't almost get married," she said. "A more accurate description would be that I almost, almost got married. I'm sure that had things not gone the way that they went that I probably would have, but as they didn't go that way, neither did I."

"But you were in love?"

She smiled enigmatically with a distant gleam in her eyes. "I really can't quite recall," she said. "I think he loved me. I suppose I probably loved him, too… quite a lot. If things had gone that way, but as they didn't…"

Chesney sighed. He wondered if his brief fling had already been fully flung; born, and died after two short glimpses. He wondered if he'd be sitting on a sidewalk in thirty years pondering the nature of love with some yet-to-be-born Potoski.

"I certainly hope that sigh wasn't for me, Chesney."

"Huh?"

"Don't heave your bosom for your poor Aunt. I haven't lived a life without love."

Chesney felt his face redden, and he fumbled for a reply. She patted his shoulder. "There's a great difference between romance and love," she said. "Both can survive quite well without the other. While I've had very little romance, the love in my life has grown with every passing year. And I've known people who have tried to live on romance, but have pursued it, caught it, only to find there was very little real love behind it. Worse than that is the people who mistake both love and romance for..."

She paused and looked around.

"...lust..." she whispered.

"Lust?"

She rolled her eyes. "Alright," she said aloud, "Sex!"

A few passers-by turned their heads. Elinor took no notice of them.

"You can live without sex, you can live without romance," she concluded, "but don't try to live without love."

They sat silently while Chesney pondered his Aunt's remarks, but he couldn't ignore the stirring within him when he thought of that girl. As if she read his thoughts, Aunt El added a coda.

"I'm very happy for you," she said. "You've gone weak in the knees, you've had a unique experience. I understand romance and love together is quite nice, in fact, it's wonderful, and I pray that for you with all my heart. But more importantly, I wish you love."

Aunt Elinor stood up.

"Now, while I respect romance, and I cherish love, more than that at the moment what I really crave is a nice cup of tea and a seat that isn't in the middle of the sidewalk. Let's go."

Chesney looked up at her and smiled, and she smiled back. He picked up his suitcase and followed her.

"It's just down this street and 'round the corner," she said. "My place. I rent from Postie."

"Oh, yes, Mr. Postlewaite? I'd like to meet him...again, under the right name."

"You'll have to excuse Postlewaite. He's a bright gentleman, perhaps too bright, and that what gets him into..."

"Trouble?"

Aunt Elinor pursed her lips. "Trouble? Oh, no, no, he gets into mischief. Trouble has a cruel, malicious connotation to it. He's quite harmless, really. He's just easily bored. So when situations arise that afford him playtime, he grabs it with both hands. He's a lot like you."

"Me? I don't go around pretending to be a shopkeeper."

She studied his face for a moment. "No, you don't have a shopkeeper's features. I meant that you're both very clever fellows with active minds.

He doesn't have your facility for puzzles, though. That's the difference. I tried to get him interested in those jumbled word things..."

"...anagrams..."

"Yes, but it didn't take. So, he finds his jollies elsewhere. I assure you though, in Postie's case, it's completely harmless."

"Harmless," repeated Chesney. "Postlewaite, Postlewaite..." He began to write in the air for a moment before proclaiming: "Teapot wiles..."

"Teapot wiles?"

"Postlewaite..." he explained. "The anagram...teapot wiles."

His aunt's face beamed. "I say, that is perfect. That's Postie down to a 't,' or should I say down to a teapot. Yes, he's a clever one, wily even, but harmless as a teapot. You are a wily one yourself, well done! Teapot wiles! So very English, too, just like Postie. And speaking of teapots, I trust there's one waiting just around this corner."

Aunt Elinor led him to a cozy side street and pointed to an entrance of a storefront half-way down the street. Above it was a hanging sign announcing: "Chuzzlewitt & Postlewaite: Effluvia Britannica."

Chesney smiled at the name the shop and started to comment upon it when he looked beneath the sign and was struck dumb by what he saw coming out of the door.

It was the girl. Or at least he thought so. He only saw her from the side as she exited the shop, but in that moment he saw the same nose, lips, glasses, and other average features. As she turned, he noted from the rearview the same hair, the same coat, the same beret, and those bright green boots. Yes, it was her! It had to be her, he thought as she walked away. He turned to Aunt Elinor, excitement welling up in his heart.

"Aunt El! The girl..." he began until his mind interrupted with a news flash. "...is walking away!"

This must have seemed self-evident to his Aunt. Yes, there was a girl, and she was walking away. What was mysterious is why her nephew would drop his suitcase and start running down the street.

"Chesney!" She called out. "Chesney, you're running right past the shop. Chesney, your suitcase!"

Chesney heard his aunt's cries but paid them no heed as he ran towards the girl. Half-way down the street, he pulled up short. Suddenly, he felt like a dog chasing a car, intent on catching it but never considering what he would do when he did. He didn't know this girl, and she didn't know him. She would think him mad and not in the benign manner of Mr. Postlewaite. While he debated with himself, the girl turned the corner and disappeared from view.

That settled it. He must pursue! He couldn't let her slip away again. He ran, running as he had never run before in his life, as if the very remainder of his life depended upon it, as fast as he could, even faster than he realized he was capable of running. Chesney ran so fast, he overshot the corner, taking it with a one-footed skid like a slapstick comic from a silent movie.

He grabbed a lamppost to keep from falling headlong into the street. From there, he saw her, the girl who made his heart flutter and his knees buckle, getting into a taxi cab and speeding away. He had lost her again. He had only known of her existence for less than an hour, and in that span, he had loved her and lost her not once, but twice.

– 23 –
The Brief Life and Sudden Death of the Gossamer Perspective

The suspense was killing Valerie Fierro. It was like waiting for the jury to return with the verdict: life or death. Except, she thought as she sat on her bed, it was much more important than that.

Someone waiting in a courtroom might live, in which case they would just get up and go on with their dull little life. On the other hand, if they got the death penalty, she thought, well, they'd just go die, and that would be that. No, Valerie was waiting for something much more important than just some boring matter of somebody else's fate.

She strained to hear the muffled voices downstairs where her whole future was being decided. Her mother, as usual, was prosecuting the case against her. Her kind, sweet, loving father, was defending Valerie's cause.

There was a gentle scratching at her door. Valerie hopped off the bed and opened the door for Reggie, the collie.

"Poor Reggie," she said, closing the door behind him. She sat on the bed and invited Reggie to join her because she knew her mother wouldn't approve of the dog on the bed. She'd take her victories wherever she could find them, no matter how small.

"Reggie, Reggie, you could tell me what they were saying, couldn't you?" She squeezed the dog's head between her hands. His pink tongue flicked out to lick her on the nose, and she ruffled his fur in appreciation. "It's so frustrating, isn't it, Reggie? Some people just don't have a sense of priorities, do they? You know how important the right dress is, don't you, boy?"

Whether the dog had a genuine appreciation of haute couture could never be established; nevertheless, Reggie responded with a sympathetic whimper that elicited a fresh round of hugs from his mistress.

"At least someone in this house understands," said Valerie. "Too bad you don't have a credit card, Reggie. You'd do the right thing, wouldn't you, boy?"

As she petted Reggie, Valerie thought back on how it had all unfolded. It had worked like a charm, at least at the outset. She was terribly pleased with her job gluing the perfect, sophisticated dress, out of *Cosmo* over the girly prom dress in *Tiger Beat*. Even icky Albrecht Eckner's rubber cement worked, though she wasn't surprised. It was a sneaky trick. Sneakiness and Albrecht's beady little eyes just seemed to go together like, well, like beady eyes and sneakiness. The mere thought of that icky store and his grotesque old grandfather made her shiver.

"*Einfalt,*" she said aloud. It was a strange word, German or some weird language that people spoke in places where they didn't know English. For some reason, the word stuck in her mind. Maybe it was the way the old pig said it or Albrecht's reaction; either way, she remembered it: "Einfalt."

Valerie forced the thought from her mind and returned to the dress.

She showed the doctored *Tiger Beat* to her parents. As she flipped through it, her mother seemed to be falling for it. She was fine with any dress she'd seen so far, setting her up for the last dress, the pasted photo, the coup de grace! As her mother turned the last page, Valerie could hardly contain herself.

"That's my dress!" she said exuberantly, so much so, that her father, who had been watching TV, looked up.

"What? That?" said her mother in a prejudiced tone.

"That one," repeated Valerie, though less forcefully. "That, uh, that's the dress I'm going to wear to the prom… please."

Connie Fierro's eyebrows attainted such a height Valerie almost expected them to fly off her head. She looked at the dress, and then at Valerie, and then back at the dress, and then sideways at her husband. The prejudice had swelled into a full-blown indictment of all that was glamorous and refined.

"Do you see this?" asked Connie to her husband.

"What?"

Connie handed the magazine to her husband. Being a stranger to fashion, Giorgio's head bobbed around the two open pages, unsure of which one he was supposed to be judging.

"There!" said Connie, spearing the dress with her index finger.

Her father stared at the dress for a good half-a-minute. At last, he emitted a low whistle.

"That's some… dress," he said.

"There you see…" began Connie.

"But, Daddy…" whined Valerie simultaneously.

His mouth twitched as if he were formulating replies that would satisfy both of them. After several seconds of contortions, Giorgio exhaled so forcefully his lips buzzed.

"Con," he said, to his wife, "it's not so bad." Valerie's heart leaped with hope until he added: "Is it?"

There followed a debate which Valerie stayed out of. Instead, she sat on the couch, looking as demure and virginal as she knew how. She reverently folded her hands in her lap and adopted a wide-eyed gaze.

The tactic worked, at least on Giorgio. The dress, he said, wasn't *that* provocative. His wife differed. But, Giorgio countered, their daughter was a good girl. Connie agreed and wanted her to stay a good girl. It was a short hop, she assured him from a good girl to a bad woman

"After all," noted Giorgio in his final summation, "a bad girl could be bad even in a nun's habit, but a good girl will be a good girl no matter what she's wearing."

"...Or not wearing," muttered Connie, pointing at the dress' daring décolletage.

Despite this last dig, Valerie's mother consented – conditionally – to take Valerie shopping for the dress.

"I don't even know where you'd buy a dress like that around here," said Connie.

Valerie knew all the shops within a fifty-mile radius of their home where the dress could be purchased, and she almost blurted out the nearest one. Wisdom, or maybe it was cunning, dictated that she hold her tongue. She didn't want her mother to become suspicious. Instead, Valerie reinforced the patina of innocence plastered upon her face. She shrugged her shoulders as if she were a newcomer to the area and the subject of dress shops was beyond her grasp.

"Oh, well," said Giorgio, "It's just a dress. How hard can that be to find?"

Valerie smiled inwardly. Poor sweet oblivious Daddy, he really had no idea. He thought that stunningly sophisticated gowns were strewn about in every store in bins, like the roofing nails he bought by the bagful. Her mother merely sighed as she retreated to the kitchen.

As savvy as Connie Fierro was, she still was laboring under the misconception that they were shopping for an ordinary, albeit provocative, dress. The next day they made the rounds of all the mall shops, though Valerie already knew none of them had the dress. It was all part of her plan.

"Valerie," said Connie Fierro wearily, as they drove home, "you're just going to have to find another dress." She paused, expecting at least a token protest from her daughter. Valerie remained silent. "We've looked over every shop in two malls, and haven't found a thing."

Again, Valerie sat in mute martyrdom.

"Frankly," resumed Connie, "I think it's just as well. I mean that dress wasn't right."

Silence: save for a faint sigh of agreement, resignation, and disappointment. Out of the corner of her eye, Valerie could see her mother glance at her. Valerie just looked ahead wearing her bravest outward expression of inward suffering.

"Honey, I know you had your heart set on that dress," continued her mother falling into the trap, "but we'll get you something else even better. Something nice and cute…"

She was almost there. Valerie blinked a few times, as if her eyes were welling up with tears, took a sharp intake of breath, and nodded; her focus still straight ahead.

"If we could find that dress, we'd get it…"

The moment had come, the concession, just in time, too.

"You're right, Mom," Valerie started, before looking up. "Hey, what about there?"

Fatigued from hours of futile shopping, her mother was caught off guard. "What? Where?"

"There! There!" said Valerie, waving her arm and pointing to a store just up the highway. "Kirchendorfs! They might have it!"

"Kirchendorfs? Oh, Valerie…"

"But, Mom, it wouldn't hurt to look, and we're here…" said Valerie, reminding her of her words of thirty seconds ago, "Besides, you said, 'if we could find it'…"

Too tired to argue the point, Connie Fierro steered the car into the parking lot of the boutique.

Ten minutes later, Valerie was sheathed in her dream gown, feeling every inch as mature, sophisticated, and womanly as she imagined it would make her feel. Twelve minutes later, after her mother had seen the price, Valerie was unwrapped, and feeling as humiliated, and miserable as anyone possibly ever could – ever! Her mother's calm, polite explanation to the haughty saleswoman – that the dress was just too expensive – was the most stinging blow of all. Valerie stood petrified as they took away her dress. It was only after the second tug that she realized her mother was physically – physically – pulling her out of the store as if she were a child. All the way home, neither mother or daughter said a word. Valerie would have resorted to tears, but she knew that's just what her mother wanted, the proof that her daughter was still a little girl who only deserved a poofy, cute, girly dress for the most important night of her life. Instead, Valerie sat up straight and pointed her chin upward at a superior angle. She was prepared to stay that way the rest of her life as an eternal judgment on her mother's petty, penny-pinching ways.

Valerie maintained this pose for two hours until Giorgio Fierro returned home from work and asked: "What's new?" This innocent question produced two simultaneous eruptions; for not only did Valerie's stoic exterior explode into a torrent of tears, but her mother began with a rapid-tongued indictment of their daughter's profligate tastes. Moments later, Valerie found herself running up the stairs to the sanctuary of her bedroom. Downstairs, Giorgio was thrust into an argument in which he had very little interest.

Not certain how long they would take to decide her fate, Valerie waited nearly an hour for the verdict, and then in an attempt to relieve the suspense, decided to get a shower. She had taken off her clothes and slipped on her robe when it seemed to be all over, downstairs. She tip-toed to the door. Reggie the Collie whimpered. Valerie signaled for him to be quiet as she listened. Someone was coming up the stairs. It was her father's plodding tread. She looked around the room, not sure how she should be found, and started in several different directions before she opted for the relatively neutral position of sitting on the edge of the bed. As if he were an accomplice, Reggie jumped up to her side. A moment later, there was a soft tap on the door.

"Hello, *Principessa*," he said, sticking his head in, "can I talk to you?"

"Of course, Daddy," she said, though from his downcast expression she knew that they had lost.

Giorgio sat down next to his daughter on the side not occupied by the dog. He looked around the room, examining the posters and pictures on the wall as if he were there for the first time. Finally, as if he were finishing aloud a sentence he had begun in his mind, he said: "growing up so quickly." Having made this observation, he placed his rough hand around her shoulder.

"Principessa, Principessa," he began. It sounded like an apology.

That was it, thought Valerie: Cheap had won. Her mother had won. Sophistication was dead in Delaware.

"...I know, Daddy," she said.

"Your mother..." he started, but unsure of what to say next stopped. After several moments of painfully awkward silence, he tried again. "That's a lot of money for a dress."

"...I know, Daddy," she said. She almost began to argue that it wasn't just a dress, in fact, it wasn't a dress, but a gown and gowns cost more than dresses. But it wouldn't have done any good. He had tried his best, but he just didn't understand.

At that moment, unexpectedly, a thought occurred to Valerie. It wasn't a very big thought. It certainly wasn't a very strong thought, but just the glimmer of a thought. Perhaps it was barely a notion, but there it was in the corner of her mind.

Perhaps, thought Valerie, perhaps it wasn't her father who didn't understand, but perhaps, maybe, perhaps... she didn't understand. What if it wasn't the end of the world if she went to the prom in a different dress? The very concept was jarring, almost akin to an out-of-body experience. It was as if she could see herself, not like looking in a mirror, but like she was another person looking at herself. Suddenly, for the briefest of moments, she saw herself in a new light. It was like they said in art class. What was it that they called it? Perspective? Yes, that was the word. It was like she was seeing it all - her life, the prom, the dress, everything - from a different angle, and an angle where all those things weren't front and center, but were off to the side where they held a less prominent position. Viewed from that point, it wasn't all that important, not in the grand scheme of existence. It wasn't even that important in her own life. Viewed from this different point of view it was just a dance, just a dress, and she...

Valerie's brief pondering, stopped as she came up against a cold hard fact. It was just a dance, just a dress, and she was just a girl. At that moment, Valerie Fierro felt a chill down her spine and the hairs at the back of her neck prickled. For the first time in her life, she realized that maybe she wasn't the center of the universe. That concept was quickly followed by the idea that perhaps she wasn't even the center of Delaware, or Hockessin, or even the family. Maybe... the ember of a thought struggled for life... maybe she had been just a little, tiny bit selfish. Just maybe... perhaps.

These ego-shattering revelations flashed through Valerie's mind in less than a quarter of a minute. Even so, it stabbed at her very core, and like most self-inflicted wounds hurt all the more because of it. What made it worse was that her father was there, with his arm around her, trying to comfort her, and being so kind and understanding. She wasn't precisely sure why, but at that moment, Valerie began to cry.

She had used tears before, particularly on her father, on whom they were particularly effective. But these weren't those types of tears, not the loud, dramatic sobs. These were honest tears, and they were quiet, soft tears, only shed to give vent to her true feelings. At first, Valerie herself was surprised by them, and even tried to stop them, but could not.

"It really is very important, isn't it?"

"What?" Valerie looked up into her father's loving eyes.

"This is very important to you. Isn't it?"

"I, uh..." she tried to put into words her thoughts, but as they were still half-formed in her mind, she found that impossible. What did she want to say? Thank you? I'm sorry? She wasn't sure what she was feeling and began to look away.

Her father took her chin between his calloused fingers.

He smiled and muttered something in Italian that she didn't understand.

"What's that mean?" she asked, wiping her eyes.

He shrugged. "Oh, you just reminded me of someone. You're getting so grown up. Almost a lady..." He looked in her eyes in a way that he had never done before. A slight smile graced the corners of his mouth as if he were looking at someone else, somewhere else.

"She would have been so proud of you," he whispered.

Valerie almost asked who, but before she could, the faraway gaze in his eyes was replaced by a more practical look.

"I can do some extra work," he said.

"What?" Valerie wasn't quite sure what he was saying.

"It will be okay," he said, stroking her hair. "I can pick up some overtime, do some freelance jobs. I've been asked to before. It would only be a few weeks working nights, no more than three, or maybe four."

Valerie looked up at her father, who smiled. Behind the smile, which was so loving and sincere, she could see the weariness in his eyes, no less real. She almost stopped him. She almost said it wasn't that important. But then he spoke again.

"After all," he continued, "you are my *Piccola Principessa,* aren't you? It's like the stories I used to read to you, like Cinderella, isn't it?"

She looked at him without saying a word.

"What was it they said in that story? Oh, yes, 'you shall go to the ball!'" A distant look crossed Giorgio Fierro's face as if he were seeing back over a great number of years; as if he were gazing on something very precious in the distance. It only remained there a moment. "Well, yes, I have no magic, Principessa, other than hard work, a strong pair of hands, and a good strong back. And as there are plenty of roofs that I can repair, and gutters I can hang, and tar that I can spread, you will go to your ball…"

"Prom," corrected Valerie, still not entirely convinced to accept this offer. Her father worked hard enough…"

"Oh, yes, prom," said Giorgio. "Well, you do not get to go to a prom every day. You will go, and you will be the most beautiful Principessa, the only Principessa, there, and in the most beautiful dress, right?"

The dress, he had to mention the dress, didn't he? The gossamer thread of selflessness that had briefly twined around Valerie Fierro's soul snapped at the mention of the dress. She sat numbly for a moment before reaching out and embracing his offer.

"Yes," she said, faintly at first, as if she were acclimating herself afresh to the idea. "Yes! Oh, Daddy, you do understand. Yes, it is very important, thank you, thank you! You're sure it's not too much?" This last question was asked rhetorically and was smothered in a hail of hugs and kisses for her father. She promised him between kisses than she would be eternally grateful, that she would be a good daughter, and that she would help out around the house in whatever she was asked to do. She promised him so many things by way of thanks, promises that she knew would never be redeemed, and so she offered them up lavishly.

After several minutes she calmed down. A thought crossed her mind.

"What about, Mother?" she asked.

Giorgio Fierro grimaced slightly. "Oh, well, your mother… your mother loves you very much. Well, I will just have to explain it to your mother…" His voice trailed off as if explaining it all to his wife entailed the heaviest job ahead for him. A worried expression began overspreading his features until he looked back at Valerie and relaxed once again into a smile.

"It will be okay," he assured her. "After all, this is an important day for you. It is a day that I never had."

"You never went to a high school prom?" asked Valerie, though she knew he hadn't even attended high school.

Giorgio shook his head. "No, no my Principessa, no prom. At your age, I was still in Germany."

"Germany," said Valerie, recalling the incident at the Eckner's icky store. "Daddy, you know German, don't you?"

He nodded.

"Well, what is a..." she thought for a moment, trying to recall the exact word. It might be a useful insult someday if ever she had to deal with Albrecht Eckner again. "What is an *Einfalt?*"

The blood ran out of her father's cheeks. His mouth dropped open, and his eyes grew wide.

"What did you say?"

"Einfalt?" she repeated innocently.

"Einfalt!" he whispered.

"I'm sorry," she said, shaken by his reaction. "Is it a bad word?"

"No, no," he said after several seconds of silence, "no, it's not nice, but, but, well, you shouldn't use it. Don't say it again, ever. Do you hear me?"

"I won't," promised Valerie, not certain why her father had reacted so. She smiled at him, and he stroked her hair, and kissed her on the top of her head.

"That's a good girl," he said, rising from the edge of the bed, "that's my Principessa. Now, I'll go talk to your mother. Don't worry, everything will be okay."

"Thank you, Daddy."

Giorgio Fierro exited, closing the door behind him, leaving Valerie with Reggie. She waited until she heard his footsteps retreat down the stairs before she gave a silent scream of triumph and began kicking her legs in victory atop the bed.

"The dress, the dress, Reggie," she cried in a hoarse whisper. "I got the dress! I got the dress! I got the dress!" Reggie knew little from dresses, but he did know a celebration when he saw one. In one bound the collie jumped up, nearly smothering Valerie in her short robe. Quickly her excitement turned into a wrestling match as the dog got carried away as dogs will. Valerie pushed against the dog and tried to reprimand him quietly while still making her scolding effective. Finally, she succeeded in shoving him off the bed, hurriedly closing her robe, and going off to take a shower. Moments later, her thoughts were of dresses, rather than dogs. She would have the opportunity to recall it all later.

– *24* –
An Old Phrase Returns

Einfalt!

When his own daughter said the word, he could hardly believe it. At first, he thought he had misheard. But when she said it again...

Einfalt!

Giorgio Fierro tried to shake it off as he walked downstairs, but the word kept repeating in his mind, not in Valerie's soft voice, but in the way he used to hear it. That harsh, rasping Teutonic inflection rang through his head as if he had only heard it a day before; an hour before.

Silly, he told himself. That was years ago. He hadn't thought of him for the longest time. Still, that word brought back all the memories, and again he was a frightened war orphan in a strange place where they spoke a strange tongue. And in that severe-sounding language, where every word seemed a precursor to a punishment, the first word he had learned was that one: Einfalt.

"Well?" asked Connie Fierro as he returned to the kitchen.

Giorgio stared at her for a moment; so lost in the past that he had forgotten there was a present. Oh, yes, he reminded himself, that was his wife. He lived in America now. She looked at him as if she expected some answer.

"I'll, I'll be alright," he said, slowly looking around the room to reacclimate himself to his current life. He patted the chair like it was some sort of comforting talisman.

"Did you fall down the stairs and land on your head?" asked his wife facetiously.

He reached up and touched the top of his head, then shook it.

"No, I'm fine, I'll be…alright." He sat down slowly.

"Well, what about it?"

Giorgio looked around for a clue to what they had been talking about. Connie rolled her eyes, placed one hand on her hip, and thrust the other one towards the ceiling.

"Did you tell her about the dress?"

"Dress?" He stared at his wife. She was wearing slacks.

"The dress, Giorgio," she said, "Valerie's dress."

He stared at her for several more seconds thinking of the war, and *Captaino* Zimmer, and Bavaria, and Einfalt!

"You're going soft in the head," she scolded him. "You're working too hard. You…"

"NO! Don't say it!" he clapped his hands over his ears, certain she was about to use the word.

"Say what?"

"That word."

"What word?" she asked.

"The word you were about to say…"

She looked at him sideways. "that you… need a rest?"

"Rest?"

"You need a rest."

He heaved a sigh of relief and managed a weak smile. He tried to forget that other thing, that thing Valerie had said. An accident, he told himself, it was an accident. Valerie hadn't really said that. She must have been trying to say something else. He would just forget it.

Connie Fierro broached the subject of the dress again.

"Oh, yes," he said more back in the present, "yes, I told her she could get it."

His wife stood motionless except for her eyes. In less than thirty seconds, her eyes launched a series of emotions including confusion, disbelief, anger, frustration, annoyance, distress, and resentment. Her last expression, the first to have an audio accompaniment, was scorn.

"So, you told her she could get that dress, eh?"

Giorgio looked down and nodded.

"After all we discussed; after we agreed that she wasn't going to get that dress, you went upstairs, caved in, and told her she could get it. Is that what you're telling me?"

Evidently, yes, thought Giorgio. But in his wife's current state of agitation, he wasn't going to admit as much. He just kept his head down and continued to nod at the appropriate pauses. Giorgio loved his wife. Maybe not like he loved other women in his past, but that wasn't Connie's fault. She was a really good wife. She kept the house really well. She raised their daughters well. She was a good cook. She rarely turned down his requests for sex. No, as wives went, he thought, he couldn't ask for much more. Well, except at these moments. She could talk, and rant and argue, and wear his ears down to the nub. Though he spoke three languages, Giorgio was amazed at the number of words his wife could wring out of her tongue when she really got going. And right now she was really going. Boy! Was she going! When she was in this sort of a mood, the best he could hope to do was keep his head down and not get clipped in the verbal volley. Occasionally, he would make some gesture of submission, a nod, a shrug, a grunt that he hoped would be appropriately placed.

The rant was interrupted only once. Rose started to enter the room, realized what she was stepping into, reversed course, and disappeared. Finally, like a battery-powered tape recorder losing juice, Connie started slowing down. She briefly regained momentum for a short summary of all her points, and then folded her arms across her chest, as if she were closing a book. Thus endeth the lesson. It took Giorgio several seconds for his wife's tirade to stop ringing through his ears, and then, cognizant of the return of silence, looked up from his metaphoric foxhole.

His eyes met his wife's. They still contained enough fire to scorch, though no longer enough to incinerate him. He ventured a smile, not quite a smile, but rather a barely perceptible upturn to the corners of his mouth. The couple remained locked in this pose for the better part of a decade, though, in reality, it was only twenty seconds. Then Connie tilted her head to one side (she opened her mouth only slightly as, he thought, her jaw must certainly be sore after chewing him down to the bare stump of his soul), and spoke one word.

"How?"

It was a fair question and one he wished she had started with.

"I'll work some overtime," he said softly.

"Overtime? Giorgio! You already work overtime."

"So, I'll work some more," he shrugged.

Connie was a wizard of household finance. She started manipulating her fingers as if they were beads on an abacus. In less than ten seconds, she announced her results.

"Do you know how many hours of overtime that will be?"

Giorgio bobbed his head. "What does it matter? A lot. I'll do what I need to do."

"Do you know how many roofs that is?"

Again he motioned that was of little consequence.

"It's nearly..." Connie consulted with her fingers again. "...seven and a half residential roofs..."

"Nobody wants half a roof..." he mumbled.

"...Or five and three-quarter tar roofs..."

"I'd have to do six."

"And these roofing jobs just hang on trees?"

"I'll get them."

"Where?"

Giorgio thought a moment. "I did that job on that store in Newark, on the main street."

"And?"

"And I could see," he said with professional confidence, "that some of the other roofs around needed work. I could do a special deal, line up some hot tar jobs, and go down the whole side of the street... bop, bop, bop!"

"Bop, bop, bop? What is that?"

Giorgio shrugged. "You know, one, two, three, down the road... bop, bop, bop."

"I'll give you bop, bop, bop," said his wife. "Bop... you're working too hard! Bop... you're never home! Bop... you'll undercut your pricing and run through six months of jobs in four weeks and then dry up all your prospects! I could bring up all that, but I won't."

Giorgio nodded. He knew she was right, but this was not a matter for logic. Connie didn't understand. She couldn't. She didn't see Valerie the way he saw her. He wasn't just doing this for the present but in honor of the past. For a moment, he tried to form the explanation in his own mind, but it just wouldn't come together. Instead, he just got up and kissed his wife on the forehead.

"It'll be okay," he said and walked out of the room.

He hoped it would be. Later that night, while Valerie couldn't sleep for planning the most perfect night of her life, and her mother couldn't sleep for worrying about how that night would be paid for; Giorgio Fierro quickly fell into a deep slumber.

The nightmares started that night.

Einfalt!

– 25 –
The Economic Acumen of
a Hot Commodity

Like most sixteen-year-old virgins, Valerie Fierro was an expert on sex. She was a good girl in all the best definitions of the term. Her parents saw her as eternally virginal, while all the boys saw her as hotter than a heatwave in the middle of July. Boys wanted her, and she knew it. She had worked hard to cultivate her appeal. She was careful with her weight, she was meticulous with her skincare, and she wore just the right amount of make-up (which, as a teenaged girl, meant enough to plaster the ceiling of the Sistine Chapel).

Most importantly, Valerie knew economics. Not useless stuff about credits, debits, and those boring things. Instead, Valerie knew better than any Wall Street trader the concept of buying and selling at maximum market value. Though she had but one item in her portfolio, she had nurtured it, guarded it, and increased its value. Her stock was her virginal body.

Other girls in her circle had better "portfolios" and more lucrative assets. But these girls didn't have her trading acumen. Those girls had sold too soon and too cheaply with regrettable results.

In her circle of friends, Angela Bartoldi was the first girl to reach first base with a boy, or rather to have the boy reach first base with her. Not surprisingly, she also gave up second base in the same inning. And while Angela was still stranded on second for several months, another competitor, Donna Reilly, wound up on third. Meanwhile, because of her parent's strict rules, Valerie hadn't even got a turn at bat. Then came the day when Susan Hanrahan produced the first home run.

Susan became a celebrity or at least a curiosity. When Susan lost her virginity, she was like a visitor from another planet. The other girls pumped her with questions more vigorously than Susan's boyfriend had in their inaugural encounter. Most of their questions had some connections to romance and everlasting love. The more adventuresome girls asked how pleasurable it was. The more cautious girls asked if it hurt. After a few minutes of this intense barrage, it was evident that poor Susie would rather not be subjected to such scrutiny. Her replies were all brief and softly spoken. Finally, Valerie stepped in.

"Come on, girls, please, be a little sensitive, will ya," said Valerie as she herded Susan's inquisitors away. "Can't you see she doesn't want to talk about it now, come on, give her a little space, okay?"

The girls slunk away, leaving only Valerie to comfort Susan. She put her arm around Susan's shoulder. That sat in silence for several minutes.

"Thank you, Valerie," Susan finally sighed.

"Oh, they should have known better. Honestly, they were coming at you like a bunch of bulldozers!"

Susan smiled weakly. "I'm sure they were just concerned."

"Nosy is more like it," said Valerie.

Susan sighed. They sat in silence for at least another minute.

"So…" started Valerie as if she were tiptoeing on eggshells, "what was it like."

"Huh?'

"You know…with a boy, what was it like?"

Susan sat for a moment as if she were recalling memories from years ago rather than days.

"It was…it was quick."

"Quick?" Valerie was disappointed.

"It didn't take very long," said Susie.

"Oh." Valerie thought again. "Quick bad or quick good?"

Susan shrugged her shoulders. "I don't know, just… quick. I mean, when something's so quick, and you don't expect it to be so quick, you don't have time to think about it. It was just over fast."

Valerie sucked on her lower lip for a moment and nodded.

"But it was good, while it lasted, right?"

"It hurt, at first," she admitted. "And I guess it was starting to be okay after that, but then he was done."

"That quick, huh?"

Susan nodded, followed by another minute of silence.

"But…" Valerie said, breaking the silence, "you'd do it again."

"Well, yeah, I guess," said Susan. "I mean, I don't plan on becoming a nun. I mean, I'm going to get married someday."

"But, I mean, you'll do it again… with Jimmy, right?"

Susan inhaled one of those juicy, watery types of sucking of breath that come just before or just after a really good cry. Valerie braced for a flood, but Susie kept it under control.

"No," she said after a deep exhale. "I won't."

"Oh." Valerie was afraid to ask the next question, but even more afraid of not asking it. She did it gingerly. "Why not?"

"Because we broke up," said Susan, turning her head away.

"Oh."

Valerie sat there, wondering what if anything at all she should say. She wanted to ask her why they had broken up. If they had broken up for a reason other than the sex, then she wasn't interested. If on the other hand, they broke up because of the sex, well, that didn't really matter either. It could have been, Valerie thought, that Susan wasn't good enough, or didn't...what was the word...satisfy? If that was the case, it didn't much help Valerie. Susan was bright, but not smart. She got good grades but wasn't savvy in the really important matters of life. Valerie shook her head. It was too bad that Susan had been the first. It was like sending a girl to an important lecture in Paris only to learn upon her return that the only French she knew was *"oui"* and *"parley vous."*

Valerie stroked Susan's hair, and, like Jimmy probably had a few nights earlier, promised to call her tomorrow, and then went home.

It was several months until other girls had "The Experience." Only one girl, Nancy Falcone, actually had her relationship with the boy survive for more than a few weeks after the deed. Valerie tried to learn how Nancy and her boyfriend managed to succeed where others had failed, but try as she might, Nancy seemed to resent Valerie's attempts to wheedle it out of her. Valerie concluded that they were only together because each was the best the other could hope for.

By the previous Christmas nearly half the girls in Valerie's circle had experienced "it" as they came to refer to the act. Valerie, usually a trendsetter in their group, was starting to feel that she was falling behind.

Her best response, she figured, was to act superior, which was her way of dealing with any social challenges. Besides, Valerie's standing was safe as long as Angela was a virgin, too. Valerie and Angela were the leaders of the group. What one didn't know about style, or relationships, or music, or anything important like that, the other did. In tandem, they were the undisputed experts of their class in all things feminine. As long as Angela held out, Valerie was safe.

Fortunately, like Valerie, Angela was Catholic which gave her at least an extra twelve-month breathing room.

"Some girls can't wait until the time is right," was Valerie's standard reply when she felt her own chastity was being belittled. This was effective since more than half the girls who had had "it," meaning sex, wish they had "it," meaning their virginity, back.

It was then that Valerie perfected her theory of sexual economics. She hadn't sold cheaply when the market first opened and now she was literally sitting on a commodity which would only increase in value. No, Valerie Fierro was not going to give it away to the first horny boy who asked for it. She was going to use her allure to get something of greater value in return. When she sold, she would be left with more than a quick kiss-off and a used condom. She wasn't going to "lose" when she lost her virginity. Her friends' experiences had taught her how appropriate that phrase was. They had lost boyfriends, lost respect, and lost self-esteem, and had received very little in return. She was going to have it all and on her terms. She hadn't been the first one in the game, but she was learning from the mistakes of others. She was going to win and do it at the biggest venue there was: the prom.

After herculean efforts, Valerie had secured the perfect dress. The next piece would be much easier: the boy. Valerie had been looking forward to the prom for ten years, ever since she had seen one of her baby sitters attend her prom. Back then, she had seen it all as fairy tales and princesses. It was all innocence, like something out of a little girl's favorite Disney cartoon. Only years later did she comprehend it was a vitally important rite of passage, a giant step into adulthood. The prom would be the demarcation line between being her Daddy's princess and her own woman.

Her notions about the boy who would escort her had evolved with her changing ideas of the prom. At first, the boy was a cardboard Prince Charming, not much more animated than the Ken doll slavishly at the beck and call of her Barbie. Now she realized that the boy would have to be good looking, but he would also have to be mature; mature enough as not to be silly but still be fun. He couldn't be so mature, however, as to be too set in his ways. He would also have to be pliable, but that went without saying. The last component, social status, grew in importance as Valerie began to understand how the world worked. The boy to whom she was going to bestow her greatest prize would have to be a boy with a future. Like picking out a fine show dog or a thoroughbred stallion, breeding could not be overemphasized. She wanted a boy whom, if it worked out that way, she could marry; a boy who had a head start on the competition in life because of his family background.

Once, Valerie made the mistake of sharing these views her sister Rose. Rose merely laughed.

"What?" asked Valerie, "Why shouldn't I want to marry a boy from a good family, with good connections, and a good future?"

"No reason at all," said Rose. "But why should such a good catch want you?"

Valerie seethed for a moment as her sister continued.

"Why do you think some rich boy would give you more than a passing glance?"

Valerie's eyes narrowed. If they'd been a few years younger, she would have put her fist up Rose's big nose. Good thing for Rose she was more mature now.

"You... you're just a... a snob!" Valerie concluded.

"Me?" laughed Rose. "You're the snob. I'm perfectly happy being who I am. I'm not ashamed of my family. I'm not trying to land some fancy guy. I'm not the one..."

"Peas!" Valerie blurted out from the recesses of her brain.

"Peas?"

"Yes, smart-ass, peas! That's what I learned about in science, at least I think it was science... maybe it was home-ec... no, wait, yes it was science. I'm not ashamed of my heritage, and I'm not a snob. I'm doing these people a big favor!"

"What people?"

"Whatever people... the family I decide to marry into! I'll be doing them a big favor, and it's all because of peas!"

"What are you going to teach them: how to eat peas with a fork?"

"No, snotty," said Valerie, "I'm going to restock their pool."

"Oh, that kind of pee... you're going to start dating a rich boy and then pee in their swimming pool."

Valerie gave Rose another withering look. "I won't dignify that... idiot! I'm going to restock their gene pool."

"Really!"

"It's a well-known scientific fact proven by some guy who was breeding peas!"

"Actually the 'guy' was Mendel, and he was cross-pollinating them."

"Whatever, but he found that adding different peas made better peas."

"And you're just the kind of different pea these lucky people need to make better peas?"

"Obviously," said Valerie smugly, "you understood all along. You really shouldn't pretend to be so stupid, Rose."

"Let me get this straight," said Rose, "you're going to help out some needy, affluent, socially well-heeled family by adding the rich minestrone of your Italian heritage to help stir up their stagnant genetic soup. Is that about right?"

Valerie almost said that Rose would be more like adding a can of extra thick tomato paste to any family she married into. She decided to ignore her sister's remarks. "That's about it."

Rose walked away laughing, and shaking her head. Valerie resolved right then and there that Rose would be the last bridesmaid in her bridal party, but only if she could be paired with a particularly grotesque toad of an usher. No, she wouldn't do that. It would ruin her wedding pictures. Rose's punishment would be seeing her fabulously happy and married to an extremely upwardly-mobile hunk.

But she was getting ahead of herself. First, there was the prom.

She needed the right sort of boy. After all, she was going to give him her virgin body. Early on there were scores of candidates, many from the football team, though most of these were eliminated. Oh, these athletic boys had good physiques, but there were very few she could see having successful careers unless there was suddenly a severe shortage of human fence posts, and that became a six-figure occupation. Even the smarter football players, and there were some of those, were dropped from consideration because their families were too common. Valerie refused to contemplate a married name more than ten letters in length and with more y's and z's than vowels.

Finally, the perfect candidate emerged by surprise. She had known him since elementary school, though he was a grade ahead of her. He had what seemed at the time to be a funny name. He wore thick glasses. He was short. At times he would gasp for breath and then have to suck on one of those asthma things. But then, somewhere between his sophomore and junior years, a remarkable thing happened. The shortest kid in the class went away for the summer and came back as one of the tallest. He got contact lenses, and he outgrew his inhaler. The effect was amazing. At first, Valerie didn't recognize him. When she did, she was relieved that she had ignored him during all his awkward years. His sudden ripening, coupled with the fact that he came from the fringes of a very prominent family completed the picture.

Yes, now that she had the perfect dress and the perfect body to pour into it, she would go to the prom and afterward shed that perfect dress and offer her perfect body as a down payment on her future to W. Buxton Dorning.

– 26 –
The New Old
Curiosity Shop

Chesney Potoski clutched the lamppost for what seemed like several hours. The cab seemed to drive away in slow motion, though it would have done no good to run after it. The very air had turned to treacle. It would have been like running a marathon through molasses with a broken leg and a rubber crutch. Chesney was deflated and defeated. He would stand there, his arms around the lamppost until they petrified and he became one with the wrought iron, an eternal testament to broken dreams, dashed hopes, and bad timing. He resolved to do all that, and would have, had not he been tapped on the shoulder.

"Chesney," a familiar and caring voice said, "you've run right past my flat. The shop is back there."

He turned and saw his aunt.

He blinked and then blinked again. The lethargy of disappointment fell from his shoulders, and he became animated once again.

"It was her, Aunt El! It was the girl! I saw her again. She was walking down the street. She was walking, and I was running, and she turned the corner, and she got in a taxi. But it was her. She really was…" he looked down at the pavement. "…she walked right there! Aunt El!"

His aunt reached out and gently smoothed his anxious brow. Then, finding her palm still open and in the vicinity, she delivered a sharp slap to the side of his head.

"I'm not hysterical!" he said.

"You don't have the advantage of my viewpoint," she said calmly.

"But Aunt El," he cried, "it was the girl, and she went that way…"

"And, I will repeat," said Elinor, "that the shop is back there…"

"But she went…"

"The shop," she said, lowering her voice for effect, "the shop, Chesney..."

"Who cares about..."

"The shop your mystery girl came out of," she said resolutely. "The shop the girl stepped out of, Mr. Postlewaite's shop, is back there. The shop that she emerged from carrying a shopping bag."

"She bought something..."

"Yes, she made a purchase," said Aunt Elinor.

Chesney released the lamppost.

"She made a purchase?" repeated Chesney as he regained the full strength in his legs.

"Either that or Mr. Postlewaite gave her a shopping bag," said Elinor, "but in the quarter-century that I've known Postie, he's never given away a shopping bag. He's part Scottish, you know."

With his aunt at his elbow, Chesney crept back up the street, repeatedly glancing over his shoulder lest the girl should return. She did not.

"I thought," Aunt Elinor muttered as she prodded him along, "that love put a spring in a young man's step." She tugged at her nephew's elbow. "Whoever first voiced that opinion didn't formulate it by observing a Potoski in love. Come along, Chesney we're almost there. Stop turning around, will you?"

Chesney apologized but kept looking over his shoulder.

Finally, Elinor hauled her nephew in front of the shop. Chesney's suitcase was where he had dropped it.

"Chuzzlewitt & Postlewaite: Effluvia Britannica," said Chesney looking up at the sign over the doorway.

"There is no Chuzzlewitt," said Elinor.

"Yes, there is," said Chesney. "It's in Dickens."

"Well, there's no real Chuzzlewitt around here," she remarked. "No Chuzzlewitt, but Postie makes up for his absence. He's what you might call a Chuzzle-half-witt." She nodded to a door off to the side. "That's the doorway to the flats. Do you want to settle in first?"

Chesney thought for a moment. Settle in? No, he wanted to find out if that girl left a clue to her identity. "I want to find out about her."

Aunt Elinor nodded as if it were her sole purpose in life to escort love-struck nitwits. She told him to pick up his suitcase, grabbed his free elbow, and entered the shop. A small bell over the door announced them with a cheery tinkle. A shadowy figure emerged from the back room, though at first, his form was difficult to make out in the crammed shop. True to its sign, the small, musty shop was filled with a vast array of effluvia and ephemera, most of it British. There were books, magazines, posters, prints, toys, games, dolls, signs, records, sheet music, advertising pieces, and just about anything else imaginable that had been part of the popular culture of the British Isles over the past two-hundred years. Aside from the sensory overload that the store's stock imposed, there was another reason the shop's proprietor was difficult to make out: he was standing between two human replicas. The first was a mannequin of a London Bobby from the 1920s and the other a life-sized cardboard cutout of Freddy Garrity from 1963 promoting *I'm Telling You Now*. After his eyes adjusted to the light, Chesney noticed the figure in the middle moved.

"I see you there, Postie," said Aunt Elinor. "No use hiding. You've already pulled enough tricks on my nephew for one day."

The real Postlewaite stepped forward. It was the man who had introduced himself as Witherby in the haberdashery shop.

"Who told you it was me," said the man.

"You did, you twonk," said Elinor. "Remember? You're the one who came and told me my nephew was being arrested."

"Oh, yes, that's right, I did," beamed Postlewaite, before a more remorseful look overspread his face. "I'm sorry, my boy. You see," continued Mr. Postlewaite, "I know all this…" he pointed around his shop, "…seems fascinating. But even the most wondrous spots on earth, like my shop, would seem commonplace if you had to sit in the middle of them ten hours a day. Do you do like cake?"

"Yes, sir," said Chesney. "Yellow cake with chocolate icing…"

"Well then," said Postlewaite, "it would be like sitting on a cake ten hours a day, no wait, that's not it." He rolled his eyes. "No, it would be like eating your favorite cake three times a day. After the first year or two, it would get very monotonous. Don't you agree?"

"What's your point, Postie?" asked Elinor.

"Hmm? Oh, yes, as I was saying, as interesting as my little shop appears, it can get a bit boring. That's why I have to make my daily routine a little more amusing whenever I can. That's what I was doing in Witherby's shop. You see when he goes to the bank I go and watch his shop."

"And who watches your shop?" asked Chesney.

"I do," said Aunt Elinor.

"Yes, that's right," said Postlewaite. "It gives Witherby a chance to get out and run his errands, and it gives me a little break, as well. Naturally, to make the whole thing a bit more interesting, when a customer does come into Witherby's shop, which doesn't really happen all that often at that time of the morning, but if someone does venture in…"

"You take the Mickey out of poor unsuspecting customers!" said Aunt Elinor, before turning to Chesney. "That means teasing, dear."

"Me? Now, that's not very kind," said Postlewaite.

"Nevertheless, Postie," insisted Aunt Elinor, "I would be cross with you if I thought that you had singled out my favorite relative for such treatment. However, years of observation have shown me that you behave in such a manner to anyone fate drops in your bored, little path."

"Aunt El," moaned Chesney, "what about the girl?"

"And another thing," she continued, ignoring his plea, "you almost landed this boy in the nick…"

"The nick?" asked Chesney.

"The nick, old chokey, the hoosgow, in the hands of the Old Bill, a guest of Her Majesty…" offered Postlewaite.

"Thank you, Thesaurus of Britain," said Elinor, "if you had only been that helpful when you first encountered him, he wouldn't have nearly been arrested. An unsuspecting young man wanders into England…"

"…I thought he was here to do some writing job…"

"…Wanders purposely into England," she went on without missing a beat, "and the first person he encounters is a shopkeeper who gets his jollies impersonating other shopkeepers. Really, Postie, what possible enjoyment could one shopkeeper have pretending to be another shopkeeper?"

Mr. Postlewaite looked at her intently, then stared into space, as if this were his cue to deliver his soliloquy.

"It's quite liberating to be another person," said Postlewaite, "even if only for a few minutes. I suppose it's why actors enjoy what they do. But I've never wanted to go up on a stage. Still, when I watch Mr. Witherby's shop every morning for ten minutes or so, I can be someone else, if only for a brief moment. Some days I'm the slow-witted shop assistant, other times I'm the disgruntled cousin who got cheated out of his share of the shop in a dodgy inheritance scheme, once I was the Oxford Don who was working the shop after he'd been driven from the university in disgrace. And other times, like today, I'm just Witherby himself."

Aunt Elinor stared at her friend with a blend of bemusement and admiration and then shook her head. "Postie, you never cease to amaze me, even after all these years." She turned to Chesney. "I'm sorry that your introduction to this specimen was so unconventional, my dear, but then I suppose it was the most typical way to meet Postie. Still, in spite of running smack dab into the full force of his quirkiness, there was no real harm done…"

"But Aunt Elinor…"

"Your Aunt is a very generous soul," smiled Mr. Postlewaite. "It's why we all love her and why I've regularly proposed marriage to her over the past twenty-odd years."

"Odd years! That's a perfect description of our acquaintance, Postlewaite, but I wouldn't marry you, not in a million years. I'd have my head examined first."

"But Aunt El…"

"There you have it, Chesney," said Mr. Postlewaite, "that's why I'm the way I am. If your dear Aunt had consented to be my bride years ago, I wouldn't have developed these peccadilloes to add a little color to my dull existence. I would have been a complete individual with her by my side."

"You'd be an even more complete idiot," said Elinor. "Don't you believe it, Chesney. He's bad enough with me renting a flat over his head without spending life at his side…"

"But, the girl, Aunt Elinor…"

"Not just a girl, my boy," said Mr. Postlewaite, "Your Aunt Elinor is a lady. That reminds me of a song. I've got the record here somewhere." He began to rummage through a stack of old vinyl albums.

Chesney sat down in a heap on a nearby bundle of magazines and emitted a low moan as he thought of the girl driving further away.

"Don't sit there on the *Beanos*," said Mr. Postlewaite, abandoning his search for the record album. "If you want to sit on magazines please sit on the *Dandy*…"

"Postie," said Elinor putting her arm around Chesney, "can't you see he's upset."

"But you explained to the constable…"

"Nothing having to do with that, well, not directly," she said. "Chesney saw a girl, that's why he ran from the haberdasher's. He was chasing the girl he saw."

"Did he catch her?"

"Do you think he'd be sitting here in your chamber of nonsense looking like that if he had? She got away."

"Poor boy, still, it's better to have loved and lost…"

"Yes, well," she continued, "he may have gotten over that disappointment, but then he saw her again coming out of your shop."

"My shop? Then he did catch her!"

"No, she got into a taxi and got away again."

Postlewaite stroked his chin and nodded. "Sounds like a case of reverse stalking on the part of the young lady."

"Perhaps," said Aunt Elinor, "but you can be of help. She was walking out of this shop carrying a bag, one of your bags."

Mr. Postlewaite stared into space for several seconds as his mind seemed to be turning over the facts presented to him. Then his jaw slackened, his eyes darted around his shop as if to complete a quick inventory, before closing his mouth, snapping his fingers, spinning around and pointing to a shelf to his left.

"Sheet music," he said. "Yes, she bought a piece of sheet music."

Chesney looked up, hopefully.

"A girl with medium to dark brown hair, sort of, well," Chesney waved his flattened hand just below his shoulder, "sort of average length?"

"Yes."

"And sort of, well, very, very beautiful in a…stunningly average way."

"Astoundingly attractive," agreed Mr. Postlewaite, "in a completely nondescript manner that would go unnoticed to all but the most discerning hearts, my boy."

"And glasses," said Chesney, his excitement rising by the moment, "she had glasses?"

"But only over her eyes," said Postlewaite.

"That's her! Who is she?"

"*Even a Twerp Needs Love…*" he exclaimed. "That was the piece of sheet music she purchased."

"*Even a Twerp Needs Love!*" said Chesney, clutching his hands to his chest. "Aunt El, it's a Hugh Goode song! *Even a Twerp Needs Love!* Don't you see what that means, Aunt El? She not only is the most beautiful girl in the world, but she likes Hugh Goode. We like the same things or at least one of the same things. It's, it's…"

"Kismet?" offered Postlewaite.

"Fate?" suggested Aunt Elinor.

"More than I ever hoped for in life," said Chesney. He leaned over the counter, imploring Mr. Postlewaite with his outstretched hands. "She was in here."

"Yes, she was," he said with a broad smile.

"And you know her?"

He nodded his head. "That I do, yes, I know her, very well, exceedingly well. She's been in here more than once. You could say that she was a semi-regular customer."

Chesney released a deep sigh of relief.

"Well?" asked Aunt Elinor, "Postie, what's her name?"

"Name?"

"Yes, the girl's name," said Elinor.

He shook his head. "I haven't the slightest idea."

"But you said you knew her."

"Oh, yes, I know her exceedingly… that is very… well, pretty well… for the most part." He paused for a moment of reflection and then concluded: "I'm almost certain I'd recognize her if I saw her again."

"If I weren't non-violent I'd knock your block off," she said.

Chesney shook his head. "This is painful enough, Aunt El, without splitting infinitives: you 'knock off one's block.'"

"He's lucky I don't split his skull right down the center of his silly sconce! He's the one who said he knew her."

"I do," said Postlewaite defensively, "she bought *Even a Twerp Needs Love* today. Two months ago she bought a very nice poster from the 1941 film: *Hugh Spins the Axis*. It really was very popular during the war. In it, Hugh Goode gives a hot foot to Mussolini, not the real Mussolini, an actor playing Mussolini. I saw it as a small boy. The whole theater broke out into gales of laughter and cheers at that one."

Chesney thought a moment. "Mr. Postlewaite, you said she's been in here at least twice."

"Oh, yes, that's just the two latest occurrences. She comes in here quite often, has for several years, whenever she's in town."

"So the girl doesn't live in London?" asked Elinor.

"No, she mentioned that she stops in whenever she's in London on other errands."

"And always for Hugh Goode items?" asked Chesney.

"Yes, yes, I've tried to interest her in some Flanagan and Allen, or Arthur Askey, but she won't wear it. It has to be Hugh Goode. I set them aside for her. She comes in fairly regularly, every few months, or so it seems. When you run an establishment that's packed with years' worth of memories, it's easy for the weeks and months to run together. Oh, there's one more thing. I think she's in service."

"Army or Navy?" asked Chesney.

Mr. Postlewaite chuckled.

"He doesn't mean in the armed services," said Aunt Elinor. "He means in domestic service."

"You mean like a maid?" said Chesney.

"No," said Postlewaite, "I'd say more like the housekeeper, or the head of the staff, that sort of thing. She's mentioned an estate at times, and she always wears a white blouse and a black skirt, like her uniform, as it were."

"At least," concluded Aunt Elinor, "if Chesney waits here long enough there's a good possibility this mystery girl will return. How long do you think that writing assignment you're on will take, Chesney?"

"It's hard to say. I haven't even met his Lordship, yet."

"Lordship, eh?" said Mr. Postlewaite impressed.

"Yes, I'm ghostwriting the autobiography of Lord Bagnall of Staffordshire."

Mr. Postlewaite grimaced.

"Do you know him, Postie?" asked Aunt Elinor.

"That's Lord Bog Roll!" laughed Postlewaite.

"Bog roll?" said Chesney.

"The toilet tissue king, the Lord of the Loo, the... well, I can't recall any other of his titles, but he's often mentioned in the papers, especially the tabloids."

"I never read them," said Aunt El. "Are you saying this Bagnall, this person who my nephew has to write for, that he's notorious?"

"Well, let's just say..."

"Stop," said Chesney. "I don't want to know. I've got to write his life story. I'd rather not go into it with any preconceived notions about notorious pasts or toilet tissue."

"He's a life peer," said Postlewaite. "That's nothing he wouldn't have told you himself. That just means he's been made a Lord, by services to the nation, such as military bravery, or charitable work, or by selling tons of bog paper."

"I knew he was some sort of industrialist," said Chesney, "but I'd rather not know any more details. It's bad enough that I have to go to Staffordshire."

"I thought you were looking forward to it," said Aunt Elinor.

Chesney frowned. "Well, I was, but I wish I could stay here in Mr. Postlewaite's shop..."

Postlewaite stood erect. "Thank you, my boy. It's always gratifying when a newcomer recognizes my humble establishment for the world of enchantment that it is."

"Sorry," said Chesney, "it's a wonderful shop, but I wish I could wait here for when she returns." He grabbed Postlewaite's arm. "Look, if she comes in, could you ask her to wait."

"Wait? For what?"

"For me," said Chesney, "and then you can call me up, and I'll rush right down."

"From Staffordshire?"

"Is it far?"

Postlewaite shook his head. "Relatively speaking, it's around the corner when you compare it to the Galapagos Islands or Alpha Centauri. Still, it would take you close to three hours to get back here if the traffic's with you. I doubt I could hold a girl here much longer than that without the authorities accusing me of abducting her."

"Don't worry, Chesney," said Aunt Elinor dear, "if this mystery girl returns…"

"If?" Chesney felt his heart sink.

"When she returns," she corrected, "when she comes back in, Postie will get her name and address." Aunt Elinor looked at the smiling Mr. Postlewaite and after a moment amended her promise. "Even better… when this young lady returns, Postlewaite will fetch me. Then I will get the name and address of your mystery girl."

"Mystery girl," his mind spun anagrams. "Try my leg, sir." No, that wasn't right.

"Come on, now, Chesney," said Aunt Elinor tugging him by the elbow, "let's get you some rest. You have a big day tomorrow."

"Yes," laughed Postlewaite, "a long drive to a life peer."

– 27 –
A Long Drive to a Life Peer

English motorways were as monotonous as the Interstates back home. The seemingly endless asphalt ribbons offered only passing glimpses of more interesting vistas just beyond their boundaries. Chesney imagined the charming English countryside, the quaint old villages, and the fascinating relics of a thousand years of heritage just over the horizon. Each exit might be the gateway to a lovely British scene or a far greater treasure.

One of those exits, he imagined, led to the Mystery Girl. She was out there somewhere. Or maybe she was still back in London. Maybe every mile north took him further from her. Or perhaps the lorry was moving in her direction. Or maybe he was passing her at that moment. He tried not to think of it, but from his vantage point high above the roadway, he could look down into every passing car. The briefest glimpse of a young woman, especially an average brunette, made him think that it was her. If he closed his eyes so he wouldn't see the passing motorists, he saw her in his memory. If he looked out of the window, above the traffic, he imagined her face in the clouds. Any glimpse of a roadway rest stop, a far off town, any kind of shelter, made him wonder: is she there? Has she ever been there? Has she traveled on this very same road in the past? Will she in the future?

I should have taken the train, he thought, but if he were on a train, he would walk up and down each car scrutinizing the face of every passenger. He would probably get arrested for stalking strangers on a train. He would have to content himself with riding to Staffordshire in a tractor-trailer truck.

"I do appreciate the ride," said Chesney, just to say something. He grimaced, certain that he had made the same comment at least a dozen times between London and Birmingham.

The driver nodded sagely, but then, he did just about everything sagely. He had never known a truck driver to downshift with inscrutable wisdom, but then, he hadn't known many truck drivers. Perhaps the majority of them jammed their gears with that same sagacity.

"Brummies..." said the driver.

"Brummies?" asked Chesney, looking at the vehicle ahead of them on the M6 motorway. "You mean that car?"

The driver chuckled, not in a demeaning manner, but as an introduction to the forthcoming explanation. "No, though it could just as well be the name of an automobile. Brummies are what people from Birmingham are called."

Brummie, thought Chesney. Perhaps the girl was a Brummie.

"Still," continued the driver, "I wouldn't call any of them that if I were you, especially not in your American accent."

Chesney felt self-conscious. Would the girl, if he ever found her, be repelled by his manner of speech? "Is it that obvious?" he asked.

Again the hint of a smile crossed the driver's lips as he changed lanes. "The noblest frog may feel ill at ease amid the lowliest company of toads."

"Oh," said Chesney as he turned and looked out the window.

"I am in earnest," said Li Gao, "you are fine, Chesney. You come with the most glowing of references which one-hundred miles of motorway have only burnished more brightly."

"Thank you," said Chesney.

"I'm thankful to you," said Li Gao, "after all, I've made this journey alone thousands of times. I'm grateful for the company. I'm especially grateful to meet a young man of whom I've heard so many good things for so many years. You hold a cherished place in the heart of your aunt."

"She holds a pretty special place with me, too."

"Ah, yes..." Chesney waited a moment for another nugget of wisdom from Li's venerable lips, but the sage kept his own counsel.

After a quarter of a mile of silence, Chesney felt the need to say something but was at a loss for what it should be. He started, for lack of anything else, to again thank him for the ride, but realized that now that voicing his gratitude yet again would be ridiculous. He wished that he could bare his soul to the driver. Surely, Li Gao would have some words of encouragement on life and love. Perhaps he knew the ways of the universe beyond the grasp of physicists and philosophers. He might even know if his friend Postlewaite would remember to tell the mystery girl that there was an American boy dying to meet her. Every time, however, his lips began to form these seminal questions, Chesney recalled the parting advice of his aunt.

◆

"Now, a word," Aunt Elinor told him just before he climbed into Li Gao's lorry, "you're in England now."

Chesney started to say that was obvious, but Aunt Elinor cut him short.

"And you're an American. The English are a wonderful people. They've made me feel very much at home here, in fact, this is my home now. They are a wonderful nationality. I'd want no other group of people on my side in a fight. But don't mistake politeness for friendship."

"Don't trust them?" asked Chesney.

"I didn't say that, did I? No, an Englishman's word is his bond, for the most part, but Americans tend to be more open and more readily embracing. The English are more cautious. They come by it honestly. You'd be that way too if you had a continent full of foreigners at your doorstep that's been trying to bump you off for more than a thousand years. You'll never find a more resolute, stalwart bunch of people, but it takes a while to become intimate with them."

"I don't expect Lord Bagnall to want to be my friend," said Chesney. "I'm just going to ghostwrite his biography."

"I'm not talking about Lord Bagnall," she said, and she glanced in the direction of Li Gao who was just out of earshot fiddling with something under the bonnet of his lorry.

"Li Gao?" said Chesney loud enough to elicit a hush from his aunt. "But he's Chinese."

"He was born there, but he's been living here since he was two. So he's got double politeness – English, and Eastern – but just don't get too personal with him."

"But I thought he was your friend."

Aunt El rolled her eyes. "One of my dearest friends; after you, I consider Gao and Postlewaite my family, but it took a long time with both of them to win that position of trust and affection. Why, I didn't know that Gao played the accordion until I had known him for nearly ten years."

"The accordion?"

"Yes, well, he wanted to learn to play the zhonghu, but do you know how hard it is to find a good zhonghu instructor in Marylebone?"

Chesney confessed he didn't. He barely recalled that it was a two-stringed Chinese fiddle.

"And I didn't find out about the zhonghu, either until I had known him for another five years," said Aunt Elinor. "And don't let him know that I told you, please. I suppose my point is that you're going to be spending more than three hours in the cab of a lorry with him. Just don't get... personal."

"Could I ask him about, well, about Mr. Postlewaite?"

"What about him?"

"Oh, I don't know," said Chesney, "about his shop, and how reliable he was."

Aunt Elinor stroked his cheek. "Stop worrying about that girl, Chesney. She'll show up again, probably. And when she does, Postie will do his duty."

"Can I be sure of that?"

"I've said it before, and I say it once again," she vowed, "I will remind him daily. And beyond that, I will check with him hourly on the visitors to his shop. And whenever possible, I will keep watch myself. So, just relax and don't worry. Do your job with Lord who's-his-face, and I'll do mine with Postlewaite. And for your own peace of mind, don't reopen the whole can of worms by burdening Gao with it. Okay?"

"I won't say anything," promised Chesney. "I'll just keep my mouth shut all the way to Staffordshire."

"Well, don't be a waxwork either, for goodness sake," she said. "You two will get along. He's a very deep thinker. You can talk philosophy, he loves to talk theology, just don't get too familiar. Do you understand?"

Chesney said that he did, though he still wasn't quite sure.

"Now, you've got your grip?"

He looked down at his hand, before recalling his aunt was using her antiquated term for a suitcase. He picked up the leather satchel she had loaned him for the short trip, leaving most of his luggage with her for the time being. To him, it looked more like a tool bag. She reached over and fussed at his lapels, and started to reach for his cap, before stopping and shaking her head.

"That hat!" she said to herself. "Still you look like an Englishman. But that doesn't make you one. Just remember what I said."

"About Li Gao…"

"Him, too, but everyone you meet," she said. "Be polite, be respectful, but be a little…"

"Reserved?" he offered.

"Yes, I suppose." Aunt Elinor sighed and gave him a hug. "I wish I were going along, but I don't particularly want to go to Wigan with Li Gao after he drops you off. Now, you have enough money?"

Chesney assured her that he did, though he wasn't exactly sure how much money he would need, how long he would be staying on his first visit with His Lordship, or indeed what expenses he would have.

Li Gao signaled that they were ready to go. Chesney climbed into the cab of the lorry, first getting in on the driver's side, forgetting that British vehicles had their steering wheels on the right-hand side. And off they went.

◆

Now, three hours later, having exhausted all general conversation, he sat looking out as the outskirts of another city retreated, and they approached open countryside. He preferred the rural scenery. For unless the girl was living in a treehouse or down a badger hole, there were few places she could be in those open spaces.

"A penny," said Li Gao, raising his calm voice above the roar of the engine, "for your thoughts."

"At the current rate of exchange," noted Chesney pedantically, "that's about two-and-a-half cents in American money."

"I'm sure your thoughts are worth that modest investment."

"I was just thinking about... Aunt El." Chesney felt his face redden and turned away. He was thinking about Aunt Elinor, but not her alone.

"Ah, yes..." another heavily-laden pause from the inscrutable lorry driver, this time, however, he managed to complete the sentence. "Such thoughts are worth far more than a penny."

Apparently, Li Gao so liked the subject of Aunt Elinor that he hoarded it. He spent the next two exits in solitary contemplation, leaving his passenger to do the same.

Chesney wondered if Li Gao was romantically interested in his aunt. Mr. Postlewaite had seemed to be, but his declarations, while out in the open, had a facetious air to them. Perhaps that was just his way, as it was Li Gao's to be stoic. He also wondered why Li Gao was now a truck driver. He had once run a Chinese restaurant, or at least that's what he thought Aunt Elinor had once told him. If only they had been driving down Interstate 95 instead of up the M6 and Li Gao was an American truck driver instead of an articulated lorry driver, Chesney could ask him all these questions. As it was, however, he would have to sit politely and wait for Gao to direct the conversation. Before this, however, Gao steered his lorry off the motorway.

"Cresswell," noted Li Gao, as they passed a sign indicating the same. "It's not too far."

Chesney nodded and swallowed hard.

"Whenever I am nervous," said Gao looking straight ahead, "I recall the Sermon on the Mount: 'do not worry about tomorrow; for tomorrow will care for itself. Each day has enough trouble of its own.' And then I feel peace knowing things will work out." Then, he fell silent, concentrating on the road.

Li Gao may have been referring to Chesney's anxiety surrounding his assignment for Lord Bagnall, but Chesney was worried about the girl. But worrying would only drive him to distraction and possibly affect his more immediate responsibility. The trouble of today? Well, he didn't have any trouble; he had a job to do. He had to go meet this Lord Bagnall and start working on his autobiography. And the girl? It was unlikely, according to her past visits to the shop that she would turn up again so soon; so that probably was not a concern for today. No, he could worry about that in a few days, or maybe next week. He would return to London in a few days, and even if she did show up in the meantime, Aunt Elinor would handle the situation.

Chesney nodded to himself and sighed, feeling much more at ease. He glanced over at Li Gao. His eyes were still on the road.

They passed through various small towns, some not more than a cluster of two or three homes. Even in the less populated areas, Chesney was taken by the neatly maintained hedges, walls, and fences which somehow seemed distinctly English.

"I've not often been this way," confessed Li Gao, referring to directions written on a pad of paper. After a quarter of an hour, they made another turn through a gate in the middle of an old stone wall.

"This should be Bagnall Hall," said Li Gao.

Chesney looked at the stone house, just beyond the gate. "It's very… nice," he said, though it was larger than the average house, it was much smaller than he imagined the home of a lord to be.

"I believe you're looking at the caretaker's cottage," said Li Gao. "His Lordship more likely resides there…"

Chesney looked up. Beyond a small hillock was what was obviously Bagnall Hall. He'd never seen anything like it, at least not in person, though for a country estate or the home of a Duke or a Lord it may have been quite average. The house was of brick and stone, three stories high, though the hip roof had a railing that could have easily hidden another floor. On the front alone, Chesney counted over thirty windows. He thought of his father, who would have loved all those windows, and his mother, who would hate cleaning them. As they neared the large house, a well-tended design of low-hedges became apparent beyond the front entrance. A drive of small white stones led around the front of the house, circling back out again to the main road.

"I think they'll be able to offer you accommodation," said Li Gao with a dry understatement. "At least on the settee."

Chesney smiled at the comment but wondered if he was up to writing the story of anyone who lived in so grand a home. Especially daunting was the fact that he was only ghostwriting it. The words would have to seem as if they were springing from the mind of Lord Bagnall. Thinking of his little apartment, Chesney wondered how he could even begin to imagine the lofty musings of a member of the aristocracy.

The lorry's brakes came to a squealing stop, jarring Chesney from thoughts of his own inadequacy. He stared at the front door. It threatened dire consequences to any boy from New Jersey who dared to knock upon it. Chesney gave a jump when he felt a gentle prodding at his shoulder.

"My friend, houses do not bite," said Li Gao with a smile.

Chesney inclined his head as if to indicate this one may be the first to do so.

"Do not be in awe of stones and bricks. Your home is made of much the same."

Chesney looked up at the imposing façade. "Yes," he admitted, "but there's so much more of it here, and it's arranged much more impressively."

"Your humble spirit will stand you in good stead," said Li Gao. "Two things I will leave with you. First, to walk in humility, but without shame."

"And the second?"

"Knock on the door. They rarely open by themselves, except in supermarkets."

Chesney nodded, shook Li Gao's hand, thanked him yet again, grabbed his satchel, and climbed out of the cab. Gao nodded him towards the door, and Chesney walked slowly over the gravel. Even the stones crunched under his feet in an intimidating manner. He reached the door, put down his bag, straightened his long tan coat and his flat cap, and then picked up his bag. The door was a double-hung and double-paneled affair, like two vertical jaws primed to bite. Both featured heavy brass knockers, leaving Chesney to wonder whether he should strike the left or the right, or just turn and run away. He glanced back at Li Gao, who nodded encouragement.

Taking a deep breath, Chesney started to reach for the right-hand knocker, but then recalling that they drove on the opposite side of the road in England changed his mind and raised the left and let it fall with a heavy metal thud.

Gao smiled approvingly. Chesney was smiling back sheepishly when he heard the door open behind him. He turned, but not in time to wipe the silly grin from his face. A man with a severe look met him. It was either this look, or the man's ramrod straight posture, or the fact that he was standing in the doorway of a grand estate that made Chesney feel that he was at least six-and-a-half feet tall, though he was barely taller than Chesney.

"Yes?"

"Oh, uh, your Lordship, I'm here, to work for you." Chesney hoisted his satchel containing, in addition to a few changes of clothes, his notebooks, and pencils.

The man looked up and down Chesney twice, spending an inordinate amount of time on the satchel and the cap.

"Tradesman's entrance is around the back," he said coolly.

"Oh, right," said Chesney, flashing another sheepish grin. "Yes, your Lordship, I'm sorry, I didn't..."

"I am not Lord Bagnall," said the man.

"Oh, sorry," said Chesney, widening his grin in proportion to his expanding embarrassment. "Yes, round the back..." he looked to the right and the left before returning to the man. "Would that be back to the left or the right?"

The man, who was already standing painfully erect, stiffened visibly while stifling a sigh. "Either way...and remove your vehicle from the front of the Hall."

"Vehicle? Oh, right, yes, absolutely," Chesney turned to look at the lorry. That's Li Gao, he's not staying, he's going on... to Wigan..." Turning back around, Chesney discovered the door was already shut. For some reason, he tipped his cap to the closed door and jogged back to the lorry.

"Got to go 'round back," he explained to Li Gao. "Maybe they just waxed the floors up front."

Chesney exchanged another round of thanks and waved as the lorry drove around the drive, over the hillock, and into the distance. He waved until Li Gao's truck was out of sight, then feeling quite alone, started towards the back of the house. As with the door knockers, he began to go right, and then switched to left. Navigating around the large rectangular building, Chesney stole a few peeks at the side of the house. He didn't want to take a prolonged gaze lest he should find someone looking down at him while he was looking up. Around the back of the house, Chesney reached another door. It looked much more welcoming than the one up front, almost like a real home. It was less forbidding and much easier to knock upon.

After two raps with his knuckles, he noticed a doorbell and started to reach for it when the door opened.

"Yes?" asked a motherly woman wearing an apron. The woman's "yes" was warm and friendly, the direct opposite of the frosty "yes" he had received around the front of the house.

"I'm here," said Chesney tipping his cap, "to do some work for His Lordship."

The woman's face, which was welcoming to begin with, lit up even more. "We've been expecting you," she said, beckoning him to enter, "my you got here quick, didn't you?"

"Uh, yes, *quickly*," said Chesney. "I came by truck, that is, by lorry."

"Oh, yes? Well, I wouldn't have expected you any other way, dearie."

"No?" said Chesney. He had considered coming by train. Perhaps it was customary to travel to English country estates in tractor-trailers.

"Come in, come in," said the woman who began to chatter on about some sort of difficulty and the necessity of meal preparation as she led him through a pantry into a large kitchen.

As he entered the kitchen, all sounds, and indeed all sights but one disappeared from his consciousness.

There, sitting in the kitchen, looking up at him and smiling was the girl in the lime green wellies.

– 28 –
Paradise Found... in the Kitchen

Chesney stood with his mouth agape. The girl whom he had found and lost, and found and lost, was found once again.

He turned around to verify the location of the nearest exit. Should this girl attempt to run out of his life a third time, Chesney was well-positioned to stop her. Standing between her and the outside world, he could now devote his full attention to appreciating the girl at close range. Previously he had only admired her from afar. In the back of his mind, he feared that her plain beauty would not stand up to close scrutiny. Now, as he looked at her less than ten feet away, he set his mind at ease. She was stunningly ordinary, even up close.

The girl was sitting there in a white silk blouse and a plain black skirt. Her brunette hair hung straight upon her shoulders, and kissed her forehead in soft bangs, framing her delicate face of completely average proportions. Her nose was not too large as to be demeaned as a beak, nor small enough to be dismissed as a button. It was just average. Her cheekbones were neither too high nor too low, but just normal. In fact, as he stood savoring her features, it was apparent that the only sub-par feature were her eyes which were weak enough to require a pair of glasses. This was more than just all right with Chesney, however, as he had always had a weakness for girls with weak eyes. Together the entire ensemble recreated the initial effect it had had upon him back in London: he felt himself go weak in the knees. Fortunately, he was holding the satchel which served as a counterbalance and allowed him to steady himself.

All the while, the woman in the apron kept talking about fixing something or dinner being late. Whatever she was saying wasn't important. Chesney was too busy looking at the girl. She must be the head of the staff for Bagnall Hall. Wasn't that what Postlewaite had said, that she was in service or something like that? Wonderful Postlewaite, he had it right.

Li Gao was right, too. He had just advised Chesney not to worry about tomorrow. He had taken that advice, and now tomorrow's worries had suddenly changed into today's blessings. And as far as the current day holding any problems, he couldn't imagine a one. No doubt some poor sap somewhere else had got a double helping of woes on this day. For Chesney Potoski the score was now: Chesney:10; Woes: 0.

Close on the heels of these thoughts was Aunt Elinor's admonition about the English temperament: don't mistake politeness for friendship. Chesney's first impulse was to profess his undying devotion, propose marriage, and then introduce himself. That would have been the plan in New Jersey, and no doubt it would have ended badly. No, the flinging of oneself at a girl was not a winning strategy, especially not in the middle of an English manor. He would follow Aunt Elinor's advice and respect the British reserve.

"So, is that clear?" asked the cook.

Chesney turned to the cook and nodded, for no other reason than it was probably what she expected him to do. He smiled and looked back at the girl and smiled even more broadly. Thankfully she smiled back. Their eyes met for a moment, and Chesney took hold of the butcher block in the center of the room to steady himself. Her eyes glanced up to the top of his head, and he realized he still had his cap on.

"Sorry," he said. He removed the cap and proceeded to mangle it in his hands.

She smiled again and then spoke.

"Oh, you're from America," she said. Her voice, like the rest of her, was soft, sweet, and devastatingly average.

"Yes," he said bashfully, "New Jersey."

"New Jersey," she repeated with a degree of interest.

"Have you ever been there?"

"No."

"Oh." It was as Aunt Elinor had warned. She was being polite, and he had mistaken it for something more. He must not, he reminded himself, be overly familiar. He retreated to verifiable facts. "Yes, it's between New York and Pennsylvania," he said, looking beyond her eyeglasses and into her soft brown eyes. "It was the third state to ratify the Constitution. And of course, it was named after your own island of Jersey in the Channel."

"I'd never thought of that, but that makes sense."

"In turn, the Island of Jersey was named after Julius Caesar."

"You certainly are well-informed," she said.

"Thank you," he said. "In my line of work, you tend to pick up lots of little facts like that." This, he thought, was an opening to a conversation about his work. Then, he could ask her questions about her work. From there it was a straight line to how many children she wanted and the number of tiers on their wedding cake.

"How extraordinary," she said. "I wouldn't think that your profession would afford many opportunities for learning those sorts of things."

Chesney felt a puzzled look knit his brow. How could she know that he was a book editor? Then he realized that as the housekeeper she was well-apprised of the people coming and going from the manor, and of course, he was expected. Or perhaps she wasn't the housekeeper but was His Lordship's private secretary.

"Yes, well," he said, "um, well, I, I hope I'm not late."

"Late?" she said.

"Late? I should say not," piped in the cook. "I only just called. That's quick service I'd say."

Chesney gave her a quizzical look.

"Yes, well," said the girl standing up – Chesney noted she was of average height as well, about five foot four – "now that you're here, we'll leave you to your work." With that, she started towards the interior door at the other end of the room.

"Wait," said Chesney, the girl stopped and turned. "I mean, I'll see you again, won't I? I mean, of course, I will"

The girl exchanged looks with the cook, and then looked back at him.

"I don't expect so," she said, then asked the cook. "Do you think so, Miriam?"

The cook shrugged her shoulders.

"I mean," said Chesney, "this is a pretty big job, isn't it?"

"Is it?" said the girl.

"Well, I mean, yes," said Chesney. "It's the job of a lifetime, isn't it?"

"Is it?"

"Well, someone's lifetime," he said.

"You would know better than I... Mr...."

"Potoski," he said, "Chesney Potoski."

"Mr. Potoski, as I say, you're better acquainted with this sort of thing than I. How long does it usually take?"

How long, he thought. He exhaled and scratched his head. "Well, I don't want to shake your confidence in me, but I've never actually done this sort of thing." A look of concern spread across her face, and he rushed to dispel it. "I've done very similar work, and I assure you I'm fully qualified. But there's a first time for everyone for everything... just about. Isn't there?"

"Yes," the girl said cautiously. "I suppose that's true."

"And I've known other people who have done similar jobs. Based on their experience..." Chesney thought for a moment. "I'd say starting from scratch, that is, from the very beginning, this will probably take at least a month or two."

"A month!" she said.

"Or two?" interjected the cook.

"Yes, well," said Chesney, "that's to be expected."

"What about dinner?" said the cook.

Chesney didn't know if this meant he was invited to dine with Lord Bagnall or the staff. He looked over at the girl.

"Yes," said the girl, "Miriam does have to prepare dinner."

Chesney looked at the girl, then at the cook, and then back at the girl, and then back at the cook. He shrugged his shoulders, not knowing what the writing of a biography had to do with the cook's plans for dinner. Still, he thought, best not to act like a big shot to the staff, especially when he had fallen in love with one of them. Magnanimity was the best approach under the circumstances.

"Well," he said, scratching his head and smiling, "I'd say, yes, by all means, this nice lady should go ahead and prepare dinner. And I'm sure it will be delicious." He felt quite generous at this compliment. Instead of appreciation, however, his magnanimity was met by hostility.

"And what do you expect me to cook on?" said the cook.

Chesney smiled and pointed to a nearby range. "On that stove?"

The cook rolled her eyes. Chesney was afraid to look over at the girl to see her reaction.

"It's not connected," said the cook.

Chesney bit his lip and rubbed the side of his head.

"And what do you think a representative of UK Gas would do with this cooker?" said the cook.

That was an easy one. "He'd probably grab his tools, dive right in and connect it right up for you," beamed Chesney.

"And how long would that take," asked the cook.

Chesney approached the range which on closer inspection he saw was sitting a few inches away from the wall, and next to the gas pipe. Though he wasn't an expert, it seemed an easy job. "Oh, no more than a few minutes," he said with assurance. "It seems very straight forward. No more than twenty minutes tops!"

"Excellent," said the girl, and she once more started for the door.

"Wait," he said. He wanted to ask her name. Still, it didn't matter. Now he knew where she worked and presumably lived. He wouldn't lose her again.

"I'll leave you to it," she said as he exited. "Miriam will give you everything you need."

Chesney watched her leave, admiring her from the back almost as much as he did from the front. He continued to stare at the closed door, her door, the door she had used, drinking in the residual memory. His reverie was broken by a nudge at his elbow.

"One or two months," said the cook derisively.

"Pardon?"

"Now that you've finished the tomfoolery, perhaps you can get to work, so I can get to work."

Chesney nodded but stood there. He didn't know how she expected him to start writing right there in the kitchen and without even first meeting Lord Bagnall.

"Well," she nodded at his satchel, "get cracking."

"Get cracking," he repeated.

"Do you have any questions?"

He brightened. "Yes, yes, I do!" He pointed towards the door. "What is that young lady's name?"

"Miss Goodhue?"

"Miss Goodhue!" said Chesney with a smile and a nod, as if somehow he should have known all along. "Miss Goodhue." He closed his eyes and appreciated this for several seconds. When he opened his eyes, he noticed the cook looking at him askance.

"Sorry, sorry," he said, "it's only that, well, it's such an apt name, such a fitting name, such a, a... likely name... Miss Goodhue." He thought for a moment and realized that in rushing to the "Goodhue," he had neglected the essential introductory part: Miss. Miss Goodhue, oh yes, what a wonderful name."

"Yes, sir," said the cook taking a step away from Chesney and toward the knives.

"Does she have a Christian name?" asked Chesney.

"Of course..."

"And what, sorry... what did I hear your name was?"

"Miriam..."

"Yes, of course, Miriam. I'm sure Miss Goodhue's first name is quite lovely."

"Yes, sir."

"And what would that be?"

The cook looked around. Chesney wasn't sure what she was looking for.

"If, if I tell you," said Miriam skittishly, "do you promise to get to work and stop acting like a... a..."

Chesney could tell she was groping for just the right phrase to describe a young man in love. "...like a... mooncalf?"

"I was going to say like an imbecile," confessed the cook.

"Forgive me," said Chesney. "You probably think I'm behaving very strangely..."

"Not half!"

"Not half, you're right, not half at all, but full, full from a full heart. But please, don't think I'm crazy. You see, I know this girl."

"You know her?"

"Yes, oh, for a very long time, or at least that's how it feels."

"But you don't even know her name?"

"Um, no."

The cook looked at him with a skepticism usually found in the eyes of traffic cops and retail clerks.

"Do you promise to get cracking if I tell you her name?"

Chesney crossed his heart with his index finger. "I promise to get cracking, immediately."

"Right," said the cook, "Miss Goodhue's Christian name..."

He nodded.

"Verity."

"Verity?"

She repeated it.

"Verity," he said in a hushed, almost reverential voice. "Verity. Verity Goodhue."

"Okay, then?" asked the cook.

"Okay? Okay?" said Chesney, "It's more than okay. It's a wonderful name. Thank you, Mrs..."

"Gertz."

"Thank you, Mrs. Gertz."

"Now what about the gas?"

He smiled. They could turn on the gas, lock him in the room, and he would die happy!

Chesney nodded. "How about the gas?"

She folded her arms. "You promised you'd get to work, so get to work!"

Chesney looked at her and then towards the door. "I'd be happy to get to work. Shouldn't I go see His Lordship?"

"His Lordship? Stone me! Just reach into your gear, and get to work."

"Here?"

"Here and now," she said.

Chesney nodded. The cook seemed so adamant he put his satchel on the counter, opened it up and fished through his clean shirts and socks until he found his notebook and a pencil. He flipped open his notebook, exhaled, and began.

"Now, uh, Mrs. Gertz, when did you first come to work for Lord Bagnall?"

The cook's jaw dropped, and she grabbed the nearest implement, which happened to be a cast-iron skillet.

Chesney wondered what the pan had to do with his question, but jumped back when she brandished it in a menacing fashion.

Fortunately for Chesney, the door opened, and the man who had answered the front door entered.

"Mrs. Gertz!" The voice though not raised, carried great authority.

The cook lowered the skillet and her eyes.

"Mrs. Gertz," said the man. Although he had just said the same two words, each time they carried a totally new meaning. The first time his "Mrs. Gertz" was translated: "Woman! Put down that pan!" The second clearly meant: "What were you thinking? This sort of behavior is not acceptable." Chesney marveled at the depth of meaning that the man injected into proper nouns.

"Sorry, Mr. Towson," said Mrs. Gertz.

"I should think so," said Mr. Towson frostily. He punctuated his reprimand by pulling down on the lapels of his coat. He eyed the woman severely, and then as if by warning, delivered a frigid glance in Chesney's direction. His look served as a thorough indictment of Chesney's role in the incident.

"Mrs. Gertz," said Towson, "the gas company has called to say that their installation crew has been detained. They won't be here until tomorrow morning."

Mrs. Gertz's jaw dropped, and she waved her hand at Chesney.

"But, but 'e's the man from the gas company!"

Mr. Towson cocked a sharp eye towards Chesney.

"Me?" said Chesney. "I'm not from the gas company."

"You are!" asserted the cook, and then appealed to Mr. Towson. "'e told me 'e was 'ere to work!"

"Did he," said Mr. Towson. He took a determined step towards Chesney.

"But I am here to work," pleaded Chesney.

Towson took another step towards Chesney, this one even more menacing.

"I'm not from the gas company," said Chesney, "true enough! But I never said I was from the gas company. I'm here to work for Lord Bagnall."

"His Lordship," sniffed Towson, "is not expecting anyone today."

"He's expecting me," said Chesney, "at least, I thought he was. I'm... I'm Chesney Potoski."

This information failed to impress anyone, not even Chesney, who, though he believed himself, was starting to have his doubts.

"His Lordship does not entertain sales solicitations," said Towson, taking another step forward, presumably with the intention of tossing Chesney out the kitchen door.

"But I'm not a salesman. I'm the writer from Marlton Press... in New Jersey."

Mr. Towson, hands outstretched, poised to grab Chesney by the collar, stopped at this piece of news. "The representative of Marlton Press is expected from London on the Wednesday morning train."

"I got a lift," said Chesney, "with Mr. Gao... in his truck, uh, lorry..."

Towson lowered his fingers and scanned Chesney from head to toe. Without uttering a word, he cast the vilest aspersions on Chesney's coat and hat. The corners of the butler's mouth turned almost imperceptibly from a threatening scowl to a smirk of superiority.

"Mrs. Gertz," he said, addressing the cook, but still eyeing Chesney, "prepare tea for Mr. Potoski. Mr. Potoski, if you'll allow me to take your coat and, ahem, cap. I will inform His Lordship that you've arrived... prematurely.

– 29 –
The People Who Gain the World Selling Toilet Rolls

Chesney enjoyed a cup of tea courtesy of Mrs. Gertz and her electric kettle. Now that she no longer thought him a lunatic gasman, Mrs. Gertz returned to being the friendly soul Chesney had met on his arrival. As welcome as the tea was, Chesney was more interested in information on the housekeeper, Verity Goodhue.

After some very roundabout conversation about the estate, the staff in general, His Lordship, Mr. Towson, the grounds, the tea, Chesney subtly steered the topic back to Miss Goodhue.

"So, you all live here, in the manor house?" asked Chesney sipping his tea. "I mean the staff lives here, too? You're all live-in staff?"

"Oh, yes," said Mrs. Gertz, who was busy shucking peas. Her shucking was more out of habit since she had no way to actually cook them. "We're all of us here."

"One big happy family…"

Mrs. Gertz grimaced. "More or less."

"One big happy family," he repeated airily, pausing for a moment, not wanting to appear too anxious. "And Miss, uh, Miss Goodhue. She lives here, too… of course."

The cook didn't reply for several seconds. Chesney wondered if she hadn't heard. Perhaps he had been too casual. He started to open his mouth to restate the question when Mrs. Gertz shook her head.

"Oh, no, Miss Goodhue doesn't live here, not any longer…"

"Oh," said Chesney. Perhaps he had been wrong. Maybe she didn't work there. Maybe she used to work there. Doesn't live here any longer? Maybe she used to work there, and this was her last day. Perhaps she had been in the kitchen to say goodbye. Perhaps she was already out another door, driving away forever. He panicked inwardly. Still, he knew her name, and she must have left a forwarding address. Chesney was reviewing the options for his next move when, Mrs. Gertz, engrossed in her pea shucking, completed her sentence.

"...no, she lives in the cottage now..."

"Oh," he said as nonchalantly as he could, "is that the caretaker's cottage?"

"Yes, that's right, mind you..."

Mrs. Gertz started on some tangent that had something to do with the estate, but nothing directly with Verity Goodhue. Chesney nodded, while his mind wandered out the door, down the drive, and over the hill to the cottage that served as the cozy home for the lovely Miss Goodhue.

Verity Goodhue: Chesney's mind constructed anagrams: "Thieve Your Dog?" No, she wasn't a dog-napper. "You Drove Eight." Eight what? Eight horses? She wasn't "comin' 'round the mountain when she comes!" She could be driving an eight-cylinder car, but those were becoming as rare as teams of horses. Verity Goodhue: "Erode Tough Ivy." That was more fitting. He recalled the caretaker's cottage had some ivy around it. Yes, her beauty could erode the toughest ivy, it could make the clouds roll away, make the roses bloom...

Chesney's reverie on ivy-covered walls giving way to English roses was halted by the reappearance of Towson.

"His Lordship will see you now," he sniffed.

Chesney followed the butler through paneled halls and stately rooms, while still trying to construct a more fitting anagram to her name. "He'd Give You Rot?" "Huge Video Tory?" Best to leave rot and politics out of it, thought Chesney. "Her Devout Yogi?" No, he'd leave religion and baseball out of it as well.

Following Towson in this distracted state, Chesney soon found himself in the library. The room was two stories high, with floor to ceiling bookcases built into the wall. A wrought-iron walkway provided access to the upper level. This was reached by a spiral staircase. The shelves were filled with leather-bound volumes. The walls not occupied by books were paneled in dark walnut. On one side of the room, three large windows ran the full height of the room, with rich dark green draperies. A large oak desk was at the far end of the room in front of a large marble hearth. In the middle of the room was a massive table surround by enough chairs to hold a board meeting. The effect of it all on an ardent bibliophile was breathtaking. It was just the type of library Chesney imagined an English Lord would have.

"His Lordship," said Towson, "will be with you directly."

Before he could finish, Lord Bagnall entered from a side door at the far end of the room. If this was just the type of room in which to ensconce an English Lord, then the man who had just entered it looked every inch a Lord. He was tall, ramrod straight, with a strong jaw tilted proudly upward in a manner that deftly concealed the beginnings of a double chin. His head was narrow, his forehead high, and looked even higher due to his receding hairline. Still, he did not try to vainly disguise this trait, which others might see as a flaw. Rather his hair was neatly trimmed and carefully combed back. His aquiline nose suited his distinguished demeanor, as did the thin mustache beneath it. He stood for a moment, allowing the room to acclimate itself to his lordly presence before he looked directly at Chesney, and then at Towson.

"Your Lordship," officiated the butler, "Mr. Chesney Potoski of Marlton Press, New Jersey, USA. Mr. Potoski, Lord Bagnall of Staffordshire."

Lord Bagnall moved with military bearing towards Chesney, eyeing him carefully as he came. Chesney noted the cut of his clothes, meticulously tailored to his frame which only just revealed the beginning of a middle-aged paunch around the waist. Yes, thought Chesney, this was exactly how an English Lord looked; this was how he dressed; this was precisely how he lived.

Lord Bagnall stopped an arm's length from Chesney smiled in a condescending way as he looked down upon him, extended his hand, and spoke.

"Potoski? Wot sort of kind of name is Potoski? I h'ain't never not knowed no Potoskis before, 'ave I, Splatterguard?"

Chesney weakly shook his hand. After a moment, he realized that his mouth was hanging open. The estate, the library, the butler, the physical bearing of the man, all were blown to bits in his imagination more effectively than a ten-ton bomb could have done it, all by the uttering of a single sentence.

He continued, not at all scandalized by his own speech patterns. "I h'ain't not, 'ave I, Splatterguard, never not known no Potoskis, 'ave I?"

Towson tilted his head deferentially. "No, your Lordship, I believe not."

Lord Bagnall snorted in triumph. "No, never 'ave. Didn't think not."

Chesney recovered sufficiently from the shock of a torrent of double and triple negatives along with a plethora of "h's" dropped from where they belonged and others inserted where they had no business being, to answer the question.

"It's Polish," he said, but Lord Bagnall had moved on.

"First name sounded alright," he said, looking towards Towson. "What ya say it t'was, Splatterguard?"

"Chesney, your Lordship."

"Chesney, eh, Chesney?" His Lordship began marching up and down in front of his desk, repeating the name as if he were considering it for purchase. "Good name, British sounding..."

"Actually," said Chesney softly, "it's French. It means oak..."

"Yes, like that, solid, British name," said his Lordship, before catching the tail end of Chesney's utterance. "Wot? Oak, you say? Oak! Yes, good stuff oak, solid. Makes good furniture." He slapped his palm upon the desk. "Deal with wood, wood is me business, wood made me wot I am. Not oak, though. Can't not make no bathroom tissues from oak. Still, good stuff oak. Chesney, Chesney..." he turned again to look Chesney up and down. "Good name. British. But Potoski..." here he made a sour face as if he had just sucked an unripe greengage. "Ever think of changing that?"

"Change my name?"

"Yes, h'ain't not nothing to a name," said Bagnall. "Changed me name, actually 'er Majesty did that for me, but still, eh? She can't not be bothered to go around changing everyone's names. Wouldn't not hurt you none to change your name, not necessarily all the time, mind you..."

"You mean, Sir, I should change my name some of the time?"

"No, no, no, yes," said His Lordship, "sometime, like wot is for professional reasons, you know, for like on me book. 'By Lord Bagnall, as told to Chesney so and so. Suspect these 'ere author types do it all the time."

"And actors with stage names?"

"Yes, yes, yes, no! Well, yes, those types do that 'ere sort of thing, but you don't not want to be like them. Actors! No, no, you don't not want to be like one o' them types. Actors? Boo! Actors! Bunch of right 'nanas!" He jabbed Chesney's shoulder. "Still, something to think about, just a bit of friendly advice... from the chap wot you're working for."

"For whom you're working," muttered Chesney.

"Wot?"

"Nothing, Sir."

"Good, right, don't not have to do anything with it, just a suggestion, take it or leave it. Still, just could shorten it, yes, shorten it."

"You mean, like Chesney Toski?"

"Toski?" He made a face even sourer than the first.

"Or Potts?"

"Potts," Lord Bagnall's face brightened, "Splatterguard, whatcha think, eh? Potts! Didn't we know a Potts way back when?"

"A Corporal Potts, I believe it was," said the butler.

"Potts, yes! That's it, Corporal Potts." Here he paused for another disapproving tic. "Can't stand creepy crawly corporals, can I?"

"No, Sir," said the butler.

"You can go, now Splatterguard," said Bagnall. "We've got work 'ere."

"Very good, Your Lordship," said the butler backing out of the room.

After he had gone, Lord Bagnall invited Chesney to take a seat in front of the desk, while he planted himself behind it. Chesney noted a bronzed toilet roll mounted on a small pedestal, giving credence to Mr. Postlewaite's assertion that he was working for "Lord Bog Roll."

His Lordship jerked his head towards the door. "Splatterguard, top butler, first-class crawler..."

"Excuse me, Your Lordship," said Chesney, "may I ask a question?"

Bagnall's eyebrows shot up. "Certainly, that's wot you're 'ere for, h'ain't it? That's why I wanted someone from outside the country, so's they could ask questions. So they didn't not have no notions, not no prefabricated ideas. Start from scratch on me life. Ask away..."

"Your butler... Splatterguard?"

"Yes, good butler, good crawler, got to be a real good crawler to be a top-notch butler..."

"Yes, but you called him Splatterguard..."

"So?"

"Your cook, Mrs. Gertz, called him Mr. Towson."

"Yes, that's 'is name, but Towson... Towson..." Bagnall made another disagreeable face, "that h'ain't not no good butler's name. Splatterguard, that's got a flare, panache, style. See?"

He wondered if the other people he'd met there were using their proper given names. Mrs. Gertz? Verity Goodhue? He hoped Verity Goodhue was really Verity Goodhue. He realized he was daydreaming, and Lord Bagnall was still talking.

"...I hope you h'ain't that type," he said.

"What type would that be, Your Lordship?"

"One o' them young types that h'ain't not got no panache. You h'ain't, h'ar you?"

Chesney had never thought to check on his supply of panache, and even if he had, he wasn't sure if his definition of the term agreed with Lord Bagnall's. Instead, he just said he hoped he had the necessary skills for the task at hand.

"Youngsters today," Bagnall snorted. "Not like when I was young. We was older at that age, not in years, of course, but we was more, uh..."

"Mature?"

"Spot on," said Lord Bagnall with a snap of his fingers. "Too many of these younger people today they don't not know they've been born! When I was their ages," he continued not specifying any particular age, "I had already been demobbed..."

"Demobbed?"

"Discharged, from the h'army."

"Oh, yes, I see."

"And I was on my way to putting up me second factory." He grabbed the bronzed toilet roll on his desk and proudly waved it. "Last year, last year, Potski, I sold over 400 million of these little beauties..."

Chesney winced.

"Not bronze ones, of course! 400 million rolls! That's almost eight for every bottom in the UK! Or four per cheek!"

"Yes, sir," agreed Chesney.

"Proves what youth can do, 'cept young youth these days. They don't not know they've been born!"

Lord Bagnall went on to apply similar disparagements to the generations that had preceded him. By the end of the monolog, Chesney was left with the impression that humanity had only succeeded in a brief window of time corresponding with Bagnall's time on the earth. As he rambled on, Chesney's mind drifted to thoughts of Verity Goodhue. He wondered where she was at the moment. Perhaps just through the door, or walking by in the hallway, or above on an upper floor, or maybe she was in the garden, trimming the roses, of course. This daydream was interrupted as he realized that Lord Bagnall had ended his philosophical musings and was now back to more practical matters.

"...so if you needs something, you just h'ask," said His Lordship. "Splatterguard or any of the other staff will see you straight. 'Ere's a schedule of when I'll be available for interviews and such. The rest of the time, you can research, look through that pile..." He pointed to a stack of papers, clippings, and albums on the large table, "that'll give you a place to start. Just ask if you need anything, paper, pens, cups'a tea. You'll be staying close, I 'ope, 'least most of the time..."

"Yes, that's very kind, I would like to go to London, perhaps on weekends. I have an aunt who lives there."

"Aunt, eh?" Lord Bagnall nodded as if he were weighing the wisdom of having an aunt in London or anywhere. "Suppose that's all right. She a whatchacallit, too?"

"A Potoski? Yes, Sir."

"Mmm," he simply nodded, scrutinized Chesney for a moment, before slapping his palms on the desk. "Good, good, well, must go, got meetings, warn't not expecting you 'til tomorrow, still, glad you came 'ere, glad to 'ave you, an' all that. Look forward to digging into all this stuff, me life, all that..."

As he spoke, Lord Bagnall made his way to the door. He was halfway out when Chesney recalled his resolution to be more assertive.

"Just one more thing, Your Lordship, please?"

Lord Bagnall stopped, a slight shadow of concern crossing his brow as if he was not accustomed to being stopped once he'd set himself in motion.

"Yes? Wot?"

From that tone, Chesney had almost wished he hadn't stopped him. He almost wished that he was back in his cubicle in New Jersey flipping one page every two minutes. Then he recalled the reason for his interruption and continued with renewed boldness.

"Your housekeeper, Your Lordship..."

"Yes, wot about her?" His voice was ripe with suspicion. Chesney swallowed hard.

"Would you object..."

"Yessss?"

"Being as I'll be almost working here, that is," said Chesney, "that I'll practically be a member of your staff, for the time being, would you have any objection if I... if I asked your housekeeper out?"

"Out?" The look of suspicion was replaced by one of genuine puzzlement.

"Yes, to see... socially?"

A puzzled look crossed Lord Bagnall's face. Then he shrugged his shoulders.

"Objection?" He half chortled, half puffed. "h'ain't not no skin off my knees. Go right ahead; on your own time, of course!"

"Yes, my own time, naturally," beamed Chesney, "yes, thank you, Your Lordship."

Before Chesney could finish thanking him, the benevolent Lord Bagnall was well out of the room. This was ideal since Chesney immediately jumped up in the air in exhalation.

"Yes! Yes!" cried Chesney. While it wasn't technically necessary to have his permission, Lord Bagnall's blessing certainly couldn't do any harm. He punched his fist into the air and added one more exuberant, "Yes!"

"Mr. Potoski."

Chesney froze as an emotionless voice came from the doorway behind him. It was Towson, or Splatterguard, or whoever. Chesney turned slowly, feeling his cheeks redden as he did so. It was a basic fact of human nature that calm, stoic exteriors tend to make emotional outbursts seem foolish by comparison, no matter how justified they were.

"Uh, yes, uh..." Chesney was unsure what to call the butler, so he let any personal pronouns die upon his lips unspoken.

"Telephone, sir," said the butler.

"For me?"

"They did request 'Mr. Potoski,'" said the butler.

"Here?" said Chesney, though as soon as he spoke, he realized it was a silly question. Towson undoubtedly thought so, too, and gave Chesney a sharp censure with his eyes.

"Yes, sir," he said, pausing to further emphasize the obvious nature of the question. "You may take it in the kitchen."

Chesney nodded and slouched off after the butler. He actually didn't slouch, but in comparison to the stiff and proper Towson, he felt as if he were dragging along like a Neanderthal. His posture revived a bit knowing that he might run into Verity Goodhue on the way and didn't want to be seen skulking down the hall.

They reached the kitchen unobserved with Towson pausing only to pick up the phone's handset with two hands, as if he were cradling a bottle of fine wine, and placing it in Chesney's hand. Then he bowed obsequiously and seemed to fade away in that disconcerting way that butlers have of never letting you feel that you're safely rid of them.

Chesney waited a moment, to make sure the butler had indeed gone and then lifted that phone to his ear.

"Hello?"

"Chesney? Where have you been?"

"Aunt Elinor? I'm in Staffordshire."

"Of course you are! I didn't think you were on the other side of the county when I called, though."

Chesney began to explain the size of Bagnall Hall when his Aunt interrupted.

"Never mind all that," she said, "Postlewaite's remembered something, nothing as important as the girl's name..."

"I know it," he said in very guarded tones lest he be overheard.

"You do?"

"Yes," he lowered his voice even more, "she's here... she..." he lowered his voice further, "...works here..."

"Oh, well, how about that! Well, still, Postie's remembered something that might help anyway."

"Yes?"

"Yes, look, remember she was buying that memorabilia?"

"Yes, *Even a Twerp Needs Love.*"

"Yes, well, he remembered something else that I think you'd be very interested in."

"In which I'd be very interested," he corrected. "Sorry, please go on. I mean, continue..."

- 30 -
The Song of the Substitute Twerp

A musty smell permeated the hall courtesy of fifty-years' worth of old hymn books, some threadbare robes, and the aging scenery from several decades worth of church pageants. Added to this eclectic mix were some freshly-minted fish paste sandwiches and the bodies of nearly seventy-five ukulele enthusiasts.

Chesney Potoski had to experience it primarily by smell. He couldn't see much from behind the curtain on the stage of the church hall. He gripped the neck of a borrowed banjolele he peered through the small hole in the curtain. Through the room was crowded, he couldn't see the person promised by Mr. Postlewaite.

"All right then, lad?" a hand grasped Chesney's shoulder.

"I'm okay, Mr. Pilchard," said Chesney. "I'm just a little nervous."

"No need to be worried, lad," said the man. Though his hair was almost all gray, Chesney guessed that he was still younger than most in the gathered crowd. "We're a friendly bunch. Oh, and you don't want to be leaning too close to the surpluses." The man nodded towards the clothing rack. "Only the vicar just had those dry cleaned, and he gets quite shirty, especially if we muss the orpheys on his clean chasubles."

Chesney sidled away from the vestments.

"Yes, sir, I'm sorry..."

Mr. Pilchard waved away the apology. "Not to worry, stuff the chasubles! After all, like I said, we're a friendly bunch."

"Yes, sir," said Chesney. "Thank you again for accommodating me on such short notice. Thank you also for the loan of your uke."

"Not at' all," said the man. "After all, not many Yanks come through here; even less come to our meetings, and even fewer of them come to play."

"How many Americans have you had at your meetings?"

"None, actually," declared Mr. Pilchard. "Still, nothing to be nervous about. We're a convivial bunch. We're all here for fun and to enjoy ourselves no matter how bad anyone plays or how off-key they might sing."

Chesney smiled and swallowed hard. Mr. Pilchard excused himself, leaving Chesney to return to the hole in the curtain. There was still no sign of her.

Being well-connected with the nostalgia crowd, Mr. Postlewaite had suddenly remembered that there was a meeting of the Staffordshire branch of the Huge Goode Appreciation Society. That was the reason for Aunt Elinor's call. Postlewaite also recalled he learned of the meeting from the young lady Chesney now knew to be Verity Goodhue. It followed that if she were promoting the event, she would be attending it. Now, after tracking down the location for the meeting, being welcomed into the same, and even being asked to be a guest performer, he discovered much to his dismay that Miss Goodhue was nowhere to be seen. Perhaps Postlewaite was wrong, he thought. Or maybe something happened to her.

He sat down on a crate. He had imagined coming to the meeting and pretending to casually bump into her, impressing her with his extensive knowledge of Hugh Goode, and then clinching the deal with a performance on the ukulele. Each revelation, he anticipated, would be a greater surprise than the one preceding it. By the end, she would be so impressed that she would allow him to escort her back the half-mile to Bagnall Hall.

Now he'd just have to make a fool of himself in front of a bunch of genial strangers, impress no one, and find his way back alone. His miserable pondering was interrupted by the sound of applause, and the beginning of Mr. Pilchard's introduction.

As listened, he hoped the introduction was not for him.

"...and we have a very lovely guest with us here tonight," he heard Pilchard say through the curtain. "She's been with us before on many occasions, and we're always happy to see her. She can't stay long, but she wanted to stop by just the same and bring special greetings from her granddad."

Fresh applause broke out.

"As I said, she can't stay long but let's give a big Hugh Goode Appreciation Society welcome to the granddaughter of our very own Hugh... Miss Verity Goodhue."

Even more boisterous applause burst from the members in the church hall, and those with ukuleles began to strum. Chesney for his part couldn't clap nor plunk but only managed to fall backward on to the crate as if he'd been struck by a lorry load of banjolele picks.

Of course! How stupid could he be? Hugh Goode was only his stage name. His given name was Herbert Goodhue.

What a complete nincompoop he was! If previously he'd only been a partial nincompoop now his personal set of nincompoopery was complete.

Verity Goodhue! Not only the most captivating girl in the world, but also the granddaughter of his favorite musical artist of all time. By the time he stopped slapping himself on the forehead, Miss Goodhue was nearly done with her short talk on the other side of the curtain.

"...and grandfather was very appreciative of the many cards and remembrances you all sent him a few weeks back on the occasion of his 87th birthday. It means so much. He only wishes he felt well enough to join you here this evening, but he sends you his love and his warmest wishes to you all, and a deeply felt: 'that'll do yer good!'"

The crowd echoed back that last greeting, the catchphrase of their beloved Hugh. A fresh round of applause broke out. By the time it had begun to die down, Chesney had overcome his stupefaction, wobbled to the gap between the curtains and peeked out. The lovely Verity was making her way towards the exit at the back of the hall, stopping to exchange greetings with various members. His view was suddenly obstructed by the backside of Mr. Pilchard.

"Thank you again, Miss Goodhue," said Pilchard, "as always we appreciate your visits and know you'll send the greatest best wishes and appreciation to your grandfather, the great Hugh Goode from all of us here at the Goodhue, uh, great, the uh..."

"Hugh Goode Appreciation Society," shouted one member from near the front. This impromptu contribution resulted in a hearty laugh from the other members and several more crescendos from their ukuleles. At least, Chesney thought, the delay would allow Miss Goodhue to leave before he had to perform. He had looked forward to meeting her at the event, but now that had all changed. Now he wasn't just singing to a beautiful girl who shared his appreciation of Hugh Goode. Now he'd be singing to the granddaughter of the great man. No doubt Verity would have heard all the songs from the time she was an average little girl, sitting on her grandfather's famous knees. How could a...a...his mind groped for a low adjective...

"A Twerp!" he muttered aloud to himself behind the curtain. "She's got the real thing for her grandfather. How can a little twerp from New Jersey hope to impress her?"

By now, Mr. Pilchard had regained control of the meeting and was halfway through his introduction of Chesney, a mercifully brief description that ended with: "And so here's our Goode pal, from across the pond, which is where they usually keep the States, a Hugh Goode fan and a uke player like us..."

"Oh, not as bad as all that!" shouted one wag. Good-natured laughter followed.

"A uke fan and a Hugh Goode player..."

"You got it backwards!"

"Oh, 'eck! Just give a 'round of applause to Chesney..." There was a slight interruption as, through the curtain, Chesney could see Mr.

Pilchard searching his pockets, presumably for the card containing his last name. Finally, he gave up, pushed back the curtain, put his hand behind Chesney's shoulder, and pushed him out. "Uh, here he is, our Goode pal... Chesney."

The crowd applauded, and Chesney found himself in the middle of one small, but blinding spotlight. He raised his hand, partially to wave, and partially to shelter his eyes. Even so, it was difficult to see beyond the first row.

"What are you going to sing for us, lad?" asked Mr. Pilchard.

Chesney began to speak, but his throat had gone dry. He swallowed as hard as he could and found enough spittle to croak out the song title.

"Even... uh... Even a Twerp Needs Love."

"Even a Twerp Needs Love," repeated Mr. Pilchard in a voice much more audible. "A favorite of us all. So then, let's all listen to... all the way from America... Even a Twerp Needs Love."

Mr. Pilchard clapped. The audience followed suit and then grew quiet. Chesney squinted out, trying to see anything aside from the glare of the spotlight. Seeing anything was futile, as no doubt were his chances with Verity Goodhue. Chesney emitted a deep, heartsick sigh, and resolved to get it over with.

He looked down at the ukulele's fingerboard, located his first chord, closed his eyes, lowered his hand for the starting strum, and began to sing.

I've always been gormless chap,
An ordinary, formless sap,
A fellow without any sophistication,
Of no particular social designation.
My oysters never hold a pearl,
And I never ever win the girl.

I hate to complain, but it's not quite fair
In romance, even a dog will get his share
Even the wee slug finds a mate,
I'd like my chance before it's too late.
Like lonely fingers looking for a glove
You know that even a twerp needs love,

The song was one of Hugh Goode's more popular tunes and had been the hit of his 1938 film *In Love With Hugh*. Chesney chose it because he thought it might be a favorite of Verity Goodhue's. After all, she just purchased the sheet music from Mr. Postlewaite's shop. He imagined he would sing it, and her heart would melt.

Now, however, his fanciful hopes seemed but hollow dreams. In just a few minutes it had all come undone. Thankfully she had left. After living with the original, anything else would have been a flat imitation; quaint at best, ridiculous more likely. Fortunately, Chesney knew the song well enough not to have to think about the performance. His left hand ran automatically through the chord changes. His right hand kept up a rhythmic strum. And while his throat felt dry and constricted, his mouth managed to run through the lyrics by rote. Meanwhile, his mind dwelt on another missed opportunity with the girl of his dreams.

After what seemed like several hours, he finished the four-minute song and made a short bow. He thought he heard the audience clap, but their response was far from his mind. He felt himself shaking Mr. Pilchard's hand, and then he saw something that made his heart sink even lower. As his eyes readjusted to the light, there at the rear of the auditorium, standing in the doorway, he saw Verity Goodhue. He stood frozen for a moment. His legs were ready to spring into action, but his mind was unsure of which way to direct them. His bolder nature wanted to leap from the stage and rush towards her. His more craven side wanted to run away and hide. As with most decisions forestalled, the choice was taken from him. While he pondered, she left.

He was vaguely aware of Mr. Pilchard nudging him off the stage, and only slightly more cognizant of trudging up the side aisle towards the back of the hall. Some of the members shook his hand. Others patted his back as he staggered past them like an extra from *The Revenge of the Zombies*. It was only as he reached the doorway that his mind began to reanimate. There stood the man who just moments before had been speaking to Miss Goodhue.

The man shook his hand and was saying something.

"Pardon?" said Chesney his mind still fogged in.

"I said," repeated the man, "thanks for coming. We don't often get people even from London, let alone all the way from America."

"Yes," nodded Chesney. As far as he could tell, the man seemed impressed more at the distance he had traveled than his performance. It was understandable. Most people wouldn't cross the street to make total fools of themselves. He had crossed an ocean to do it. Just then he realized this was the man who had been talking with Verity. Hoping against hope, he decided to ask if she had said anything.

"...and Miss Goodhue?" said Chesney.

"Yes, she was here," said the man.

"Did she hear my... the song?"

He nodded in a way that confirmed the fact but gave no indication of her reaction. Perhaps the man was just trying to be kind, but at the moment Chesney didn't need kindness.

"Did she..." Chesney didn't quite know how to put it. "How did.. did she have any... reaction... to my... to the song?"

He again nodded. Again, Chesney couldn't interpret the gesture.

"And?"

"Oh, she said she was chuffed."

"…chuffed?"

"Yes, to be precise, she said she was 'dead chuffed,'" he said quite clinically, much as a doctor would give a terminal diagnosis to a condemned patient.

"Thank you," whispered Chesney. He then staggered out the door into the chilly night. The bracing air helped to clear his head enough to look in both directions. To the left was the way back to Bagnall Hall. To the right, and just up the road was the railway station. A train was just approaching pointing south. For a split second, he remembered Lord Bagnall and his long-term assignment and took a half step to the left. Then the words rang afresh in his mind: "chuffed… dead chuffed"

She was dead chuffed, completely mortified. How could she help but be chuffed at this doughy, little American coming all the way from New Jersey to do an embarrassingly poor imitation of her legendary grandfather? Though he had just heard the term for the first time, Chesney was feeling dead chuffed as well. It was a succinct, pithy term, he thought, encompassing all the nausea, embarrassment, and self-loathing he was feeling.

Chuffed! That settled it. Lord Bagnall or no Lord Bagnall, Chesney couldn't face any life peer or death peer, or any peer knowing that he had chuffed a lovely girl to death. He knew what he had to do. He darted towards the station, just making the last train for London as it pulled out of the station, and making good his retreat from the scene of his greatest disaster.

– 31 –
Fishing without Worms

Valerie Fierro sat in the cafeteria, ignoring food. Aside from skipping lunch to keep her perfect figure for her perfect prom dress, she was too preoccupied with important matters to think of anything as mundane as eating. Valerie's plan for the perfect prom experience was entering its final phase: being asked to the event by the boy of her choosing.

Valerie smirked as she pretended to read a dull textbook. She found it ironic that boys thought they invited girls to the prom. Technically they did, but in reality, boys had as much say in the matter as a fish did dancing on the end of the baited line. Left to their own devices, the average young male would swim through life as oblivious as a dumb fish. Like a fish, they had no concept of the real world, of the things that actually mattered in life such as designer fashions, parties, looking good, and marrying well. It didn't take that much skill to hook a boy. In most respects, it was easier than catching a fish. The difficulty lay in landing the right one.

She went fishing once with her father. It was totally smelly and revolting. What other activity could begin with touching a slimy worm and, if successful, end with handling an even slimier fish? Her sister, Rose, actually like going fishing with their father. That annoyed Valerie. Supposedly Rose liked sitting on the ground, getting grass stains on her clothes, and keeping quiet for hours on end. Rose said it was nice to just sit there and think. Rose said that she and their father could enjoy each other's company without either of them saying a word for an entire morning. Rose was full of crap, Valerie concluded.

The one time Valerie had gone fishing, her normally attentive father kept telling her to be quiet. He used the flimsy excuse that it would scare away some idiotic fish. Then he actually got upset when she screamed. She wasn't really afraid of that bug. It was more of a warning shout. Valerie couldn't help it if she had a perfectly modulated voice in a higher register. Then her father accused her of kicking the bug, which was sitting in his stupid tackle box. It turned out to be some fancy fishing lure. Well, that was enough of fishing for her lifetime. If fishing came with icky worms, slippery fish, and disgusting fake bugs, then Rose could have it. Valerie would go angling for different prey. And her catches wouldn't need to have the scales scraped off of them.

Valerie looked at the boys in the cafeteria. The majority of them would have to be cleaned and scraped before they would be fit for consumption.

Fish or men: the fact remained that neither had the sense to realize they were part of a sporting competition. Still, a girl had to be particular when it came to boys. A fish was just a fish. Any bait would work, and her father didn't seem very choosy about what he caught. Valerie looked down at her body. She was confident of her bait, but here's where the skill entered into it. She didn't want just any boy, especially not for her prom plans.

Just that moment, her fish entered the cafeteria: W. Buxton Dorning. W. Buxton Dorning: moving towards the stack of plastic trays. W. Buxton Dorning: hardly looking to the right or the left, as he waited in the serving line. She watched him while pretending to read. There was W. Buxton Dorning, doing what he could be expected to be doing at a quarter past twelve on a normal weekday afternoon: looking to feed. And here was Valerie watching him, careful to remain invisible to her prey. She wasn't making a sound. She was just trying to blend in with the surroundings. She didn't want to scare him away, not while he was feeding. Let him feed. After his belly was full, he would move on to the next most immediate need: spawning.

Oh, but he was a magnificent specimen, thought Valerie. He moved gracefully, or at least as gracefully as a boy could through a cafeteria serving line. He stood at least a head taller than the pimply sophomore in front of him and was positively statuesque compared to the fat greasy freshman behind him.

"W. Buxton Dorning," she muttered under her breath, as he purchased his meal, "you're mine."

As if drawn by the sheer strength of her will, W. Buxton Dorning began to move in Valerie's direction.

"Come on, come on," she thought, as she pretended not to notice him while never losing sight of him. "Come on, boy..."

◆

Valerie had been playing him for over a week. She had "just happened" to be there when he had lunch, always in the same place, always at the same time. W. Buxton Dorning was more regular than the sun. The sun changed its rising and setting each day – not W. Buxton Dorning. He was more reliable than the atomic clock over in England that they'd learned about in science class. If he wasn't so cute, and such a good prospect, Valerie would have said he was in a rut. Since he had such nice teeth and came from a good family, he was merely reliable.

She worked herself into his lunchtime routine over several days. She wanted W. Buxton Dorning to come to expect her to be there. She wanted to become a regular fixture in his world without him realizing it.

Lunchtime, cafeteria, tray, food, drink, cash register, table, chair, salt, pepper, napkin... Valerie. That was how she wanted him to expect life on any given weekday between twelve and twelve-thirty.

Once Valerie learned his routine, she placed herself in the middle of it. That first day W. Buxton Dorning stopped short at his usual lunch table. There, in his seat, his regular spot, was a girl.

"Uh, um..." W. Buxton Dorning stood there, unsure of what to do. He looked around, trying to reorient himself to otherwise familiar surroundings. Valerie sat motionless, pretending to read a book, but in reality, not missing a twitch of his movements.

"I..." he looked around again, but could only come to one conclusion: this girl was sitting in his seat. "Um, are you sitting there?"

Valerie glanced up at him, at first seeming to look through him, and then looked back down at her book. Then, she looked up at him again; this time as if he were an actual human being. Her eyes met his, and she held his gaze for several seconds before flashing her most alluring smile.

"Oh," she said, raising her voice half an octave for effect, "am I sitting in your seat?"

Of course, she was. He knew it, and she knew it. And she knew that he knew it. But he didn't know that she knew it. Besides, it was a silly question. It was his seat, and at the same time, it wasn't. No one had an assigned seat in the cafeteria, though in practice most of the students did. Still, he couldn't assert his claim to the molded plastic chair. A guy could have said to another guy, "Hey, get outta my chair." But a guy demanding the same rights from a young woman, especially an attractive one? It wasn't done.

"My seat?" he said, glancing around, "uh, no, it's not..."

"Would you like to sit down?" she said, with another flash of teeth. She sat there, the smile frozen on her face. This was a critical moment, one that could well determine everything. Would he return the smile and sit down? The bait was presented, and for a moment, the poor fish is contemplating his next move. Will he see through the game? Will he sniff at the worm, and swim away?

Valerie wondered: did the fish see the line? Did boys see what was behind the pretty smile and the batting eyelashes? Did they realize where all the perfume and the enticements led? No, there was something seminal in both fish and boys that made all the enticements irresistible and all the dangers invisible. It was how nature must have intended it, or else there would never be any bridal magazines or tuna sandwiches.

Nature took its course. W. Buxton Dorning returned her smile and sat down. Though he didn't have a clue to the significance of what had just happened, nor did he recognize his own footprint on the first step down a dangerous path, but Valerie did. She nodded. He wasn't sitting in his seat anymore. He had ceded that to her. A small gesture, granted, and one that W. Buxton Dorning would chalk up to chivalry, but to Valerie, it said the contest had begun, and she was in the lead.

Starting with a seemingly innocent conversation, Valerie reeled him in, and then, so as not to tip him off to the contest, she would ease off. This process played out over the space of a week of lunches. By the end of which time she had become a part of his noonday routine. He came to expect her there and seemed glad to find her waiting there in his former seat. He didn't seem to notice that Valerie never ate in front of him. This too was part of the plan. Nobody looked good while chewing. Besides, it made him think that his company was sustenance enough for her. On about the fourth day, he offered her a chocolate chip cookie. She took it, but then laid it aside after a cursory nibble.

She would let him do most of the talking, of course. This built up his ego, bolstered his confidence, and made him think that she was genuinely interested in his activities. Valerie marveled how a boy became dependent on a girl while thinking she relied on him. She proved this by deliberately breaking the routine once she had established it.

After joining W. Buxton Dorning for seven consecutive lunch periods, Valerie stayed away.

It was quite satisfying as she watched from a secluded vantage point outside the cafeteria. There was poor Bucky, as she had begun calling him, striding through the serving line, proudly holding up his tray, making his way beyond the cash registers, as if he hadn't a care. That patina of self-assurance, however, was barely a smear on his young psyche, for as he approached his regular table, he came up short. She wasn't there. Disoriented, W. Buxton Dorning looked around him as if the world had tilted off its axis. In less than two weeks, without realizing it, Valerie Fierro had become the center pillar, the load-bearing wall of his lunchtime. Now without her, his eyes betrayed a lost glaze. From her place of concealment, Valerie smiled as he looked about him trying to orient himself in a strange new universe, a Fierro-Free zone, a world without her.

Poor helpless Bucky, she thought, he was nearly ready. Tomorrow, or perhaps the next day, she would be back in the spot where he had grown accustomed to finding her. She wondered if he would bring up her absence. If he did, she would pretend that she hadn't realized that she hadn't been there. The poor sturgeon, the simple little carp; he would use her reappearance as the motivation for asking her out formally. From there it was only a few dates until the subject of the prom was bound to come up.

Valerie was nothing if not kind. Bucky had suffered enough the day before, stumbling around with his tray like a rudderless ship cast adrift in an archipelago of Formica-topped islands. She would only deprive him of her presence the one day.

◆

Now, as she sat, pretending to be engrossed in a book, Valerie mentally coaxed W. Buxton Dorning towards their table.

"Come on, just a little closer boy," she thought, rooting on his progress, "don't rush. No need to trip." After her absence yesterday, he would hurry to her side.

As she saw him walk closer out of the corner of her eye, Valerie put her head further down. Any second she would hear his voice. Bucky always said the same thing. It was their personal joke. Once they started dating, it would be their own cute little pet phrase, the type that would cause them to chuckle and smile when no one else understood.

"Are you sitting there?"

Valerie started to look up where she expected Bucky Dorning to be standing but immediately realized that instead of his pleasant baritone, spoken in his self-conscious delivery, another voice had uttered the line. It belonged to a tenor and was slippery, smooth, and altogether confident in itself. She turned her head to the right to find the speaker almost in her face. He had sat down next to her and was using the back of her chair for an armrest.

"Can I join you," he said with that serpentine smile and those little piggy eyes. It was a rhetorical question since he was already seated. He hadn't waited for permission, and obviously didn't care.

Valerie sat; her mouth agape. She turned back in the direction of W. Buxton Dorning. Seeing another boy with his arm around Valerie, Bucky had turned and was walking away. Enraged, she turned back to the still smiling face beside her.

"What do you want... Albrecht Eckner?"

– 32 –
The Alizarin Crimson Gastropod and the "So Do I" Factor

Valerie Fierro had heard the expression "seeing red." She knew it meant being very angry. But as she glowered at the flabby face of Albrecht Eckner, she realized the phrase was wrong. To a person familiar only with primary colors, "seeing red" may have sufficed, but to one well-versed in fashion "red" was hardly enough. Valerie traded in "cerise," "burgundy," "carmine," "flame," "magenta," "raspberry," "vermillion," "wine," and a dozen other neighboring shades. "Seeing red" must have been coined by some colorblind individual. More accurately, anger should be called "seeing alizarin crimson," cooler than mere red with a definite leaning towards the purple. Still, she hadn't the time to reflect on this distinction. Right now, she was too freakin' angry.

She seethed while Eckner looked at her placidly. The fact that she could have spit carpet tacks only made his peaceful expression more maddening.

"I only asked," he said, "if I could sit down."

Valerie bit the inside of her lip. She wanted to scream like a banshee and knead Albrecht's doughy head into a breadstick. The fact that W. Buxton Dorning was near kept her from acting on that desire. Instead, she sucked a strong draught of air up her nostrils and replied through pursed lips.

"I... didn't... say... you... could. Did... I?"

The corners of his mouth turned up slightly as if recalling an amusing anecdote.

"It was a rhetorical question," he said.

"Rhetorical..." Alizarin crimson deepened into Tuscan Vermillion.

"That means..."

"I know what it means..." She raised her arched fingers halfway to his throat.

"Oh, right, we were in the same English class last year, weren't we?" He paused a moment before adding: "That's another rhetorical question. We were."

Valerie closed her eyes and shook her head as if doing so would reset her vision. With her eyes still shut, she asked as calmly as possible: "What do you want, Albrecht?"

"How did that rubber cement work out?"

Rubber cement? Somewhere in her mind, it struck a chord of recognition, but as with most things in her life, such as last year's clothing styles or last week's school lessons, if she had no immediate use for it, she discarded it from her memory.

"The rubber cement," he said, "that I loaned you? About a month ago? You were going to use paste for a little... project?"

A light tripped on in her mind. She had used rubber cement to glue the picture of the perfect dress into the teen magazine. Yes, that was right, he had loaned it to her... EWWW! She had remembered too much. Her mind raced back into that icky yucky store with all the surgical corsets and wheelchairs and potty seats... EWWWW! No wonder she had blocked it all out.

"You do remember, don't you?" Albrecht pasted a knowing grin atop his usual smirk.

"Oh, yes, of course," she fumbled. "I mean, yes, the rubber cement, my... project... the school project I was working on, yes that was a big help."

She looked at him and smiled. He smiled back. He knew too much, she thought. He knew it all. He saw her buy the *Cosmo* and the *Tiger Beat*. With those basic bits of information, anyone could figure out what she was up to, especially a sneaky creep like Albrecht. She had to be nice to him.

"So," she said airily, "so, what's new, uh, Albrecht?"

He continued to smile in that irritating way he had. That look made her feel that he was not merely reading her thoughts but compiling a complete catalog of her mind.

"Going to the prom?" he asked.

He knew her whole plan, she thought. How she detested this little worm!

"Uh, yes, sure, of course," she began, but then stopped herself short. While she had no qualms about lying to some little nonentity, she realized that lying to Albrecht was not only futile but potentially dangerous in a way she didn't fully comprehend. "That is, I mean, yes, I plan on going to the prom. I'm sure, I'm going to be asked..."

Valerie fought the urge to look off in the direction of Bucky Dorning who had sat at another table. She caught herself in time, or at least she didn't turn her head. Her eye movement must have given her away, however, as Albrecht's eyes darted that way. He looked back at her, with an even more knowing look in his eyes. They sat silently for a moment.

"I'll be going to the prom," he said as if he were introducing an entirely new subject.

"You?" Valerie said.

Albrecht was a junior, like her. The only way he could go to the Senior Prom was if a senior girl asked him. There were plenty of desperate girls in the senior class, but none so hard up that they'd ask a pathetic specimen like Albrecht Eckner.

"I'm the photo editor of the yearbook," he said.

"Oh, right, that is, I thought maybe you were going with one of the senior girls."

"No," he reiterated, "I'm taking photos. But even though I'm technically working, I can bring a date."

His steady gaze met her eyes. A date? Was this spotty amphibian suggesting that he would be allowed to take her to the prom, and as an actual date? Valerie's lips began to curl back. She was about to unloading her full vitriol on this adolescent gastropod, but something stopped her. He knew too much to be verbally shredded in public, no matter how much he deserved it.

"A date?" she spat, and then caught herself. "A date," she repeated, but more kindly. "How nice, who are you taking?"

"My first choice," he said with a straight face, "is you."

Valerie was grateful that she hadn't eaten lunch. If she had Albrecht Eckner would have been wiping regurgitated canned ravioli from his personage.

"Me?" Again she had to repeat herself but with less contempt. "Me, oh how...sweet." "Sweet" being her last-minute replacement for: "repulsive." She reached out and touched his forearm. This also was the alternative to smacking him upside his fat head. Valerie now felt she had the upper hand, or at least was on an equal footing with Eckner. He wanted something from her, and now she had the singular pleasure of rejecting him. She would enjoy this. She felt her lips broaden into a satisfied smile, but before she could fully enjoy it...

"But, you're going with someone else," said Albrecht.

"Uh..."

"You're not going with someone else?"

"No, I am, that is, uh..." Her advantage was slipping away.

Albrecht shook his head. "It isn't fair, Valerie."

"Fair?"

"No, it's not fair to this other guy," said Albrecht.

"Huh?"

"He's obviously a senior," continued Eckner. "He's waited four years for his Senior Prom. What's he going to do if you leave him high and dry at the last minute?"

"High and..."

"I wouldn't dream of doing that to such a nice guy," said Albrecht.

"Nice...how..." Valerie caught herself. Albrecht couldn't read minds. Could he?

Albrecht nodded, winked, and jerked his head across the cafeteria.

"Oh," she said, "is it that obvious?"

Albrecht smiled his porcine grin. "Not obvious to the casual observer, but..." He wrinkled his nose slightly, causing her to shift uncomfortably in her seat. "He's a good guy."

"I didn't know you knew Bucky," she said, "I mean, Buxton."

A barely perceptible chortle passed his lips, leaving Valerie to wonder if Albrecht had known, or if she'd just been tricked. Now it was Albrecht Eckner giving Valerie's arm a reassuring pat.

"Buxton Dorning's a nice fellow," he said.

His odd choice of the word "fellow" made Valerie wonder what was wrong with Bucky. No one of their age called anyone a "fellow."

"You go to the prom with him," said Albrecht, as if somehow she needed his blessing. "After all, there's always next year."

"Next year?"

Albrecht Eckner raised his eyebrows and swayed his head slightly as if to indicate that next year would be their Senior Prom.

A fresh shade of red was rising in her eyes.

"I can help," said Albrecht.

"Listen, you little... help?"

"With Buxton."

"With Bucky?"

"That's who you want to go to the prom with, isn't it?"

"Yes, but..."

He nodded as if was a done deal. "Okay, then."

Rubber cement was bad enough. If she were indebted to Albrecht Eckner for her prom date, well, that was almost as bad as going with him. Besides, Buxton Dorning wasn't some stumbling nitwit. He was capable of asking her to the prom. She began to shake her head, "no."

He leaned towards her. "Don't worry, I'm not going to say anything to him," said Albrecht confidentially. "What do you think I am, some sort of clod? I can give you some tips."

"Tips?"

Albrecht rolled his eyes as if he were dealing with a slow child.

"Look, I'm sure you're doing fine with Buxton, but everyone can use some help. I know things that will give you a little boost, speed it all up a little bit. Nothing against you, Valerie, and I'm sure what I'm going to tell you is nothing that you couldn't find out on your own, eventually. But you're working on a deadline. The prom will be here before you know it. I can let you know about Bucky's likes and dislikes, things that you can bone up on so when he brings them up you'll know about them, and you can talk to him about them intelligently. You know, the 'so do I' factor."

"The what?"

He gave her a patronizing look. "When he tells you how much he likes knitting dolly clothes from belly button lint..."

"He doesn't!"

"Of course not," said Albrecht, "at least not as far as I know. But when he tells you whatever he's interested in, instead of being surprised by it, you can say: 'you like that? So do I!' That's the 'So do I' factor."

Valerie thought about it for a moment. She looked sideways at Albrecht Eckner and wondered if he was a secret lint-knitter. Still, bizarre hobbies aside, it would be very helpful to know a few details about Bucky, wouldn't it? She tilted her head as if to see Albrecht from a fresh perspective. He was a strange little creature, but what harm could there be accepting his help? After all, he said it himself: there was nothing he could tell her about Buxton Dorning that she wouldn't find out on her own eventually. Albrecht would just be helping nature along, almost like cupid. She tilted her head the other way and for a moment imagined his pasty body with tiny wings on his back. Ewww!

Time was moving on, too. She did know a few couples who had already nailed down their dates for the prom. And tickets were going to go on sale in two weeks. It would be a crime if she had to wear her perfect dress with a less than perfect boy, or... a horrible thought darkened her mind. Or if she didn't go to the prom at all! Not going to the Senior Prom when she was a junior would be devastating. It would cripple her for life. Instead of embarking on her full womanhood, she might as well buy a thick pair of glasses, some orthopedic shoes, a pack of granny panties and admit her life was over at sixteen-and-a-half.

"The 'so do I' factor, eh?" said Valerie, her eye slits narrowing to approximate those of Albrecht's.

He nodded.

"Okay," she asked, leaning forward, "what do you know?"

Albrecht's eyes darted to the right and the left, making sure they weren't overheard. "Animals."

"Animals?"

"Do you like animals?"

Valerie thought of Reggie, the family Collie.

"I love animals."

"That's good."

"It is?"

Albrecht nodded "yes," and then in the general direction of W. Buxton Dorning. "Very animal-friendly, animal welfare; all that sort of thing. His whole family is that way."

Valerie nodded. That would make sense. He came from a classy family, and those types were all into charity and junk like that.

"I didn't know," she said.

"You wouldn't," said Albrecht raising his index finger to his lips, "they don't like to make a big deal out of it."

Valerie nodded again.

"So don't bring it up," cautioned Albrecht, "well, not in so many words."

Valerie's brows knitted. "How many words do I use to bring it up?"

"Don't say you're active in animal rights or animal charities..."

"I'm not," she confessed.

"Right, his family has got that market cornered. He'd know right away that you were just feeding him a line."

"But I am very concerned about animals," again she thought about Reggie. "I love animals. I really love animals a lot!"

Albrecht nodded. "That's exactly the approach you take," he said.

"I love animals."

"You're crazy about them," agreed Albrecht. "Just keep that in the back of your mind, and anytime you even get near the subject of animals..."

"...I'm passionate about animals!"

He patted her hand and winked. "Perfect. It's the perfect starting point. Then he can tell you all about what he and his family are into and invite you into it. That way he's the real expert and you're the novice he can instruct. Guys like that. They like to feel that they're the ones leading things."

"I have a Collie," said Valerie.

He smiled in an odd way. "Oh, really?"

"Yes, I even taught him to dance," said Valerie. "He put his paws up on my shoulders, and we dance."

"Perfect," said Albrecht, "just remember, don't press it. Those types of people don't like to flaunt their charitable work. If you just let him know how much you like animals..."

"I'm passionate," offered Valerie.

"That's the word: passionate. That's perfect! Let him know that, even if he doesn't seem to respond..."

"...because he'll know that I'm passionate about animals, but he doesn't know that I know that he's passionate about them."

"Right!"

Valerie leaned back. It was all coming together perfectly, passionately.

– 33 –
To Sleep, Perchance to Scream

Valerie dreamt. She dreamt of the perfect dress. She dreamt of the prom. She dreamt of W. Buxton Dorning who would ask her to the prom. She dreamt of the perfect corsage, the perfect limousine, and the other perfect and crucial ingredients that she would tell Bucky to give her. And after all those perfect things, she dreamt of the perfect culmination to that perfect event: when Bucky would drive her away to a perfect little spot, somewhere down at the shore, where, as the first hints of the perfect sunrise kissed the eastern sky she would give him the perfect gift as a reward. And she would emerge the perfect woman.

They were such delicious dreams, so scrumptious and perfect. They were Valerie's dreams and hers alone. For now, the real world was barred from intruding on her dreams. Valerie was oblivious to any other dreams, even those playing out just down the hallway.

Her mother was well-aware of those other dreams. She had no choice. She had to share a bed with the dreamer of those dreams.

"Giorgio, Giorgio," rasped Connie Fierro as she shouted and whispered simultaneously. "Giorgio! Wake up!" She gave him a sharp poke in the ribs.

"I can do it! I can do it!" muttered Giorgio Fierro.

"Giorgio, you're doing it again," she said, jostling his shoulder.

"I can do it!"

"Giorgio..."

He fell silent. Connie held her breath for a moment.

"Giorgio?"

A pause, made longer by the darkness, was followed by a deep exhale.

"Again? Another one?" asked Connie, though she knew the answer.

"Another," said her husband.

A soft rap was heard at their bedroom door.

"Mom? Dad?"

"Everything's all right, Rose," said her mother, "go back to bed."

"Only, I heard…"

"Everything's okay, Rosie," said Giorgio sitting up. "Go back to sleep, sweetheart."

"Okay, if you're sure you're okay, goodnight."

They exchanged soft goodnights and listened until they heard Rose's door shut. Husband and wife sat silently for a moment in the dark.

"Giorgio…" she started.

"It's nothing," he said, though the tone of his voice contradicted him.

"Nothing? It's not nothing," she said, trying to keep her voice down which made her tone all the more strident. "It's the fourth time in the last week. You know the reason."

He knew what it was, but he also knew she would tell him.

"You're working too hard," she said.

"It's not that."

"You're working too hard, and for what?"

He knew for what. He'd been reminded of it for weeks. His wife was obsessed with Valerie's dress. It was just a little overtime; that was all. But anything that went wrong she blamed on that dress. If he was late coming home: it was the dress's fault. If the sink was clogged, it was because Giorgio hadn't been home to unplug it because of the dress. He expected her to start blaming natural disasters and international crises on Valerie's poor little dress. They didn't argue about it, they didn't even dare mention it, and for that reason alone the specter of the dress loomed ever larger.

Despite his wife's theories on the subject, Valerie's dress was not the cause of his night terrors; not directly at least.

"I worry about you," she said as she gently rubbed his shoulders.

"I'm okay," he said, patting her hand.

"You can't put in these long hours."

"It won't be for much longer. The work is there, I'll do it. It won't be for much longer."

They fell silent once more until Connie broke it.

"You said, 'I can do it.' In your sleep, you were saying you could do it."

He nodded.

"You're working too hard…"

"It wasn't about work," he said. Connie didn't say anything, but he had been married long enough to hear her unspoken question. He sighed. "It was about when I was a boy."

"The war?" she asked.

"Si, I mean, yes…the war…"

She kissed the side of his head.

"Maybe you should see someone about it," she suggested.

"Like who? Mussolini?"

"You know what I mean," she said, "get professional help."

Giorgio shook his head and scooted back down in the bed.

"It's over, it's done," he said, "I'll be all right."

She sighed and lay back down. He knew by the sigh and the way she turned over that she was arguing with him in her mind. She was a good woman, he thought, especially the way she restricted her nagging to certain hours.

He rolled over with his back to her and began breathing heavily to imitate sleep, but he didn't sleep. As tired as he was, sleep offered little rest.

It was the war, but not the Second World War. It was the other war that began in the middle of that conflict and continued long beyond it.

It couldn't have been him, thought Giorgio. He had been telling himself that for weeks without fully convincing himself.

He'd have to be a hundred and twenty, he thought. In actuality, he didn't know how old he was back then. From a child's perspective, every adult seems ancient. But he looked old back then, even when compared to other adults. He had to be nearly seventy back then, didn't he? Or at least in his sixties. And that was almost forty years ago. That would make him the oldest living person in the world, the most ancient living bastard. The devil takes care of his own thought Giorgio, but even the devil's own become decrepit and die in time, don't they?

Admittedly, Giorgio reasoned, he was standing on a rooftop. Still, the hot tar fumes could have blurred his view. It was a chilly afternoon, and the fresh hot tar created a shimmer of heat. It could have been like a mirage. Yes, like in the desert or on a long straight road on a hot day. But when he saw him, Giorgio walked to the edge of the roof. He put his foot upon the parapet and leaned over for a good hard look.

The man was older. He was fatter. He was already the oldest, fattest man he'd ever seen, and that was so many years ago. But, he reasoned, what would he expect him to do in those intervening years? Grow younger? Slim down? No, he would have gotten older and fatter. It was him.

In Delaware? Old fat Germans don't uproot themselves and wander off to Delaware. If they did Delaware wouldn't be known as the First State, or the Blue Hen State; it would be the Fat Old German Bastard State. The state's tourism industry wouldn't stand for that as a slogan.

But it looked so much like him; the same ruddy cheeks, the same cherry tomato nose, the same handlebar mustache, admittedly whiter now. He had heard that everyone has a double. He was so fat, however, that it was more like a quadruple. This man, the one walking down the street dressed much the same. The man's waddling gate reminded Giorgio of the way he shifted the refrigerator across the floor when his wife wanted to clean behind it.

No, it couldn't be him. That settled, Giorgio rolled over in bed.

But if it wasn't him, he thought, rolling over again a minute later, if it wasn't him why was he tortured with those nightmares.

It was Purzelbaum. Who else could it be? God was not so vengeful to inflict two of them on the Earth in Giorgio's lifetime. There was only one Purzelbaum, and somehow he had made his way to Delaware. Why not? Giorgio had wound up there. Perhaps Purzelbaum was looking for him? But why? Did he want to reunite his acrobatic troupe?

Giorgio opened his eyes. In the dead of night, everything looked menacing. Even that shadow on the wall looked like that fat old man

◆

"Fierro, you will do it, no?"

It wasn't a question. It was a command.

"I will try, Herr Purzelbaum."

Giorgio looked up. Purzelbaum must have been ten feet tall.

"No trying!" Purzelbaum snapped the pony whip. He never actually hit one of the boys. Giorgio would have preferred if he did, at least once, just to see if it would hurt as badly as he feared it would. If he were hit, just the once, much of the fear of the pony whip would go away. That was why Purzelbaum would never actually hit him. The fear was a more potent weapon than the actual whip.

The whip cracked again.

"We do not try," asserted Purzelbaum, "we do, or we fail. What do we do, Fierro?"

"Do or fail, Herr Purzelbaum," said Giorgio, "only I am smaller than the other boys…"

"The other boys can do this trick…"

"But they are better…"

The whip snapped once more and Giorgio gave a start.

"You will do it, Fierro. You will do it!"

"I can, I-I can do it. I can do it."

Giorgio put his small head down, and with a running start leaped into the air. One…two…but instead of a third flip, his little body submitted to the law of gravity. He fell to the ground with a thud, his face down in the dirt and sawdust. He would have been content to lie there, but he felt a presence overshadow him. He raised his head just enough to see the heavy boots, one of them tapping impatiently.

He looked up to see the disapproving expression. He heard Purzelbaum snort: "*Einfalt!*"

"I can do it," cried Giorgio. "I can."

– 34 –
Definitions in the Dead of Night

It was half past one in the morning when Chesney Potoski stubbed his toe on the threshold of the railcar and stumbled back into London. His bruised toe had nothing on his wounded heart. It was devastating enough that he had made a fool of himself singing a Hugh Goode song to Hugh Goode's granddaughter. But to make things even worse before Miss Goodhue left, she had shared her great displeasure with one of the other attendees. Under the circumstances what else could Chesney do but rush back to Aunt Elinor for consolation? Beloved aunts are created for such disasters. Disasters and Aunt El, unlike British Rail, clung to no timetable. His aunt would be at his disposal, even in the dead of night.

Just as there are last trains to London, that city's Underground and bus service also shuts down in the wee hours of the morning. Thus, Chesney had to find his way from Euston Station to his aunt's flat without so much as a *London A to Z* to guide him. What would have been a thirty-minute walk, had he known where he was going, turned into a ninety-minute meander.

When he arrived, he knocked on Aunt Elinor's door, and only then glanced at his watch. It was now past three. He knocked again, and then again, and only then wondered if Aunt Elinor would be angry with him. Still, it was too late. He could hear someone on the other side of the door undoing latches and throwing bolts.

"Chesney!" said Aunt Elinor. Even through sleepy eyes, she knew her nephew anywhere.

"Aunt El," mewed Chesney, who was also spot-on at relative identification.

"It's Three O'clock in the morning," she said.

He re-checked his watch. "Actually, twelve past, now," he noted pedantically, before moaning: "Oh, Aunt El, it's all ruined. I've made a total mess!"

She looked around on the landing outside her door. "Well, don't make a mess out there." She pulled him inside and steered him into one of the easy chairs in her parlor.

"Now," she said, "suppose you tell me what's messed up. Where's your luggage."

"I left it with you," he said, looking around.

"Just like your mother," she muttered, "takes everything literally. All right, have it your way, let me rephrase the question. Where is my satchel? The one I loaned you when you went off to Lord Bogie Man…"

"Bagnall…"

"My satchel?"

"I suppose it's still up at Bagnall Hall," he said as he pondered the question. "At least, that's where I last saw it. Yes, I'm almost certain it would still be up at Bagnall Hall."

She smiled. "I see, well, that's the major issue settled. Just one minor point remains. Why aren't you up there with the blessed thing?"

He stared at her for a moment and then burst into tears as he tried to explain what had happened. Within several minutes she had gained a fairly clear, if soggy, sense of the situation.

"So you don't think this Miss Goodhue appreciated your singing?" she asked.

"Either that or my ukulele playing, or both."

"And she left right after you finished?"

"As if she were running the 100-yard dash."

"Hmmm, not easy to do in dress shoes," agreed Aunt Elinor. "I know, I've had to beat several hasty retreats in my time. Until a young lady settles down, she'd be well-advised to forget the dictates of fashion and wear nothing but plimsolls."

"Plimsolls?"

"Sneakers to you," explained Aunt El. "Until she's finished with romance a girl often finds that she's got to run at a moment's notice. Heels only get in the way."

Chesney smirked. "Well, they didn't seem to get in Verity Goodhue's way. She looked like she could have been in the Olympics. She would have won a medal, too."

"Watch out for fast women, Chesney," she cautioned. "But let's look at the facts. You sang, she ran, but it could be just a coincidence. Maybe she had to catch a train."

"I caught the last train, and she wasn't on it."

"I'm just trying to say that the young lady might have had somewhere else she had to go. Perhaps she had stayed later than she had intended because she was listening to you. Perhaps she enjoyed your little show. Did that ever occur to you before you jumped to conclusions, hopped on trains, and burst through my front door?"

"As a matter of fact," he said, "yes, I thought about those things all the way to London. I kept trying to convince myself of those possibilities."

"And?"

"It's all a load of baloney, a lorry full if you prefer."

"Why?"

"Because the man at the door told me what she thought of it."

Aunt Elinor leaned forward. "And what did she think of it?"

Chesney emitted a deep sigh, hung his head in shame: "He said that the phrase she used was 'dead chuffed.'"

"Dead chuffed? This girl said she was dead chuffed?"

Chesney nodded, still looking at his feet.

"Those were her exact words?" asked Aunt Elinor.

"That's what he said that she said. Why? Do you think he was lying?"

"I certainly hope not!"

Chesney looked up at her in puzzlement.

"Chesney," she said, her face beaming, "Chesney, my love. You're in!"

"In what? Aunt El, what's going on?"

"You've got it made! This is your lucky day, and you don't even know it. Chesney, my dear dope, what do you think 'dead chuffed' means?"

He shrugged his shoulders. "From the context, I figured that chuffed meant 'irritated,' you know, like 'chafed." Adding 'dead' to it only made it worse."

"You've got the wrong end of the stick. Chuffed means 'pleased.' Adding 'dead' to it only means the girl was extremely pleased. This Verity Goodhue is tickled pink with you. She's enchanted, pleased as punch, ecstatic, over the moon. Can I put it any other way?"

Chesney stared at his Aunt, trying to absorb what she was telling him. She kept smiling and nodding as if she were encouraging him to not only buy what she was selling him but to throw away the receipt.

"You mean," he finally said, "she probably... likes me?"

Aunt Elinor grabbed his head and kissed him hard on the forehead. "Absolutely!"

"Really?" He was trying to adjust to this ascent into happiness. It was like a diver coming up from the ocean depths. He was afraid if he rose too quickly to her level of joy, he'd get a case of the bends in his head.

"Really, Chesney," Aunt El assured him. "The girl obviously loves her grandfather very much, and here comes this nice young man from halfway around the world, and how does she know he's a nice young man? Because she's already mistaken him for the man from the gas board. And now, with a favorable impression firmly ensconced under her little beret, she runs into him again, and he's singing songs in honor of a man she already loves very much."

"But she ran out," noted Chesney.

"Probably to go tell her grandfather, or write it in her diary, or put a down payment on a wedding dress."

"You really think so?"

Aunt Elinor reached down and pulled him up by his lapels. "I really think so, you pudding head! Now, I suggest you..."

"I've got to get back there," interrupted Chesney.

"I was just about to say..."

"I've got to get back there, now, right away, Aunt El. What if she comes to work tomorrow morning and she finds I'm not there? I'm supposed to be staying at the Hall. If she comes to work in a few hours and I'm not there what will she think? I've got to get the next train back, or else..."

"Chesney, Chesney," said Aunt El, grabbing his shoulders, "it's four o'clock in the morning. The first train won't leave for another hour.

"I'll miss it then," he wailed, "it took me over an hour to get here from Euston Station."

"Nonsense, I've walked it in less than thirty minutes." She took him by the arm. "Alright, come on, I'll take you there."

Within ten seconds, they had rushed out the door. In another five seconds, the door reopened as Elinor realized she was still in her robe. In another three minutes, properly dressed, she escorted her nephew out the door once more.

The pair arrived at Euston station in plenty of time for Chesney to catch the first train back to Staffordshire. While they waited, Aunt Elinor bought him a cup of tea and a buttered roll, and coached him once again not to be too much of an American to this English girl and thus scare her away. At the same time, he was to be himself, but not so much of himself that he would, in her words, "put the mockers on everything." Essentially, her advice was to doing everything right and nothing wrong.

He arrived back on the first morning train after having left there on the last evening train. As he walked back to Bagnall Hall, he debated whether or not he should try and sneak in to make it seem like he'd spent the night there. Or he could go into the kitchen and tell Mrs. Gertz that he was just coming back from a morning constitutional. Yes, that would be a good excuse, he thought, until he realized he was wearing the same suit he had worn yesterday. This thought was followed by the recollection that he only had the one suit with him anyway.

In his preoccupation, Chesney neglected he would have to walk past the caretaker's cottage to enter the estate. This only crossed his mind after he had walked past the cottage, and then, it came to his attention via a lovely, but totally average voice. The voice was calling his name.

– 35 –
The Act I've Known for All These Years

"Mr. Potoski?" she said.

"Oh, hello, Miss Goodhue," he said shyly.

"Out for a morning walk...Chesney?" She hesitated before saying his name for the first time, almost as one takes a few tentative steps around the shop when trying on a new pair of shoes.

"Yes, I suppose I was, Miss Goodhue...Verity." He rationalized to himself. It was morning. He was out. He was walking. And it avoided the explanation that he was returning from a panicked retreat to London.

They stood for a moment, the only sounds being those of the country morning.

"I wanted to say...Chesney...how much I enjoyed you last night...that is, your performance." Her hesitation was slightly less at this second use of his name. His name was a pleasant fit for her English accent. It was remarkable how a name that had always sounded so clumsy and odd through nasal American accents now seemed almost lyrical. For the first time in his life, he appreciated his name.

"Did you really enjoy it...Verity?" He could feel the blush rising to his cheeks.

"Rather!" She smiled. His knees softened to the consistency of tapioca. "I was dead chuffed!"

He felt himself return the smile. Dead chuffed! Amazing how the words that had made him scurry away in the night now seemed so beautiful in the morning light.

"Dead chuffed," he repeated.

"Yes, rather," she said. "It was awfully good."

"Really?"

"Oh, yes," she agreed. "I wouldn't say so if I didn't mean it, Chesney." There was no hesitation this third time around. "I'm sorry I couldn't stay and tell you last night how much I enjoyed it. You see, I had to return home and give grandfather his medicine."

She pointed over her shoulder at the cottage.

"Grandfather? You mean Mr. Goode? Hugh Goode?"

"Yes, he's my grandfather."

"Yes, I know, I mean, I found that out last night, Miss... Verity. Do you mean he lives here, with you?"

"Yes," she pointed to a window in the peak of the gabled roof. "That's his room, up there."

Chesney stared at the window. Not only did she live there, and not only was she the granddaughter of his musical hero, but he lived there with her. "Gosh," was all he managed to say in awe.

"I told him about you."

"Wow," he gulped.

"I told him all about your wonderful tribute, and how it was the most beautiful, heartfelt rendition I'd ever heard, after his own, of course."

Chesney exhaled. *"Even a Twerp Needs Love,"* he said.

She lowered her eyes in a way that was terribly attractive. "Not such a twerp, I think."

He looked away. For the next several moments, two people who very much wanted to look at each other stood within a few feet of each other, not daring to do so.

"Would you like to meet grandfather," she said, breaking the awkward silence. "That is if you have a moment?"

"I'd love to," he said, "I don't... that is, His Lordship doesn't need me until..." He looked at his wrist without actually seeing his watch. He barely noticed that he still had a hand. "...sometime."

He followed her as she walked towards the cottage.

"He'd love to meet you, Chesney, after all I told him about you."

Chesney grinned bashfully. "I only hope he doesn't need a gas cooker connected."

Thankfully she laughed at his little joke. Her laugh was just as delightful as her soft voice and so charmingly ordinary.

"Yes, that was a rather silly little mistake, wasn't it? Towson told me about it later."

"Yes, I don't work for the gas company. I'm from New Jersey. I'm a writer."

"Yes, Towson said as much, that is, about being a writer."

"Actually, I'm writing Lord Bagnall's autobiography for him."

"Yes," she agreed, "that's what he said. Isn't that what's called a ghostwriter?"

He nodded. "You're not afraid of ghostwriters, are you?"

He cringed at such a silly joke, but relaxed when she actually laughed.

"Just as long you promise not to haunt my library," she said, before adding: "at least not uninvited."

She opened the door and called out to her grandfather that they had a visitor. A frail, but familiar voice called from a sitting room encouraging them to come along.

"Grandfather," said Verity to a little man ensconced in an oversized easy chair, "this is the boy I was telling you about. Chesney Potoski, this is my grandfather."

"Mr. Goode, it's a great, great pleasure, I'm, I'm…"

Hugh Goode smiled and shot a playful glance at this granddaughter. "Nice fellow, but he says everything twice." He then laughed at his own observation.

Chesney resisted the urge to say that he laughed the same way as he did in his films. Instead, he just grinned and nodded.

"Sit down, sit down," said Hugh. "Ha! Now you've got me saying everything twice. You know, I don't have enough time left to me to pick up that sort of habit so late in life.

Chesney sat down.

"Verity tells me you're from the States," said Goode. "Never cracked the States. Suppose they had enough daft singers and silly comics that they had nowt need of a gormless goof the likes of me."

Chesney tried to insist that wasn't the case, but Hugh Goode had already changed topics.

"And you sing and play the uke too, eh, lad? Our Verity tells me you did a bang-up job last night."

Chesney nodded and said she was just being very kind.

"They're a fine bunch of lads at the appreciation club. Can you believe there's over twenty such clubs all over the country? Of course, their numbers are getting pretty thin." He looked down at his own body. "I'm getting pretty thin, too." He laughed his trademark laugh. "We're all of us growing older." He reached up and took Verity's hand as she stood behind him. "Those boys, well, I guess most of them are O.A.P.s…"

Verity noted Chesney's puzzled looked and interjected: "Old Age Pensioners."

"Yes, an' all," agreed Hugh Goode, "they were just boys when they first saw me films. 'Eck! I wasn't much more than a boy meself at the time I made 'em. Still, not many youngsters who listen to the uke anymore. And that's fine; everyone to his own tastes."

"I love your music, and your films, Mr. Goode," interjected Chesney.

"That's grand of you to say so, Mr. Pot…"

"Potoski, Grandfather," said Verity.

"Yes, of course, Mr. Potoski."

"My Aunt Elinor used to send me your records when I was a boy. She lives in London."

"Well, when next you see your aunt, please send her my kindest regards, my deepest thanks, and tell her I owe her a royalty for helping me gain a foothold across the pond."

Chesney lost all track of time, his fascination alternating between listening to the reminiscences of Hugh Goode and gazing upon his lovely granddaughter. It was only when Mr. Goode made a particular comment that he even recalled why he was in England.

"Yes," said Hugh with a sigh, "it's been a grand life. I even set out to write me story, even had the title: *'Even a Twerp Has a Life.'*" He laughed. "Well, at least I liked it. Still," he pointed to an antique desk in the corner, "I started scratching it out, but never did much with it. It's all over there."

Chesney's eyes lit up. "Mr. Goode, I'm a writer, or at least, I'm a book editor..."

"Ee, I thought you were uke player."

He tilted his head to the side. "That's just a hobby."

"Aye, I've heard some people just play uke for hobby," he noted leaving out the definite articles, as was often the way with those from the North of England. "But you say you can write?"

"Yes, in fact, that's why I came here, you see..."

"Grandfather, it's nearly time for your morning nap," interrupted Verity. She looked at Chesney and signaled that Hugh needed his rest. "After all, you're not used to visitors, at least not in the mornings."

Hugh Goode began to make a contrary expression, but it melted into a compliant smile as he looked into his granddaughter's face.

"Aye, well, she's right, lad," he said, "Got to do what she says." He patted Verity's hand. "But you'll come back, eh? Maybe we can talk about making that mess over there into a book."

"I'd like that very much."

"Are you working nearby?"

"Yes," laughed Chesney, "in fact..."

"You'll be late for work, Mr. Potoski," said Verity, before amending that to "Chesney."

Chesney glanced at his watch and gave a start.

"Oh, is that the time? I'm late! I've got a nine o'clock appointment with..."

"Then you'd better hurry," said Verity rushing him out of the room. "Sorry, we kept you so long."

"It was a pleasure, an honor to meet you, Mr. Goode," said Chesney over his shoulder as Verity escorted him from the cottage.

Outside, Verity smiled at him.

"Well," said Chesney, "I want to thank you, and I'm very sorry if I overtaxed your grandfather."

"No, not at all," she said, before adding, "well, maybe a little bit, but he enjoyed your visit... we both did."

She led him up the cottage path, back towards the main drive.

"Do you think," said Chesney, "he'd really want to write his autobiography? I mean, if it wouldn't be too much of an exertion. I'd be happy to help him... free of course, and in my spare time, when I'm not working on Lord Bagnall's book, that is."

She stopped walking just as they reached the end of the path and lowered her eyes.

"Yes, well, I should tell you something about Lord Bagnall..."

"No, not yet."

"Pardon?"

"I've just started the research," he explained. "There will be plenty of time to get your impressions of him, but this isn't the right time."

"But..."

He smiled and raised his palm.

"I'm sorry," he said, "but I must insist. I promise when I start interviewing the household staff, you'll be the first person I interview."

"The staff..."

"Sorry, I don't know much about English estates, so forgive me if I got that wrong. I don't know if the housekeeper is considered part of the staff. I imagine it's a managerial position, but again, this sort of thing is all new to me."

"Housekeeper..."

"Still," he said, looking back at the cottage, "it's awfully nice that His Lordship allows your grandfather to live here with you as well."

"Chesney, about Lord Bagnall, I think you should know..."

"Please, all in good time." He now looked down at his feet and then up again into her eyes. "There is one thing I'd like to ask you now."

An amused look graced the corners of her mouth.

"Are you sure," she said, "that this question wouldn't prejudice your book... on His Lordship?"

"Oh, no, he wouldn't mind," said Chesney, "in fact, I got his permission first."

"His permission? To do what?"

"To ask you out," he grimaced realizing that he'd brought up the subject before actually asking her.

Thankfully she smiled and not at all as if she were going to laugh at him, but rather it was a lovely expression.

"And what did His Lordship say?"

"He said if I wanted to, I could."

"Take out his housekeeper?"

Chesney smiled. "Yes. That is if you'd like to go out with me?"

She looked at him intently. He wasn't sure what she was thinking.

"He said," continued Chesney, "that it was all right with him if two people in his employ dated."

"Very generous of His Lordship," said Verity.

"I hope I didn't step in it, you know, do something wrong, only I knew the first time I saw you that I'd like to know you better. But I didn't want you to get in trouble with…"

"My employer?"

"Exactly," he said, "and especially now…" he nodded towards the cottage.

"Now?"

"Now that I know your grandfather is living here with you. I wouldn't want to do anything to jeopardize the positions of either of you, Miss Goodhue…Verity."

She continued to stare at him for a moment, and then as if drawn by some irresistible impulse, she leaned over and kissed him on the cheek. He had been kissed before, and more passionately, but never so tenderly. He watched her as she moved slowly back from him, and his eyes met hers. Verity smiled softly as a perfect complement to her kiss. It was as if by that kiss, and with that smile, she was giving him a pledge of something yet come. He touched his cheek.

"I'd be delighted to go out with you," she said.

He smiled and nodded. "Dead chuffed, eh?"

"Dead chuffed," she repeated.

"That would be wonderful." He spent another moment wandering around in her gaze before he remembered his appointment with Lord Bagnall.

"Oh, no," he said with a start and another look at his watch, "I won't be able to take you out if I get fired. I'm nearly an hour late as it is." He bolted away in the direction of the main house, and then stopped and looked back. He wanted to confirm that she was still there, that her cottage was still there, and that it wasn't all just part of the most fantastic dream he'd ever imagined. When he saw her standing there, and her neat little house had remained as real as before, he smiled again, and then gestured over his shoulder at Bagnall Hall, as if to beg her pardon before dashing off as fast as he could, late for his appointment with the benevolent Lord Bagnall.

– 36 –
Lysander and the Star-Crossed Chump

For some reason, as he jogged towards the manor house, Chesney thought of Lysander's observation from *A Midsummer Night's Dream*: "the course of true love never did run smooth."

Despite his repeated loss of the mystery girl and the brief confusion over the phrase "dead chuffed," Chesney concluded that Lysander was all wet. Those minor potholes aside, Chesney had never seen a smoother path to love in all his life.

After his brisk run, Chesney stooped over, catching his breath at the kitchen door. Slipping inside, he found the room unoccupied except for a plate of cookies. Having had a very early breakfast, Chesney pocketed a handful of the goodies before creeping to the library.

To his relief, that room was also empty. As gingerly as a safecracker, he tip-toed across the carpet and sat down at the large center table, in front of a pile of newspaper clippings. At last, where he needed to be, albeit an hour late, Chesney sat back, reach into his pocket, bit into a cookie, and start reading.

He was halfway through the first cookie and two paragraphs into the first clipping when he heard a voice booming from above.

" 'Aving a little snack, are we?"

Chesney spat crumbs all over the table as he jumped to his feet. He looked around, having heard the voice of Lord Bagnall, but finding no other evidence of him.

"I h'ain't not paying you, Potsky, to scarf biscuits all morning."

Chesney turned and looked up. There was His Lordship on the walkway. Towering ten-feet above him, Bagnall looked even more imposing.

214

"I hope you h'ain't not one of these types," he continued as he descended the spiral staircase, "wot 'as always got his nose down 'round the cookhouse door."

Chesney couldn't help but notice that when he said "cook," Lord Bagnall somehow managed to pronounce at least four "o's."

"We had a chap like that in the h'army," he said as he reached the main level, "Grubber McCann, we used to call him, he was always 'round the mess, skiving away…"

"Skiving?" interrupted Chesney.

"Yes, skiving, that's wot I said…"

"What is that?"

"Skiving?"

"Yes," said Chesney.

Lord Bagnall scratched his prominent forehead. "Skiving, well, everybody knows wot skiving is…"

Chesney silently appealed that this was obviously not the case.

"Skiving, well," Bagnall made a face as if he were tasting something of indeterminate quality. "Oh, well, it's like slacking."

Chesney grabbed a pencil and pad and began writing.

"Wot are you doing?"

"Is that s-k-i-v-i-n-g?"

"Yes, I suppose," said Bagnall, for a moment distracted by the proper spelling of the word. "It don't not matter no how! Skiving is one of them words which is spoke but not writ. You don't not need to write it down."

"I just thought you'd want to include him in your memoir."

"Who?" asked Lord Bagnall but pronounced it more like "Ooh?"

"Grubber McCann."

Bagnall made another face as if that thing he had previously tasted turned out to be rancid. "Ooh, 'im?!"

"Was that a question or an expostulation, Your Lordship?"

"It warn't not neither! It whar pure revulsion. Look, I'm paying you to write my story. I don't not want it all mucked up with the likes of Grubber McCann. Wot would you put 'im in that for?"

"You brought him up, Your Lordship," said Chesney.

Lord Bagnall's pupils retreated into his brow as he tried to re-board his train of thought. After a moment, he had caught up to it. "Oh, yes, I was asking if you was one of them types, like Grubber McCann?"

"No, Your Lordship," said Chesney, "I've never been in the army."

Bagnall made another face as if he were dealing with a particularly thick private. "I warn't asking if you'd been in the h'army, I was asking wot cher doing sitting there, scarfing biscuits."

Chesney looked down at the half-eaten cookie on the table.

"Oh, sorry," he said, picking up the cookie. He raised it towards his mouth. Lord Bagnall's eyebrow shot up disapprovingly. Chesney shoved it back in his pocket.

Somehow mollified that the cookie was now out of sight, Lord Bagnall took a more indulgent tone. "You know, my boy, I hain't running a work camp 'ere. We do have elevensies…"

"Elevensies?"

"Yes, you know, wot you Yanks call 'coffee break'… a snack."

"Oh, I see," said Chesney.

"So you don't 'ave to be sneaking Mrs. Gertz's biscuits."

"I'm sorry, Your Lordship, only I haven't eaten since around five o'clock."

"You mean," said Bagnall, "you'd been up since five?"

"No, sir, I was up all night. I only had something to eat around five."

Any trace of condemnation fell from Lord Bagnall's face as he broke into a smile. As glad as he was to see his client pleased, Chesney couldn't help but note that His Lordship's grin was positively ghastly.

"By Jove!" said Bagnall, putting his arm around Chesney's shoulder and pulling him to his side. "By Jove! You mean you h'ain't not been to bed?"

Chesney confirmed that he had not.

"By Jove! Soldiering on! That's wot that is: soldiering on! And here I was putting you on a fizzer for 'aving a little nibble!"

Chesney had no idea what precisely a "fizzer" was, but the context, along with the fact that Lord Bagnall was wiping a tear from his eye, led him to conclude that in the future he could scarf biscuits at will.

"My boy, you've been working 'ard, 'aven't you?"

"I mean to do my best for you, Your Lordship," he said, neither confirming nor denying his effort so far.

"Good lad!"

Lord Bagnall, Chesney concluded, was chuffed, perhaps even dead chuffed. He began to ask about Chesney's progress. Had he, for example, read through the mountain of clippings on the desk?

Chesney stared at the pile. He was tempted to skirt the issue but decided honesty was the best policy.

"Actually, Your Lordship," he said, "I've barely touched the stuff."

Lord Bagnall's beaming face suddenly switched off its light.

"But I said I mean to do my best for you," Chesney added, "and I promise that much. You see, anyone could write your biography from press clippings, and then that wouldn't be your story."

"Oos would it be then?"

"It would be their version of a story about you. I've got to confess, I know very little about you, but that's why your autobiography is going to be honest, fresh, and reflective of your greatness…"

The gleam returned to Lord Bagnall's eyes.

"…if there is any greatness," said Chesney.

"Whotcha mean, if?"

"No disrespect meant, Your Lordship. But to be perfectly honest, if you were walking down the street I wouldn't know you from Adam or the street sweeper, except perhaps that you'd be better dressed than either of them.

You may be famous, a known commodity to your fellow countrymen, but how do they know you?"

The question sent Lord Bagnall into spasms of pops and squints, which he soon put into words. " 'Ow? 'Ow? Everybody knows me!"

"But how?"

His lips buzzed as he spluttered and crossed to the stacks of newspapers and grabbed a handful.

" 'Ere! 'Ere's 'ow they know me! It may not be known to a Yank, but I'm in the papers every week, and 'ave been for years! People can't not go in no store without seeing me products. They can't not go to the loo without... well, I've made their lives better, and I've made this country better, and that's wots in these 'ere clippings."

"Yes, Sir," said Chesney, trying to calm the roiling peer, "but that goes back to my point. Up until now, you have been defined by the press and your products. The whole point of an autobiography is for you to tell the unknown story, to give the public that thinks they know you a truer picture of the real man."

Chesney picked up the one clipping that he had begun to read and offered it as exhibit A.

"It says here you were in the army."

"Quite true," said Bagnall sticking out his chest. "Sergeant Major I was!"

"Yes, it says as much here," said Chesney. "But it doesn't say anything about, Grubby what's his name. "

"Grubber McCann! I should jolly well 'ope not! What would they be putting that skiving little 'ound in my story for?"

"Well, they wouldn't," said Chesney brandishing the article, "but you might want to include him."

Lord Bagnall looked at Chesney sideways through narrow eyes as if he were sizing him up anew. As he did so, one eyebrow slowly rose, as if a fresh revelation was dawning upon him. Then, a sly smile spread across his lips, elevating his trim military mustache along with it. He nodded and wagged his finger at Chesney.

"That! That," he said, "that's the kind of thinking wot made me wot I 'ere am now! I tell my story, my way."

"Exactly, Your Lordship."

"And I tell it 'onestly, or as 'onestly as 'onestly as 'onestly as I wonts to," he crossed to the pile of clippings. "Tell me, Pitstock..."

"Potoski..."

"If you like. Tell me, lad, you read much of the British papers?"

Chesney admitted he hadn't.

"Well, let me tell you something to h'enlighten your h'education in that area. They's mostly rubbish!"

"Rubbish?" asked Chesney looking at the pile on the table.

"Mostly," continued Lord Bagnall. "Go in for a lot of tittle-tattle from gossipy malcontents, and, and..."

"Skivers?"

Lord Bagnall snapped his fingers. "Precisely! When a fellow writes 'is h'awtobeeography, you'll get a flood of stories from a bunch of these skivers what was left out of the book. Or they'll be saying 'that h'ain't the way it was,' and putting their own version out."

Chesney nodded in spite of the split infinitive.

"They's looking for a bit of dosh or a bit of fame or both. But that h'ain't going to happen to my book! I like your plan of attack, young Potstick..."

"Potoski, Sir..."

"Wot? Oh, yes, well, so I don't keep mucking up yer name, let's just make it Potts, for now, right?"

Chesney smiled weakly. Potts was better than Potstick or Pitstock.

"Good, that's settled!" Lord Bagnall rubbed his hands together. "I'll tell my story the way I wants to tell it, and I'll include all them skivers. I knows which ones just want a mention, so I'll mention them. And I knows which wants an ax to grind, so we'll mention them in a way that takes it out of their 'ands. Yes, this'll be an 'onest book!"

"And presumably tell your whole story, as well, My Lord?"

"Oo's else? It will tell the story of a 'umble boy's rise to greatness."

"So, you came from poverty?"

The enthusiasm drained from Bagnall's face.

"No, not h'exactly poverty," he looked around him for a moment, almost as if he were expecting to be contradicted by some eavesdropper. "But, but I'll tell you this much, young Potts, this..." he waved his arms at his magnificent estate, "I may not 'ave been poor, but neither did I grow up in all this!"

"What about your parents?"

"They didn't not grow up in this neither."

"I meant, what were your parents like?"

Lord Bagnall sat behind his desk and placed his hand over his heart.

"Me mother was a saint," he whispered. "She died when I was a little nip."

"Oh, I'm very sorry," said Chesney.

"Thank you, Potts. I was barely six."

Chesney waited as Lord Bagnall blew his nose in his handkerchief.

"After that, you were raised by your father?"

The tenderness which had filled Bagnall's countenance was replaced by revulsion.

"Me father? Don't make me laugh. 'E didn't 'ave the time. Put me in a school 'e did! 'E was too busy. Did you 'ave a father, Potts?"

"Me?" replied Chesney, "yes, of course."

"Put you in school, did 'e?"

"Yes, well, I was enrolled in the local school, but I lived at home."

"Didn't not put you in no school until you was 15 and then you scarpered off, lied about yer age and joined the h'army, eh?"

Chesney confessed, to the best of his recollection that his father had not sent him away to a boarding school. He also admitted under the circumstances he had little motivation for joining the army.

Lord Bagnall nodded as if that proved his point. "Well, good for you, Potts," he said. "Just as well for you, lad! Mine did."

Chesney tried to soothe Lord Bagnall by pointing out that as traumatic as those events were at the time, they ultimately had been the making of him. Besides which, they would provide excellent drama to his autobiography.

"This will all make compelling reading," Chesney assured him, "and we haven't even gotten into all your philanthropic work."

Lord Bagnall feigned humility and nodded towards the press clippings.

"Oh, ah-ha," he said, pretending to cough modestly, "you've read about that, eh?"

"No, I hadn't read that, yet."

"Oh, well, then you just assumes, rightly, mind you, that's the sort of chappie I am, eh?"

"No," confessed Chesney, "I've actually seen it, firsthand."

Lord Bagnall sat up and looked around his library as if evidence of his largess had been indiscriminately strewn around the place.

"I had a very nice chat with your housekeeper," said Chesney. The mere thought of Verity Goodhue caused a bashful grin to spread across his face.

Bagnall, being a man who had evidently dallied in the fields of romance, knew the look. "Ah, ha, young Potts," he said, wagging a conspiratorial finger, "my bee-ography h'ain't all what you've been working on, is it, eh, is it?"

Chesney blushed and lowered his head. "No, sir..."

"Ah, ha, quick little worker, and with me old 'ousekeeper. You sly little, Potts, you! I only 'ope you make such fast work on me book!"

"Yes, sir," said Chesney. "And I think, Sir, this may be it."

"Wot? Over so quick?"

"Quickly," corrected Chesney. "No, Your Lordship, when I said this may be it, I meant that it might be true love... a lifetime of happiness... forever."

Lord Bagnall seemed confused. "Really Potts, steady on, boy. Take it from an old soldier oo's sown enough wild oats in 'is day to supply the 'orse guards. These sorts of things 'ave their place, but I wouldn't not call it a lifetime of 'appiness. Listen to the 'ol Sergeant Major, these May-December romances h'ain't not the stuff of wot true love is made of."

Now it was Chesney's turn to be confused. "I wouldn't call it May-December."

"Oh, then April-November," conceded Bagnall with a worldly air.

"Sir?"

"Wot then, Potts, would you call it?"

Chesney thought a moment. "I'd estimate it was May-May, Your Lordship."

"May-May?" asked Bagnall incredulously.

"Well, I'm not sure of the lady's exact age, but even given a few years, either way, the most I'd be willing to concede is early-May on her part and mid-to-late-May on mine."

Lord Bagnall leaned over his desk and scrutinized Chesney's face. "You been at this long, Potts, this book racket?"

"About five years, why?"

"Lot of close work, reading, that sort of thing?"

"Of course," said Chesney, "why?"

Bagnall shook his head. "Your eyesight's shot, lad."

"I admit my eyes aren't 20-20, but that's why I wear glasses. But with them or without them she's one of the most lovely, beautiful creatures I've ever seen."

"Me 'ousekeeper?"

"Yes, Sir."

"The woman what does for me 'ere at the 'all?"

"Yes, Sir. And I may proudly add, the woman who has consented to have a date with me. And I hope I'm not being ungallant to mention this, but the young lady who kissed me just this morning."

"Young lady?"

"Yes, Sir."

"Where did she kiss you?"

Chesney pointed to the side of his face. "Right here, on my cheek."

"In this 'ouse? In Bagnall 'all?" asked His Lordship fidgeting as if his shorts were riding-up on him.

"No, Sir," said Chesney pointing towards the windows, "she kissed me outside her house."

" 'er 'ouse?" Lord Bagnall stood up and started squirming like a man who suspected his pocket had just been picked but wasn't quite sure. "Wot 'ouse?"

"The caretaker's cottage," said Chesney, still having no idea what was wrong. "The cottage by the gate, where she lives with her grandfather."

"Grandfather," said Bagnall, the pitch of his voice rising, "did you meet that old, uh... old gent?"

"Yes," said Chesney, "and I think it's wonderful what you're doing for him."

"Wonderful, is it?"

"I can understand your modesty, but you won't have to brag about what you're doing for them in your book."

At his point, an odd sound, a combination chortle, choke, and gurgle escaped from Lord Bagnall's throat.

"He can put it in his book," explained Chesney.

" 'oose book?"

"The grandfather's..."

"Is that... is 'e writing a book, as well?"

"Yes, well, he's asked me to help him with it... entirely free-lance, mind you, Your Lordship. I wouldn't do it on your time. It would be, well a labor of love, I suppose. I hope you don't mind. I wanted to tell you at the first opportunity, and I guess this is it."

"A labor of love. Love, eh? Love?" There was a strained quality to the peer's voice. "Love for oom?"

Chesney bashfully lowered his eyes. "I suppose more admiration for one of them and love for the other."

"And," he said almost in a whisper, "you're helping the old man write 'is book."

"On my own time..."

"'E gets it free, while Muggins 'ere," he pointed to himself, "pays through the..." Lord Bagnall stopped in mid-sentence, finishing his thought with a shudder.

The fit of apoplexy towards which Lord Bagnall had been working for the last minute burst forth all over his face into its full Technicolor glory. Had Chesney witnessed the same colors in a sunset, he would have marveled in his appreciation of God and nature. On the face of a man who moments before had been amiably chatting, however, it was disturbing. He tried in several halting sentences to try and placate the life peer, but whatever was disturbing Lord Bagnall only found release when he reared back his head and bellowed at the top of his lungs.

"SPLATTERGUARD!"

Splatterguard, or Towson, did not appear until midway through the third bellow. While they waited, Chesney stood dumbfounded.

"Splatterguard," said Lord Bagnall when the butler appeared, "Splatterguard, throw this blackguard out of me 'ouse, off of me estate, out of the 'ole bloody country if you can manage it."

"But, Your Lordship," said Chesney, "what about your life story?"

"I'll do without a life story, either that or you'll do without a life, Putterstick! Never did trust the Poles! Splatterguard... ah, Mrs. Willows..."

This last remark was addressed to a rather spinsterish woman who had just entered the room in response to all the shouting.

"Mrs. Willows, see this little snake in the grass, this little bosom-dwellin' viper?" He was pointing at Chesney. She nodded her head, her mouth agape. "Did you kiss 'im?"

"Kiss him, Your Lordship?!"

"Ha! I thought not! Not no 'ow!" Lord Bagnall turned back to his butler and pointed at Chesney. "Splatterguard, toss 'im!"

"Very good, Your Lordship," said Towson. The butler grabbed Chesney by the back of his collar and the rear of his trousers and began frog-marching him from the room. He only paused a moment as Verity Goodhue appeared in the doorway.

She wore a very distressed look, which served as a bit of consolation to him. What he heard next, however, wiped away any of that solace, for as she rushed by into the library, he heard her sweet voice exclaim: "Father! What have you done?"

"Father?" gasped Chesney as he was rushed by.

Lord Bagnall's reply was muffled to Chesney as his whole person was flung out the grand entrance to Bagnall Hall by Towson, the butler.

Chesney had the relatively good fortune to land in a fresh planting of peonies. His head was swimming, least of all from his short flight from an English manor house. As best as he could piece together, the events of the last few minutes had revealed that not only was Verity Goodhue the granddaughter of Hugh Goode but that she was Lord Bagnall's daughter and not his housekeeper. His mind tried to make the connections between the absent father who had sent Bagnall to a boarding school and Hugh Goode's life on the road as an entertainer. Atop all this, Chesney recalled afresh Lysander's observation the course of true love. He concluded that somewhere that character was having a good laugh at the expense of another star-crossed, love-sick chump.

– 37 –
Wilmot and the Penang Assam Laksa Uprising

It was an important night. Valerie Fierro was meeting the Dornings for the first time.

W. Buxton Dorning had already met her parents. Giorgio Fierro wasn't going to hand his daughter over to some teenaged boy, no matter how fancy his name sounded, without first getting a good look at him. Bucky performed as the thoroughbred Valerie expected him to be when she had selected him. He was respectful to her parents. She was also pleasantly surprised that her parents didn't do anything to embarrass her. Like most teenagers, Valerie was laboring under the impression that her parents had no idea how to interact with anyone born after the Precambrian era. Though she loved her father, his slightly broken English and his working-class manners always held the potential for social disaster. She forever forgot the fact that the man spoke three languages and had traveled throughout Europe by the time he was her age. It impressed Giorgio Fierro that every time Bucky picked up his daughter, he not only came to the door but insisted on paying his respects to Valerie's parents. These occasions always resulted in pleasant chats of at least five minutes, since that was the minimum time Valerie would purposely keep him waiting. Tardiness was a necessary part of the dating ritual and helped to raise the boy's sense of anticipation. Rather than being rude, Valerie was doing Bucky a favor.

Before they left the house, Valerie insisted on showering affection on Reggie the Collie. Remembering Albrecht Eckner's advice, she made a great show of petting him, hugging his neck, and even showing off her trick of dancing with the dog.

Tonight was different, however. Valerie didn't have to worry about her parents. They weren't being scrutinized, she was. She would have to rise or fall on her own merits... dancing solo as it were. She had changed her clothes at least three times. Starting out with a nice pants outfit, but then realizing that was too casual. She imagined that any people with a name like "Dorning" who christened their son "W. Buxton" weren't casual people. She was having dinner at their home, presumably in a dining room and not around the kitchen table. She would have to be as classy as possible. She would have to wear a dress. She tried on the first dress, viewed herself in her full-length mirror, and smiled. It was a fun dress that showed off her figure. Then she doubted whether Mr. and Mrs. Dorning would appreciate a fun dress. Valerie rifled through her other dresses. None had a high enough neckline for the chore at hand. She could wear a skirt and a turtleneck sweater, she thought, but then looked down at her boobs. For the first time in her life, she regretted Mother Nature's generosity which a tight sweater would only enhance. She couldn't afford to be voluptuous tonight, not for this first meeting.

Then she saw it, at the back of her closet: the suit. She hated the suit. Her mother had bought it, and Valerie only wore it when threatened. It was horrid, she thought. It was a pastel shade of coral with a short little jacket, and a knee-length skirt and it made her feel like she was about eight-years-old. Still, it was perfect for a first impression on the Dornings. They would see her as sweet, innocent, safe, and virginal. It was just what she wanted them to think. If she went in showing too much flesh, it would announce that she was some kind of man-eater who was going to rape their little boy. That was her intention, but the last thing she wanted to signal in advance.

Next to the hated suit hung the blouse that went with it, and thus, by association was equally loathed. It was white with terminally cute little eyelets and nauseating embroidered accents around its Peter Pan collar. Valerie sighed and began to get dressed but found that in the year since she had last been forced into the wretched garment her figure had outgrown it... across the bust. She scrutinized herself from various angles in the mirror and came to the conclusion that she looked like a refugee from a softcore porn film: a zaftig woman masquerading as a schoolgirl. Rather than tone down her sensuality, the outfit accentuated it. She thought for a moment and then came up with a solution. Twenty minutes later, she came downstairs.

"Oh, Valerie," said her mother, "I've always liked that little suit."

Valerie smiled weakly. She would have to call it a "little suit." She almost sarcastically asked her mother to braid her hair into pigtails.

"Oh, yes," said Connie Fierro circling around her daughter and fussing at her outfit. "Doesn't she look nice, Giorgio?"

Giorgio was wolfing down a meal before another overtime job. He looked at his youngest daughter and smiled. He looked away, and then looked back again, this time with a confused expression.

"Something's different," he said.

"It's just a different suit," said Connie, "Valerie doesn't wear it too often. You should wear it more, dear."

Valerie grinned condescendingly as if to say: "over my dead body." In fact, she imagined pouring kerosene over the monstrosity later that night and reducing the suit to a pile of adorable ashes.

The impromptu fashion show was cut short by the arrival of Bucky Dorning.

"Hello, Mr. Fierro, Mrs. Fierro," he said politely, "is Valerie…"

The young man was stopped short. For the first time since he had been dating her, Valerie was ready to go at the appointed time.

"Valerie?"

She grinned. "Hello, Bucky." He was staring at the suit while trying not to do so. His eyes were concentrating, or more accurately, trying not to concentrate on one portion of her body. His eyes betrayed a puzzled look. She knew what he was thinking, but hoped he was too well-mannered to voice his thoughts, especially in front of her father.

"Well, we'd better be going," said Valerie, as she crossed the room and then stiffly bent over to give her father a peck on the cheek.

"Are you feeling okay, *Principessa?*" asked Giorgio.

Valerie smiled wanly and assured her father that she was fine. They had almost made it out the door when Reggie the Collie came bounding into the room, and rushed for Valerie, putting his paws up to her shoulders.

"Down, Reggie, down Scoreggia, bad dog!"

"He probably wants to dance," said Bucky. "You two dance together every time I come over."

"I can't… I mean, I don't have time to dance with you now, Scoreggia." Valerie softened her tone and petted the confused collie, then kissed him on the head. "Sorry, Reggie, we'll dance…" she exhaled, "…later."

Maneuvering into Bucky's car was difficult. It reminded Valerie of walking around with a book on her head the summer she had decided to develop poise. W. Buxton Dorning, being a gentleman, didn't ask what had happened to her youthful flexibility, which was just as well, since she wouldn't have told him. Even a refined boy like Bucky would never understand why a girl would use Ace bandages to bind her breasts. As she sat there, her torso reacting to each bump in the road, Valerie wondered if perhaps she was wound too tightly. When she was sure that Bucky wasn't watching she would glance down at her flattened boobs and sigh, or at least she would try to sigh. The constricting nature of the bandages barely left room for shallow breathing, let alone a deep exhale. Still, she told herself, it would be worth it. She thought of her prom dress with its daring décolletage. She could do all the heavy breathing she wanted to in that outfit. In that dress, there would be no doubt that she was a full-fledged woman. If she had to regress tonight for the sake of progress, that was fine.

Valerie's mind was taken off her discomfort as she noticed their surroundings. In the matter of a few minutes, they had left the world of the Fierro's modest middle-class neighborhood to a more affluent, upscale, upper-middle-class area. In fact, it was upper-upper-middle-class, even lower-upper class. She rarely noticed the deficiencies of her own home, not until she rode past ones like these. The lawns were larger with nicer shrubs and plantings. She imagined they were all tended to by professional landscapers or at the very least by stay-at-home women who only gardened because they liked to, not because they had to. The trees were larger, too, either because the homes were older and the area more established, or the existing trees had been carefully preserved when they built the houses. Valerie's development - the one where she lived with her parents, not the one currently beneath the Ace bandages – had very few large trees. Before those homes had been slapped up, the area had been leveled by an army of bulldozers. There was something special about these houses, too. They were not only larger but of a better quality of construction as well. Valerie was hard-pressed to see one bit of vinyl siding, or even aluminum. No, these homes all had wooden shingles with clapboard, brick, and even stone in evidence. She looked at these homes and imagined the only member of her family who would be welcomed in any of them would be her father, and then just to patch the roof. That would all change tonight, she reminded herself. Tonight she was dining with the Dornings.

Twilight was falling as they drove down the winding road where the Dornings lived. Unlike her development, all the houses were different in style and construction, as if they were independent of each other. Valerie sat in awe of the homes. Although they were less than five miles from her home, she might as well have been on another planet.

"This is it," said Bucky as he made a right-hand turn and past a mailbox with "Dorning" painted on it in script. The mailbox was on a fluted column painted white. Her mailbox was on a plain black steel tube, and "Fierro" was written with stick-on letters. The "F" always seemed to come off in the rain and was secured with a piece of packing tape. The Dorning's driveway was curved and rose slightly to the house which sat on a small crest. Valerie shook her head. Her house was the same level as the curb with a straight driveway perpendicular to the street. It was a different world, but one in which she knew she not only belonged but would reign over someday.

With Bucky's help, Valerie rose from the car, her Ace bandage constricting the simplest movement and reminding her of its presence with each breath. Fortunately, Valerie had regained her poise by the time they reached the front door. The door swung open, and a large, friendly man who looked like an older heavier version of Bucky greeted them.

"So, we finally get to meet this little lady," he said as he shook Valerie's hand in whip-cracking motion. She tried to smile through the pain and caught a glimpse of her face in the hallway mirror. Good, her wince looked very demure. She smiled.

"Dad, this is Valerie," said Bucky.

While Mr. Dorning rambled on with some boring remarks, Valerie pretended to hang upon every word. Actually, she was trying to imagine if Bucky would look like this in thirty years. His father wasn't repulsive, she concluded. Her eyes wandered slightly to take in the rest of the house. It was a lovely house, very nicely furnished; a bit stuffy, but with lots of expensive things. She looked back at Mr. Dorning – he was saying something about school, either Bucky's school, or his, or some other school, it didn't matter. Still, she nodded her head, not in reaction to his remarks, but in agreement with her own thoughts. Yes, she concluded, even if Bucky turned out looking like his father, but could attain the same level of income, she could see herself with him. She looked at the elder Dorning's paunch. If Bucky tried to sprout one of those she would have him work it off. Yes, she could handle all this.

Mr. Dorning guided them into the living room while saying something about business. Valerie maintained a polite, diffident expression, while generally ignoring him but keeping an ear out for any relevant data such as annual income figures. Mr. Dorning was interrupted by the entrance of his wife from the direction of the dining room. One look at Bucky's mother made Valerie thank the inventor of the Ace Bandage. Mrs. Dorning was a plank, a carpenter's delight, flat as a board. Valerie had seen two pimples in relative proximity to each other do a better imitation of cleavage than this poor woman managed. Still, it didn't seem to matter.

Money, Valerie concluded: if you had money, you could be cheated by Nature, passed over by puberty, and still look like a million dollars. It wasn't just her dress, which was expensive and very tasteful, or her perfectly matching shoes, or her rich but understated jewelry, or even her simple but elegant hairstyle that set her apart. But all of it together, along with the confident air with which she carried it, was pure class. Valerie was even surprised, on second glance, to notice that the woman was wearing an apron on top of it all. Not one of those big, over the shoulder jobs that her mother wore all the time splattered with tomato gravy. No, Mrs. Dorning was wearing a cute little apron that went around her tiny waist and seemed to complement her ensemble. She imagined the woman had as many aprons as she had entertaining dresses.

Mrs. Dorning greeted her warmly and gave Valerie one of those glancing little air kisses that cultured women chuck at each other. Valerie tried to return the gesture without committing the transgression of actually putting her lips on the woman's face, while still making the correct corresponding lip-smack sound. She did okay but made a mental note to practice that move later when she was alone.

After exchanging a few more trite pleasantries, Mrs. Dorning put her arm through Valerie's and led her into the dining room. Valerie even smiled when Mrs. Dorning remarked that her horrid suit was "simply darling." She also made subtle compliments on Valerie's slim figure, which she interpreted to mean her apparent lack of a chest. Valerie thanked her while wondering if she would have to continue to wrap up her boobs as long as she was dating Bucky. Would Mrs. Dorning throw her out when she discovered Valerie was not a fellow member of the "Itty-Bitty Titty Committee?"

If Valerie's breath had not already been taken away by the Ace bandage, the dining room could have done it. There was cut glass and crystal everywhere, including in the chandelier, and what wasn't crystal was silver. There were a linen table cloth and linen napkins, and the table was set with some very expensive china.

"Oh, I love," Valerie almost said 'everything,' but settled on "your china."

"Always thought it was funny," remarked Mr. Dorning, "that they call it 'china' when I bought it in Japan."

Valerie's eyes must have opened wide at this remark, for Mrs. Dorning jumped in to explain.

"Clifton often goes to the Far East, on business," she said. "He brought back the Noritake."

Valerie looked around the room until she realized that the Noritake referred to the dishes. As they sat down, Valerie felt self-conscious. There was so much more that these people knew. They moved in circles at least one or two revolutions above hers. But as quickly as this realization formed in her mind, a stronger one took its place. She may not be as refined as the Dornings. She may not have started as high on the ladder as any of them. But, she told herself, she was as good as any of them, if not better. She would observe it all, digest it, and master it. She may be a princess in her father's world, but she would become a queen in this one.

After enjoying the salad, which was already set on the table, Mrs. Dorning announced she would get the soup. Valerie started to rise slowly, constrained by her binding and was relieved when she was told to sit down, although the next thing out of her hostess' mouth was as equally disconcerting.

"Wilmot will help me," said Mrs. Dorning.

For a second Valerie looked around expecting to see that a butler had slipped into the room. A butler would have been startling enough, but what was even more jarring was when Bucky stood up and followed his mother to the kitchen.

Wilmot? The "W" in "W. Buxton Dorning" stood for "Wilmot?" Uncertain whether to laugh or gasp, Valerie took a sharp breath and was rewarded with an equally sharp pain in her chest. Apparently, some sort of reaction registered on her face. With mother and son out of the room, Mr. Dorning explained.

"That was one of the little compromises that make up married life," he said, nodding toward the door.

"Oh?" said Valerie, trying to recover with a smile, but not sure what he was talking about.

"Wilmot," said Mr. Dorning.

Valerie nodded.

"Abigail... Mrs. Dorning... Buxton's mother," he said, "her family's descended from David Wilmot."

"David Wilmot?" Valerie wondered if this also had something to do with Japanese plates.

"The Wilmot Proviso," said Mr. Dorning. "American History?"

"Oh, yes, of course, the Wilmot Proviso, yes, of course, Wilmot," said Valerie. "And... his proviso, of course, we learned about that in History class."

"Anyway," sighed Mr. Dorning, "Buxton was the firstborn of his generation on my wife's side of the family. As I said, it was a silly tradition, but life is full of such customs and conventions. Lord knows they're ridiculous to anyone else."

"I notice," said Valerie, "he just uses the first initial."

Mr. Dorning leaned back with apparent satisfaction. "You noticed that, eh," he said, although Valerie had already admitted as much. "Yes, I suppose that's a bit of a compromise on the part of Abigail. Oh, well, Buxton's a much better name, isn't it?"

"It's a very different name," said Valerie feeling as she was verbally groping through a dark room. "There aren't any other Buxtons in the school."

"No," he beamed, "it's a grand old name, from my family. We've always had a Buxton in every generation... good solid name."

Valerie smiled while thinking that in the International Naming Competition, "Wilmot" and "Buxton" would be in close competition for the coveted Golden Kleenex of Drippy-ness.

The discussion of names was cut short by the return of Mrs. Dorning and Wilmot Buxton. Bucky was carrying a soup tureen while his mother held the door and directed his progress.

"Ah, you'll enjoy this," said Mr. Dorning slapping his hands together as if summoning his satraps. "My wife has become quite expert in her conjuring up of Penang Assam Laksa."

Valerie nodded and smiled. She had never before heard the words Penang, Assam, or even Laksa: either together or individually. That Mrs. Dorning conjured it up, whatever it was, suggested that she was some sort of enchantress who was about to magically produce one of those little foreign dogs, like a Shar-Pei or a Lhasa-Apso. She hoped not. While she was hoping, Valerie also wished they would open a window, or turn down the heat. Not able to catch a breath in that constricting bandage, she was feeling quite flush.

"Wilmot's father," said Mrs. Dorning, "picked up the recipe on one of his many business trips to the Far East."

It occurred to Valerie that people in China ate dogs, or so she had heard. They weren't going to serve her a bowl of dog soup, were they? Valerie felt her throat constrict. The mere thought of a steaming serving of Fido activated her gag reflex. She felt herself become lightheaded and reached for her water glass.

"It's pretty good," assured Bucky as he placed the large china tureen in front of his mother, and removed the lid.

The Dornings were big animal advocates, weren't they? They wouldn't be rescuing household animals only to eat them, would they? No, she told herself of course not. With these outlandish thoughts running through her mind, she said the first thing that popped into her head.

"I love animals," she exclaimed. The three Dornings stopped and looked at her sideways. "I mean," she clarified, "I'm very passionate about animals. Dogs, I love dogs, very much... very, very much... passionately."

After an awkward silence, Mr. Dorning piped up. "We had a great dog..."

Valerie almost expected the conclusion of the sentence to be: "...the other night for dinner." Thankfully, it was not a culinary reminiscence.

"...his name was 'Boswell,' had him when I was a boy. He used to sleep at the end of my bed."

Being a bit more sensitive than her husband, Mrs. Dorning put a different interpretation on Valerie's outburst.

"Oh, my," she said, looking concerned, "Wilmot didn't tell us that you were a vegetarian."

"Vegetarian? But, I'm not, I..." Valerie stopped. She almost said: "I just don't eat dogs or even cats for that matter."

"Well," said Mr. Dorning, "I'm sure you'll enjoy my wife's Penang Assam Laksa..."

"It's Malaysian," said Mrs. Dorning, though this was little help.

"From Malaysia," adding Mr. Dorning, providing even less assistance.

Valerie looked across the table at Bucky, who smiled in subtle condescension toward his parents. "It's fish," he said. "Don't worry, it's pretty good."

Valerie smiled. She liked fish, and though she had never sampled Malaysian fish soup, she figured it must be better than Malaysian dog soup. She thanked Mrs. Dorning as that lady ladled a portion of Penang Assam Laksa from the tureen into the Noritake soup bowl and handed it to Valerie.

"It looks delicious," said Valerie, mainly to have something to say while waiting for the others to be served. She tried not to look down at the soup, as she was feeling woozy enough without staring into what looked like a bowl full of kitchen scraps. "It smells... wonderful, too," she added.

After serving everyone, Mrs. Dorning sat down, and with a demure expression that reeked of class, silently signaled that they could begin.

Carefully selecting the proper silver spoon from the cutlery in front of her, Valerie dipped it into her bowl and tasted it.

"Mmm," she said, "it's delicious." Valerie wasn't just saying this to be polite. It was good. This Penang Assam Laksa stuff was really good. She smiled and took another spoonful. In was in between the second and third tastes that the full potency of the dish manifested itself in a blazing dart of fire down her throat.

"I'm glad you like it, dear," said Mrs. Dorning.

Mr. Dorning was on his third mouthful, which, despite his income level, he made with a healthy slurp. "A bit milder tonight, dear?"

"I used less tamarind this time," replied his wife.

"Still, excellent as always," he said, taking another spoonful. "Not as much tang as usual, but great Penang Assam Laksa."

Not as much tang, thought Valerie. She could feel the beads of sweat break out on her forehead. Her throat felt as if a tiny mule with Ben Gay coated hoofs was stuck in her gullet trying to kick his way out. Everyone else was sitting there, calmly eating away, and making small talk, while Valerie felt a burning sensation working down her neck towards her chest. She started to reach for her water glass, but as she did so, the room began to sway. Valerie grabbed the edge of the table with her left hand to try and steady herself, the roof, the world, and whatever else seemed to be rocking. She looked up through watery eyes at Bucky. He was calmly eating that damned soup, chatting about some sporting event with his father, oblivious to the fact that his girlfriend was spontaneously combusting. She tried to take a deep breath, but the Ace Bandage around her breasts morphed into a boa constrictor intent on squeezing the air out of her like some helpless mouse.

She was about to mew for help, but suddenly and without warning, Valerie found the Noritake dish full of Penang Assam Laksa was rising up off the table to meet her face. And at that moment everything went black.

– 38 –
Sofas Are for Vapors,
Couches for Bloodbaths

She was on her back, looking at the ceiling. Bucky Dorning came into view standing over her.

Where was she? Was it after the prom? Had they done it? Was it over? Did she enjoy it? Was he good? She would have been terrific, naturally. Bucky was smiling. Yes, that must be it, thought Valerie. She was about to ask him for details when another voice intruded.

"Is she coming to, then?" It was Mrs. Dorning.

Valerie tried to sit bolt upright, but her tightly bound chest held her back. Over Bucky's shoulder, Mr. Dorning came into view.

"Funny, it was a real mild batch, too," he said, "but it must have been the soup."

"Pish tosh!" said Mrs. Dorning. "People don't faint from soup."

The soup, thought Valerie. It was coming back to her now. That bowl of Chinese dog, or whatever it was, soup, that Napalm Lhasho Whatchacallit; rising up to her face. No, the soup hadn't come up. She must have gone down. She fainted into the soup! She almost wished she were dead, but then she wouldn't want to be dead for the prom. She could wish that the people staring at her were dead, but that included Bucky, and she needed him for the prom. No, she wished she wasn't laying on this couch. As it was within her power to fulfill that wish; so she got up, with difficulty.

"I'm sorry," she mewed, though she knew nothing was her fault.

"There's no need to apologize, dear," said Mrs. Dorning

"I feel so foolish," she said. That was true enough.

"For what?" asked Mr. Dorning kindly. Though the answer to that question was obvious, Valerie replied anyway.

"For passing out in your... soup," she said, forgetting the name of the atomic concoction. "For lying down on your couch..."

"You didn't lay down," noted Mr. Dorning, "Buxton carried you there."

Valerie suppressed a smile. Bucky had carried her. She would have enjoyed that if she had been conscious. Still, it was good to know he could manage it, and it was good practice. She imagined him carrying her, in her perfect dress, after the prom, gently placing her down, and then passionately tearing the perfect dress to shreds.

"And," interjected Mrs. Dorning, "it's a sofa."

"Excuse me," said Valerie.

"You said 'couch,' dear. It's not a couch. The proper word is 'sofa.'"

"Oh, yes, of course," said Valerie, "I meant, sofa, of course." She made a mental note. Rich people, refined people, her new people didn't say "couch." The word was "sofa." She vowed she would never say, sit on, or own a couch from this moment forward.

"Are you okay, Valerie," asked Bucky. "Do you think it was the soup?"

"Oh, of course, it wasn't the soup," said Mrs. Dorning. "I know what it was."

For a split second, Valerie panicked. She reached up for the top button on her blouse to confirm that it was still fastened. Did Mrs. Dorning really know? Had she seen the Ace Bandage? Her husband and son exchanged puzzled looks. It was still a mystery to them. But Mrs. Dorning wore a knowing smile on her skinny lips. Perhaps, thought Valerie, after Buxton had dropped her on the couch – damn, the sofa – perhaps the men left the living room leaving Mrs. Dorning to conduct a thorough examination. No, thought Valerie, upper-upper-middle class people who had expensive china and sat on sofas didn't strip search their unconscious guests. Did they?

"Well, if it wasn't the soup..." said Mr. Dorning

"Let's just say..." Mrs. Dorning paused to exchange a conspiratorial look with Valerie. "...let's just say Valerie has a touch of... the vapors."

Mr. Dorning got it. His son was still confused. Mrs. Dorning offered Valerie the subtlest of winks.

The vapors? Eww, thought Valerie, this woman, this emaciated, flat-chested, extremely mannered lady thought Valerie was having her period. She would have laughed if her son, her prospective prom date, her planned de-flowerer wasn't standing there, still looking befuddled. Had they been alone, and had Mrs. Dorning not been the mother of W. Buxton Dorning, Valerie would have told her off, but good! Valerie may be upwardly mobile socially, but she didn't come from such weak stock. One day she would have a nicer home with even nicer dishes from even farther away than Japan, and twice the number of sofas, but she was, and always would be an Italian woman. She was there to restock their obviously weakened gene pool. The vapors? It would be laughable if it weren't so insulting. While poor Mrs. Dorning might be a martyr to that time of the month, Valerie would never admit to such weakness, certainly not to some man and certainly not with such ridiculous phrases as "the vapors." She and her girlfriends used euphemisms like: "the Crimson Tide," "Waving the

Red Flag," "the Bloodbath at the Y," and a dozen other grosser sayings. If any of them ever dared to use such a limp-wristed phrase as "the vapors," they would be laughed out of their sex, drummed out of the corps, and carried out on their last panty shield.

She just nodded at Mrs. Dorning. Valerie resolved, however, when she was running things, these women would toughen up and stop falling victim to "the vapors."

"What about dinner?" asked Mr. Dorning.

His wife tilted her head sympathetically at Valerie. "Do you feel up to having dinner, Valerie, dear?"

Valerie studied the woman's face for a moment. She was looking at Valerie as one would a daughter, or, at the very least, a favorite niece. Mrs. Dorning saw her as a kindred spirit. After living alone with a husband and a son here finally was someone to whom she could relate; someone with a slight figure (or so she thought), and a martyr to women's complaints. Her work here was done. She had won Mr. Dorning on the doorstep, merely by showing up. And now, with Bucky's mother showering her with sympathy, she knew that she had won her seal of approval. Staying for the rest of dinner could only jeopardize what she had already achieved. Besides, she couldn't wait to get home and grant her boobs the freedom they craved.

"If you don't mind," said Valerie making sure her voice quavered, "that is, I'd hate to be rude after all the trouble you went through with dinner, but I think I'd really like to go home."

"Of course, dear," said Mrs. Dorning extending a hand to Valerie and helping her off the sofa. "I understand. They'll be other dinners."

Valerie smiled weakly and made a mental note to buy some loose tops and a good flattening sports bra before she came back to the Dornings.

"Thank you for being so understanding," she sighed.

"Not at all, dear," said Mrs. Dorning. She leaned forward to hug Valerie. Thankfully her hugs were like her kisses, more intent than actual contact. Valerie returned the gesture, rather well, she thought. Too tight a squeeze would have been painful, plus Mrs. Dorning might have felt the bandage.

"Wilmot will take you home."

Twenty minutes later, Wilmot Buxton Dorning stopped his car in front of the Fierro home. He switched off the engine and turned to Valerie, his face visible only in silhouette from a nearby street light.

"Thank you," he said.

"For what?" she asked.

"For being so good with my mother. It must have been," he paused, groping for a word, "I don't know… intimidating."

Intimidating? It had been damned intimidating. It would be intimidating under normal conditions. She merely replied with noncommittal: "Oh?"

"I mean, they're different from your parents. Oh, I don't mean better, or anything like that, but I don't know, I was pretty scared the first time I met your parents."

"Oh?"

"Sure," he said, "they're great. Your Dad's got this, I don't know, this wisdom or something, like he's lived a lot. I don't mean he goes around bragging about all the places he's been or the things he's brought back from around the world, but it's there on his face, somehow, you know?"

"I guess," said Valerie. She hadn't heard such a perceptive description of her father before. In fact, she'd never heard him described at all.

"And your Mom," he continued, "she's a really good cook, you know, of real food."

"Thanks," said Valerie.

"So, anyway, I know it's hard meeting different people, and I wanted to thank you for going to so much trouble to impress my parents, especially my mother."

Valerie looked down at her mashed torso. Did he figure it out?

"I mean," he said, "You picked out that dress..."

"My suit?"

"Yeah, it's not really, you know... you. But you somehow knew that was what my mother would be comfortable with."

Comfortable, thought Valerie, as she rolled her eyes.

"I just wanted to say, thanks."

"Oh," she said with a shrug, "you're welcome." She started to open the door, wanting more than anything to get inside and change while she still had feeling in her chest.

"And I wanted..."

He leaned over, pulling her towards him. Valerie winced with pain, but only emitted a slight whine. Then, in the darkness of the Fierro's driveway, W. Buxton Dorning kissed her. It was a pretty good kiss. Actually, it was a really good kiss, so good that it made Valerie forget about any feeling other than his lips pressed against hers and a warm itchiness elsewhere. She returned the kiss, pulling him back, just as he began to relax his grip. Their passions momentarily slaked, the two teenagers came up for air. Fortunately, Buxton exhaled loudly enough to mask Valerie's panting. Kissing was a lot like buying a car, she thought: you didn't want them to see how much you wanted it.

"So," said Valerie, "that's what you wanted, hmm?"

"No, I mean, yes, that was great, but what I really, I mean, I wanted to ask you to..."

She sat, holding her breath for what seemed like a shadowy eternity.

"...the prom."

Yes! YES! Inwardly she was pumping her fists and doing flips and imagining how incredible she would look in her dress. Outwardly she played it so cool she could have sunk the Titanic.

"Oh, the prom? When is that?"

"I, uh, I'm not sure of the exact date."

"Oh, well," she said coyly, "I'm sure I can arrange my schedule."

She could just make out his boyish smile in the dim light.

"That would be great," said W. Buxton Dorning. "It's going to be a great night."

Oh, thought Valerie, you've no idea how great.

– 39 –
Confessions of a Delicate Watercolor

I love your nephew," said Verity Goodhue.

Chesney Potoski rolled over on his aunt's couch. He had been working so hard that he had fallen asleep during the visit. He could hear the two women talking in the next room at the kitchen table.

"But..." said Aunt Elinor.

"I didn't know you could hear a 'but.'"

"Oh, maybe not a big one, but there's something more to that sentence, isn't there, dear?"

Chesney kept his eyes closed and clutched the little throw pillow. A fear, unimaginable moments before, suddenly gripped him. The silence that ensued, while only lasting a moment, was torturous.

"But I'm afraid," said Verity.

"Love can stir up a lot of emotions in us, not the least of which is fear."

There was a prolonged silence.

"I do love him, really," continued Verity. "he's... Candle-ends."

"Pardon?"

"Lewis Carroll," she said, and then recited:

'His intimate friends called him "Candle-ends,"
And his enemies "Toasted Cheese."'

"I never thought of my nephew as a candle-end," said Elinor, "but if you say so, I suppose it fits."

"Yes," said Verity, "there's something very sweet, very special about him, something different," her words trailed off. A moment later, she began again with renewed enthusiasm. "One evening we came out of a cinema, and it was pouring down rain by the bucketful. All the patrons were huddled under the marquee. No one had an umbrella or even coats.

Every minute or so, a couple would dash off trying to reach their automobiles without getting soaked, but none of them came close to succeeding. After seeing the effect this had, your nephew said: 'don't they look silly running around like that? They're all getting drenched anyway.' Then after watching this for a few more seconds, he said: 'Let's stroll back to the car, just as if it were a beautiful evening.' And that's what we did. Of course, we got soaked through, but as we walked, I could feel the eyes of all those huddled people watching us, probably with their mouths hanging open. If anything, the rain came down harder, but Chesney just held my hand and strolled along. It was as if he were made of something different from all those other people who were cowering a few yards away, afraid of the rain. And a little bit of that special quality, whatever it was – perspective, or the courage to be different – a little of it passed to me because I was holding his hand. Once we got in the car, we burst into laughter. We were soaked. My hair was a mess. And then he told me how lovely I looked and then we kissed. It was so very romantic."

Aunt Elinor said nothing. He could hear her sipping her tea.

"And," Verity added, after another minute, "he has a smile that reminds me of the Cheshire Cat."

"My, you do like your Lewis Carroll."

"Yes, I read a lot of it as a girl. Chesney's smile… it's very mischievous, but in a very innocent way," from the cozy sound of her voice, he guessed that Verity was smiling the smile that charmed his heart. Then he heard her sigh, and he felt the smile slowly vanish.

"But you're afraid?"

Verity sighed. "I know it's silly…"

"Fear isn't a silly emotion," said Aunt Elinor. "Sometimes it's irrational, but at those times, especially at those times; that's when it's scariest. It's like being awakened in the middle of the night when there's no one there but you. And some little thought creeps in with the darkness, the kind of thought that if you had it in the light of day, you'd blow away with a puff of breath. But in the middle of the night, when you're alone in the dark, that thought seems huge. It can sit, crouched on your mind like the weight of the world."

Verity sighed again. "Sometimes I imagine we're two paintings, hanging side by side. Only he's a bold Impressionist painting, something like a Degas or a Monet, full of daring, striking colors…"

"And you?"

Her voice grew soft. "A delicate watercolor…"

"More tea?" asked Aunt Elinor and then rose to put on the kettle. The kitchen was filled with domestic sounds for nearly a minute, while Chesney waited for a continuation of the conversation. He almost tried to go to sleep, so as not to eavesdrop any more, but he was too anxious, his heart beating loudly in his chest.

"I wouldn't have thought to compare him to a painting," said Aunt El. Chesney could hear her stirring the tea in the pot. "I'm only his aunt, and I don't mean that to sound like any more or less than that is, but I probably know him, the real boy, better than anyone on the face of this Earth. I would have called him 'sweet,' 'thoughtful,' 'insecure,' and a lot of other images that would fit your first description of, what was it?"

"Candle-ends."

"But I've rarely known him to be bold," said Aunt Elinor. "Of course, that could be him just being an American as compared to your Englishness. I speak from a unique perspective. I was born in the States, but I've lived here so long that I feel I'm an expert on both cultures but belong to neither. It could be that, but knowing Chesney as I do, there's a much more simple explanation."

"Oh?"

"He's madly in love with you, my dear."

"And I love him."

"But, you're afraid."

Chesney could hear the delicate clink of a teaspoon against a cup rim, almost as if it were the sound of the wheels turning in Verity's mind.

"We've been seeing each other for almost six months," she continued, "and in that time I've seen how loving he can be, more loving, and romantic, and attentive than anyone I've ever met before. The problem is that it's all almost too loving."

"Sweeping you off your feet, that sort of thing?" asked Elinor.

"Yes, as you say: 'madly in love.' The only time we've been apart was when I had to go away for a short trip. I was only away for two weeks."

"Well, that must have given you a chance to come up for air and give some perspective on your feelings."

"It would have," said Verity, "but the day I left, he handed me fourteen letters, all dated, one for each day I'd be away. I'm sure I would have missed him terribly…"

"…if only he'd given you the opportunity."

There was another painful silence, painful at least to Chesney.

"My nephew," continued Aunt El, "is all those things you say, and I can see how they would be scary. I doubt if many girls could help but wonder if it were all genuine, if he were sincere. After all, there are not many of us who feel worthy of such devotion and adoration."

"Yes, that's it. I wonder if he's in love with me, or …"

"…in love with love?"

"Precisely," said Verity.

"Knowing the boy who has grown up into that lump that's dozing away on my settee, I can safely say he loves you, dear. I see it in the way he looks at you when you're looking the other way. I see it in the way he acts when you're not there, and the way his eyes light up when you come into the room. I see it in a hundred little looks and a thousand little gestures that speak in tones softer than a breeze but with a passion beyond a gale. And at the same time, the boy is a romantic, not some great lover, but an idealist who believes."

"Believes in love?"

"Believes in love, believes in life, believes in joy even when he's most downhearted, believes in hope when he's suffered a crushing disappointment. I've never known anyone who could seem so shattered when he's knocked down, and yet after a brief wallow in self-pity, he throws it off and rises again with even more optimism than before. I don't think even he realizes he possesses half of these qualities, but they're there. St. Paul could have been writing about Chesney when he said 'love bears all things, believes all things, hopes all things, endures all things.' Chesney does all that, too, and he loves, and he loves love, but more than that he loves you, my dear. And if he seems to be sweeping you off your feet, if you don't feel deserving of all that surge of emotion, if you think it can't be you, believe that it is you, and consider it a truly wonderful blessing."

There was another moment of silence.

"Oh, yes, and, I nearly forgot: he's an idiot," added Aunt Elinor.

"Pardon, did you say…"

"Idiot, yes, a complete idiot, in the nicest way, of course, scaring a sweet girl like you with all that sloppiness."

"Well, it wasn't all that unwanted, just…"

"Too much," said Elinor concluding the sentence. "How did Shakespeare put it: loving not too wisely, but too well? Yes, I think that was it. The dumbbell! Still, and this is no excuse, but he's not had very much practice in romantic affairs. He's like a starving man visiting a smorgasbord for the first time. He's so flippin' hungry that he goes overboard and looks like a gluttonous fool."

"Oh…" there was a bit of trepidation in her voice.

"But that's not to say that he doesn't truly savor every morsel," she paused. "Do you understand?"

"I think I do."

"He may have done it clumsily and like total nincompoop, dear," said Elinor, "but never doubt that Chesney has put everything he has, all his trust and love on the line at your feet… the dope! Oh, not that he's a dope for loving you, but, well, I think you know what I mean."

"Yes, I believe so."

"And you're right. You are a delicate watercolor, and he is a bold painting. You're a gentle English rose, and he's an aspidistra, or whatever other comparisons you want to draw. But I've seen many a wall that was graced and beautified by two very different paintings hanging side-by-side, serving as a joyful complement to the other. The most beautiful gardens are those with the greatest variety of plants. I'd like to think that, oh, never mind…"

"No, what was it?"

"Nothing," said Elinor falling silent for a moment, "but when I was a girl, in our town, there was a very rich man who was plagued with very bad feet. Did I ever tell you about him?"

"Bad feet? No, you never did, Ms. Potoski."

"Please, Elinor, Aunt Elinor, if you like."

"Aunt Elinor," Chesney could hear the smile in Verity's voice, and he smiled himself, albeit into the couch cushion.

"There was a very rich man who lived in our town, back when I was a girl. As I said, he was a very rich man, but for all his wealth, he had terrible feet..."

Chesney, after pretending to be asleep for the past quarter of an hour, gave too good an imitation and dropped back into a sound slumber.

◆

On their way to London, Chesney had kept up a steady stream of conversation. He hadn't noticed Verity's quiet. She was naturally reserved, and he talked enough for both of them. Now, however, on their return to Staffordshire, the only sounds were that of the tires on the road, the hum of the engine, and the replay in his mind of the overheard conversation.

"You should learn to drive," she said, breaking the silence.

"Yes," he agreed until he realized what he was saying. "I mean, I know how to drive."

"Yes, excuse me," she said, "you should learn to drive a manual transmission."

"Oh, why?"

"So, you could drive my car," she said. "I could teach you."

He hummed in weak assent. "I'd have to learn how to drive on the correct side of the road."

She took her hand off the steering wheel and caressed his cheek.

"That was very nice," she said.

"What?"

"Implying that we drive on the correct side of the road. Most Americans come here and say we're driving on the wrong side of our own roads."

"They're your roads, after all," he said, and then fell silent for another mile or so.

"A penny for your thoughts," she said.

Chesney looked at her profile as she drove, and was, as always, taken by her simple beauty. Now, however, he also studied her face for traces of the fears that she had confessed to his aunt, fears he had put there. A penny? No, he wouldn't reveal what he was thinking at the moment, not for half the Crown Jewels in cash. He forced himself to think about something else.

"Oh, I'm just thinking about your grandfather," he said, "and the book."

"Oh," she said, and he felt there was something left unspoken in the brevity of her reply.

"Yes," continued Chesney. His throat felt dry. "It's going very well. I can't believe we're almost done. It's been a great pleasure and honor working with him on his memoirs. It's the second greatest pleasure in my life."

"Oh, what would be the greatest pleasure?" she asked.

Chesney looked away. Had she asked him that on the drive down, he would have blurted out: "you are the greatest pleasure in my life." But now, as he watched the setting sun, he dared not reply from his heart. Instead, he just mumbled that he hadn't really thought about it, after all.

"Oh," she said. And they retreated into to silence.

Had he been a dope, and idiot, and a dumbbell, as his Aunt had said? He thought back over the past six months, beginning with the moment that Towson had tossed him from Lord Bagnall's front door. In retrospect, it was all wonderful. Not landing in the flower bed, but what had happened next. He had picked himself up, dusted the peat moss from his trousers, and had started limping away from the hall. He wasn't certain where he was going. Perhaps he would go back to Aunt Elinor's. Chesney was reviewing his possibilities when he heard a voice calling after him. He turned around to find Verity following him.

"I'm very sorry," she said, as she caught up to him.

"Yes, I'm sorry, too," said Chesney.

"For what?"

"I suppose I'm sorry that I didn't know the whole situation around here," he said. "Not only didn't I know that you were Hugh Goode's granddaughter; I didn't know Lord Bagnall was your father. I thought you were the housekeeper."

"Yes, I know, I tried to explain..."

"It doesn't matter now," he said.

"Because I'm his daughter?"

"Well, it was easier when you were the housekeeper."

"But I never was the housekeeper," she said.

"I suppose I meant it was easier when I thought you were the housekeeper."

They walked over the crest of the small hill between the manor and the caretaker's cottage.

"Why did you think I was the housekeeper," she asked.

"I don't know," he said. "No, wait, yes, I do. It was because you lived in the caretaker's cottage and because you spoke so nicely to the cook, and to me when you thought I was there to fix the stove, and because of the way you're dressed."

"The way I'm dressed?"

"You always look so right."

"For a housekeeper?"

"To tell you the truth, I've never met any housekeepers, but you always look, oh, I don't know. I suppose I could have thought you looked like any person in any profession, but whatever it was you looked right to me."

"Thank you, I think."

"You're welcome, I'm sure," they walked a few more feet, and then Chesney stopped and snapped his fingers. "I know where I got the idea that you were a housekeeper. It was Mr. Postlewaite."

"From the shop in London? But how?"

"Well, I have to confess, I saw you there."

"In Mr. Postlewaite's shop?"

"Well, not exactly in the shop. It was outside the shop, and you were walking away, and I ran after you. I wanted to meet you. I had to meet you after I saw your face."

"But how could you see my face if I were walking away. I didn't see your face. I didn't even see you."

Chesney sighed and asked her to sit down on a nearby bench. He then confessed how he had first seen her in the mirror of the haberdashery shop, and gone weak in the knees. He explained how he had tried to chase after her but had been stopped by the police. Chesney tried to convince her that he didn't normally chase strange girls, get stopped by the police, or even go weak in the knees.

"In fact," he admitted upon reflection, "I've never done any of those things before in my life."

"I am honored," she smiled. The tension of confessing it all just melted away. This made it easier to tell her even more. His despair over losing her twice turned to ecstasy over meeting her again in the kitchen, then his confusion over the phrase "dead chuffed," and all the bits and details in between.

"And," he said, exhausted by the full recounting, "that brings us to the latest twist..." He jerked his thumb over his shoulder at Bagnall Hall.

"You have been on something of a roller-coaster, haven't you?" she asked.

"I guess, but I'm not complaining."

They rose from the bench and walked the short distance to the cottage in silence.

"I suppose, this is goodbye," he said once they'd reached her front door, "Miss Goodhue."

"Oh, I'm back to Miss Goodhue, am I? After all, you've been through I think the least you deserve is to call me by my Christian name."

"May I... may I write you, Verity?"

"Why? Are you going away?"

He thought a moment. "I assume so, after all, Lord Bag... that is, your father didn't seem like he wanted his ghostwriter to be dating his daughter."

"Does that mean you're out of a job?"

"Most likely."

"And you would give up your job over a girl?"

"No, not just a girl," he said, feeling his cheek redden. "But I suppose I would over a really good housekeeper." She laughed, and he was very glad. "Besides, maybe I can get a job in London working with Mr. Postlewaite, or with Li Gao."

"Li Gao?"

"He's a truck driver, another friend of my aunt."

"Why don't you get another position writing? Or have you forgotten your promise to help grandfather write his biography?"

"Yes, but..."

"Not to mention your promise to me," she added.

"...to you?"

"You asked me out, Chesney," she said with mock severity, "and besides, you have the permission of His Lordship to take out his housekeeper."

He was about to remind her that was all a misunderstanding when she leaned over and kissed him.

– 40 –
Love on the Reel

O nly six months, Chesney thought as he stared out into the dusk
that was descending on the passing landscape. It seemed he had
known Verity for a lifetime, while at the same time, it all felt like
just a moment.

After his ejection from Bagnall Hall, Chesney devoted his full energies
to Hugh Goode's autobiography. The dear old entertainer was delighted
to have a genuine editor taking over the project, and Verity was dead
chuffed to see the vigor the effort infused into her grandfather.

That same day Chesney called Beverly Marlton to apprise her of
the situation. The publisher told him she had already received an irate
call from Lord Bagnall. Chesney held out the possibility of getting
Bagnall to relent. Meanwhile, he assured Marlton of the potential for an
autobiography by one of the UK's greatest stars of yesteryear. Ms. Marlton
conceded that to bring Chesney back immediately would represent a total
loss. She allowed him to stay on as sort of sabbatical. He was to devote
the majority of his energies toward the Hugh Goode book, while trying to
mend fences with Lord Bagnall, and would be at partial pay while he did
so, with the understanding that he would receive a royalty if and when
the Goode biography was published. Chesney accepted the arrangement
as it would allow him to remain in England with Hugh Goode, Aunt
Elinor, and especially Verity.

While he was offered lodging by Hugh Goode, Chesney didn't think it
proper to live under the same roof with the girl he loved. Instead, he rented
a room nearby with Mr. and Mrs. Pilchard of the appreciation society.
Chesney threw himself into the effort as never before, spending all his
days with Hugh Goode, and all his evenings with Verity. And he fell even
more deeply in love. At every opportunity, he expressed his feelings for

her, in little notes, in funny drawings and sketches, in flowers picked from wild patches. Every thought, every gesture was captive to her.

Only now, after overhearing Verity's conversation with his Aunt did Chesney realize he in danger of smothering her with love.

He was moodily silent all the way back to Staffordshire, and more than once, Verity asked him if he were feeling well. He answered that he was fine, though he had no idea whether he really was or if she believed him.

That night, in his tiny rented room Chesney lay awake, uncertain of what to do. The work on Hugh's story was nearing an end. Twenty-four hours earlier, his plan had been to finish the book and propose to Verity. Each night as he drifted off to sleep, Chesney rehearsed how he would ask her. No matter what words he imagined using, or where they were spoken, the end was always the same: she said "yes."

Now all those dreams were in jeopardy.

The next morning it didn't take long for Mr. Goode to perceive a change in his biographer.

"Ee, lad," said the old gentleman, "are you all right?"

"Hmm?" Chesney looked up. "All right? I suppose, sir, why?"

"Only you've been staring at paper for last five minutes."

"Just checking for errors."

"Oh," said Hugh, "didn't think blank sheets of paper had many errors, but I'm just an old uke strummer. You're the book editor."

"Yes, quite," said Chesney.

"Good, that's settled," said Mr. Goode. "Now, maybe you can tell me why you're looking more miserable than a pig at trotter eating contest."

"What?" Chesney looked up again at the old man. "Miserable? Is it that obvious?"

"And then some, lad."

Chesney stood halfway up and craned his neck to either side. "Are we alone, that is, is your granddaughter around?"

"Verity? No, she's out I think. Why is something wrong with Verity?"

"No," said Chesney bowing his head, "no, she's perfect. There's something wrong with me."

"You're not sick, are you, lad?"

"No, as far as I know, the medical associations haven't classified stupidity as a disease. In my case, it's just a chronic condition."

"I see," said Hugh. "And you're wrong, lad."

Chesney looked up. "About being stupid?"

"No, you're probably that," said the old man, "or at least I won't argue the point as you seem so comfortable with it. I mean you're wrong about Verity being perfect."

"She is to me," he said.

"I won't argue that either," said Hugh, "I'm too old to argue. But I can say what I know, or at least what I think I know, and remember, I'm only a bit of puddin' meself. But I do know this. You're not perfect, I'm not perfect, and Verity's, though she's the most precious thing in my life, is not perfect either."

Chesney conceded his point and then explained the reason for his worries. "So that's it," said Chesney when he came to the end, "I'm afraid I've scared her off, and I've ruined my chances with the perfect girl, or at least the girl who was perfect for me."

Hugh Goode nodded as he stroked his chin. He didn't speak for several minutes, only raising Chesney's anxiety.

"Once, during the war," he finally said breaking his silence, "I was overseas, out in Middle East it was, entertaining the troops - did more of those shows than I care to recall. I was too scrawny to be of much good in the service. They figured I was more dangerous with uke than with a rifle. I was in ENSA, that was like you Yanks' USO. It stood for Entertainments National Service Association, only the troops joked it stood for Every Night Something Awful." Hugh Good laughed at his own reminiscence. Chesney had heard it all before but remained respectfully quiet waiting for the point he hoped was coming.

"Where was I? Oh, yes, in the Middle East, out in the desert with ENSA. Well, I would do a show, nothing fancy, sometimes it was just me, standing on the bonnet of a tank playing the uke and singing some songs. Sometimes it was a bigger show. No matter what it was, the boys all seemed cheered by us showing up and doing what we could. Sometimes we used to bring films with us too. Watching films then was nowt like watching them now what with tapes and video thingees. Back then we had a projector and screen, but then you know all that. Sometimes we just had a projector and no screen. They used to show film on sheet or side of a supply lorry. Any road, one night out in the desert they showed one of my films, I think it was *Hugh'll Catch It*, remember that one?"

Chesney nodded. He'd have a poor memory if he'd hadn't since they'd watched it together two weeks before.

"Silly stuff," said Hugh, though with an underlying pride and fondness for his own work, "but as I said, folks then liked it… except that night in the desert."

"They didn't like it?" asked Chesney.

"Oh, they liked it fine in parts, lad," said Hugh, "only it confused them something awful."

Chesney was taken aback. He'd seen all of Hugh Goode's films, and while they were enjoyable, none of them were difficult to follow. They all had rather simple plots fleshed out with cheery songs and comedy.

"How could they be confused?" he asked.

"It warn't difficult," explain Hugh, "not if the film were shown all which way around. You see, back then films were in reels, about ten minutes long each and you had two projectors, and one would end, and the next would start. Or if you had but one projector you'd wait for reel change. The night I'm telling about the fellow operating projector was a bit…" here he paused and mimed someone drunk. "…you know, tiddly… and he got it all wrong. Well, not all wrong. He started out fine, but somewhere in the middle, instead of reel three, he put on reel six. Now that film's in seven reels, seven parts you understand. Then from six, he went back to four, and then he showed the end second to last and finished with five. So I was kissing the girl for the happy ending while the spies still had her tied up in the scene before; and after I'd had the fight with her, but not with the badduns yet. Understand?"

Chesney looked at him. The old man smiled.

"I've gotten my reels out of order?" said Chesney.

Hugh Goode wrinkled his nose. "Just a bit, lad."

Chesney sighed and shook his head.

"Now, it's not as bad as all that," said Hugh.

"You didn't hear what she said," said Chesney. "And what makes it worse, she didn't think I heard it."

"And you've nowt heard what she's said to me, and more important what I've seen. I'm just a twerp who got lucky being gormless for a living, but I've also been around a bit. You're a fine lad, and our Verity is a fine lass. You just need to give her a bit of time to sort out the story. You wanted to jump to the closing kiss and happy ever after too early. She needs to catch up with the plot, sort out the players, that sort of thing."

"Wait then."

"A bit," he agreed.

"How long?" asked Chesney. "How will I know when she's… caught up."

The old man smiled enigmatically, as if he knew something, or perhaps didn't. Then he shrugged. "Oh, she's a bright lass, yes, a very bright lass. If you give her brain some space to catch its breath, I suspect she'd sort things out right quick."

It made sense to Chesney. It had to. He didn't see any other way. Still, he thought, it would be the most difficult thing he ever had to do.

– 41 –
The Gladiator's Bustier

She hadn't thought of it at the time. After all, when you're scheming for the perfect prom dress, you don't worry about what you'll wear under it. Now, however, as she was getting dressed for the prom, Valerie Fierro paused to admire her selection of lingerie.

The dress was only the outer layer. Everyone would see that. The girls would die with envy of her style and her perfect figure. And while the girls were seething, their dates would be jealous of Bucky Dorning because he was the lucky boy escorting her to the prom. But, later, for Bucky's eyes only, it would have to be perfect beneath her dress. After all, how would it look to have the perfect dress, the perfect body and between them some dull, baggy cotton underwear? How anticlimactic! No, her dress would just be the appetizer. After they left the prom and drove down to the beach, and she removed her dress, he would be driven wild when he saw the next course. And then, once that layer was removed, he would get her virginal self, the first and last boy to receive that honor. He'd better appreciate it.

Valerie paused and tried to sort out the analogy that she had formed. If the dress was the appetizer, was she the dessert? Really, shouldn't she be the main course? No, dessert was a good fit, but then her lingerie, no matter how alluring, couldn't be the main course, could it? Underwear, even sexy underwear wasn't a main course? Perhaps the dress was the appetizer, and she was both the main course and the dessert. That would leave her underwear as…the salad? Valerie shook her head and decided that no matter how it was served up, W. Buxton Dorning was getting one hell of a feast.

She gave up thinking and went back to admiring herself in the mirror. Running her hands down the curves of the strapless satin and lace bustier, her fingers paused over the delicate embroidered flowers before running down to the attached garters. She had never worn stockings and garters before. They made her feel very mature and sensuous. She only hoped that Bucky would pause if only for a moment, to appreciate her underwear before tearing it from her body.

After a few strategically placed daubs of fragrance, she took one last look at her half-clothed body. When next she viewed it again at such leisure, she would be a total woman. Next, like an ancient Roman warrior girding for battle, she donned her prom gown. Ideally, she should have had attendants helping her, pulling up the gown, adjusting it, zipping it closed while she stood there motionless like a perfect marble statue. The only attendants available were her mother and her sister, and she didn't trust either with the honor. She didn't want her mother to see her in her underwear. Her mother would figure out that a sexy bustier wasn't there to keep her warm. And Rose, well, Rose couldn't have fit one leg in the gown. She might accidentally on purpose damage the dress out of some deep-seated resentment that Valerie had gotten the good body and not her.

Due to its location, Valerie had a minor struggle doing up the zipper. No matter, she noted, she would have another set of hands to help when it came time to get out of the thing. Another two or three minutes to admire herself in the dress, and Valerie was almost ready. She glanced out of the window and looked down into the driveway. Bucky's car was there, as it had been twenty minutes ago. Valerie had always imagined she would be driven to the prom in a limo, but Bucky's car was almost as good. To be precise, it was his mother's car, a new Jaguar. Poor Mrs. Dorning, thought Valerie as she adjusted the neckline around her cleavage. If she could get a load of this rack that flat little woman would have a heart attack, but not before locking her son away from the girl who was going to devour him after the prom. A quick adjustment to her up-do which had been set in place hours before at the area's top salon, a slight tug on the curling tendrils which cascaded teasingly beside her ears, and she was ready... nearly. There were just the shoes, the perfect shoes that went with the perfect dress the perfect lingerie, the perfect clutch, the perfect earrings, she could go on over every detail, but after all, Bucky had been on time and that was almost a half an hour ago. She wanted him to be on edge with anticipation, but if she kept him waiting too long, he'd likely become a basket case; of no use to anyone, least of all her.

Valerie slipped on her four-inch heels and tottered for a moment towards the bedroom door before gaining her equilibrium. She opened the door a crack to see if she could hear any references to herself from the voices downstairs. They were talking, but too low to hear the topic of conversation. It didn't matter, she told herself, whether they were talking about her or not. They soon would be. Valerie opened the door, took one step outside, then turned back for one last look at the room of her girlhood. She wasn't feeling sentimental. Rather it was as if she were leaving her past behind with disdain. She was saying good riddance to the girl who had brought her to this point but now, no longer needed, was to be discarded. You've served your purpose. Just make sure you're out of here by the time I get back. And of course, that girl would be gone, never to be seen again.

– 42 –
A Princess, Almost a Woman

Giorgio Fierro's wife told him he was exhausted and nearing a breakdown. He was just tired; okay, very tired. The fatigue of the extra jobs, the freelancing and moonlighting had crept up on him relentlessly. Still, he thought it was almost over, and it hadn't been that hard, had it? Except for…

All fatigue, all doubts, every other thought vanished when he saw his daughter

"*Principessa,*" he whispered. His wife and the boy in the room turned to see what Giorgio had been the first to witness. Connie gave a grudging smile and admitted that her daughter looked nice. Bucky Dorning, himself looking sharp in his tuxedo, stood up and grinned. Giorgio noticed the hands in which Bucky held the corsage trembled. As a father, he almost gave the boy a precautionary warning. But as a man, Giorgio understood. He would have been more disturbed if the boy hadn't reacted. He knew Bucky well enough to know that he was a respectful young man. And he was fairly confident that Bucky Dorning knew that he was a father who would castrate any boy who laid an inappropriate appendage on his daughter.

Valerie stopped atop the last step, like an actress on the stage, or a princess on a platform.

"You look great, Valerie," gasped Bucky.

Connie added that her daughter looked beautiful, but there seemed to be the hint of warning as if she were transmitting unspoken advisories in some secretive mother code. Valerie must have picked up these signals for she did her utmost not to look her mother in the eye. It didn't matter. There was enough parental approval coming from Giorgio Fierro to support Valerie's ego.

"Ah, Principessa," he said, standing back and admiring her. "I can no longer say *Piccola Principessa*, for you're not little anymore, you are almost a woman."

"Almost," Valerie agreed.

"You look like…" Giorgio's voice trailed off. The way his daughter looked, so grown-up, so mature, took his mind back over forty years. He had no picture of her, and the image in his mind had faded over the years as memories will, but for a brief moment, looking up at her with her head turned just so, Giorgio could see his own mother there. He turned away to staunch a tear.

Bucky Dorning presented the clear plastic box to Valerie containing her orchid.

"For me," she said feigning surprise. She had told Bucky the exact style and color she expected.

"No, for me," muttered Connie.

Bucky assured her they were for Valerie. She asked him to pin the corsage on her while maintaining her lofty perch. On the step, and in her four-inch heels, Bucky was left staring into her neck. He fumbled with the box and removed the corsage. It wasn't the orchid that made him anxious. Rather his discomfort was caused by the corsage's intended resting place: directly over Valerie's left breast. The low-cut design of the gown made this effort all the more daunting.

Valerie maintained a frozen smile as if she were posing for a magazine cover, all the while watching her date as he approached his target. Bucky moved in slowly, followed by several tentative parries and retreats. Valerie almost grabbed the flower from his hands. There was so much potential disaster, she thought. The whole pinning of the corsage was such a stupid tradition to leave to the inexperienced. He could ruin her dress, demolish the flower, or make her the first girl in her class to have a pierced nipple. At this point, all she could do was to hold her breath and remain as steady as possible. After two or three attempts, Bucky somehow managed to attach the flower on Valerie with no discernible damage and only about four inches from where it should have been. She would fix it in the car.

Giorgio Fierro stood out of the way in his work clothes as his wife took pictures. Valerie looked so beautiful, so regal. She must be very happy. The boy looked nice, standing beside her. By squinting, Giorgio could imagine how Valerie would look someday as a bride. It also increased the resemblance to her grandmother.

He watched as Bucky escorted Valerie to the car. Some car, Giorgio thought, a Jaguar, but then it was no less than a Principessa deserved. He watched with his wife by his side as the couple drove away and out of sight.

"You're a big softy," said Connie, half affectionately, half scolding. It was only then that he realized that a tear was rolling down his rough cheek.

"So what if I am?" he said defensively. "I think she looks beautiful."

"She should," said Connie, apparently in reference to the expensive gown. "And you, you look like hell."

Giorgio looked up the road to where he had last seen the car.

"It is worth looking like hell if I can give her a little bit of heaven."

His wife snorted in reply.

"I'd better get going," he said, looking at his watch. "I'm nearly done, you know. Only a few more nights."

"Ummm," said Connie.

He had been living with her long enough to know the translation. She was saying he was a fool; that he spoiled Valerie; that the dress was a waste of money; that they could have put the money to a dozen more practical uses. And, he reminded himself, it also meant that she loved him and was worried about him. It was this last thought unspoken to which he replied.

"Don't worry," he said, kissing her on the forehead as he left, "It'll only be a little while longer. I love you, too."

– 43 –
Bosworth Fields Forever

It was a doubly notable occasion. It was the first time Chesney Potoski had driven a stick shift, and it was the first time he had driven on the left-hand side of the road.

He had only mashed the gears on Verity Goodhue's car twice, only stalled the engine once, and only made one wrong turn. After a few initial winces, Verity was careful to compliment him on his progress. Every bit of encouragement helped.

"One of them should be around here," she said looking down at the map, and then up again at the road. "You could pull in there and park."

Chesney did so, then got out of the car and went around and opened her door.

"You did very well," she said.

"Thanks, I've been practicing opening doors."

"You know what I meant," she said, offering him an affectionate smirk. "Your driving was good on both the shifting and the English roads."

He resisted the urge to tell her she was a good teacher. In the last month, Chesney had made a conscious effort to temper anything that sounded like fawning. She paused, almost as if she were expecting a reply, and then continued without it.

"This is one of the possible sites," said Verity, glancing at the small book in her hand. "Of course, they aren't exactly sure where the battle was. There are at least three possible locations."

Chesney looked around at the field. "Well, we're near Market Bosworth. This could be it."

They walked along the path by a stone wall. Verity reached out to take his hand and squeezed it. He returned the gesture.

"One would think you'd be tired of English history by now," she said. "After all you've been saturated with it for the past six months with Grandfather."

"Oh, that's not history," he said. "Well, it is or will be someday. I've just enjoyed working with him. I don't consider it work, not most of it. It was just spending time with a wonderful old gent."

She twined her arm through his and pulled him close to her side.

"And he's enjoyed it, too," she said, and then leaned over to kiss his cheek. "And I've enjoyed it, too."

He almost returned the compliment, but stopped himself and made light of it. "Yes, I suppose it kept me out of your hair." He glanced at Verity and resisted the urge to add: "Your soft, silky hair…"

"That's not what I meant, and you know it," she said. "Are you trying to pick a fight with me?"

"I'd never want to fight with you," he said. "Besides, I'm finished."

She released his arm and faced him.

"Finished? With the book? When?"

"Early this morning," he said.

"Oh, Chesney," Verity threw her arms around his neck and hugged him. "Why didn't you say so? This is wonderful."

He just nodded.

"But you don't think the book is any good?" she said.

"No, I think it's very good. Your grandfather has had a great life, and he shared a lot of wonderful stories about it."

"Then why are you acting as if you'd just finished a grocery list and a boring one at that?"

Chesney turned, leaned against the wall, and looked out into the field. He felt her at his side, but neither said a word for several minutes. Finally, feeling the need to break the silence before it became unbearable, Chesney reached for the farthest thought from his mind.

"So," he said, "this might be the site of the Battle of Bosworth Field, eh?"

She got in his face. "I don't know, but I can assure you that in the future it will be known as the site of our battle if you don't tell me what's wrong."

He looked into her eyes and blinked away a tear. Then he took a deep breath and exhaled. He felt a lump catch deep in his throat.

"I…I heard you talking…to my aunt," he said. "That time we went to visit her."

"Go on…"

He looked down at his feet and bit his lip. "I had been asleep, but I woke up, and I heard what you said."

"About what?"

"About being afraid and being a delicate watercolor, and me being…" his voice trailed off.

"I see," she said. "Is that why you've been so... different since then, so less..."

"A jerk..."

"I was going to say: 'so less you.'"

"A jerk," he confirmed.

An angry expression darkened her face. He thought this was it. She was going to dump him right there, at the possible site of the Battle of Bosworth Field.

"Don't you dare..." she started.

Chesney braced himself.

"Don't you dare call the man I love a jerk!"

"Love?"

"Yes, you, you... twerp! I love you!"

"But what about..."

"What about my fears, and my anxiety, and all those things?"

"Well, yes..."

"Perhaps I thought them through," she said. "Perhaps someone gave me a little space, and it made me realize I didn't want any space between us, ever again. Perhaps, I don't want to break in anyone else's shoes."

He understood her up to that point, but the last reference confused him.

"Shoes? What shoes?"

"I thought you said you were eavesdropping."

"Yes, well," he confessed, "I did that, but I fell back asleep."

Verity laughed and kissed him. "That will teach you to wake up and listen to things that you shouldn't overhear, and then fall asleep again before you listen to it all. Your Aunt Elinor told me the story about a rich man in the town she grew up in..."

"The town in which she grew up."

"I'll ignore that," she flicked the end of his nose. "She told me there was a man who was very well off, and whenever he bought a new pair of shoes, he would pay another man to break them in for him."

"I don't understand," said Chesney.

"Your Aunt Elinor explained that even though he was getting paid, the man who broke in the rich man's shoes was being paid to take all the pain the rich man would have suffered if he had to break in the shoes himself. Elinor pointed out that you weren't perfect..."

"Thank you, Aunt El."

"...but that love was a lot like a pair of new shoes. There was bound to be some discomfort and some blisters involved in the best of relationships before the relationship is truly 'broken in.' She said that I'd have to determine for myself whether or not I love you, but if I did love you to be careful not to break you in for someone else. And that's what your aunt said after you fell asleep." Verity waited a moment, and then asked: "Well?"

"I'm not sure what to say," he said. "I've never been compared to footwear before, least of not by my favorite relative. But I suppose... wait..."

"Yes," she smiled.

"Shoes, you don't want anyone else to wear the shoes after you've broken them in?"

"That's right," she said, her grin widening.

"I'm the shoes... and you want me?"

"Yes, please, very much so."

"And the blisters, I mean, me, you're not afraid?"

Verity Goodhue shook her head.

"Does that mean," he said his mind racing faster than he could verbalize his thoughts, "I mean, if... you don't... I mean... will... will you..."

"Will I what?"

He took a deep breath then looked around at the field for a moment, and then looked back, and took both her hands in his.

"Will you marry me?"

It was only a moment, but seemed like an eternity before she said: "Of course I will."

Chesney kissed Verity and couldn't help thinking that if he died that moment, he would die the happiest person who had ever stood on the possible site of the Battle of Bosworth Field, or in fact, the happiest person who ever set foot on the British Isles. After he kissed her, he embraced her, and then kissed her again, and then he thanked her, and then kissed her again. Then he looked around once more at the surrounding fields.

"Why do you keep looking around?" asked Verity.

"I'm trying to remember this spot," he said. "I wish I could have asked you at someplace a little more romantic. To tell the truth, I didn't even expect to ask you at all, at least not today. I'd always hoped but..."

She placed her fingers over his lips. "I think it's perfect," she said. "It's a beautiful spot. It's been here untouched for over a thousand years, and it's historic."

"It might be historic..."

"No, it's definitely historic," said Verity. "Not for some battle that may or may not have happened here hundreds of years ago, but for what just took place today." Verity looked around and then looked back into his eyes. "I will forever cherish this spot in my memory. I shall never forget it as long as I live, and I shall bring my children here someday, and tell them how a good and kind boy came from across the sea and unexpectedly found the treasure of his heart, and how once he had found it he set out to win her with a silly song and a thousand small acts of gentleness. I will tell them of an overly exuberant exterior that masked a sensitive heart full of love and consideration. I will tell them of his patience and his steadfastness. And when I am done telling them all that and a hundred other things I will have learned between now and then, I will tell them that boy is their father, whom I will love forever and to the end of my days."

Chesney wiped a tear from his eye. "Wow."

Verity smiled. "Wow indeed."

"I suppose," he said, trying to lighten the moment for fear if he didn't his heart would burst for happiness, "I suppose you'll tell them his name was 'Candle Ends.'"

"No," she said, squeezing his hands. "No, you're not 'Candle Ends' any longer, not even the Cheshire Cat."

"I'm not?"

"No," said Verity, "from now and forevermore, you are My Beloved."

– 44 –
A Legend Exits the Stage

In his current euphoria, Chesney couldn't remember that he wasn't driving an automatic, or that he needed to stay to the left side of the road. He even confused the accelerator and the brake. While Verity found his enthusiasm quite charming, she preferred to return her car, her fiancé and herself back home in good condition.

From the passenger seat, Chesney recited all the romantic words and feelings that he had suppressed over the past month, while also apologizing for being too effusive. Verity merely smiled, occasionally laughed, and seemed to be enjoying herself nearly as much as he was.

"And I promise," he said after a particularly heartfelt declaration, "not to be so... mushy."

"Oh?"

"No, I mean it," he said. "For example, I'll never write you all those letters the next time we have to be apart."

"Well, that's something you won't have a chance to prove," said Verity. "I don't plan on letting you out of my sight long enough to find out. From now on Mr. Potoski: 'wither thou goest, tither I.'"

It was nearing nightfall when they reached the caretaker's cottage. Chesney insisted on sharing the news with Hugh Goode.

"I know he'll be pleased," he told Verity, "It will also give me a little strength for facing your father, and breaking the news to him."

"Either way," she assured him as they neared the front door, "whether Father likes it or not, I'm going to..." She stopped short, and a look of concern crossed her face. "Something's..." she began, before cutting herself off, and hurrying into the house. They were met in the sitting room by the grim figure of her father's butler.

"Towson," said Verity, "what's wrong?"

"He's had a bad turn, Miss," said the butler in the same solemn tone he used for announcing everything from calamities to afternoon tea.

"Who..." Chesney began to ask, not sure if he were referring to Lord Bagnall or Hugh Goode.

Verity needed no clarification and bolted up the stairs with Chesney close on her heels. She broke stride before softly entering Mr. Goode's bedroom.

"Hullo," came a weak, almost disembodied voice from the bed, "oh, it's you, dear. I thought it was the doctor again or that stuck-up butler. How are you, dear?"

Verity knelt by the old man's bedside and reached out to smooth his tousled hair. "How am I? How are you? I leave you for a day, and..." Her voice broke off.

"Now, now," said Hugh, "no fretting over a clapped out old ham."

"You said the doctor was here. What did he say?"

"Oh, not much," said Hugh, "where do you want the final bill sent, that sort of thing."

Verity bowed her head on her grandfather chest and began to sob.

"That was supposed to be a joke," he said. "Eee, if me timing's shot perhaps it's all for the best that I go." He waited a moment before continuing in a more serious tone. "Verity, love," he said, lifting her chin. "Don't cry, dear. I've known I was living on a bonus for a while now. My heart, you know. It was always willing but ne'er as strong as I would've wished. But I want you to know, it's been grand, simply grand. Who's that," he asked, raising his head towards the doorway. "Is that our Ches?"

"Yes, sir," whispered Chesney.

"Well, good, I couldn't bear not seeing you again, and thanking you one last time, come here, come here."

Chesney drew closer. "Thank me?"

"Aye, lad, right here, come right, here, sit ye down," the old man patted the opposite side of the bed from where Verity was kneeling. "Don't worry, sitting on the bed won't break me. It might break this cheap old bed though. Sit."

Chesney did so.

"Now, I want to tell you it's been wonderful reliving me life with you, these past months, lad. You're a grand writer, and I want you to put your name on the cover, along with mine. Mind you, I don't often demand top billing, but it's business, you understand."

"But..."

"No, I won't hear another word, that's my wish, and if you have the least bit of regard for an out of tune uke player, you'll do me that favor."

"I'd be honored..." said Chesney. He didn't dare look at Verity for fear they'd both break down.

"Good, that's settled," said Hugh patting Chesney on his forearm. "Telling my story was a tonic, lad. It's what kept me going, but now that's done, and just in time. I'm very tired."

He closed his eyes slowly. Without taking his eyes off the old gentleman, Chesney reached across the bed and found Verity's hand meeting him halfway. They slowly turned towards each other and then back to Mr. Goode.

"I guess..." Chesney began in a soft voice.

"Oh, one more thing, Ches, lad..." they were startled by Hugh Goode's voluble interruption.

"Yes, sir?"

"Did you ever, you know, do anything 'bout what we'd talked about that time?"

"Sir?"

The old man rolled his eyes. "You know..." he mimed what was meant to be a subtle gesture, a nod in the direction of his granddaughter. After years on the stage, his expression could have been read in the last row of the balcony. "You know, about the film reels all mixed up... did you straighten them out?"

Chesney looked over at Verity and then back at her grandfather.

"Yes, sir, that's all straightened out now," he said, "all the reels are in the proper order."

"And it's going to be a happy ending?"

Chesney looked at Verity and nodded.

"Grandfather," she said, releasing Chesney's hand in favor of Hugh Goode's, "Chesney and I are going to be married."

Hugh Goode smiled broadly, and then his face fell. "You're wouldn't just be telling me that because I'm almost done, would you? I mean, just to make me happy?"

Verity smiled and squeezed his hand. "No, dear," she said, "I'm saying it to make me happy."

"Champion!" said Hugh. "Proper champion! That'll do yer good, and bless you both. All reels are right way 'round. As it should be. Right way 'round."

He closed his eyes, and the smile that had once cheered war-weary audiences shone forth one last time. Then, with his granddaughter holding his hand, Herbert Goodhue, better known as Hugh Goode, breathed his last.

Verity held his hand for a minute and then feeling for the pulse that had faded away, softly confirmed her grandfather was gone.

"I'm sorry," said Chesney squeezing her hand.

"He went out very happy," she said. "He was quite pleased about us."

Chesney nodded.

"And I think he was delighted to have completed the book," she said, "thank you for all that, My Beloved."

"I suppose we'll have to inform your father," said Chesney.

"Yes," she agreed, "we'll have to tell him about grandfather, and about our engagement."

"I wonder what he'll think."

"'E's most like to think of them two h'events that one was h'inevitable, and one's h'avoidable."

They turned to see Lord Bagnall standing in the doorway.

"Father," said Verity, "how long have you been there?"

"And the h'inevitable h'event should be right and proper buried with full honors," said Lord Bagnall ignoring his daughter's question. He then cast a withering eye on Chesney. "And the h'avoidable one…well, that one I'll deal with."

– 45 –
The Queen of the Barbie Nation

The du Pont Country Club was just as Valerie Fierro had imagined it would be: rich and classy. And as elegant as the club was, Valerie knew that she was not outdone by the venue.

The other couples looked nice, but they looked like kids at a high school prom. As for her, she would not only have fit into any event the club hosted, she would have been the center of attention. The hardest part was pretending that she belonged with the rest of them. She didn't want to appear stuck-up. Still, it was hard to be humble.

As a little girl, Valerie and her friends played "prom" with their Barbie dolls. In the Barbie Nation, all the girls looked the same: same cold frozen expression, same perfect figures, only the dresses were different. They all took turns being elected prom queen. But that was a little girls' game. Now they were grown up and while it was still a game, fairness no longer entered into it. Though she was a junior, in the back of her mind… who knows… she might be prom queen. After all her hard work, it would only be fitting if she were selected.

Jealous girls, those with flawed complexions who hefted in over a size ten, might argue that being a junior disqualified Valerie. They would say it was the Senior Prom. Still, she reasoned, any girl there was in the running.

These thoughts retreated slightly, as Valerie glided into the ballroom on the arm of W. Buxton Dorning. Bucky looked good, too, she told herself, but then most of the boys all looked the same, as they should. The only real distinguishing difference between them was the girl on their arm. By that standard, Bucky Dorning had the best-looking arm in the place.

On their arrival, they got in the line for formal portraits. Best to get the professional photos out of the way first, Valerie reasoned. Anything could happen: someone could spill punch on Bucky's white jacket, or worse, on her gown, or her make-up could become smudged, or her perfectly coiffed hair could get mussed. And although photos had been taken back at her house, this was the official portrait, the one that she would cherish for the rest of her life. Like everything else, it would have to be as perfect as possible.

"Are you sure you don't want me to get you a drink?" Bucky asked for the second time as they stood in the line.

"No, not yet," snapped Valerie. Really, would boys ever understand? She looked up at him. He looked so handsome. She had done a marvelous job grooming him for this important job. Valerie looked around at the other boys scattered around the ballroom. Some were beefier, a few were cuter, some may have even had better future prospects, but all in all, she couldn't have made a better choice than Bucky Dorning. He was deserving of the honor she would bestow on him later.

"You really do look beautiful," he said. Valerie smiled until she realized he was starting to lean over towards her face.

"Please!" She said, putting up her hand. "What do you think you're doing?"

Bucky glanced around the room where more than a few couples could be seen kissing. "Uh, I was going to kiss you."

She arched her brows. "There will be plenty of time for that after the picture." That's all she needed, an eternal record of smudged lipstick. Her grandchildren, great-grandchildren, and generations yet unimagined would only shake their heads and wonder. She noticed a pout on his face. It reminded her of Reggie the Collie after he had been scolded. She smiled and coyly twirled her index finger around his lowest jacket button.

"Not right now," she said in her throatiest, sexiest tone. "I promise you, I'll make it up to you later. In fact, I'll give you a lot more than just a…" She blew a kiss at him. His reaction was perfect. His eyes widened, his mouth dropped slightly and then rose again in a hungry smirk. What was unspoken was apparently in both of their minds, and now understood. It was all going to be perfect.

Into this perfect moment was interjected an imperfect intrusion.

"Valerie…"

Valerie heard the voice behind her, she recognized it, and she tried to ignore it. But the voice was insistent.

"Valerie. Valerie, you look great, can I get a picture."

She glanced over her shoulder, confirming what she had thought. "We're in line to get our pictures taken," snapped Valerie.

"I mean, one for the yearbook," said Albrecht Eckner.

Valerie turned again. There stood Albrecht with his expensive-looking camera which did nothing to compensate for his garish tuxedo. She stared at the pastel coral cummerbund just below the pastel coral ruffled shirt and the matching pastel coral jacket. She used to like pastels and coral. Not any longer.

"Just a quick few shots," said Albrecht. The expression was his usual mixture of groveling and grand larceny. "A few candids, for the yearbook... when you're done with the formal portrait, of course. I wouldn't want you to lose your place in line. You're a lucky guy, Buxton. She looks very nice."

"Uh, gee, thanks, Albrecht," Bucky Dorning smiled. Valerie couldn't believe how guys could bullshit each other and never realize it.

Having disarmed her escort, Albrecht returned his attention to Valerie. "Very nice dress," he said in an almost conspiratorial tone.

Valerie was about to tell him to dry up and get lost, or get lost and dry up - she wasn't sure which order she preferred - when Albrecht lowered his voice.

"Really, a great dress," Albrecht continued as if he knew something about haute couture, or as if he knew something about something else. Then he stuck in the fork. "It's amazing what can be done with some fabric...and rubber cement."

Valerie's mouth dropped open. She had forgotten about the rubber cement and the magazines and the visit to the Eckner's store. It all came back on a wave of guilt. She felt the blood rise to her cheeks. She turned to look Albrecht squarely in the eye, trying to detect a trace of the intent behind his comment. He looked back at her with that disturbing look that was both innocent and menacing. She looked up at Bucky, who smiled benignly. He had no idea that there was a dramatic struggle going on right before his eyes. If he had, Valerie could have asked him to punch in Albrecht's face somewhere out on the elegant veranda. As it was, however, W. Buxton Dorning was oblivious and thus, for the moment, useless. She made a snap decision.

"Bucky, darling," she said, pulling on his lapel and bring his ear into whisper range, "can you hold our place, while I... powder my nose?"

"Uh, sure," said Bucky.

"Well, I'll see you later, Albrecht," said Valerie as she hustled off towards the ladies' room, but kept going into a small lounge tucked in an alcove. She only had to wait a moment before she was joined by Albrecht. Before he could speak, she grabbed him by his pastel lapels.

"Alright, what do you want?" she said.

"Me?"

"Yes, you, what was that crack about the rubber cement."

"Nothing," he shrugged, before adding in a conspiratorial tone, "but I did want to ask you something."

"Now?"

"It's about the prom queen voting."

"Oh?"

He leaned in towards her.

"How would you like to be prom queen?"

She assumed an innocent air. "Me? But I'm only a junior."

Albrecht's eyelids fluttered agreeing to her charade, but not believing it for a second.

"Yeah, well," he said, "I didn't ask if you thought you'd win it, or if you were qualified, or your class ranking. I asked if you'd like to be prom queen."

She dropped all pretenses in the face of such a direct offer.

"Sure, I'd like… I'd love to."

"I'm not just here to take pictures," he said. "I'm also on the planning committee. The seniors always put juniors on the prom committee to do all the grunt work. I collect the ballots, I help tabulate them. How would you like it if I fixed it so you'd be prom queen?"

Valerie couldn't quite believe her ears. Of course, she wanted to be prom queen. And winning in a rigged vote didn't bother her. After all, she reasoned, there probably hadn't been a fair election in the history of the world. If she didn't take advantage of this opportunity, it would just mean that the fix would go to some other girl, one with a much less attractive gown and figure. It was a no-brainer, except…

"Wait," she said, "what about you?"

"I'd make a rotten prom queen," he said facetiously.

"I mean, what do you want?"

"Me?" Albrecht looked around to verify he wasn't overheard. "I want revenge."

"Revenge?" She hadn't thought about that.

"Revenge on these stuck up snotty seniors, especially the girls," he said sneering even more than usual. "You don't know what it's like working with them on the prom for the last six months. They act as if they're the center of the universe and that this is the whole culmination of their stupid, shallow little lives. Do you know what I mean?"

Valerie nodded. "That sounds like them."

"Sitting through all those meetings," he continued, "listening to them come up with all their big plans, and then making me do all the work. It's so demeaning. Then they tell you that next year when you're a senior you'll have the next crop of juniors do it for you. Like that's some sort of payback. 'We'll torture you, but don't worry, next year you can torture somebody else.' No, thank you. Now I want them to get theirs. Cheryl Delaney, Priscilla, and Mary Beth, you know them…"

Valerie nodded her head. They were popular seniors, all very pretty, too.

"Well, they were the worst ones," said Albrecht. "And they're so positive that one of them is going to win. But it would serve them right if a nice girl won, a junior girl, a sweet junior girl…"

Valerie looked at him vacantly for a moment until she realized he was referring to her.

"So," he said, "do you want to be prom queen," he said. "Will you help me out? If you don't want it, there are a few other junior girls…"

"No, wait... I don't know..."

"It will really help me out," he said.

Help him? Valerie suddenly felt very altruistic. She would be doing a favor for another human being. And after all, Albrecht did loan her that rubber cement. It was the least she could do for him.

"What do I have to do?"

"Nothing," he said, "just win. Oh, and act surprised, and modest, all that, which you would, anyway, of course. Well, do you want to be prom queen?"

She smiled. It was a practiced smile, just like the one she'd use when they called her name. "I'm honored to be selected queen of the prom."

"Shh, not so loud."

"Oh, right. Sure. I'd be glad to... if it will help you out."

"It will," he said. "More than you know."

– 46 –
I'll Pretend That I'm Flipping
The Flips I Was Missing

Giorgio Fierro gazed at the setting sun and wiped the sweat from his eyes. Another roof done. Weeks of overtime, often six nights a week and half days on Sundays, and now he was nearly done.

You do what you have to do, he told himself. It wasn't a burden, it was just what fathers did, and that was that. His wife didn't understand. She wouldn't; she was never a father and wasn't likely ever to be one either. That's just the way it was.

He shook his head. Poor Connie, she thought it was just about some expensive dress. Giorgio knew almost nothing about dresses. Women wore them. That was the beginning and end of it. He wouldn't work a minute of overtime spreading hot tar for a dress. It wasn't about a dress.

Didn't Valerie look every inch a princess? He smiled as he spread the rapidly coagulating goop. He'd always called her his little princess, but tonight he realized how close he had been to the truth. She looked regal, beautiful, and pure. He would spread tar a hundred years for his princess, or for anyone of his little family. Valerie looked so happy, but she wasn't half as happy as he was seeing her like that, and when she turned her head just so with her hair up the way it was, he could almost see his mother. We live on in our children and their children. Life goes on with each passing generation peeking out from their descendants. Everything was as it should be. Life was good. Giorgio was happier than he could ever remember.

Almost done. Giorgio leaned the squeegee against the chimney and then joined it in repose. Just a minute, he thought just a short rest. As he sat there, Giorgio closed his eyes, just for a moment. As much as his body craved it, his mind had begun to shun sleep. The nightmares had grown worse since he had seen that fat old man walking down the street. It couldn't have been him; not after so long, not more than half a world away. From the rooftop, anyone could look like anyone else. Any fat old man with a bristling mustache could have been him. As much as he didn't want to, as the twilight shadows lengthened over the rooftops, Giorgio fell into a deep sleep.

◆

"Fierro," said Herr Purzelbaum, "you come back to try again, eh? Will you do it finally, Fierro, or will you forever be the...*Einfalt?*"

Once more Giorgio was a boy but at the same time, an adult in that strange mixture of fantasy and reality that constitutes dreams.

"I... I will try again," said Giorgio.

The fat man snorted. "I will believe that after I see it, and then even if I see it, I will not believe it."

"I will try! I will do it, or my name isn't Giorgio Fierro!"

"Your name, ha!" said the fat old German, his cheeks aglow. "You may be Giorgio, but I made you Fierro. Who knows what you were before? Fierro? That means fire in your native tongue. Fire? I should have named you Giorgio Einfalt! That would be a more fitting name!"

"No," shouted a voice.

They turned, and the scene changed. They were no longer in the old barn but were in some sort of amphitheater, grander than any they had ever performed in before. This theater seemed to be constructed of clouds. There, above him stood the source of the objection.

"Mama," cried Giorgio. She was there, looking as he had remembered, except instead of her simple peasant dress and apron she was now wearing a beautiful gown.

"My boy is not a simpleton," she said. "He is a good boy, and he is a clever boy, you fat old thing!"

Purzelbaum sneered and waved aside her protests.

"No, he can do it," said another voice. Giorgio looked up into the mist. There was Uncle Roberto, and not only him, but Cousin Rosa by his side. And there were more behind them. It seemed that half the village was there; faces that he hadn't thought of in years, but they were there encouraging him, rooting him on; and not just them but there was *Captaino* Zimmer, the kind-hearted pilot. They were all on the side of the little orphan boy.

"See, Herr Purzelbaum," said Giorgio. "They are all for me. They know me. It is just you who are against me."

Purzelbaum sneered. "So, all your friends are here to tell me you can do this little trick. This trick is so simple for any of my boys, any of my boys who are not an Einfalt, that is! But life is not a vote. It is doing! They say you can do your triple somersault. That is fine, but even if a million people say you can do it that does not make it so. You must do it by yourself, or forever fail... by yourself."

The great cloud tried to shout down Purzelbaum, but the fat German merely stood there with his hands outstretched as if to say: "It is no good until he proves it by his actions."

Torn between past failures and the support of so many witnesses, Giorgio was gripped by fear. He had failed before, but only in practice, only in front of his tormentor. He had grown used to that. He could fall a thousand times in front of Purzelbaum. But how could he fail in front of such a cloud of encouragement? Giorgio tucked his head between his shoulders and waited for the voices to die down.

The celestial bowl grew quiet, but though he dared not raise his head, Giorgio still felt a thousand eyes trained upon him.

"So, there you see," said Purzelbaum, "he cannot. He will not even try. He is an Einfalt. I am sorry that you all had to come to see a performance that will not even end in failure. It will not even start, this boy..."

"He can do it," said a new voice.

Giorgio looked up. There beside his mother was an unfamiliar face but instantly recognizable.

"That boy is my son," said the man. He was tall and stood straight, he wore a soldier's uniform. "He can do it. He will do it, and then everyone here will see that you are the simpleton."

The crowd cheered. Giorgio's eyes were fixed on his parents, standing side by side and smiling at him. Giorgio felt himself rise to his feet. The cheering grew louder, and then hushed once more as he went to the edge of the springboard. Giorgio took his place. To his side was Purzelbaum daring Giorgio to even attempt that at which he had so often failed. Giorgio looked back up at his mother, beaming proudly at him and at her side, his father signaling his faith in his boy.

"I can. I can. I can do it," said Giorgio. He bent his knees slightly and could feel a new-found strength building up in his muscles. He rocked slightly, counting to himself. Every eye was trained upon him, every breath baited on his behalf. He tucked his body into a tight coil and then in one great burst of energy let fly.

Giorgio soared into the air, higher and higher, and then almost as an afterthought, recalled his purpose for doing so. He rolled. Once, twice, three times. He had done it! But Giorgio wasn't finished. He continued to spin: four, five, six times! The great cloud roared like a flood bursting through a dam. They seemed to rise as one to join him in celebration.

And he was one with them.

– 47 –
How a Lord Loses Gracefully

It h'ain't never was nothing, ahem, not nothing of no personal nature. Not no how."

Chesney Potoski unconsciously rubbed his bottom and recalled the last time he'd been in Bagnall Hall. That is, until today.

"Father, how can you say it wasn't personal," said Verity. "You threw poor Chesney bodily from the house."

Lord Bagnall went through a series of uncomfortable grimaces. "I don't recall tossing him…"

"No, you ordered your butler to do it," she said.

"Splatterguard always was a bounder," said Bagnall. "Always taking liberties, overstepping his bounds. I didn't not want the lad harmed…"

"And is that why you only had him forcibly thrown out…"

Chesney raised his hand, half encouraging calm, half seeking permission to speak; both went ignored.

It was an unseemly ending to what had been a touching memorial service for Hugh Goode. In addition to the national outpouring of affection for the late entertainer, the occasion was especially meaningful for the members of the immediate Goodhue family. Lord Bagnall, after years of estrangement from his father, delivered the eulogy. His Lordship revealed that just before Hugh Goode's passing father and son had been reconciled. Sitting next to Chesney throughout the service, Verity gripped her beloved's hand.

Now, with the last of the mourners leaving, Lord Bagnall was attempting to extinguish the fire on yet another burning bridge in his life before it was irreparably damaged.

"All right, then," said Lord Bagnall, first in a loud, angry voice, and then in more civil tones. "All right, this h'ain't not no time for such goings-on. Look, my dear, let me rephrase all that. I, me, your father, I'm a rotter.

Yes, it was me what had this..." he paused as he looked at Chesney. His nose twisted as if someone had neglected to put out last night's trash. He caught himself, forced a smile, and continued. "I had this boy tossed out on his ear..."

Chesney rubbed his posterior. "You missed," he muttered. Verity patted his arm.

"It was I wot had it done," continued Bagnall. "If I h'ain't not learned nothing in my years in the Queen's service it was that there is what is called a chain of command. As some American said... one of your type, I think..." this parenthesis was addressed to Chesney. "Some American said if a buck is going to stop it might as well stop 'ere. I h'admits it, yes, I threw the little... threw him out, or would 'ave 'adn't I not 'ad someone to do it for me. It was done just as if I 'ad done it myself and not that rotter, that Splatterguard. Any road, I owns it, I done it, and..." here he lowered his head momentarily before raising it again. "...and I admits me loutish behavior. It was done in the 'eat of the moment, and warn't not directed at this... fine lad... though it whar his bum that got the bruising. What say, uh... Chesney, lad, shall we let by-going go by?"

Lord Bagnall extended his hand to Chesney, who smiled and began to reach for it until Verity intercepted his hand.

"Just a minute, Chesney," she said. "I think we need to settle a few things first. Father, you fired Chesney from his assignment."

"Oh? Wot assignment would that be?"

"As your biographer," she said. "What I'd like to know is why you fired him."

Lord Bagnall contorted his face in a way that made his mustache perform a dance interlude. Then he jerked his head to the side. "My bee-ography? Ha, I 'ad almost forgotten that, yes, I suppose I was going to jot down just a few notes on my life h'experiences."

"Just a few notes?" She said, "Your library is filled with research for it. Did you fire Chesney and toss him out because he told you that he was working on grandfather's book, or because he told you he was seeing me?"

The question seemed to cause His Lordship discomfort. He ran his index finger along the inside of his collar and kicked at the marble floor with the toe of his shoe.

"Well?" said Verity.

"I don't quite recollect."

She glowered at him. He refused to look at her.

"Well, it doesn't matter," Verity finally concluded with a dismissive air.

"It don't?" said Lord Bagnall.

"It doesn't?" said Chesney.

"No, it doesn't matter," she said, "not really. If you fired Chesney and threw him out of your home because he was writing grandfather's biography that didn't stop him."

Lord Bagnall grimaced.

"And if you tossed Chesney out because he was going to date me," she continued, "that is a moot point as well because I love him and I'm going to marry him. Of course, any girl would want her father's blessing and support in such an important undertaking. But that is what is going to happen with or without your approval, Father."

For a moment His Lordship's teeth seemed to be bothering him as if he had just bitten another unripe greengage. He digested her disagreeable declaration before forcing a smile.

"Haw, haw," he said, "I can't fool me own flesh and blood, can I?"

"Can you?" said Verity, sweetly, but skeptically.

"No, no, of course not, no how," he said. "Daughter, you prove yourself worthy of the proud lineage from which you've been sprung. Not to put too fine a point on it, you've got a good brain in that pretty 'ead of yours."

She just smiled. Bagnall coughed a few times before continuing.

"Uh, yes, as I was saying, I can't not pull the wool over yer eyes. I'm a proud man. No, no, I h'am..." he paused here as if he expected to be contradicted. Receiving no argument, he continued. "Ah, well, as I was saying, pride comes and goes and then ashes to ashes we all's fall down, as the rhyme 'as so aptly put it. Your grandfather and I 'ad what you'd call a complicated relationship. 'E was what you'd call beloved..."

At that word, Chesney couldn't help but look at Verity.

"That's what Verity calls me," he said. "My beloved."

Lord Bagnall grimaced. "Does she? Well, I h'ain't never been beloved, not by nobody no 'ow..."

"Mother loved you, she was devoted to you," protested Verity. "And I love you."

Bagnall wagged his head. "Yes, well, I know that, but that's not wot I meant. Yer grandfather was loved by strangers. 'E dumped me in a boarding school when me mother died, and went around singing them silly songs, and people loved 'im for that. Wot all did I do? I just went into the h'army, and then built a big business conglomerate. I give thousands of people jobs and done a great lot for my country, but I h'ain't not wot you'd call 'beloved.' Then the same man, the man wot shunted me off to the side when I was just a little nip goes and nicks me own bee-ographer... one wot I'm paying, and 'e gets what I'm paying for... for free, clear and gratis." He stopped and put his hand on Chesney's shoulder and looked him squarely in the eye.

"Boy, would you have come all this way to do my bee-ography for free?"

Chesney bristled, not only because "free" didn't require the preposition "for," but because of the answer. He shook his head.

Lord Bagnall nodded his head and smirked, patted Chesney on the shoulder. "Well, thank you for yer h'onesty. I suppose now you'll finish me father's book."

"It's all finished."

Bagnall seemed surprised. "Well, then wotcher gonna do now?"

"I'm going to marry your daughter, and I suppose I'll go back to work."

"Work? Where?" A look of panic was in His Lordship's eyes.

"New Jersey."

"But that's in the States! All the ways over the ocean!"

"Yes, sir," agreed Chesney.

"That's thousands of miles away," he turned to Verity. "That's thousands of miles away. What are you going to do?"

She looked at him as if it were an odd question. "Father, I'm marrying him. Wither he goest, thither I."

"Thit... thit... thit..." spluttered Bagnall.

"Thither I," said Verity firmly.

"Why couldn't he not work 'ere," he said, "in England?"

"Because I 'aven't not got no work here, not no 'ow," said Chesney, imitating His Lordship's colorful speech patterns. His Lordship cast him a forbidding look.

"He had work here," said Verity, "but someone fired him."

"Well, uh, wot if that someone, re-hired 'im?"

"I suppose I'd have to stay where my work was," said Chesney.

Lord Bagnall's eyes twitched as if his mind were making rapid calculations. "I suppose someone," he said, "namely meself, needs to resume 'is bee-ography. If I can find me a good writer, that is." He looked at Chesney.

"I'm sure something can be arranged," said Chesney.

His Lordship wedged a hideous grin beneath his mustache and turned to his daughter.

"There, that's that," he said.

"I see," said Verity, though Chesney seemed to detect some reserve in her reply. "So you're happy for Chesney and me?"

Again, there was a pause as His Lordship seemed to be forcing down another sizable pill, but once swallowed, he broke into a smile.

"I couldn't not be more 'appy," he said and reinforced his grin to confirm it. "I'll be man enough to admit that I've lost."

"Father, you've never lost," said Verity skeptically. "You hate to lose."

"Well, I've lost this time, 'aven't I?" said Bagnall. "Of course, it's always 'ard to lose a daughter, but, like they say I'm, uh, getting a son. Besides, I always liked young, uh, Potoski 'ere, 'aven't I?"

"Potts, Sir," said Chesney. "I've changed my name... legally."

Both father and daughter looked at him.

"Potts, yes, Potts, always liked that, simpler, cleaner, more, well, British," said Lord Bagnall with his first sincere smile of the day.

"Chesney, why?" asked Verity.

"I believes it was my idea," interjected His Lordship. "It was me what first called 'im 'Potts,' eh?"

"Well, yes, you did first call me that," admitted Chesney. The look of surprise on Verity's face was hardening into displeasure. Chesney turned to Verity. "He did first call me that, but it was something your grandfather said that really gave me the idea."

"Grandfather?"

"'Im?" said Bagnall.

"Yes," said Chesney glancing at His Lordship before turning his full attention to Verity. "It was when we were writing his book. I asked him why he changed his name from Herbert Goodhue to Hugh Goode. He got that twinkle in his eye and said that it was almost magical. He had only been performing for a few months, and it wasn't going at all well. He was doing two-a-days at small music halls, trying to make a go of it as a performer and still send enough money home to his wife and baby."

Chesney pointed to Lord Bagnall. His Lordship, smirked.

"As I said," Chesney continued, "it wasn't going at all well. He tried new material, he tried changing around the order of his act, but nothing seemed to help. That's when he realized that he was afraid, afraid of looking foolish, afraid of being rejected by the audience, afraid of a dozen different things. But most of all, he was afraid that he, Herbert Goodhue would be a failure at the thing he most loved to do.

"One night, while he was trying to sort out his problem, your grandfather was asked to fill in on another part of the program. It was a one-act play, and one of the troupe had fallen ill. It was just a small part, and he was familiar with it from having seen it done for weeks, so he agreed to help out. That night he went on playing another person, and though he was only on the stage for a short time, he was a success. Afterward, he realized that he did so well because he didn't have to worry about failing because he was playing someone else. That's when he decided that from that point on he wouldn't go out on the stage as himself, but he'd be someone else."

"Hugh Goode," said Verity with a smile.

"Exactly," said Chesney. "He created Hugh Goode, and though no one could tell the difference between Herbert Goodhue and Hugh Goode, deep down it gave Herbert that extra confidence of not being alone on that stage. From then on it was Herbert and Hugh up there together, backing up each other.

"Your grandfather told me that made all the difference, and from that day on whenever he was afraid of failing or had any kind of career setback he would tell himself: 'Well, at least Hugh's on my side, and we'll get by together, Hugh and I.'"

"And that's why you changed your name?" asked Verity.

Chesney bowed his head and nodded. "That was around the time when I was afraid I'd lost you. Your grandfather helped me a lot during that time. We talked about his life, we'd just talk about life, and of course, our favorite topic: his granddaughter. When I was afraid of having messed up everything, he suggested that I get an ally on my side. Just as he had created Hugh Goode, he suggested that I create an alter-ego that would always be with me. I couldn't really change both names; after all, I didn't want it to be too obvious, or too confusing. So I just shortened my own name, Anglicized it a bit. Your grandfather called in his solicitor, and we did it. It's all legal."

Lord Bagnall curled his lip around his mustache. "Better name, anyway," he concluded.

"So I'll be Verity Potts, not Verity Potoski," she said.

"I'm sorry," he said. "Does it make that much of a difference?"

"Of course not," she smiled, "you've got a perfect right to change your name. After all, I've changed already changed your name, too, haven't I, My Beloved?"

They embraced. Lord Bagnall merely scratched his head.

"Who's hugging me now," asked Verity. "Chesney Potoski or Chesney Potts?"

"Both of us."

"I think I'll like having the two of you around."

Chesney smiled. He had been worried that Verity might object to the change. Now there was only one more person to tell. He hoped she would understand, as well.

– 48 –
Packing for My Destiny

Potoski or Potts, I couldn't care less. I've never called you by either, Chesney. You could change your name to Creamed Spinach, and I'd love you just as much. Hand me that… thing… that… case, please, dear."

Verity Goodhue did so and then sat down again in the armchair beside the bed.

"Thank you, dear," said Aunt Elinor. "I want to apologize again for not being able to attend your grandfather's memorial service."

"I understand," said Verity. "After all, you didn't even know him."

Elinor stopped her packing for a moment and looked at her. "No, that's true. And I can't even say that I felt I knew him. But, I sincerely wished that I had, if for no other reason than the kindness he showed to my dear boy…"

Chesney blushed.

"There he goes," said Aunt Elinor pointing at his face. "He never could take a compliment. Why should you go all red in the face like some… one of those things… tomato? Because I call you 'my dear boy?' I could have easily said 'our dear boy,' but you probably would have blushed an even deeper red, and you'd be even more useless… hand me those papers, Chesney. Chesney Potts! Yes, I think that suits you, as much as anything else. It certainly was a favor to this sweet girl. Imagine lumbering a gentle flower with such a lovely first name with a last name like 'Potoski!' I've had my whole life to get used to it, and still, it chaffs at times. Verity Potoski? Why it would be like putting kielbasa inside of a… what do you call it? One of those batter things…

"Toad-in-the-hole?" Verity suggested.

"Oh, yes, that's it: toad-in-the-hole, like a kielbasa in a toad-in-the-hole. No, it was probably the best wedding present you could give to the girl."

"I'd love him no matter what his name," said Verity.

Elinor looked at her and smiled, and then studied her face. "Verity Creamed Spinach. No, I can't see it."

"You don't think Dad would mind, then?" asked Chesney.

Aunt Elinor looked up from folding a sweater. "Your father? No disrespect, but I don't think he's in a position to object or even comment, at least I hope not. You're not Hamlet, after all. That's all you'd need at this point, ghosts walking around and you holding up skulls and wondering to be or not to be. It's all right for some old play, but it wouldn't do nowadays." She picked up another sweater. "I wish I could have come to your grandfather's memorial, dear, I'm so sorry."

"Please, Aunt Elinor, don't feel badly," said Verity. She then brightened. "You did send Mr. Postlewaite."

Aunt El adopted a somber expression. "Yes, I'm sorry for that as well. I hope he behaved himself."

Verity assured her that Postlewaite had behaved.

"I wish you didn't have to leave, Aunt El," said Chesney.

"It seems of all the phrases that run through my mind," said Elinor, "I can hear you saying that more than any other." She crossed to the corner of the room and hugged him. When she released him, he could see tears in the corners of her eyes.

"Aunt El…"

"Oh, don't mind me," she said. "I think as we get older, we get soppier."

"You're not old," he said.

"I feel… I feel all at once as if I were a mere child and at the same moment as old as Methuselah. But you know none of us is getting any younger. That's why I need to take this trip now, while I'm still young enough to enjoy it."

"But all the way to Tibet?" asked Chesney.

"It will make a… oh, what is it… an honest woman of me, you understand, don't you Verity, dear?"

Verity confessed that she didn't, leading Aunt Elinor to relate the story of how she had first come to London."

"Over thirty years is long enough for a layover, don't you think?" asked Elinor. "I have to go on now that I have the chance."

"Sort of fulfilling your destiny," said Verity.

"Precisely, yes, my destiny! My word, you've found a treasure, Chesney. Take good care of this one. An absolute treasure! My destiny!"

Chesney stood behind Verity and rubbed her shoulders, she reached up to clasp his hand. "She's one in five-billion, Aunt El."

"I'm no book editor, Chesney, dear," she said, "but isn't the usual phrase: 'one in a million?'"

"That's the approximate population of the world," explained Verity, half-embarrassed, half-delighted at the hyperbole.

"I see," said Aunt Elinor.

"It's my way of saying she's the only girl for me," he beamed.

She smiled at them and then returned to her packing.

"Yes, destiny," said Elinor, "apparently each of us has one. And that's why I have to go on my little, what's the word… journey?"

"All the way to Tibet?"

She shrugged her shoulders as if Tibet were just another Tube stop on the Picadilly Line. "Li Gao offered to escort me, and so I feel I must go."

"Couldn't you wait until after the wedding?" asked Chesney.

"Yes, the wedding… when is it again?"

"April 19th," he said.

She paused and seemed to be making mental calculations. "No, no," she concluded, "I couldn't wait until after that."

"But you'll be back for the wedding."

She looked at both of them. "I'll be there," she promised and placed her index finger over her heart. "I will be there."

As she resumed her packing, Chesney noticed she seemed to be packing an odd assortment of clothes.

"Aunt El…"

"Yes, dear," she said without looking up.

"Tibet is rather cold this time of year, isn't it?"

"I expect so," she said, still intent on her work, "what will all those mountains, and such…"

"Then why are you packing these things," he said. "those look like summer clothes. In fact, it looks as if you're packing everything you own."

She stopped and stared down into the box. "Yes, well, it appears that way," she said. "But only… because I am."

"But why?"

"I want to be ready," she said slowly at first, but then with more conviction. "I'll be moving soon."

"After you return?"

"You see, Postie wants to rent to a new tenant," she said.

"Moving? But you've lived here forever. Have you and Mr. Postlewaite had a fight?"

She seemed scandalized at the notion. "Fight with…" Aunt Elinor stopped in mid-thought.

"Aunt El?"

"Sorry," she said, "I just lost my train of thought. I must have been thinking of something else. What was I saying?"

"I asked if you had a fight with Mr. Postlewaite."

"A fight with Postie? Of course not! That would be like fighting with a puffy cloud, or one of Santa's elves, or even a congenital idiot. I'd never fight with dear, dear Mr. Postlewaite… argue, sometimes. Once I even chucked a tea cozy in his general direction when he was being obstreperous. But no, we've never fought."

"But then why are you…"

She raised her hand. "It's nothing to be concerned about. No one is angry, nothing is amiss, God is in his heaven…"

She left the end of the quotation to dangle.

"And all's right with the world?" added Chesney after a prolonged silence.

Aunt El looked up and smiled. "Absolutely, now bring your bottom over here, and sit on this case so I can shut it."

When he did so, and she snapped shut the latches, she kissed him on the forehead, and then looked down in dismay.

"Oh, I've left this out," she said and held up a gray pinafore dress. She then looked over at Verity. "It's nearly new; would you like it, Verity?"

"Thank you, but I couldn't," she said. "It's lovely, but…"

"Nonsense, here, try it on. That blouse you're wearing will go fine with it. I'd like you to have something… that is I'd like to give you something. I've never had much in the way of jewelry or heirlooms. Go ahead, try it on, for fun."

Verity agreed, and Aunt Elinor ushered Chesney out of the room and into her kitchen, where she began to fix the tea.

As Chesney sat watching her fill a plate with biscuits, his thoughts grew unsettled once again as to her odd preparations and why she would be moving.

"Aunt El," he said, "about all this packing…"

"Chesney, open this tin, please," she said, thrusting a tea canister into his hands. "About this trip I'm taking. I don't want you to worry. There's nothing to fear. I'll have Li Gao with me, and he knows where I'm going."

"Where you're both going, you mean."

"Yes, yes, of course," she said. "So, there's nothing to worry about. There's nothing to fear."

"Fear?"

Aunt Elinor stopped as if he had introduced the word and not her. She cocked her head to one side as if she were listening for an outside sound, and then continued. "No, that's right, nothing to fear. It's just an ordinary trip; the kind ordinary people take every day."

"Then why would you say not to fear?"

She shrugged her shoulders as she put the kettle on the stove. "Because I suppose it's something we all do so very well… be afraid, that is. Your grandfather, you don't remember him, do you?"

"Only that he seemed a million years old, had a wooden leg, and a military medal."

She thought for a moment and then nodded in agreement. "Yes, that was him," she said. "He was a bundle of fears."

"But I thought he was a war hero."

"Oh, certainly he was, he had been extremely brave, extraordinarily courageous, and scared out of his mind, as well."

"Is that why he never spoke about his heroics," asked Chesney. "Dad said that he'd never talk about it."

"Yes, your father was always bothered about that. He didn't know the full story, and Daddy, our father, would never tell him. I only found out years later. You see, he was afraid of that, as well. Perhaps 'afraid' isn't the word. He was more embarrassed. And I guess he was afraid: afraid that people would find out…"

"…that he wasn't a hero?"

Elinor seemed stunned at the suggestion. "Oh, no, he was absolutely a hero, saved his entire platoon, single-handedly. He lost his leg in the process. No, he was a great hero, your grandfather was."

"I'm afraid I don't understand."

"That's the point," she said, "don't be afraid." She stopped. "You know, your grandfather was afraid of the bathtub."

"You mean the water?"

"No, if I had meant the water, I'd have said the water. Your grandfather was afraid of the bathtub. As he grew older, he started growing weaker, in his arms, and his one leg. He was afraid that one day, he would sit down in the bathtub and not have the strength to get up again. I suppose that would seem a silly thing to fear, but most of our fears are silly, which is why I said: don't be afraid."

He looked at her as she set out the teacups. "Are you afraid, Aunt El?"

She stopped fussing with the tea implements but didn't look up.

"I used to be afraid," she admitted, "but I'm not anymore. Your grandfather was afraid of growing too old and too weak, and that can be quite fearsome. I used to be afraid of being alone, of growing old, but I see those are nothing to fear. The day I can no longer walk, well, that day, I will simply learn to fly." She smiled at him so placidly that he couldn't help but smile back and love her all the more.

"Well?" The door opened, and Verity stood there in the gray sleeveless dress with the white blouse beneath it.

"Oh, yes," said Aunt Elinor. "Oh, she's a perfect eight, isn't she Chesney?"

"I'd say a perfect ten," said Chesney.

"Eight is the dress size, you silly clot," said Elinor. "Do you like it, Verity?"

Verity smiled and pushed her glasses back up on to the bridge of her nose. "Yes, rather. How do I look, Chesney?"

Chesney looked her over. "I've never not liked the sight of you." He embraced her, and she kissed him, as Elinor watched.

"You can't know how happy it makes me to see you two together," she said. "I know you'll take good care of each other, won't you."

"I'll take good care of this boy," said Verity, "until you get back from Tibet, and beyond."

"Whither thou goest…" said Chesney.

"Thither I," said Verity.

Elinor smiled and shook her head. "I'm sure you two understand each other."

"No fear," said Verity.

– 49 –
The Dog Lover and the Negative Reaction

There was a knot in Valerie Fierro's stomach. It wasn't a little knot with a cute little bow. It was a big ugly knot with an ugly garish bow bigger than the hideous bows plaguing half of the dresses scattered around the ballroom. They were about to announce the prom queen. Albrecht had assured her she would win. Could she trust him?

Valerie sat with her back to the stage as they announced the winners. She didn't want to seem anxious; also, Albrecht could be full of crap.

The girls at the table, were surprised by Valerie's indifference.

"Don't you want to see who's going to be called?"

"Don't you want to see them go up?"

"Don't you care?"

"Oh, no," she replied, "this isn't my prom. I'm just a junior. I'm only a guest. This is the seniors' big night."

W. Buxton Dorning was very sweet through it all. "I voted for you," he assured her as if he was worried about her fragile feelings. "You look so beautiful, Valerie, I'm sure you'll be elected to the Queen's court, at the very least."

Valerie smiled and shrugged. As the winners were announced in reverse, order Valerie's name went unspoken. Bucky was disappointed and then annoyed. He was even more upset when he was named as the second runner-up to the King of the Prom.

"If they're not going to call you," he said, "I'm not going up there."

Valerie commended his loyalty but assured him that it didn't matter to her. She told him that she was proud that he had been chosen for so high an honor. High honor, she thought as he went up on the stage. Second runner-up! Second place loser! But she wondered if the fix were really in, as Albrecht had promised her. How could he rig the prom queen voting? But then, he was such a weasel, maybe he could. He was motivated by revenge. It didn't really have anything to do with her. She was just the beneficiary of his scheme. Her mind volleyed back and forth between the two alternatives, like a Ping-Pong ball on amphetamines.

Then Valerie had an idea. She would get up and walk out as if she were going to powder her nose. That would look good, wouldn't it? She would have to time it just right. She would wait until they announced the king and then start towards the back of the ballroom. That way, she would reach the exit just as they announced the queen.

The king was announced. He was the quarterback of the football team. A predictable choice: tall and good looking. He was popular with the jock crowd, but was not overly jockish and thus well-liked by his classmates. Valerie had even considered him in the first round for her own prom date. Still, she reasoned, being prom king was a nice consolation prize for him.

Valerie looked over at the table nearest the stage where all the stars of the senior class sat. It was now half empty. The other half was now standing on the stage. Sitting there, sticking out like a lone flower in a vase full of ferns was Cheryl Delaney. With most of her friends and even her date standing on the stage, it seemed a foregone conclusion that she would be the queen. She was the most beautiful non-Italian girl there, Valerie estimated.

Maybe Cheryl was going to win, she thought. After all, how could a loathsome little beast like Albrecht Eckner fix such an important election? The idea was preposterous. Elections were rigged all the time, but those were elections nobody really cared about: mayor, congress, things like that. People expected those to be set-ups. How could anyone, least of all spotty little Albrecht Eckner rig the election for prom queen?

He had made a fool of her. No one knew about it, of course, except her and Albrecht, but that was enough. She felt embarrassed and angry. Rising to her feet, she decided to leave, not just to make a show of it, but actually leave. She would come back, but she needed a moment to collect her thoughts. After all, she told herself, the entire evening wasn't ruined. She still looked spectacular in her dress, and she still had plans for later with Bucky. She just needed a moment.

She was half-way out of the ballroom when the applause started. Valerie began to walk more quickly. Good for Cheryl, she thought. It was her prom, after all.

She had almost reached the door when several hands grabbed her. She began to pull away when she heard them speak.

"You're going the wrong way."

"Congratulations, Valerie."

"Valerie, the stage is that way."

She stopped and turned. At the front of the room, she could see Cheryl Delaney sitting slumped over her table as if she had just been knifed in the back. She could see the master of ceremonies for the night standing by the microphone on the stage, repeating her name, "Valerie Fierro," and urging her to come up and receive her crown. She could see Bucky applauding as if his arms would fly off. And off to the side, standing there with his camera and his dorky little camera bag was Albrecht Eckner. Albrecht looked completely normal, even innocent. But, in the corners of his beady eyes, Valerie could see that he wasn't surprised. Those piggy little eyes had held the knife, the one that had just been buried between Cheryl's shoulder blades.

Valerie walked, almost staggering at first, but by the time she approached the stage, she was gliding.

It all came true, she thought, it all happened. Much to her surprise and great delight, Albrecht Eckner was true to his word. And there he was, happily snapping away with his camera. And there were the other girls, the runner-ups, the losers, all looking very pretty, but of course not as pretty as their queen. And there they were, those pretty girls, all seniors, placing the plastic tiara on Valerie's head and placing the velvet robe around her shoulders. And they were all failing, just barely, to hide the fact that they were all terribly envious of Valerie. The king didn't seem to mind, especially not as he kissed Valerie and handed her the bouquet of roses.

The rest of the evening went by in a blur. There were pictures. There were dances. There were congratulations, some of them even sincere. Sincere or not, it didn't matter. She had won. She had beaten them all. She was the queen, not just of the prom, but at that moment in time, Valerie was the queen of all teen-agers everywhere. She almost wished that Delaware had an active volcano. It would have been perfect if suddenly the du Pont Country Club had been inundated by rivers of molten lava and magma and all that other stuff. Valerie would have been satisfied if all that hot goo had burst through those French doors, and buried them all, preserving the entire prom in a suspended state for all time. Then, thousands of years hence, archeologists would unearth them and gasp and marvel.

"This must have been a celebration," the future archeologists would exclaim, "a celebration for a young and stunning queen...and just look at that perfect gown!"

She would be a greater sensation than King Tut and much cuter. No, she reminded herself, as perfect as this evening was, there was more to come. Soon, escorted by W. Buxton Dorning, they would drive off together in his mother's Jaguar, and they would drive down to the beach. There in his parent's seaside condo, they would consummate the evening. It would be perfect, simply...

Valerie's reverie was nudged, then prodded, and then completely knocked off its foundations by an insistent worm.

"Can I see you a moment... your majesty." Those last two words were spoken with an oily mixture of groveling and sarcasm. She only knew one person who could produce that tone: Albrecht Eckner.

She turned to see him standing there with his camera in his ugly pastel suit. His tuxedo seemed to glow. Valerie took a step back as if the aura would somehow stain her gown.

"Albrecht," she said coolly with a faint smile. She hoped he would see this was a subtle signal for him to just go away. He didn't.

Albrecht sidled closer.

"I have something for you, Valerie."

"Now?"

"Yes, it will only take a moment."

"But I... we'll be leaving in a few minutes, can't it wait until next week or sometime?"

Albrecht Eckner smiled his insidious grin, and his eyes narrowed.

"It will only take a moment," he said, "and it's very important."

Valerie turned to the girl with whom she'd been chatting and excused herself. She took a step to the side, he pulled her elbow, and she glowered at him. He ignored the look.

"What?" she snapped.

"Not here," said Albrecht calmly, "believe me, not here."

With a subtle darting of his eyes, he directed her behind a partition.

"What?" she repeated even more impatiently once they were out of sight.

"Congratulations on your election as prom queen," he said.

It sounded so genuine that Valerie abandoned her annoyed tone. "Thank you," she said.

"Yes, precisely," he said. "Thank me."

That was it, she thought, the bill was coming due. There was a string attached.

"Okay," she said, "what do you want?"

He feigned a hurt expression and then smiled as they both knew it was only an act.

"I just wanted to extend my invitation to you."

"For what?" she said.

"Just a little post-prom party," said Albrecht.

Her lips curled into a sneer of disgust. She could only imagine what type of people would populate a party thrown by Albrecht Eckner. For one thing, he'd probably be wearing the nicest suit there. Eww!

"I have plans for after the prom," she said.

He smiled.

"I'm going out with Bucky... Buck," she said. "Buck"sounded more macho and more threatening to a slug, like Albrecht.

"I think you really should attend my party," he said with a more menacing edge.

Valerie reached up and fingered her tiara. She thought of how upset Cheryl Delaney had been, and how annoyed all those senior girls were, and how uncomfortable Valerie would be if they discovered how she had won.

"Well," she said softening, "I suppose we can stop by your party. I'll ask Buck, and I'm sure he'll..."

"Come alone," said Albrecht.

"What? Who do you think..."

Albrecht Eckner raised his hand for silence and then pointed to his camera bag. He undid the latch to reveal a small tape recorder.

"It's all on tape," he said.

"What is?"

"Your plot to fix the voting."

"But that was your idea," she protested.

"In which you were complicit," he said with a smug grin.

"But..." Valerie's mind raced. She could tell Bucky to beat him up. Yes, that was it, and then she could take his tape, and... No, she thought, a bruised and battered Albrecht Eckner would only scream all the more. She would compromise.

"Can I do something for you?"

"I want to escort you to my party."

"I mean, something, some other time, not tonight. Not tonight, please."

"I'm sorry," he said, "it has to be tonight. I'll give you the tape at the end of the party."

Wild scenarios rushed through her head. Running over Albrecht with a steamroller until he was flatter than a crepe was enticing, but few proms committees had the forethought to include steamrollers in their preparations. She gave one last shot at defiance.

"What if I say no? What if I say I won't go to your party?"

He shrugged. Ha, thought Valerie, all she had to do was call his bluff. But then he reached into his jacket pocket and pulled out a rice paper sleeve.

"I didn't want to have to do this." He said it in a way that told her that he couldn't wait to do it. "But I think you should see this before you decide."

He handed her the sleeve. She examined it. It was the type of envelope for photographs. She looked at him. He cocked one eyebrow as if to say: go ahead, see for yourself, it's your funeral.

Though that last phrase was unspoken, no truer words were ever unsaid. It was Valerie's funeral. For there on a three-by-five glossy print was a picture of Valerie, half-naked, half-wearing a robe. And it looked like she was in the middle of an illicit act with Reggie the Collie taken through her bedroom window.

Valerie gasped, then covered her mouth, and then looked at the picture again, and then raised her hand to strike Albrecht.

"I wouldn't do that," he cautioned. She dropped her hand.

"What? How did you..."

Albrecht looked towards the ceiling. "I always was very good at climbing trees," he said in a bored tone. "A good tree, a telephoto lens, a girl who doesn't close her curtains..."

"You little pervert..."

"I'm not the one having sex with the family dog," he said.

"I'm not!" She began to blurt out an explanation. She tried to explain how the dog often jumped on the bed and how any movement under the blankets could drive Reggie into fits of passion. She tried to explain that the look on her face in the photo was one of shock.

"If you had a picture another second later, you'd see I was kicking him off the bed."

"Oh, I have that photo, too," he admitted. Then he wrinkled his nose in a devilish manner. "It's not nearly as interesting, however."

"Oh, really, well…" Valerie ripped up the photograph into confetti.

He shook his head. "I have the negative and plenty more prints. I think W. Buxton Dorning will find it interesting. I do hope you kept telling him how passionate you were for animals. This will only prove how passionate." He took another copy of the photo from his pocket and flashed it in her face.

Valerie thought the times she raved about animals in front of Bucky, and all the dances with the dog in his presence. Now, what would he think? "Well, no one will believe it," she said.

"Probably not," he conceded, "but that's an awful lot of explaining to do, and besides, I'm sure everyone will want to see it. Don't you think so? And then, even when it dies down everyone will remember you as: 'Valerie the Dog Humper.'"

Valerie's shoulders sunk to her sides. He had her. The little rat, the disgusting little beast, had her.

"All right," she sighed. "I'll go to your party. But what will I tell Buxton?"

"That you're not feeling well; that you've called your parents; that they're picking you up. Then you'll go out the side door. I'll be waiting for you in my car. Understand?"

Valerie nodded in resignation. "I'll be there."

She emerged from behind the partition in a zombie state. All around her, people were having a wonderful time. Now she had to leave it all, leave the scene of her greatest triumph. She had to tell W. Buxton Dorning, the man whom she had planned on offering her greatest treasure; she had to tell him she was sick.

She knew he would believe her. He had to. She felt so sick she could die.

– 50 –
The Discounted Wedding Presents and the Forever Promise

A little more than three weeks to go."

"A little more than three weeks," she repeated.

"And we'll be married," he said.

"And I will be Mrs. Chesney Potts."

"Verity Potts," he corrected. "I never was crazy about my first name, but I love yours."

"And I love you."

"And I love you."

"And I wish the pair of you would come up for air, so's Potts could get some work done on me book."

The couple sat bolt upright as Lord Bagnall barged into his own library.

"Sorry, your Lordship," said Chesney, pretending to return to work.

"Oh, Father," said Verity, "don't be such a stuffed shirt. You were in love once, I know you were."

A wistful expression crossed Lord Bagnall's face. "True, true," he looked at Verity and smiled. "And you is a constant reminder of that, daughter." He glanced over at Chesney, and his expression dropped. "Try and get some work done if it h'ain't not too much bother."

"Yes, sir," promised Chesney as Lord Bagnall left the room. He made an effort to return to the biography, but Verity interrupted.

"The tailor's shop in the village found that lace I was looking for."

"Tailor's in the village?"

"Yes, you know the one," she said, "they're the ones with the funny little sign in the window. The one that reads: 'Alternations Done on Premise,'" she laughed. "Instead of 'premises,' as if you needed grounds or evidence before you could have a hem done. I always thought it was cute."

"Do you want me to go and tell him they need an 's' on their sign?"

"No," she said, "I always thought it was so charming. I'd hate to see it corrected."

Chesney looked toward the door.

"Do you think your father's upset? I was working on his biography the other day, and he asked me again about my future."

She entwined her arm with his. "That's 'our future.' What did you tell him?"

Chesney shrugged. "I explained that aside from the wedding and the honeymoon, there are no plans after I finished his book. That's what I think may be upsetting him. He asked if I was going to stay here in England. He asked as if it were a rhetorical question, with the only possible answer being that I would stay. I explained that I didn't know. After all, I'll have a spousal visa when we get married, but that's not good forever. I said you and I would have to decide where to live."

"Wither thou goest, My Beloved..." she kissed him.

"Hmm, yes, thank you, but I don't think your father's too happy with the 'thither I' part."

She kissed him again on the cheek. "You worry too much. Father will just have to accept whatever happens, and I think he already has. After all, he did give us those lovely wedding presents."

Chesney nodded. "Yes, but why does a married couple need two sports cars? Does he think we're going to have a race?"

"Knowing Father," she said, "he probably got a two-for-one deal with one of his business contacts. Anyway, he didn't even play favorites."

"No, they're identical," admitted Chesney. "Aside from the personalized plates, you can't tell them apart."

"And they're very sweet," she said.

"I suppose, but..." Chesney was interrupted by the butler at the doorway.

"Pardon me, Mr. Potts," began Towson. "His Lordship wishes to remind you that you have your appointment with his solicitor in London this afternoon." The butler then made an obsequious show of stifling a cough on the back of his hand for seemingly no other reason than he was an obsequious butler.

Chesney attempted an obsequious smile in return but failed by half.

"I suppose I'd better get going," he said, rising and looking at his watch. "Thank you, Towson..." the butler bowed slightly and backed out of the room. "Thanks again, Igor..." muttered Chesney after he had disappeared.

"Be nice," said Verity with a smile.

"That guy just gives me the creeps," said Chesney. "I think I saw him in an old horror film. I wish you were going with me."

"I know, but I have a wedding dress fitting," she said.

"I wish I were going to that," he said, "on the premise."

"Which premise would that be?"

"On the premise that I don't want to go to London just to talk to your father's lawyer about immigration, and being integrated into the family, and all that sort of thing. I don't know anything about that stuff. And why couldn't the lawyer come here? After all, he comes up here to talk with your father."

"But you're not Father," said Verity. "Honors to honors and all that. Now you run along to London, I'll go to my fitting, and I'll pick up those maps from the auto club so we can start mapping out our honeymoon wander through Britain."

"But not Skegness," he said, reminding her of Lord Bagnall's suggestion since that was where he had spent his honeymoon.

"For you, My Beloved," said Verity, "I would go even to Skegness, even to Clacton-on-Sea, but just the same, I'd rather avoid them both."

She kissed him on the lips and then escorted him out to his waiting car, where they kissed again. He stepped back from her. She was wearing the gray dress Aunt Elinor had given her.

"I really like that outfit on you," he said, before adding, "don't change."

"The dress?" She laughed.

"No, just you," he said. "Stay as you are."

"For how long?"

"Forever, please?"

"I promise not to change if you don't," and kissed him on the cheek.

Chesney started to climb into the red Triumph convertible when she pointed out that he was taking her car by mistake. He looked at the other car's plate, which read "POTTS-7." He climbed out of her car, kissed her goodbye again, climbed into the correct automobile, received another kiss from Verity, and started the motor.

"I love you," she said as she waved him goodbye.

He returned her love and drove away. Pulling out of the estate, he began to turn left but was stopped by a work crew digging up the most direct route to the village and the motorway beyond.

"Drains," said a middle-aged man in overalls.

"Pardon?" asked Chesney.

"The drains," he said, pointing to the hole across the road. "Old drains, we're digging them up. You can take the detour," he said, motioning off to the right. Goes 'round the back of the estate, through the woods."

"Right, thank you," said Chesney.

The back road was narrow and included many dips and sharp turns. Fortunately, Chesney had left early enough that he wouldn't be late for his appointment.

The detour was the only interesting part of the journey, and that had only taken up ten extra minutes. The appointment with the lawyer was as boring as he had anticipated it would be and twice as confusing. Lord Bagnall's solicitor was as dusty as one of his law volumes. He droned on concerning the finer points of immigration laws and the possible pitfalls and their potential solutions involved when an American boy married an English girl. Once those matters had been discussed, the lawyer apologized in advance before launching into a discourse on the complexities involved when a relatively poor American married an English girl with the potential for being stinking rich on the death of her father. This came as something of a surprise to Chesney, for though he had been researching and writing on the material success of the man, Lord Bagnall's wealth had been merely an academic consideration. He had never completed the thought that one day, Verity would fall heir to Bagnall's fortune.

"Do you want me to renounce it?" he asked chivalrously. "I will. I don't care about his money. Give me a paper to sign. I'd give up any claim on it in a second."

The solicitor waved him down and assured him that would not be necessary, though a few points would have to be addressed.

These points, none of which Chesney understood, consumed another forty-five minutes. The lawyer promised he would have all the proper formal papers drawn up for Chesney to sign within the week. Then like a bored schoolboy, Chesney was released from the solicitor's office. Also, like a freed schoolboy, Chesney hurried to the playground: more specifically to Mr. Postlewaite's shop.

Postlewaite had located a rare Hugh Goode film poster for Chesney to give to Verity as a wedding present. The shopkeeper held up the beautifully mounted and framed item as Chesney entered the small shop.

"Magnificent, Mr. Postlewaite," said Chesney reaching for his wallet. "How much do I owe you?"

"Nothing, it's a wedding present." The ordinarily ebullient Postlewaite seemed strangely subdued.

"No, I want to give it to Verity as a wedding present, you can't give it to me as a wedding present, and then expect me to turn around and give it to her as a wedding present."

"It's not from me," he said. "It's from your aunt for both of you. She took care of it before she…" he looked away. "…before she left."

Chesney clapped Postlewaite on the shoulder and asked him to wrap it up. Mr. Postlewaite promised he would but first asked Chesney to step into the backroom for a moment.

"Another surprise," asked Chesney. Postlewaite said nothing but directed him to the rear of the store. There, sitting at a small table, was Li Gao.

"Chesney, please sit down," said Li.

"Mr. Li," said Chesney with a smile, "you're back early. Aunt Elinor said she'd be at the wedding. How are you? How was your trip? How was Tibet? Where's Aunt Elinor? Is something wrong?" These questions were delivered in rapid succession, though by the final question, Chesney was aware of an uncomfortable anxiety.

"Please, sit," said Li Gao solemnly.

"Don't tell me," he said, the words catching in his throat. "Something happened to Aunt El in Tibet. I knew she shouldn't have…"

Li raised his hand. "We never went to Tibet."

"But you've been away for over a month," said Chesney. "I got letters. Mr. Postlewaite forwarded them…"

"Your Aunt was in hospice," said Li Gao. "I took her there. I stayed with her."

"Hospice, then she.."

He nodded.

Chesney dropped his head on to the table and burst into tears. After a few moments, he felt Gao's hand on his shoulder.

"I'm sorry…" said Chesney raising his head.

"It is I who should apologize to you," said Li Gao. "After all, we deceived you with that story about Tibet."

"But why?"

"Your dear aunt had a form of Creutzfeldt-Jakob disease…"

"Mad Cow disease?"

"Yes, the human form," said Li, "It was particularly aggressive in her case. She deteriorated rapidly."

"But I didn't notice," said Chesney, before stopping. "Wait, the last time we saw her when she was packing, she seemed out of it, a little disoriented, forgetful…"

"That was the dementia," he said. "She had tried to conceal it from you. It grew rapidly worse. She didn't want you to remember her that way."

"She thought… she said she would be at the wedding."

Li Gao nodded and tapped his chest. "She will be there, I assure you. She loved you very much, my boy."

"I loved her," said Chesney, "she and I…she was the only person…" He checked his thought as he glanced at his watch. It was later than he thought. Verity. Verity would be worried. He needed to call her. He needed to tell her about Aunt Elinor. He needed to be with her. He asked if he could use the telephone. Chesney dialed the number. As it rang, he thought of Aunt Elinor, and how he would miss her. At least he had Verity and immediately scolded himself for such a selfish thought. But, he reminded himself, he had been a comfort to Verity when Hugh Goode had passed away. She would be the same to him now.

"Hello, dear?" he said as soon as he heard the receiver pick up at the other end.

"Chesney, lad, thank goodness, it's you," it was Lord Bagnall.

"Your Lordship, may I speak to…"

"We tried calling 'round at my solicitor's, 'cept you'd already gone."

"Yes, but, please, I need to speak to…"

"Boy, are you sitting?"

"Yes, look, please, may I speak to…"

"Chesney, boy," said Lord Bagnall gravely, "there's been an accident."

– 51 –
Lost on a Technicality

Valerie Fierro never thought she'd be there again, not willingly. And, she certainly wasn't there willingly now. "I thought we were going to a party," she said.

"Keep your voice down," whispered Albrecht Eckner. "Do you want to wake up everybody?"

"I really don't... OW!"

"And don't trip over the stock," he said as he led her by the hand through the darkness of his family's store.

"Marvelous!" she grumbled.

She still couldn't believe Bucky's reaction when she told him she had to leave the prom without him.

"I understand," he said, before adding, "let me know how everything works out."

Valerie stood there with her mouth agape. This was the boy who was going to gorge himself on her pristine virginity. Now he'd have to wait. He so readily bought the excuse that she didn't feel well. No disappointment. Instead, he said: "you'd better hurry," and almost pushed her out the door.

Now it was all ruined, she thought. She would lose her virginity some other time, but it wouldn't be as special as tonight. She wouldn't be wearing her incredible gown. As perfect as the dress was, she couldn't go around wearing it on casual dates on the off chance that the evening would end in sex. Now the first time she'd have sex, she would be wearing casual clothes. That would make it just casual sex. She didn't want just casual sex for the first time. She wanted incredible perfect sex, and to do that, she needed her incredible perfect dress. Stupid Albrecht Eckner, she thought, as he led her through the darkened store. She almost regretted being made prom queen.

"Okay, where's this party you're taking me to, and what are we doing here in this yucky store?"

He stopped and turned. The glow of the street lamps shining through the windows at the front of the store bathed half his face in an eerie light while leaving the other half in darkness. He smiled.

"We're here," he smiled.

"Here? Where? Here?"

"Of course, here," he said.

"Where's the party?"

"We're the party," he said as he crouched behind the counter, pulling her down beside him.

She tried to resist but was surprised at the strength hidden beneath his layers of baby fat. She hit the floor, but the floor wasn't hard. It was lumpy and squishy.

"What are you doing? What's this I'm sitting on?" With great effort, she pushed him off of her and sat up.

"Quiet," he said, "not so loud…"

"I want to see what's going on," she said.

"Okay, just keep your voice down," he said. "I've got a flashlight here…"

He turned on the flashlight, holding it down and creating an even creepier atmosphere. From the floor, the shop looked even more frightening in the harsh shadows. She looked down. The soft lumps were inflatable rubber rings.

"What are those? Beach toys?"

"Inflatable cushions," he said. "We sell them, you know, for people with hemorrhoids."

"EWWW!" she said and jumped up. He grabbed her wrist and pulled her back down.

"It's okay," said Albrecht, "you don't have to use them. I just thought it would be more comfortable. I've got some blankets here, too."

"Blankets for what?"

He smiled and raised his eyebrows at her in a licentious manner.

"You think I'd neck with you?" she said, raising her voice.

"Shh, will you be quiet…oh, what's the use," his leering expression melting into a pitiful one, and for a second, Valerie almost felt sorry for him, until the leer rekindled in his eyes.

"Don't forget the picture…" he said, the Machiavellian vigor returning to his voice. In a low growl, he added: "woof, woof!"

"Yes, and you promised," she said, "that you'd give it to me after I attended your party. So hand it over, and all the negatives." Valerie extended her white-gloved hand.

Albrecht shook his head. "Nothing doing."

"But you said…"

"Ah! We're not at the party, yet."

"I thought you said we were the party."

"We are," he said, "or you are…"

He tilted his head. Valerie followed the direction of his look. It confirmed her worst nightmare. The party was to take place between her legs. He meant her to be the hostess with himself the guest of dishonor.

Valerie opened her mouth wide, half in shock, half with a notion to scream loud enough to be heard at every prom within a fifty-mile radius. But then she paused to consider, a myriad of thoughts leaping through her mind.

The dog, the picture of the dog, her with the dog, her with hardly any clothes on, you could see her boobs, they were pert, round, and she was proud of them, but still, she didn't want just anyone looking at them. Albrecht would pass the photo around, in dozens of copies, everyone would see her boobs. That might actually enhance her reputation... no, everyone would see it, including people she didn't want to see it. But again, there was the dog, Reggie, the collie. As bad as it could be to have topless pictures circulated around, it was not nearly as bad as topless pictures with a very horny dog. And though Valerie was shouting at him to get off, it may look like she was as excited as the dog. Then there was her mother. Her mother would blame Valerie, blame the dress, blame the dog. Her mother had forty maybe fifty years left in her. Could Valerie listen to her nag about an incident that never really happened for that long? Her father, well, he would understand, he wouldn't believe it. She never had to worry about him. Rose! Rose would be so smug, and she would wear that smug look on her face long after their mother had gone. Having dispensed with her immediate family, visions of Bucky Dorning and his parents materialized shaking their heads. She began to think about the whole fixing of the prom queen vote, but it was more than her mind could take. She grabbed the sides of her head as if to slow the thoughts speeding through her brain. With her hands providing support, she moved her head up and down in assent.

"Okay? You'll... we'll do it?" said Albrecht eagerly.

"Yes, yes," said Valerie, not daring to open her eyes. That was it, she told herself. Just keep your eyes closed. Don't look at the icky store, don't look at the puffy boy, just keep your eyes closed and think of... She wasn't sure what to think of. Just think about nothing, she decided. Besides, she recalled from her girlfriend's testimony that the first time was overrated. It was painful. It was messy. She might as well have a horrible time with Albrecht Eckner than to have it with someone whom she might actually care about.

"Okay," said Albrecht rising to his knees and unbuckling his ghastly pastel-colored trousers.

"Don't talk so much, please," said Valerie.

"I only said 'okay.'"

"Shh," she said, "you don't want to disturb anybody." Especially not me, she thought.

Just as she imagined the nightmare to be at its zenith, the stakes were raised. Somebody turned on the lights.

"Oh, shit," muttered Albrecht, before adding: "keep down."

Valerie didn't even have to be told once. She pushed against the back of the counter while Albrecht stood up, hoisting up his trousers as he did so.

"*Was ist los?*"

The voice sounded like an old man mumbling through a half-pound of bacon. It must be Albrecht's fat million-year-old grandfather, Valerie told herself. He sounded as if he were descending the staircase across the room.

"It's only me, Opa," said Albrecht. "It's my grandfather," he muttered down to Valerie.

"Albrecht, wot you doing?" said the old man.

The last time she was there, he pretended not to speak English. The fat old fake!

"Uh, nothing, Opa, just taking stock, you know, helping out Dad."

"At *dieses* hour?"

"Uh, sure, why not?"

"In your fancy suit? Wot 'bout your fancy dance?" The old man's voice grew closer.

"Don't come down, Opa," said Albrecht. "I'll be done soon."

"Wot about der dance?"

"It's, it's all over. I went to the dance, and now... I came home, and I couldn't sleep... you know I'm all excited... so I thought I'd check the stock, for Dad..."

"*Einfalt!*" said the old man as if he were spitting and laughing at the same time. "You go to a dance and come home all by your alone. In *mein* day...ach, jung peoples! Einfalt!"

"Go to bed, Opa," he said, "I'll be up in a little bit."

The footsteps were going back up the stairs. The lights went out again, and she could hear a distant door shutting.

"He's gone," said Albrecht dropping his trousers again.

"What's that?" she asked, pointing to his buttock.

He redirected the flashlight beam over his thigh.

"It's just a birthmark."

She snickered. It looks like a..." she was about to say a used condom, but amended that thought. "It looks like a snake run over by a dump truck."

"It's just a birthmark," he repeated as he began to disrobe. She looked away, the sight of his bare butt being more Eckner flesh than she had ever wanted to see in her lifetime. She grabbed the flashlight and turned it aside

"There," he said. She took his word for it that he was ready. "Now, you."

Resignedly, Valerie reached behind her and unzipped her beautiful, perfect gown. She had hoped it would be passionately removed by Bucky Dorning, but as he was miles away, she was careful not to damage it. Sliding out of the gown, she handed it to Albrecht and asked him to place it atop the counter. She kept her elbow-length gloves on so as not to have to touch him more than necessary.

"What about your underwear," he asked.

She rolled her eyes and removed her panties.

"What about that?" he asked. He was pointing at her upper torso.

"It's a bustier," she said in a sigh. "You don't need that off. It's bottomless."

"Like a diner coffee cup," he snickered.

"Whatever," she said.

"Uh, okay," he said, and for a moment seemed distracted. Valerie took advantage of the lull to ask an important question.

"What about protection," she said.

"I locked the door."

"Not that kind of protection. I've had enough surprises for one night, and I don't want any more in nine months."

"I've got a rubber," he said.

"Good," she said. She had been on the pill for months in anticipation of this evening. But like her gloves and her bustier, any layers insulating her from Albrecht were desirable.

"I have something I'd like you to wear, too," he said.

"What?"

He reached into a nearby drawer, pulled something out of it, and held it up. She redirected the flashlight.

"Ewww!" she said. "That? You want me to wear that?"

It was horrid. It was some sort of white, rubbery looking surgical corset with all sorts of heavy boning, and reinforcement, and ugly white strings that looked like sneaker laces.

"Yes," he said.

"Yuck, it's icky," said Valerie, "it's almost as icky as this whole icky store."

Albrecht Eckner seemed genuinely taken aback. He glanced around the darkened store.

"Icky?" he said. "Our store isn't icky. This is life!"

"Icky life," said Valerie.

"No, there's nothing icky about it. These things help people."

Valerie almost added old icky sick people but didn't feel like prolonging the debate. He continued anyway.

"These things which you find unseemly..."

"Icky!"

"These things help people to heal. They help infirm people lead a more normal life. These things mean health and strength and independence. They're vital, they're exciting." His voice lowered into a smokier register. "They're even... sensuous." He extended the revolting surgical corset towards her. "That's why I want you to wear it."

"I'm already wearing the sexiest bustier you'll ever hope to see!"

He looked at her in the dim light. "You could slip it on over that."

"Not even if I needed it," she said, "which I never will because I'd kill myself before I got that old and ugly."

"But…"

"But nothing," said Valerie with a cold finality. Snatching the odious garment from his hand, Valerie flung it over the counter. She then closed her eyes and positioned herself on the floor for action.

"Okay," she said, "put your… thing… on your… thing."

He sighed but complied.

Through barely opened eyes, she watched as he opened the packet and prepared himself. Then he lowered himself on her waiting body and began.

She tried thinking of other things. She tried thinking of anything and nothing. For a moment she thought about shopping. That was nice. Then she felt a sharp pain. That's that, she thought, welcome to womanhood. Then she felt a few thrusts, clumsy at first, and then more rhythmic. She was almost forgetting who was supplying them. It was almost nice, and then suddenly they stopped. Valerie waited a moment. That was too short, she thought. From every eyewitness account from every girlfriend who'd gone on before, it was too brief: even for a teenaged boy.

Valerie felt his body rise off of hers, and she opened her eyes. She could see his silhouette against the ceiling. His shoulders were slumped forward, his neck craning out from his body. Reaching for the flashlight, she shone it on his face. There stood Albrecht Eckner red-faced, looking away. As much as she had tried to avoid it, her curiosity got the better of her. She moved the light down to his groin.

Albrecht Eckner had gone limp. He'd failed, sputtered out even before he had really gotten going.

Valerie shook her head. She had lost her virginity on a technicality. She had had sex: barely. A doctor would be satisfied, but she sure as hell wasn't.

"That's it?" she said

He looked away, over the counter. "I told you that you should have worn the corset." He muttered.

Valerie rearranged herself, rose to her feet, and put on her dress.

"I can do it again if you'll…"

"Forget it," she said as she zipped up her dress.

"But what about the pictures," he reminded her.

She looked at him and felt a new strength. Placing her hand on her hip, she leaned into him. "Look, you're not going to do anything with those pictures. You had your chance, and you blew it. You had your party, but you didn't come to it. You'll destroy everything: the pictures, that tape…"

"The tape was empty," he admitted.

Valerie rolled her eyes. "You'll get rid of that picture and the negatives! Because if anyone ever sees them, if even I see them again, if you even look at them again, I'll tell everyone about that."

She pointed down at his flaccid member.

After allowing him a moment to absorb her threat, Valerie started for the door.

"Wait," he said, "I'll drive you home."

She turned and held up his keys.

"I'll drive myself," she said. "You can pick up your car in the morning."

The woman exited.

– 52 –
The Lime Green Wellies
on the Shelf

Verity Elizabeth Goodhue.
The headstone was average and yet as dignified as the body over which it now stood watch.

Below were two years separated by a dash.

Beneath that was the inscription: "Dear Daughter."

Beneath that, Chesney had insisted on: "My Beloved, Too."

That was all he could think to add. "Dear Fiancée," didn't seem appropriate, nor did "Almost wife."

My Beloved, for she was and always would be.

Two weeks today, and they would have been married.

It was a secluded spot on the estate grounds. They used to walk there hand in hand. Now...

He had rushed back after receiving the news from Lord Bagnall. He hung up the phone, said something hurriedly to Li Gao and Mr. Postlewaite, and drove as fast as he could back to Staffordshire. He had to go by the detour around the back of the estate; the main road still ripped up. That was where he saw it: the emergency crew, the fire brigade, the red sports car identical to his own down in a ravine just off a sharp bend in the road. It had been a red car. Now it was a blackened shell, with everything in it burnt to an undistinguishable cinder.

He had jumped out of the car and started down the embankment when he was grabbed from behind.

"No, lad," it was Lord Bagnall. "You don't not want to go down there."

Verity was gone. Aunt Elinor was gone. He spent most of the next few days in a state of shock, sitting alone in her empty cottage. Lord Bagnall took charge of all the funeral arrangements, coming in occasionally to apprise his would-have-been son-in-law of the plans. Aside from that, his only visits were from the local doctor, who gave Chesney a daily sedative to help him sleep.

Not that sleep helped. His dreams were filled with Aunt Elinor and Verity, and that made his waking reality all the more painful.

He was brought the charred license plate: "Verity 4." He thought of her promises to him of forever. Verity forever. She had reached forever ahead of him.

Li Gao made all the arrangements for Aunt Elinor's service. Lord Bagnall had a chauffeured limousine take him to London. He even paid for Chesney's suite at the Dorchester. Aunt El's service was simple and beautiful. Li Gao spoke comforting words from Scripture, and despite it being early Spring, the ceremony concluded with her favorite hymn: *I Heard the Bells on Christmas Day*.

Two days later, he stood beside Verity's grave. Though he didn't notice it at first, Chesney was struck by the absence of familiar faces. There were a few dozen people, but none whom Chesney recognized. None of the household staff were there, aside from Towson; none of the members of the Hugh Goode Appreciation Society were there either. When he pointed it out, Lord Bagnall seemed uncomfortable.

"Ah, yes," said His Lordship, "I 'ad 'oped you wouldn't not notice that."

"But where are they?" asked Chesney. "Where's Mr. and Mrs. Pilchard, where's Mrs. Gertz, and the others? I thought they loved... her." He fought back a lump in his throat. It had become difficult even to speak her name.

Lord Bagnall put his arm around Chesney's shoulder.

"They all loved her," he assured him. "They loved 'er very much, lad."

"Then why aren't they here?"

Bagnall lowered his head and sighed. "I don't not know 'ow to brooch the subject, but..." He looked away and took a deep breath. "They didn't not want to see... you."

"Me? But why?"

Lord Bagnall looked away.

"They blame me," said Chesney.

"I..." His Lordship's voice lowered to a hoarse whisper, "I didn't not want to say, but..."

Chesney stood at her grave. He had shattered their world. He had taken Verity from them. For a moment, his mind tried to argue that it was unreasonable, but if he hadn't met her, she would probably still be alive. He tried to blame something else, the winding road, the detour, the drains, the sports car, but he kept coming back to himself.

He continued to stare at the headstone and its simple inscription. A hundred years from now, he thought, it would be weathered and faded. Would the people who lived on the estate then give it any thought? Would they understand who it memorialized, and the beauty of that life, and the love that person had shared? He had never thought about cemeteries or gravestones before. Now he would never look upon one again without wondering about the life that marker represented and the lives that person touched, and the void they left behind. He stood there, even as a gentle spring rain began to fall, even after the other mourners, the minister, and the undertakers had left. Finally, Lord Bagnall returned with an umbrella and tugged at Chesney's elbow.

"I loved your daughter," said Chesney.

"Yes, I knows that, boy."

Chesney started off away from the house, off in the direction behind the grave, but Lord Bagnall stopped him.

"No, no, no," he said gently, steering Chesney the other way. "You don't not want to go that way, the ground's too soft. Come on back with me, lad."

Chesney allowed himself to be led away.

"You don't blame me, sir?"

"Being an old soldier," he said, "I don't not blame nobody. Too many scarpers and skivers in the h'army, and in business for that matter. I've found that a real man don't not blame others. A real man does his best and takes responsibility."

They walked slowly back towards the car.

"I tried to do my best by Ver... by your daughter."

"I knows it, I knows it, lad."

They reached Lord Bagnall's Rolls Royce. Towson stood beside it, holding his own umbrella. His Lordship turned to Chesney and shook his hand, and forced a grim smile upon his face.

"I'll, I..." Chesney stopped and looked back toward the grave. "I'd like to take a little time off, sir. I just need to...but, then I'll get back to work."

"Work? On wot, lad?"

"On your biography."

Lord Bagnall shook his head. "I don't not think I could do that, not now, not after wot's all happened. I'm scrapping it all. It's too painful for me... too painful for you, as well, boy." He reached into his breast pocket and pulled out an envelope and handed it to Chesney.

"What's this?"

"A check, a bonus you might say," said Bagnall. "I've already talked to your boss, Ms. Marlton. I've explained why I've canceled the book. I told her wot a fine job you done, and I've paid all her fees and expenses, so she won't not be out of pocket for none of it. She understood."

"Then what's this?" asked Chesney, looking at the envelope.

"I've told you. That's for you, with my gratitude, my consolation, my sympathy."

Chesney stood there, not knowing what to say or do.

"Now," Lord Bagnall shook Chesney's hand, "Splatterguard here will take you back to London..."

"London?"

"Yes, you've got your room at the Dorchester, all taken care of, you just take your time. I know wot with your aunt's passing you have business in town, so you take your time and sort it all out. Splatterguard has your return tickets to the States."

"Return…"

"Yes, they's dated for a week from today. Best to move on with your life and all that."

Chesney looked back toward Verity's grave. "But, I… can I come… to visit…"

Bagnall shook his head. "Oh, no, no, no, I wouldn't h'advise it, not at all. Not that I wouldn't be 'appy to see you, boy, but you've got to put it behind you. So, I think it best that you don't not come back. I don't not mean to say you wouldn't be welcome, only just stay away. No looking back, eh?"

Chesney stared at the grave in the distance. Perhaps His Lordship was right. At that moment, he had no greater longing than to stand by her grave until he would join her.

"I guess this is goodbye, then," said Chesney turning back to Lord Bagnall. Towson opened the back door of the Rolls.

Bagnall patted Chesney on the shoulder. "Yes, it is. You'll see, lad, it's for the best. We'll all deal with this in our own ways. Good luck, boy."

Chesney nodded and started to climb into the car, then stopped, fished into his pocket, pulled out a leather key fob with only one set of keys upon it, and handed it to him.

"The keys to the Triumph, mine," he said. "I don't… I couldn't…"

"I understand, boy," said Lord Bagnall pocketing the keys and guiding Chesney into the back of the Rolls Royce. He then shut the door, muttered some instructions to Towson, and waved them off.

As they drove away, Chesney kept looking back in the direction of the grave. He kept looking, even after it had disappeared behind the trees and the bends in the road leading out of the estate. They passed the manor house, and then finally the cottage where he'd spent so many precious hours with Hugh Goode and his granddaughter. Now they were both gone, and the cottage seemed cold and forbidding as they passed.

The road was repaired now, the drains fixed. As they sped off towards London, Chesney Potts broke down in tears.

– 53 –
Requiem for a Roofer

Valerie Fierro returned home in the old car commandeered from Albrecht Eckner. She cursed him as she drove. This gown was not meant for driving in, to say nothing of her heels. Albrecht's car wasn't all that great for driving in either, though presumably, that had once been its function.

When she pulled into the driveway, Valerie was surprised to find all the other cars gone. Her father's truck wasn't there, nor was her mother's sedan. The porch light was on, as was the light in the kitchen.

Great, thought Valerie glancing at the clock on the dashboard, they're probably out looking for me. Isn't that just great? They knew she was going down to the beach after the prom.

Entering the kitchen, Valerie was surprised to see their neighbor, Mrs. Burns waiting for her.

"Thank goodness you're here, Valerie, come on, I'll drive you…"

"Drive me? Where?"

The woman stopped and looked into Valerie's face. "Why, to the hospital…your father…"

Without stopping for any further explanation or even to change her clothes, Valerie followed Mrs. Burns out the door.

Fifteen minutes later, she was ushered to the bedside of Giorgio Fierro. Horrible bruises disfigured his face and body. Her mother and his sister were there.

"He fell off the roof," whispered Connie Fierro.

"Our roof?" asked Valerie.

"The roof he was working on," said Rose, "in town."

Valerie tried to look at his wounded features but had to turn away.

"As bad as he looks," said Rose, "the doctor says his internal injuries are even worse. They don't know how he's holding on."

"Someone saw it," said her mother. "They were the ones who called the ambulance. They said it looked like he was sleepwalking."

"Sleepwalking?" asked Valerie.

"He hasn't been sleeping very well at home," said Rose with an accusatory edge to her voice. "He's been working all these extra jobs, you know."

"Apparently, he was sleepwalking," continued Connie. "The man who saw him from across the street was shouting, trying to wake him. That's when it happened."

"He fell?" Valerie buried her face in her hands and realized she was still wearing her elbow-length gloves.

"No," said Connie, "that was the strangest part. He stopped on the edge of the roof. It was one of those flat roofs, three stories up. He stopped on the edge, and he dove off the edge of the roof. Like he planned it, like he was awake, but his eyes were closed all the time."

"He dove?"

"He not only dove, but the man also said he did a triple somersault before he started tumbling out of control, and then…"

"How horrible," said Valerie. "Poor Daddy, what was he doing?"

Valerie glanced at her father. She then noticed both her mother and sister were glowering at her, as if it were a stupid question, or as if they thought somehow it was her fault. How idiotic! She was miles away at the prom. How could anyone think she would tell her father to do a triple flip off a roof with his eyes closed?

Finally, Rose spoke. "What was he doing? You asked what was he doing?"

Her mother put her hand on Rose's arm, restraining her.

"I was at the prom," said Valerie weakly.

Rose rolled her eyes.

"We tried to reach you. We called the country club. Rose spoke to your date. Didn't he tell you?"

Valerie's mouth dropped open. That's why Bucky had said he understood and let him know how everything worked out. She closed her eyes. If she had known, if he had only said, but apparently, he thought she knew.

"Where have you been, anyway," asked Rose. "That was hours ago. Where were you?"

Valerie tried to form an excuse, an alibi, anything other than: "I was being sexually assaulted by a little pervert with a surgical supply fetish." She wracked her brain for something, anything to say, anything but the truth.

"Well, I…"

A moan was heard from the bed. They turned.

"I did it, I did it…" Giorgio Fierro muttered.

"Shh," said his wife. She reached out to smooth his hair, barely touching him for fear of causing him greater pain.

Giorgio opened his eyes and looked at his family. A faint smile crossed his lips, which he paid for with a wince of pain.

"Rosie, Connie," he mumbled, before looking at Valerie, furthest away. He tried to focus his eyes before saying: "Mama…"

"He's delirious," said Connie. "Giorgio, that's Valerie."

He squinted. "Valerie?"

Valerie moved nearer to her father. He studied her for a moment and then flashed another pained smile.

"Valerie," he said. "You look just like…" He stopped. "You're all dressed up, *Principessa*, tell me, how was your dance?"

"It was… fine, Daddy."

"Ah," he smiled again and looked atop her head where the tiara was still affixed to her hair. "Look, what's that?"

Valerie reached up and removed it.

"Oh, they made me prom queen."

"Figures," muttered Rose.

"Queen," said Giorgio, with a shallow chuckle, "you're a queen now, no more Principessa."

Valerie touched his hand. "I'll always be your Principessa, Daddy."

He nodded. "Did you have a good time?"

Valerie thought for a moment. Altogether, it was the worst night of her life.

"Yes," she said, "I had a wonderful time."

He nodded. "That's good, very good." He began to close his eyes, but before they shut, he paused. He pointed at Valerie's throat. She reached up and touched the gold charm that he had given her. "Ah, good," he said. Then he closed his eyes and was gone.

◆

Valerie Fierro lay in bed, fingering the gold pendant. She'd been faithful to her father's charge all these years: look out for number one. He had looked out for her, and now that he was gone, she was looking out for herself in his place. Poor Daddy, she thought. Why hadn't Albrecht Eckner fallen off that roof? Probably because he wasn't a roofer, and he hadn't fallen asleep on the roof. Still, there were so many people who should have fallen off a roof, metaphorically speaking. Albrecht Eckner, Lorraine Innis, or any of a dozen people; she'd trade them; she'd push them off a roof herself for just a few more minutes with her poor Daddy. She did love him, and he loved her. That's something no one else could understand.

Though she never mentioned it again, Valerie knew that her sister blamed her for what had happened. As if she would ever do anything to hurt her father, as if! She loved him. And he loved her.

Valerie sighed and looked at the clock. Mike Valvano wouldn't be back for hours. She wondered what was on TV.

- 54 -
Elegy for an
Unpurchased Frozen Pizza

Towson deposited Chesney Potts back at the Dorchester: very elegant, very posh, very antiseptic. After ten minutes, he knew he didn't belong there and went out on foot for Marylebone. Without realizing it, he went the long way past Paddington Station, following the same route he had taken nine months before. Stopping to face Witherby's window, he looked over his shoulder, hoping against hope to see the beautifully average girl with the long brown hair and green Wellington boots. She wasn't there.

Neither did she emerge so full of life from Mr. Postlewaite's shop a few blocks further on. He knew it was futile, but he went to the corner of the street and looked for a glimpse of a girl climbing into a taxi. Not even the taxi was there. The kind woman with the multi-colored eyes who had consoled him on that spot was also absent. He wandered on.

Later, he wasn't sure how much later, for time didn't seem real, Chesney entered Mr. Postlewaite's shop. It was strangely bare. At first, he attributed it to the fact that the woman who had lived in the flat above it was now gone, her absence accounting for the deficit. Then he noticed most of the store's stock was gone.

Postlewaite emerged from the back room, wiping his hands.

"Chesney," he said, "I didn't expect to see you, not today, not with… I'm sorry, I wanted to attend, but I was told it was private."

Chesney began to ask who said so, but he already knew it could only be one of two people.

"I'm sorry," said Chesney. "I knew you liked her very much."

"Yes," agreed the shopkeeper sadly. He looked around. "Well, I'll be out of it soon."

"Out of it?"

"Yes," he said, "didn't you know. Oh, yes, how could you know? I've sold the shop."

"Sold it?"

Postlewaite nodded forlornly. "Yes, I wouldn't have, but..." he shrugged his shoulders. "It was such a good offer. I can retire and quite comfortably."

Chesney expressed his happiness for him.

"I'll miss it," admitted Postlewaite looking around. "I've been here for over thirty years – thirty years in the past. I suppose it's time to look to the future." But his eyes expressed wariness for that direction. "Besides," he continued, "there's nothing left for me here in the past."

"No," agreed Chesney, "there's nothing left."

"When I first opened this shop, Li Gao had his takeaway next door, and not long afterward, Elinor stumbled in..." He pointed up toward her now empty flat. "...waiting for a cheap fare to Tibet." He laughed, barely concealing the emotion beneath it.

They stood in silence for a moment, disturbed only by the door opening and a large packing crate entering with a pair of legs below it.

"Here's another one, my friend, oh, Chesney." Li Gao placed the crate on the counter and shook Chesney's hand. "I thought we wouldn't see you for several days. You surely must have other matters to conclude."

"It's all been arranged for me," said Chesney.

"And how are you, my dear friend?"

"I feel," he said slowly, "I feel as if I had just been shoved off a very high cliff, and that I'm falling in slow motion. And as I fall, I can see all the good memories and the love of the two people who meant more to me than life itself. And then just as I see those happy moments, time speeds up again, and I plummet to the bottom. Just before I hit the bottom, I find myself at the top again, only to start falling once more. And I know those people and that love will never return. All that's left are regrets." He sighed. "And that's how I feel."

Li Gao patted his shoulder, urged him to sit, and then sat beside him.

"You mentioned regrets," he said.

Chesney felt the tears well up in his eyes.

"I think of the stupidest things," he said, "like Frozen French bread pizza..."

"French bread pizza?"

"A few weeks ago, we were in the market, grabbing some dinner. Verity wanted to try frozen French bread pizza, but I didn't want to try it. We got something else." He chortled. "I can't even remember what we wound up eating, something I selected. But now all I remember is not letting her have frozen French bread pizza. Stupid, isn't it?"

"Not at all," said Li, "you regret not being more selfless. I'm sure you expressed your love in words quite often."

"At least a hundred times a day," he said.

"We are often chided for not telling others that we love them. But while verbal expressions of love are important, there are so many other ways that demonstrate our love in a more voluble manner."

"Like frozen French bread pizza," he sighed.

"Just so," Li Gao agreed.

"I wish I had been in that car instead of her," he said.

"So that she could now be mired in your regrets?"

"She wouldn't have regrets," said Chesney. "She was perfect."

"We all have regrets," he said with a sad smile. "I doubt she would recall your frozen pizza, but if she were in your place, Verity…"

Chesney winced at the mention of her name.

"…the young lady," amended Li, "would no doubt recall something that would be insignificant to you, but that she would feel she had disappointed or denied you in some way. You loved her as best you could. But love is not something that we arrive at fully formed and perfected the moment we first dare to express it in words. That is only the beginning. Those first moments represent the raw material. It represents our commitment, our willingness to present ourselves as a lump of clay or a block of stone, to give up our selfish lives. And then we allow ourselves to have the ugly self-seeking bits of our nature chipped and chiseled away, often quite painfully, until we emerge in a nobler and higher image, a greater, lovelier work of art. Your dear Aunt went through much personal disappointment and regrets in her life. Did she appear that way to you?"

"Aunt Elinor was beautiful," said Chesney. "She was so wise and optimistic, so full of life."

"I agree," said Li Gao, "but you saw the finished work. You were not there for the rough blows of the hammer or the abrasive rubbing to burnish away the imperfections. You were the beneficiary of the work of art. The masterpiece is enjoyed by many, but it is formed in solitary moments in the workshop of the master."

Chesney thought about his aunt. "I knew there were things in her past," he said, "but I never realized they were painful."

"All growth carries with it a degree of pain," he said. "But she endured it and was made a kinder, wiser person for it all, and she then shared that gift with all around her, and especially with you, my boy. Now you have endured great loss. A short while ago, you possessed everything you ever thought you required for happiness only to have it taken from you. It all seems cruel and without sense. You described it as continually falling and haunted by regrets. But I assure you this too is for a greater benefit if you do not waste your sorrow. 'We are hard pressed on every side, but not crushed; perplexed, but not abandoned; struck down, but not destroyed,' or so wrote St. Paul. Or to paraphrase a pious old coalminer whom I once knew: 'God gives his best saints the worst raps.' And though you are in a lonely place being chipped away at with painful blows, you will emerge a useful vessel, a great work of art. You cannot see it today. You may never understand why so great a tragedy has befallen you. But someday someone may be enriched and consoled by the wisdom being fashioned in you today. In that day, they will take comfort in the depth of kindness they find in you, such that can only be forged in this dark place."

"Someday," muttered Chesney, "I might be like Aunt Elinor for someone else?"

"I should be surprised if that were not the outcome," said Li. "'For our light and momentary troubles are achieving for us an eternal glory that outweighs them all.'"

"St. Paul?"

He nodded. "The labor appears long and painful, but the resulting beauty lasts forever."

"Paul, again?"

"No, that was only me."

Postlewaite was sitting behind the counter, sorting through a stack of old 45 rpm records. He held up a sleeve. "Oh, here's one I remember: Gilbert O'Sullivan, *Alone Again, Naturally.*"

"Naturally," said Chesney in a whisper.

– 55 –
An Unclaimed Piece of Heart

Lorraine Innis opened her eyes. Her cheeks were crusted with the salty residue of tears. She sat up on the sofa. Clodagh Clott was sitting in the chair beside her.

"I must look a state," said Lorraine reaching for a tissue.

"Good thing you took off your make-up. Lorraine Innis Waterproof Mascara is good," noted Clodagh, "but it's not indestructible."

"Neither is Lorraine Innis."

"Could have fooled me," said Clodagh.

"What time is it?"

Clodagh nodded toward the clock. "Half-past four," she said. "You've been under for over eight hours."

"I thought being in a hypnotic state was supposed to be relaxing," said Lorraine. She blew her nose, heaved a heavy sigh, and shook her head. "I thought I'd gotten over all that, for the most part."

"You did," said Clodagh. "But you've essentially relived it with all the joys and pains. I tried to warn you. Reliving the past is like picking a scab. You may think it's all healed, but when you pull it off, it's as sore and raw as it was when the wound was fresh."

"Even years later?"

"Even years later," said Clodagh. "Still, if it's any consolation, you were right."

"About what?"

Clodagh smiled. "You got to be your Aunt Elinor for someone else, in fact, for the world. Only I didn't think you had to copy her down to the hair and clothes."

Lorraine shook her head, "Yes, I did. I didn't even get to that part yet."

"Tomorrow," said Clodagh, "or the next day. As much as I want to hear how you became this person, I don't want to overtax your mind. You've been through quite a lot already."

Lorraine agreed, then stood and crossed to the window. She stared out at the city lights in the distance.

"Shame on me," she finally said.

"Yes, Ches?" asked Clodagh putting her hand on his shoulder.

"I'd almost forgotten how desperately I loved..." Lorraine's voice deepened to nearly a male timbre and choked.

"...Verity?"

He nodded and wiped his eyes. She rubbed his shoulder.

"Picking at scabs," said Clodagh softly. "We don't have to go on."

"Yes, we do," said Lorraine. "And don't end your sentence in a preposition."

They both laughed; then grew quiet again.

"Have you ever been back? I mean to the grave."

Chesney shook his head.

"Oh."

After another silence, he spoke again.

"Sometimes, I think I experienced a lifetime of happiness in those few months. We were only together nine months."

"Like a pregnancy," noted Clodagh.

"...ending in a stillbirth."

"But look at you now," she said, "I mean, look at all the good you've done, all the lives you've touched."

He just shrugged as if to discount her claims. "Still, there's a piece of my heart buried in Staffordshire, a piece that I'll never get back."

Clodagh studied the face reflected in window glass and then shook her head. "No, we're stopping here. I can't put you through any more of this."

Chesney looked up and gazed at the reflection as well. Once again, he saw Lorraine Innis. But beyond that, he saw all the others who had helped form her: Aunt Elinor, Verity Goodhue, and Martina Fergus. As painful as the process was, he knew that it wasn't finished, not yet.

"No," said Lorraine Innis, "we're not there yet."

"Where?"

"To the finished work."

The End of

The Girl in the Lime Green Wellies

The story of Lorraine Innis will continue in Book 5:

The Girl in the Saffron Espadrilles